Praise for

ENCHANTMENT
and
DAPHNE MERKIN

"A lively, evocative, often amusing work. Through Hannah's voice, Merkin deftly captures the concentration on self-definition—as well as the doubt and frustration—of dawning womanhood."

Los Angeles Times Book Review

"At once so heartbreaking and frightening, so memorable, funny, and tragic. ENCHANTMENT is an act of courage."

Chicago Sun-Times

"Classy . . . an intense novel."

Newsday

(more)

"Extraordinary—piercingly painful and marvelously funny at once."

Hilma Wolitzer

ENCHANTMENT

"A dense tapestry of memories, emotions, and vivid pictures. The reader will likely be startled into memories of his/her own: abrupt recognitions of experiences long forgotten, but now reexperienced."

Kansas City Star

"An impressive debut."

Publishers Weekly

"Complexities . . . boldness . . . lack of shame . . . the book fascinates one by its openness. . . . I *had* to read to the very last page."

Mary McCarthy

DAPHNE MERKIN

"Merkin writes with confidence and grace, invoking an idiosyncratic world whose rich ambiguities—of poverty in wealth, of servitude in power—become the substance of this very rich first novel."

USA Today

"A remarkable memoir."

Walker Percy

Winner of the
Edward Lewis Wallant
Award for Jewish
Novel of the Year

Co-Winner of the National
Jewish Book Award

Enchantment

A Novel

Daphne Merkin

FAWCETT CREST • NEW YORK

A Fawcett Crest Book
Published by Ballantine Books

Published in the United States by Ballantine Books, a division of Random House, Inc., New York, and simultaneously in Canada by Random House of Canada Limited, Toronto.

Portions of this work first appeared in *The New Yorker* and *Partisan Review.*

Library of Congress Catalog Card Number: 85-27235

ISBN 0-449-21425-7

This edition published by arrangement with Harcourt Brace Jovanovich, Inc.

Manufactured in the United States of America

First Ballantine Books Edition: December 1987

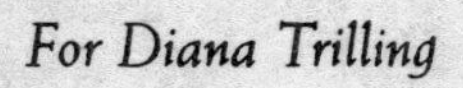

For Diana Trilling

ACKNOWLEDGMENTS

I wish to thank my publisher, William Jovanovich, for his conviction and his patience; my editor, Jackie Decter, for her enthusiasm; and Michael Brod, for his promptings and proddings.

"Everything that deceives may be said to enchant."
—PLATO, *The Republic*

ONE

I am reading aloud to my mother from Shakespeare's sonnets, trying to find one that would be appropriate to recite at her funeral. My mother is not dying. She is a relatively robust woman who looks younger than her sixty years, but she speaks of her death often and with a macabre glee. "When I am gone," she says, "I would like you to say of me that she never made mountains out of molehills." I am not sure why my mother considers this particular epitaph to be the highest form of tribute, and I cannot imagine that any of the mourners at her grave will understand it better. But I know it is important to her, a link with the hearty, hiking-shoes atmosphere of her youth.

"Fine," I say. Her implication, I suppose, is that all her children, finespun creatures, do just the opposite.

My mother and I are sitting on the bed in what I still think of as my room. I first shared it with two sisters and it finally became my own during college. The room is adjacent to my mother's, and partly because of this I have had the greatest trouble leaving it. Whenever I had one of the fierce fights with her that from early on were a constant of our relationship, I used to stand in front of her locked door and imagine my mother deep inside her bathroom, swallowing pills or taking flight from my rancor out a window. "My mother is dead," I would think, composing the sentence formally in my head as though I were a character in a play. I saw myself freed and bereft at the same time, a figure of surpassing interest: *Who is that girl in black? I hear her mother died. So young? What a tragedy! I wonder how the children feel. They say it hit that one the hardest.* I would watch myself being watched by others, wondering along with them what I was thinking. My imagination has always run to the vivid, although my mother is not the sort of woman to embrace personal drama. Sooner or later she would emerge from her bedroom, dry-eyed and stony, putting my half-hopeful, half-terrified visions to an end.

The bed we sit on is narrow, penitential—as are all the beds my mother favors for her household. The wall I lean my back against is faintly, pleasantly cold. I note the undertow of gray that sweeps through my mother's vigilantly colored hair, and the loosened skin on her neck, beneath her strong jaw. Nothing—not these or other signs—convinces me of her mortality. The bed is tightly made up, with crisp white sheets and a slightly worn wool blanket. I was reminded of my bed in an instant when I read the description of Clarissa Dalloway's in Virginia Woolf's novel: like hers, it is the unyielding bed of someone who was meant to remain a virgin.

Now, in my own apartment, I have a double bed covered with delicately flowered sheets. Taking a great wanton leap forward, I originally ordered an even larger bed, but when it arrived and was shoved against the wall by two surly delivery men, I immediately knew I was not up to it. I slept on top of the unwrapped queen-size mattress and box spring for a night. The next day I called up Bloomingdale's and told them I had made a terrible mistake—my bedroom was too small; would they please exchange the order? Both the size of my bed and the style of linen were deliberate moves away from my mother's taste, and she sniffs at them with the same disapproval she shows toward the knickknacks that clutter my window sills and coffee table. These knickknacks—a random assortment of pottery, small painted boxes, and the sort of oversize candles that are most often found in college dorm rooms—are always dusty; one ceramic bowl is filled with honey drops that are so ancient and sticky they cannot be separated from one another. I apologize for these candies, making a joke of them whenever a visitor tries to dislodge one, but I have not removed them. There is something about my dusty accumulations that pleases me.

In the living room a clock chimes.

"Hannah, have you done something to your hair?" my mother asks. "You look younger." My mother watches me for signs of bloom and decay, like a plant.

"Do I?" I say, and for a moment I feel as if our roles have been reversed—that I am old and in need of reassurance about my faded allure. "Let me see," I say, flipping through the pages of my fat college anthology, and begin reading a sonnet about cruelty. My mother stares out over my head, her eyes fixed. Her eyes are a deep-set gray-green, quite beautiful, and I sometimes pass along compliments other people have made about them. She receives such praise with a touching display of shyness.

"'Be wise as thou art cruel,'" I declaim; "'do not press/My tongue-tied patience with too much disdain.'" I listen to my own voice as I read, trying to infuse it with the ripeness that I think Shakespeare would have liked.

My mother's affection has always been unreliable, subject to whim. One day she sees fit to tell me that I shouldn't waste so much money on movies. "If you do everything now," she says, "what pleasures will be left to you when you are fifty?" The force of her illogicality holds me, even though I know there aren't a limited number of movies—of pleasures—in the world to use up, and after that you are left twiddling your thumbs.

Then, several days afterward, I call her late at night, in a sudden panic about my life. "I can't anymore," I say rather desperately, although there has been nothing terrible—no acute disappointment, no rift—to bring on this despair. "I can't go on," I repeat. "I don't see the point. I just want to do nothing. I want to lie on my bed for days. I can't always be trying to accomplish something. I *could* lie on my bed, couldn't I?"

My mother listens, or at least appears to, and this alone begins to soothe me: I want—have always wanted—her to listen to me forever. "It'll all be all right, Hannah," she says, "you'll see."

"And," I add out of the blue, as if this were the real sorrow, "I never have any clothes! I'm sick of having nothing to wear!"

"Don't worry," my mother says, "I will buy you everything."

Her answer imprints itself on my mind in capital letters: I WILL BUY YOU EVERYTHING. The grandeur of it, the complete maternalness—you are my child; I will see to it that you are clothed in happiness—silences me. I want this moment to last. Never mind that it is entirely false, that this is being said to me by the same woman who is capable of reminding me that I owe her the five dollars she lent me for a taxi weeks ago. Does she know what she's saying? And how can she say such a protective thing and a day or two later, sure enough, announce, "The trouble with you is that you're spoiled. You think too much about yourself. If you had to sell in Woolworth's all day, you'd be better off."

As a child I interpreted such vacillations as cruelty (anything else would have required an unbearable detachment), and to this day I tend to care most deeply about people who can take or leave me. Such people, I've convinced myself, can be counted on in some way that precludes trust: they will never love you or stop loving you for yourself alone.

"*That's* it," my mother says at one point, amused by my last selection. I go on reading, but pretty soon the poem meanders into universalisms and no longer applies to the specific darkness in her. I skim through a few others, trying to find one that will capture her fickle attention.

"Here's one on the tyrant Time," I announce with pedantic fervor, and my mother is willing to listen, herself a great believer in the power of passing hours.

When I am done, she says, "He was a genius, wasn't he." Jealous of Shakespeare's momentary glory, I explain that the phrase "the expense of spirit in a waste of shame" refers to sexual intercourse. "I *knew* that," she says, an immigrant from a proud line, not one to be outwitted by the primpings of the academy.

In one of my bookcases is a Lucite-framed photograph of my maternal grandfather, an Orthodox Jew, who was reading Thomas Mann's latest novel shortly before he died, in Jerusalem. His is the only photograph I have set out, and it is not entirely clear to me why I have chosen him from among my many relatives. People mistake his likeness for that of Sigmund Freud, whose was a different spirit altogether. But there is a definite resemblance, in the details if not in the whole: the same neatly trimmed beard, narrow face, intelligent eyes behind round wire spectacles. The fact of my grandfather's reading a secular writer rather than a religious book had to be kept a secret from some of his less broad-minded friends in the circle he belonged to. He was reputed to be a man to whom religious belief did not come easily. I suppose he is to be admired for having adhered to the laws in spite of this, and sometimes I wonder if the force of my grandfather's will lingers in me, and if I stray from it unnaturally.

Of my grandfather's resemblance to the father of psychoanalysis, my mother says dismissively that people of the same generation tend to look like each other; still, I think she is secretly pleased when the comparison is made. She used to quote sardonic remarks she remembers her father making, but she has stopped in recent years, as though she suddenly wondered at the implications.

My friends, especially the ones I retain from years back, always ask about my mother if we haven't been in touch for a while. I could be an astronaut now, a wielder of influence, and still they ask several minutes into long-distance conversations, "How are things with you and your mother?" When I was much younger I would leave my mother in undrastic ways—for weekend stays at the homes of friends and cousins. In my family I was considered a great socialite because of these visits; my siblings rarely ventured out. I would invariably fall in love with the homes and mothers I was visiting, whatever the actual form they may have taken. What was important was that they weren't *mine*: I could start all over again in a living room in Queens with a mother who served fish croquettes on glazed blue plates.

One weekend stood out in my mind for the longest time as being especially charmed. I was staying at the small and rather crowded apartment of some distant cousins. The cousin who was my age didn't like her own mother very much, and there was, in fact, something irascible about this woman's attitude toward her children that wasn't all that different from my mother's toward hers. Later on I would learn that "moodiness," as it was called, ran in my mother's family. But then I saw only my cousin's advantages: her brothers were far gentler than mine, and there were no sisters to contend with. On Saturday night, after her father made the blessing over the thickly braided *havdala* candle, signifying that Shabbos was over (all the families I visited were Orthodox, like my own), drove us to an Alexander's situated in a shopping center not far from their house. This was the sort of bland excursion my family never made, and it filled me with a delight that I can recall but not quite fathom. I wandered through aisles filled with racks of clothing, staring at ordinary skirts and blouses as though I were seeing such things for the first time. I watched other families shopping on the brightly lit floor around me. "How do you like that, Daddy," said one plump, blonde mother, holding up a brown suit. Something about her tone—or it may have been her windswept look—drew me, and I stood staring as her three children gathered around to study the effect of the suit pinned against their father, the most nice-seeming of men. I tried to imagine my mother calling my father "Daddy" or our many, unpeaceful selves going out as a unit to shop at a department store. Soon after this episode—I imagine my cousin's mother must have called up my mother and triumphantly informed her of my desire to come and live with them (my family was richer than most of our relatives, and we were seen in grudgingly glamorized terms)—my mother started referring to my "Orphan Annie act" whenever I went away for the weekend.

"Wish them good Shabbos," she said one Friday afternoon, standing in the vestibule as she always did while I waited for the elevator, suitcase in hand. The clamor rising from behind her—Louisa, the cook, banging an oven shut in the kitchen, my brothers yelping at each other upstairs—was already beginning to seem like tender, lost music to me.

"Should I stay home?" I asked my mother tentatively. Suddenly home—*my* home—seemed wonderful to me. Why was I always leaving it, wending my way elsewhere like a traveling salesman?

"Don't be silly," my mother said, but I could tell she rather liked my doubts. "You'll be back tomorrow night, Sunday morning latest."

"Maybe I should just stay home," I said, offering my mother a chance to declare her affection, claim me, pull me inside with operatic attachment. Some of my friends had mothers who acted that way, clinging to their offspring like vines. But my mother wasn't cut from such stuff. She was German, not Eastern European, and I had deduced from remarks made by the Polish and Hungarian parents of my friends that *yekkes*, as German Jews like my mother were called, were a fatally cold bunch—aberrant, more German than Jewish. Then, too, my mother had escaped the Holocaust—what was referred to simply as "the camps"—her family having moved to Israel in the early thirties. So I and my brothers and sisters were not her redemption, her Last Chance. (Sometimes I thought guiltily that I would have preferred a mother who *had* been in the camps, who had suffered too much to be anything other than eternally grateful that I, Hannah Lehmann, had been born to her after Hitler.)

"Don't be silly," my mother repeated. "You're all packed." She leaned over to give me a kiss. Her muted-plaid robe smelled of perfume; I could never remember the perfume's name because it was so unlikely—the name of an animal. "But do yourself a favor and don't play Orphan Annie there, okay? I know I'm a terrible mother, but no one else is interested."

I smiled, but I feared she was right. My longings would have to remain with me. It wasn't so much that they weren't recognized as that they seemed to be given mysteriously short shrift. The elevator cage groaned as it descended. While I chatted wth Lucas, who worked the old-fashioned lever as if it were the tiller of a ship, it occurred to me once again—like a shadow I couldn't dodge—that I was stuck with what I had. As what I had was stuck with me. Who else would take me for more than a weekend, I wondered, other than the family I wished to sell off like costly but damaged goods?

Over the years I have lost most of the things that have been important to me. I have a recurring dream in which all of these objects turn up again in a neat little pile: a leather-bound notebook, several watches, a stubby fountain pen with which I wrote a script full of flourishes, slips of paper on which I have scribbled crucial thoughts, a brown and white cashmere scarf that made me think of myself briefly as the mistress of an English country house. Because of, or in spite of, my tendency to lose things, I am the most intractable of hoarders. My apartment is filled with magazines and slightly faulty appliances. It is a real effort of will for me to throw even used-up items out. I check the bottoms of cereal boxes for malingering flakes and dribble out the reluctant drops in milk cartons. I watch myself at these routines and recognize that they are important to me, a way of stopping up gaps. There is one tube of toothpaste that has been lying in various medicine cabinets, untouched, for several years. The tube is cracked with age, and recently, when a friend volunteered to test it, the toothpaste squeezed out in a dried gob. "Throw it out," she said, not unreasonably.

"I might need it," I explained. "It could come in handy as a spare." This explanation, of course, had nothing to do with anything. Although it might have suited Perle Mesta or another such hostess—someone attuned to the potential hitches in the running of a smooth household, the oversights on the part of guests who stayed the night—I was hardly in the habit of seeing myself that way. No, *my* reasoning was unaccountable, embedded in the crusts of my childhood.

"Throw it out," my friend said.

I did not want her to think of me as visibly eccentric, so I threw it out. Later, after she left, I retrieved the tube from the wastebasket, and it now rests safely again on a bathroom shelf.

I suppose that for tenacious people like me the past is never really over. I sit in a psychiatrist's office, where courtesy reigns, and begin my story once again. I can't separate out the feelings from the facts: my mother is the Wicked Witch, but she is also the object of desire. Lena, our Czech nurse, once banged my head repeatedly against a wall, and when I told my mother about it in a torrent of tears I remember noting, at an age when such perceptions feel less terrible than clear, that my mother's heart was not broken. But why, then, was I made to feel special, my straight brown hair brushed by the same nurse into pigtails that were tied with bright ribbons? "Such shiny hair," my mother said. "It hangs like a curtain." My two sisters had more mediocre hair, and less attention was paid. Years later, as soon as I could, I righted the balance: I began changing the color of my hair every six months or so to a brassy off-blonde that was supposed to look, even in mid-December, as though it had gotten that way from the sun. And when the fashion for permanents presented itself, I had the straightness of which my mother had been so proud stunned into frizzy little curls. My hair is no longer admirable, but no one recognizes me in photographs as the girl with pigtails anyway.

Doesn't everyone begin happy? More or less inclined to embrace the world (I'm taking those innate differences of temperament child psychiatrists are always arguing about into account) but basically content to be born? Or are there those who sense the sorrow the world has in store for them already in the cradle, furrowing their infant brows in an adult manifestation of distress?

My mother didn't believe in cuddling babies too much, in giving them ideas. The experts like Dr. Spock may have advised against letting a child cry longer than fifteen minutes, but there I am in a baby photograph screaming myself wild. I am holding on to the bars of a playpen set in the garden, wearing nothing but diapers; I can't be more than a year old, yet my hair looks as if it has turned white and my face wrinkled from crying. Even now, in those conversations about styles of mothering that take place all around her, my mother insists on the dangers of picking up babies too quickly when they cry. "Americans," she says, "with their one or two babies apiece! Americans let their babies rule the house!"

Perhaps this Teutonic training in early self-control should have hardened me, thickened my infant skin into something reptilian, capable of surviving the jungle. But what if it has effected the opposite result, created a permanent weakening of my ability to distract myself with small pleasures? If such a process did in fact occur—and I've come to believe it has—it must have begun way back then, with the mobile of plastic ducks in cheerful primary colors that hung over my crib and failed to inspire a gurgle of joy. Without that image of consolation flashed and reflashed on my early brain like a winning ace in a deck of cards—The Mother who ran to pick me up when I cried—how was I to develop faith in the coming end of sorrow?

There are other photographs. I look at a photograph of myself as a child—a shiny, starting-to-yellow snapshot—and think, not for the first time, *It all started here*. I am a big-bellied two-year-old, my floppy hair not yet made a fuss of but butchered into bangs that stop, most oddly, in the middle of my forehead. I am wearing a pair of boy's striped swimming trunks and I am looking up at my mother, who is holding another baby. It is summer and I have probably just returned from a trip to the beach with Lena and several siblings. My mother rarely went along; my father "needed" her at home. My father worked throughout the summer—weekends, too—except for Shabbos.

On Sundays he worked at his desk in the study, in a leather chair that creaked whenever he leaned back. At some point I stopped thinking of this hardworking man with his constant supply of glasses of tea as my father; he was simply the man whom my mother, for reasons incomprehensible to me, had chosen to marry. It was easier that way.

My childhood clings to me like wet paint, blotching the picture of who I am in the present. It is summer and I stand in a train station, having missed the last train I can catch out to my parents' summer house before Friday evening turns into the prescribed inactivity of Shabbos. Their house is an hour from the city in an unstylish resort where no one whom anyone has heard of goes. I call my mother from an open pay phone; anyone can eavesdrop and draw the wrong conclusions. I am crying—I am always missing trains, and I have never liked the summer. It makes me melancholy, even though I tan for long hours in the sun. When I pictured my life as an adult, it never resembled this: I sit on the beach and watch other people's families, all the pails and shovels, and the husbands standing, talking to other husbands. I play with a little girl, my niece, who has advanced powers of concentration. We make sand pies; I bring paper cups containing water and sand meant to resemble the ingredients she has requested: sugar, milk, raisins, flour, and pickles. Together we turn over a plastic pail filled with damp sand; I give several taps to the bottom of the pail with a small green shovel, as though this will insure a better product. My niece lifts the pail off gingerly; everything depends on this. A slightly mashed-looking pie appears, and we pretend to eat it. "Dee-li-shus," I pronounce. The little girl smiles. Her hair is curly, and she is cool about bestowing her affections. I can imagine my own child on the beach with me but never a man in the role of husband.

The handle of the phone is sticky, and I am threatening to become a prostitute. "I will," I say, "you'll see," although I am a bit old to begin and am not sure how I'd go about it in any case. "All these rules," I say to my mother, "they're killing me. There's nothing holy about them." Crowds of sweating people rush by me to trains whose departures they have clocked exactly into their schedules. Nearby, a tall black man in a large-brimmed hat smiles. I try to envision sexual encounters with a stream of strangers, my thighs opening on a gray-sheeted cot, and I cry even harder.

"Don't be an idiot," my mother says on the other end of the receiver I hold wetly in one hand. "Nothing's so terrible. You'll come out after Shabbos."

My tears stop abruptly. "Don't be an idiot" has worked its caustic charm. I have become a person consoled only by the breeziest form of solace; if there is something about a lack of empathy that fascinates me, it is because I detect in it some hostile truth about myself. The men I adhere to, burrowing into their necks as though it were a way of keeping them, seduce me with the lure of denied tenderness, the endearments they do not utter. There is magic in the resistance of others, my mother's coolness transmuted, Merlin-like, into the icy glow of the unyielding lover.

An older couple, of an experimental persuasion—types I have met only since stepping out of my family orbit—invite me to a chic beach for the day. A man walks toward us along the shore and my eyes drop to below his belly, where there is no bathing suit. Groups of women sit on towels, breasts sloping downward, pubic mounds glistening in the sun. I chat gaily with my hosts. I am shocked as my grandfather would have been had he been dropped into this scene from out of his tree-lined Jerusalem street, where hats are still tipped in greeting by the polite and deeply nostalgic German Jews who live in the neighborhood. I see myself as a Victorian who has walked into a Pre-Raphaelite painting. What surprises me is not the streak of inhibition that marks me but that I don't entirely wish to rid myself of it. I remain clothed. My bathing suit is a streamlined one-piece, daring in its way, the color of champagne in a glass. I have spent some time choosing it. Naked children cavort in and out of groups of naked adults who are reading, sunning, and talking. I stand with one hand on my hip, watching. My hosts are having an argument. "I don't like your tone," he says. "I don't like the way you sound." She is as silenced by this as though he has punched her in the jaw.

My parents regularly yell at each other in argument, and my father is not one to comment on so abstract a grievance as my mother's tone. I think of their German accents, lending a slightly martial quality to everything that is said, and of the many bathrooms in the apartment in which I grew up—the vigilance about odors and uncovered flesh. One of my brothers liked to stalk around in his underpants, a habit that never failed to infuriate my mother—as though at any moment he would go mad and expose all. "Put a dressing gown on immediately!" she would hiss at him.

On the beach, close by, a little girl plays with the wrist-watch on her father's bronzed arm, twanging the strap, laughing when he grimaces as though in pain. He is sprawled out in a rickety little chair; they are both naked. I watch them and wonder what it is like to grow up with such a lack of boundaries, such clear sailing. Does it leave you free of nostalgia, with a present-mindedness that confirms the future?

It is evening on a winter Sunday and I am being driven back to the city. I do not know the people in the car with me well, but I assume their lives are preferable to mine. We pass emptied motel pools, and I imagine the guests inside, preparing themselves for dinner. One of the two men in the car, the driver, is a lawyer. He steers with great precision, as though he were applying for the role of Driver in a movie. I have never learned how to drive. Everyone excuses this by saying, "Of course, you grew up in the city."

When I was young, we were driven to school by Willy, my father's chauffeur, and my sisters and I used to take turns asking him what he had eaten for dinner the night before. At 8:15 every weekday morning, Willy's dinner menu seemed more important than the school day ahead. I was fascinated by the glass of milk that concluded all his meals. My second-oldest sister, Rachel, used to copy the way Willy pronounced his *s*'s: "A big peesh of apple pie and a tall glash of milk," she'd say grandly.

My mother has learned to drive late in life, so there is hope for me. When I am a passenger in her car, I point out oncoming cars and stop signs. She does not pay close enough attention, although she is very skilled at last-minute maneuvers. While she concentrates on twists in the road I watch her profile—the faint freckling of her skin, the straight line of her mouth, which makes me think of a child's drawings. I know her face by heart. Sometimes I think nothing will break her spell.

TWO

There's something stubborn about families, unhappy ones in particular: they outlive themselves, and then they live on. If you think about this too much, it can give you trouble. When I get sad, which is more often than not, I tend to go into coffee shops and sit at the counters. I order a cup of coffee and something sweet, a doughnut or a piece of cake—coconut if they have it—and then I drift, like an old woman, into the past. If you were to come in out of the street and notice me, it would be hard to tell if I were lost somewhere inside my head or just staring over my cup at the window where the orders are given and they shove out the plates. I like coffee shops, the hubbub of them, but it has only recently occurred to me that I gravitate toward counters rather than tables because I grew up eating at one. My mother had a white Formica board built against the kitchen wall, and it was there that my brothers and sisters and I ate on weekdays. I think of us eating quickly and silently, like a bunch of taxi drivers eager to get back to the job, but I imagine we must have talked among ourselves. There were many of us, and my mother thought it quite an ingenious arrangement. At some point the board was taken down, and we ate around a table. A visiting relative—my grandmother, I think it was—had been distressed at the sight of us eating in a line that way, but I had grown used to it and liked concentrating on the green and white kitchen wallpaper with its splotches of red.

In my family we are always gathering, like far-flung members of a fiercely loyal tribe, when in truth we all live a taxi ride's distance from each other. It doesn't seem to matter that my sisters have married and that two grandchildren have been produced; still we come back.

In my mind this phenomenon has a name, wit deflecting anxiety. *(Why has no one managed to get away?)* I think of it as More Orange Juice. A psychiatrist I saw some years ago—one of many—gave me the idea. Dr. Gross didn't appear to like me, and he liked the parents who had mangled the shape of my character even less.

"You keep going back for more orange juice," he said.

Dr. Gross had rapidly blinking eyes, as though he were caught in a constant sandstorm, but when he said something of obvious significance his eyes stopped blinking altogether; they widened and watched.

"There wasn't enough to begin with," he continued, "so all of you keep returning to the source, hoping to fill up. What you have to learn how to do is to give up on that source and look elsewhere."

I wasn't about to accept this advice from him; I

couldn't see where he was offering me anything better. I remember that I argued with him at the time, objecting fussily to his choice of metaphor.

"Don't you mean milk?" I said. "As in mother's milk? I wasn't breast-fed, if you remember."

"Either liquid will do," he said, smiling briefly. "I think you see my point."

And, of course, I did. The orange juice motif was, as it happened, an oddly resonant one. At home there was a cabinet shelf full of tiny juice glasses. Two or three sips, and it was all gone. The taller glasses were saved for water and soda. I never saw anyone in the family use these for juice, and I was at first shocked, then irritated, when friends, unguided by me, would use the larger glasses when they poured drinks for themselves from the juice bottle in the refrigerator. To this day I retain a sense of orange juice as precious, to be sipped in thimble-sized amounts.

The metaphor was right in another way—there was an acidic quality to my mother, even at her most affectionate. She was citric rather than lactic, but by this time I didn't believe in more wholehearted forms of nurturance. If I were to follow out the logic of Dr. Gross's coldly correct insights, there was a chance I'd end up saner but also, it was clear to me, alone. I saw myself floating around the cosmos like an orphaned molecule, voluntarily cut off from a chain. Besides, I didn't like Dr. Gross, either. He had an unnaturally elongated physique, and I had heard—from a friend of mine who specialized in knowing about the skeletons in people's closets—that he had divorced his wife to marry an *au pair* girl twenty-five years younger than himself. Who was he to talk of irrational needs, the holding pattern of desire?

* * *

It is summer's end, and we sit ranged along a glass-topped table on the patio. We are celebrating something. There are platters of hamburgers, warmed-over chicken, tomato salad. Everything tastes slightly stale, masked by barbecue sauce and salt. One of my brothers-in-law, the capable one, stands guard over a small charcoal grill. "Coming right up," he says, fanning the smoke as though this were a real party and he the festive chef. There are several large bottles of soda—Coke, root beer, and diet black cherry. The soda always goes quickly, and then there is an extended conversation about who will finish the last bit. My paper cup has beads of pale red soda sticking to the bottom and I stick my tongue inside, trying to suck them up. It annoys me that my mother feels it necessary to create this atmosphere of scarcity, when there is money all around us. If we were a French family, there would be wine, but we are Jewish, and Jews, my mother likes to point out with a show of unironic ethnic pride, don't drink. What, I've wondered, would happen if we *did* drink, toss down vintage bottles of red wine with picturesque labels? Would we tumble around hugging each other, lose our standards, embrace heathen ways?

Some of the food was prepared weeks ago and then frozen. Louisa, my mother's cook, is off during the summer months, so the eating is haphazard. My mother trades pieces of meat and chicken in and out of the giant freezer in the basement with happy disregard for any loss of taste or nutritional value that may occur in the process. When I show her articles detailing the dangers of refreezing cooked foods, she gives her short, mocking laugh. "Americans!" she says. "Always worrying about themselves! What a country for making a fuss about nothing!" I look around the table and envision us dying off, one by one, from tapeworm or some such infestation. The picture pleases me, my mother's Germanic unconcern shown up for all the world to see.

When I was younger, it bothered me greatly that my mother didn't cook. Real mothers, especially real Jewish mothers, cooked. Although I didn't equate cooking with love, I equated it with solicitude. My mother never said simple, motherly things like, "Are you warm enough? It's cold outside. Let me get you another sweater." I realize now that from a very early age I wanted to reform my mother, bend her to my concept of how things—she—ought to be. What I wanted was for her to stand over a hot stove, like all the immigrant mothers I had ever read about, and stir soup: I yearned for the stereotype instead of the unpredictable, powerful person I had been born to.

The refrigerator in my parents' apartment, which is emptied now of children, is barely filled except for the weekends. By Tuesday the contents have usually been scaled down to elementals: on the top shelf next to a bottle of Mott's prune juice, a cluster of grapes rests in a checked red and white carton—the same cartons in which Lisconte's, the small grocery that services the buildings in their neighborhood, has been delivering fruit for years; alongside them are plastic containers half filled with rice and coagulated gravy. A jar of applesauce and a small glass bowl containing some chopped-up parsley sit on the middle shelf, and in the crisper there is a head of iceberg lettuce, some yellowing celery, and a solitary tomato.

At the parties I go to these days, there is always very little to eat and a lot to drink. I stand around and sip potent stuff—vodkas and gins and rums. I am, in fact, a natural drinker—a Christian. It is only after three or four drinks that my tongue begins to slur. Once after one of these parties, I answered the phone, buoyant as air.

"You sound drunk," my mother said.

"Why?" I said. "I'm not at all." What I felt was happy, uncharacteristically so; perhaps that was the giveaway.

"Your voice is heavy," she went on, "and you're talking so much."

"*You* called *me*," I said, stung. "Remember?"

"I know, I know," my mother answered. "I won't call again. Just remember—it doesn't suit you."

"*What* doesn't?" By now I felt alarmingly alert, my wooziness vanished into the night.

"Being drunk. I hope you weren't on a date. It's sure to put any man off."

"Thanks," I said, "I wasn't. Good night."

I hung up the phone and was immediately besieged by an image of myself as a slack-jawed creature in a Dorothy Parker story, prey to liquor and men. *Heavy-voiced.* That didn't sound attractive. I spoke out loud, testing the judgement. I had to be careful, stop before I passed over the thin line between drink-induced cheer and vulgarity. I went over the last hour of the party in my head, trying to remember if I had said anything unnecessarily intimate to any of the people I had been introduced to.

My mother trips me up on my trajectory away from her domain and into a wider, freer sphere by highlighting the ways in which I might embarrass myself without realizing it. The method is a successful one, by and large. When I took up smoking during late adolescence, she squashed my worldly ambitions (I imagined I looked pensive and insouciant, like Albert Camus) by telling me that I looked like a lesbian when I had a cigarette in my mouth. "It looks right on some people," she said, as though I were entering a contest. "It just doesn't on you."

"What do you mean that I look like a lesbian?"

"I can't explain it," she said. "I could be wrong."

But I had already decided she was right. Her remark got to me not because I feared looking like a lesbian so much as because I feared the associations. I had always wanted the sort of undeniably feminine face I didn't have. My ideal, however retrograde, was a pouty softness, cheeks round as apples and a bee-stung mouth. My reality was a defined jaw and strong features—the sort of angularity that precluded conventional high school prettiness. Although I seemed to be less interested in boys than most of the girls I knew, I would have liked the tentativeness to be one-sided. I certainly didn't want to add to the indefiniteness of my appeal—and to my already less than firm sense of femaleness—by looking hard or masculine, the way I supposed lesbians looked. Shortly after my mother made this comment, I stopped smoking.

The odd part is that we never seemed to have any neighbors. There were vague people who lived across the hall in the city or next door during the summer, and they said, "Hello, how are you," and occasionally someone came over to use the swimming pool when we moved to a house with one, but I never had the sense that we lived among others. It always seemed to be us, alone. I do remember one family, the Daleys, who lived next to us during the summer until I was about ten. Mrs. Daley wore tube tops before they were fashionable; it amazed me that she walked around with so much flesh showing as a matter of course. Her midriff especially caught my eye; it was taut and tan between the scanty lines of her top and shorts. My mother wore one-piece bathing suits with stern wire-rimmed cups in them and loose, floating dresses. It was hard for me to think of Mrs. Daley, clacking around in her wedgies and near nakedness, as a mother, but she had, in fact, three perfectly nice children. Her husband, who wore knee-length baggy shorts and rumpled shirts, was known as Dr. Daley. I seem to recall that he was a vet, but I may have imagined that on the basis of his having a rather absent quality around people. Now that I press my memory, it seems doubtful that he was a vet because his family didn't have any pets. I was afraid of all animals, cats in particular, and would never have entered a house where I knew cats were kept.

I spent a lot of time observing the Daleys, trying to gauge the tenor of their family life. I knew for certain that it was different from mine, but I wasn't quite sure how or why. For a while I decided it had something to do with the fact that they had what was called a finished basement. *They* called it this; my mother had never heard of finished basements, and when I told her about the Daleys', she probably assumed it to be yet another American *meshugaas*. Our own basement was used for storing old furniture and toys. The one concession to us, her American children, was a green Ping-Pong table. The basement was not well lit, and I remember squinting across the table at the small white ball hurtling my way, yelling at one of my brothers that I couldn't see and we'd have to start the volley over again.

The Daleys' basement, on the other hand, seemed to have been "finished" expressly with their children in mind. When they weren't at the beach, the three of them spent most of their time down there, playing noisy games. The walls were covered in a red wallpaper that looked like linoleum, and there was a curved bar that was designated as a snacking area. At some point in the late afternoon, Mrs. Daley, her smooth brown legs appearing from under the stairwell, would descend with soda, potato chips, and a large bag of M&M's. She would divvy these out to the children and their guests, and then she would go back upstairs, heels clicking like a Spanish dancer's, and leave them to themselves.

I used to feel unaccountably shy when I visited the Daley children in their basement; it was like entering a foreign country and not being sure of the customs. The lack of overt structure—or of any tangible authority figure—intrigued me because it was so different from my own home. It took me a while to join in the rough-housing, but then they were, as I said, nice children, and they never reacted to what must have seemed to be an odd stiffness on my part. My brother Eric was friendly with the Daley brother, Charles, and he sometimes invited him and his sisters, Ann and Karen, over to our house. I wonder what they made of our quiet board games on the porch, a child or two always off in a corner with a book hiding his or her face, and our nurse, Lena, hovering strictly. My mother never appeared with snacks when the Daley children visited, but if they stayed long enough, they were invited to have supper with us in the kitchen. It bothered me that my mother refused to treat our guests the way she did her and my father's adult ones, but the division was clear. I never expected much interest to be taken in the friends I brought home; my father, to my embarrassment, failed to remember the names of even my reputedly close friends. "Aren't you going to introduce me to your friend?" he would say genially enough, coming out of his study and happening to bump into us. My friends, it seemed to me, weren't fooled; they shrank from his courtesy. Perhaps I should have taken a cue from my sisters, who kept each other company and rarely brought outsiders in.

I would have liked the Daleys to be my dream family, but Charles cried a lot, and I used to hear sudden bursts of screaming from across the fence that separated our gardens, so I wasn't convinced all was paradise over there, either. Ann and Karen struck me as happy enough but a bit drowsy. My sisters thought they were dumb, but I preferred to think of them as understimulated. Mrs. Daley, for all her niceness, spent an awful lot of time on her own pursuits, perfecting her tan or her flower beds. Her daughters consequently stood around a lot, waiting for suggestions—at which they brightened flatteringly, even for the most mundane. My brother actually claimed that the mild-mannered Dr. Daley hit his children, Charles especially, with a belt when he got angry. I tended to think Eric made this up—maybe he, too, was on the lookout for snags in the pattern—but there was a subdued tone to all of them that lent credence to this possibility.

Families are a kind of closed system; like locked trunks, they are hard to penetrate from the outside. Everyone, even the patently impious, respects the sanctity of families—their implied message of *Hands Off! Keep Away!* At which point do you buckle under and give in to the conspiracy: "my family, for better or worse"? As a child I wondered why no one meddled, why no one saw fit to step in and blow the whistle on my parents. But even today, when I ought to know better, I wonder at the wide berth we grant family doings, as though there were a righteousness in looking the other way.

* * *

We sit on the flagstone patio, at the glass-topped table, as the sun sets, dinner finished. I am part of a system that is more airtight than most, sealed from too close an inspection by money and religion and sheer number. It is the end of August, and everyone agrees that this is the best time of year at the beach. My niece throws her head back and laughs; my sister Lily is tickling her. A plate of dessert, brownies thick with homemade frosting, is passed around. My other sister, Rachel, has baked them, and compliments are heaped on her. The brownies are nondairy, so they can be served with meat dishes, and it is noted that they are creamy in spite of this. My father grabs three, and my mother protests, as usual.

What are we celebrating? What, if not the Life of Our Family, triumphant and enduring, a vaunted period in history that lasts and lasts, not giving way to a Dark Ages of the Non-Family? And is it only to my eyes that there is a chill underneath the gaiety, that we are stuck in an ancient amber of ritualized togetherness, grown cold and past its prime?

"I'm getting old," my father says suddenly. "Very old." He is in his early seventies; he has always been old to me. He reaches out and pats my hand. His hands are pudgy and dry, his nails, with their squat half-moons, are impeccably clean. I leave my hand in place for him to pat, although I barely know him. Once, long ago, I wanted to; now I have cleared the space that was reserved for him, and I wonder idly if I'd miss him. The sun goes down over the pool, casting sparks, turning the water red gold.

"Look," my nephew, Max says, "the water's shining."

* * *

Who's to say where it all starts, how and why the pattern warps? I confess I don't really believe in history, a time other than the present, which is always the past. The future I know only as something other people believe in and refer to. "Next week," they say, or "Sometime next year I hope to . . ." I nod sagely; this is not beyond my ken, but it is beyond my comprehension. What is *next week*?

What I loved about my childhood comes down to this: a sensation of coziness, a pair of washed-out cotton pajamas, long-legged and long-sleeved, bleached to a shadow of their once pink color. To change into them after being given a bath was to move from the constriction of clothes—a possible wrongness or rightness of style—into the absolute comfort of texture. What Max will love about his childhood will be so many things, a carnival of pleasures, but I wonder if any one memory will stand out: a shimmering globule. Could it be that there is something to be said for deprivation, for the way it sharpens your senses, leading to a treasuring—the preciousness of those pajamas? Or is this just a wishful belief in some naturally occurring Law of Compensation, a myth of consolation I lull myself with, like a nursery rhyme: *Hush, little baby, don't you cry*?

THREE

Children live under the rule of the comparative: we were divided up, three on each side, the Neat and Non-Neat. Lily, the oldest, had tidy, fragrant habits—I thought of them defensively as those of a spinster, but I was envious. She never seemed to acquire any laundry, balled-up socks smelling of feet, or slightly sweaty blouses. I used to peek into the underpants she had put in the hamper for telltale traces, but most of the time you couldn't detect that she had worn them. Lily and Rachel wore white cotton briefs, devoid of frills, throughout their teens; at the age of fourteen or fifteen I started buying bikinis, a bow in the direction of an eroticism I did not feel. My older brother, Benjamin, was a born clerk, forever printing numbered lists on the smallest-sized index cards while the rest of us were still scribbling into looseleaf binders or notebooks. My mother hated Benjamin's cramped style as much as I did. Although it distantly occurred to me that he was only, in fact, adopting the begrudging behavior that had often been shown toward him, I aligned myself with my mother. "Benjamin writes like a rodent," I once said to her, making her laugh. Of that group Eric's rage for order had, undoubtedly, the most modifiable quality—as befitted a middle brother. He was, simply, a boy more neatly inclined than not.

Rachel, Arthur, and I, on the other hand, were classified as *shlumps*, with Arthur, the youngest of us, leading by a wide margin. I tended to let things gather on chairs and the tops of my desk and bureau—clothes, magazines, notices from school or the dentist. My drawers themselves were a mess, and once I started to wear makeup, I hid new lipsticks or eyeshadows among my underwear. Lena and my mother were scandalized by my frequent purchases of cosmetics; I did, admittedly, have an enormous collection compared to Lily and Rachel, but I imagine I was more typical than not. The trouble was that no one bothered to compare me with the girls in my class, on whose example I tried to model myself.

Every other month or so, Lena would have enough. As her skills in the area were formidable, I continued to count on them long after I was supposed to be straightening up after myself. I would come home from school to find my part of the room, the bane of Lily's existence, spotless. The chair at my desk could be sat on once again without my having to dump everything off every evening, and there would be a short row of cosmetic items lined up on my desk accusingly, for all to see. These I whisked away, into the bathroom cabinet or back into my drawer. But my mother had inevitably sighted the evidence before I disposed of it—or, as I was secretly convinced, had been ushered in to view it by a gleeful Lena.

"I'm glad to see you have so much money to waste," she would say to me later that same night. "One or two lipsticks seems like more than enough to me but not to you, I guess. How do you ever use anything *up* this way? Buy, buy, buy. When do you have time for all this shopping? They must keep you very busy in school."

The makeup I bought, even in my most frenzied phase, never came to much more than $10, but my mother's attitude toward it and the fuzziness of her position on the issue of money generally—how we children were to spend or not spend it—necessitated a certain duplicity. Since I usually charged these items to the Bloomingdale's card that I had been given on my fifteenth birthday—the bills for which went to her—I had devised the method of throwing out my store receipts, hoping my mother wouldn't notice my signature on the copies of the bills when they finally arrived in the mail together with the ones for her purchases. She usually did notice, but I persisted anyway; it suited my vision of our being one big happy family, sharing the wealth. This in spite of the fact that I also kept a journal in which I recorded how much I hated everyone in the family, singling out one sibling—usually Lily—whom I especially disliked from day to day. But the point had less to do, in any case, with the actual expense than with its justification in my mother's eyes. In the Germany of her youth, teenaged girls didn't go around buying Revlon mascara or Biba's brown lip gloss.

Truth be told, she didn't comprehend adolescence, didn't tolerate its waywardness, and my sisters obliged by never becoming, in the usual sense, teenagers. It was only I—and to a lesser degree, Eric and Arthur—who showed these untoward tendencies. Added to this were a set of circumstances that exaggerated the situation further. One was that my mother didn't buy much herself in the way of conventional female things—she stuck loyally to a few basics from Germaine Monteil and refilled them only when they ran out—so it wasn't as though she shared my obsession with how I looked in any manifest way. True, she was always commenting on people's appearances: "My, what an ugly girl that is," she would say jovially of a particular friend of Lily's, but that was presumed to be different. The other was that since, along with her other anti-Americanisms, my mother didn't believe in giving us allowances, the whole issue of how we obtained spending money was a complex, even delicate one. If you got her in the right mood, she could be quite generous. Eric was the most talented of us at reading the signs. I'd watch, dumbfounded, as he successfully sidled up to her for something or other he wanted money for—a new basketball or pair of boots.

But depending on the day, my mother could also be arbitrarily economical; it was this possibility I was afraid of. She wouldn't order any fruit other than apples from the grocer for a week because everything else was deemed too expensive. And she would suddenly decide that there wasn't a thing I needed, just when all the girls in my fashion-conscious high school class were showing off their new spring wardrobes. Lena, who watched my closet with a hawkish eye, was always ready to support her on this score by announcing that I owned some skirt or blouse that had never been worn. If I tried to argue with my mother at one of these times, she spouted a newfound, hodgepodge Marxism: "I'm not going shopping with you for new clothes, Hannah," she would say, "and that's that. Wear what you have. *You* set the example for a change. I can't believe all the girls in your class, the ones from Brooklyn, too (Brooklyn was synonymous in her eyes with poverty, much as I tried to correct this view), drag their mothers to Saks Fifth Avenue every spring for new dresses. What about Ruth Samuel?"

Ruth Samuel was the only other person in my class at The Melamed School who came from a large family, but unlike mine, hers was genuinely penurious. Most of the girls in the snobby atmosphere of my school treated her like an exotic, someone out of *Five Little Peppers and How They Grew*, but I was intermittently friendly with her. Ruth, in a school where even the least affluent kids had self-sacrificing parents who coughed up the money for clothes, wore long farmyard skirts and men's shirts. My mother never referred to Ruth Samuel's financial condition—she wasn't interested enough in any of my friends to inquire into their lives—except for these occasions. And once she mentioned Ruth, I knew what was coming next: my mother's pet grievance against the Jewish day school we attended was that it didn't have uniforms like the Waspy private schools. Some of this was snobbism on her part, a desire to upgrade what she considered to be the deluded Jewish notion of class. But part of it was a real European-bred conviction about the principle of uniforms, their democratic anonymity. No one could patronize Ruth Samuel in a class of identically dressed girls. Of course, the majority of my classmates at Melamed came from European homes. But whereas they all seemed to have parents who rushed to embrace the American ethic of consumerism on behalf of their children (if not for themselves), my mother stood on her pride. Germany, Hitler notwithstanding, had been superior. Americans were childish, lacking in dignity, their love of education more professed than real.

"If you had uniforms in school," my mother informed me, "you'd be much better off. None of this fuss about clothes could go on. That Sharon girl and her fur skirt! Who ever heard of such nonsense in Frankfurt!"

The "Sharon girl" my mother so disdainfully referred to was Sharon Levi, the most sought-after girl in my grade. Her parents were, indeed, American—and they lived in Brooklyn. Sharon's father was a dentist; there was no one in Flatbush, apparently, who didn't bring their teeth to him. I had been to the Levis' house only once and had been struck by the mixture of wealth and casualness. Mrs. Levi served up a gourmet meal in the dinette, and Sharon's brother, Arnie, talked endlessly to his father about some tennis tournament he was competing in. They reminded me of a TV family, unfathomably happy-go-lucky. Sharon's wardrobe, mythic enough to have pierced my mother's relative indifference to the nuances of my school life, was bogglingly extensive even in the jaded terms of my peers. I had reported to my mother several months ago of her latest coup: at the start of the midwinter term, when a lot of kids returned with Miami tans, Sharon sauntered in with a Caribbean tan and a rabbit skirt.

I had told my mother about Sharon's entrance—which caused everyone to look up from their copies of *Cannery Row* (to this day I cannot think of John Steinbeck without instantly smelling raw fish)—one evening as we were looking for a coat in the Junior department of Lord & Taylor. My mother had shown up late as usual, and when she finally arrived, I wished to spur her on to greater extravagance by casually inserting the news of Sharon Levi's most recent fashion find. But I could see her heading toward a hopelessly plain navy double-breasted coat, a variation on two others I had owned, so the revelation seemed to have the opposite effect.

"It sounds hideous," my mother said. "I can't imagine why anyone—man, woman, or child—would want a fur skirt."

"Well, she certainly stands out," I said, "if that's what one wants."

Who was "one" other than me? It was *I*, not "one," who wanted, but having realized how deeply unimpressed my mother was by my feelings if they were presented as merely mine, I had hit upon the stratagem of referring to an anonymous body of opinion whenever I needed to buttress a point. How else could I get my mother to pay attention? It was an elegant solution, but it masked an essential desperation about my own significance. It also led me far astray: I ended up by ascribing most of my views to other people, claiming to have read somewhere or other that they believed what I believed. I dragged in people from far and wide, famous people whom my mother admired. "Eleanor Roosevelt," I once told her, "thought that her biggest mistake in life was in not indulging her children enough. That's why her sons had trouble later on." Whether Eleanor Roosevelt considered this to be her biggest mistake—whether she had ever said anything faintly like this or whether indeed she had been an *over*indulgent mother—was of no interest to me; I had made the remark up. What mattered was that it sounded fairly convincing and that it suited my purposes. But the person I brought in the most as an advocate of my own views was Lily. My mother, I knew, was influenced by what my oldest sister thought. I was forever quoting Lily on some matter, usually a grievance, about which she had never voiced any opinion at all. Then my mother would go off to check whether Lily had really agreed with me that she was selfish or unkind, and Lily would invariably deny it, leaving me out in the cold.

"How do you look in forest green?" my mother asked, pulling out a duffle coat with toggles—the kind five-year-old boys wore.

"Horrible," I said. "A famous designer recently said that no one looks good in forest green. I think it was Christian Dior."

"Really?" my mother said.

She hung the coat back.

"I'm just trying," I said, "to give you a sense of the competition at school. It's ruthless."

"Ignore it," my mother said. "This looks like it might suit you. What do you think?"

She held out a gray wool coat. It had a double row of shiny gold buttons and looked as if it were meant to last for years.

"It's so plain!"

"It won't hurt to try it on."

What I had in mind was a black coat with a flared skirt. Sharon Levi had recently worn a coat like this to school, but the department we were in didn't appear to carry anything nearly as flamboyant.

"I'll look like a doorman," I said, but I was already sticking one arm into the sleeve.

"Very shick," my mother said. "It fits you well."

"Shick"—which was how my mother insisted on pronouncing *chic*, even after I corrected her—was the highest praise possible as far as clothes were concerned. I was eyeing myself dolefully in the three-way mirror when a saleswoman asked us if we needed assistance. She was a timid, short woman—European, like my mother—and I knew ahead of time whose side she would be on.

"What do you think?" I turned to the saleswoman. The coat didn't look bad on me, and by now I was resigned to my fate.

"Beeyewteful," she said, clapping her hands together like a delighted child. "And vat does the mama think?"

"Hannah has to like it," my mother said with perfect insincerity.

"It's okay," I said.

"Good," my mother said. "We can always decide at home."

"Is that a take?" the saleswoman asked. "Perhaps the daughter vants to vear it home?"

I felt like killing her. Another minute and she'd suggest throwing a party to celebrate the purchase. I looked moodily out toward the elevators. It was a late Wednesday afternoon, and the store seemed strangely empty. I could never figure out why my mother loved Lord & Taylor; no one else seemed to.

"We'll send it, I think," my mother said, "if that's all right."

"Ov course," the saleswoman said. "My name, by the vay, is Eva."

"Thank you, Eva," my mother said.

"I hate this store," I said as we waited for the sales slip. I felt close to tears.

"What a nice woman that was," my mother said.

I said nothing. If I spoke, I would start crying. The saleswoman's politeness had made me feel sad; there was something forlorn about her eagerness. I wanted to tell her not to be so nice.

"What's the matter?"

"Nothing," I said.

I wanted my mother to woo me, to implore me to cheer up—"Hannah, darling, please don't be sad; tell me what's bothering you." My mother never used the conventional American endearments—"darling" or "sweetheart" or just plain "dear"—and she never used the even sweeter Yiddish ones, like "shayfele," either. *Shayfele* meant "little lamb" and it was what my friend

Sylvia's mother called her. My mother used few honeyed terms in general (perhaps, being a *yekke*, she didn't understand the point of them), but in my eternally hopeful mind, any site, however prosaic, might be the one to produce a miraculous transformation in her—even Lord & Taylor. The saleswoman brought the receipt over to us, and my mother and she thanked each other profusely, vying with each other in their expressions of gratitude.

"How about some coffee and a nice cheese Danish before we go home?"

My mother loved cheese Danish. I think they reminded her of the pastry from the corner *Konditorei* of her own childhood. On Friday morning she always ordered a dozen of them, along with a streusel cake topped with buttery crumbs, from the kosher German bakery up in Washington Heights, and by Shabbos morning the Danish were always all gone. I liked them, too, but I noticed that few American-born people had a taste for them, and I sometimes wondered if my mother was deliberately inculcating her immigrant's tastes in me—breeding me to feel foreign as she did, except that the land in question was my native one.

"Why were you late before?" I asked. "I thought you weren't coming. I almost left."

We had already been shopping for an hour, but I believed in holding grudges—or, at least, in pretending to hold them. At four o'clock that afternoon I had stood by the glove counter, as we had planned, in my red and green plaid coat. I was hot in the coat, but I refused to take it off or even to unbutton it. My mother was always late, but I was always vigilant, as though that would inspire her to promptness; I remained at the ready. For the first few minutes, I occupied myself by brooding upon the fates that smiled on

Sharon Levi, delivering her up fur skirts, but after ten minutes I had begun to feel anxious: my mother had been run over by a car or, worse yet, perhaps we had never planned to meet at all! In those next minutes while I stretched my neck, trying to catch sight of the peculiar tilt of the head, the recognizable set to the shoulders that was my mother's, I felt like a character out of Rod Serling's "The Twilight Zone"—the victim of random and malign influences. I had never forgotten one particularly scary episode I had watched several years back on a sleepover date at Sylvia's house in which a man woke up to find that everyone he knew in the world had died overnight. I was prepared to believe anything, the eerier the better. I had just decided that my entire family had moved to Sweden without informing me when my mother appeared.

"Hannah, I was only fifteen minutes late—"

"Twenty."

"—And I'm not going to argue about it. I've waited for you plenty. I thought we just bought you a beautiful coat."

"You do not wait for me plenty. And I don't even like the coat."

"All right, I don't. Shall we skip the coffee?"

I didn't say anything. I was counting on my mother's being able to read my mind. In my mind I was ready to forgive her everything; I held no grudges, offered her no resistance. In my mind my mother was my "darling" and I was her "shayfele"; we were entwined in mutual adoration.

"Come, *schatzekind*, let's go upstairs quickly. The store will close soon."

The *schatzekind*—a German approximation of "darling child" and as close to my wishes as she would ever get—assuaged me instantly. My mother took my hand, and I followed her to the escalator. Anyone watching us would have thought I was retarded—or troublingly young for my age. I stood behind my mother on the escalator and sank into my thoughts. Small efforts at persuasion were as far into cajolery as my mother would go, but I wanted more. Wasn't I her child? And if I were—a twinge of doubt always lingered in my mind—how could she live knowing I was so unhappy, so starved for confirmation?

We got off on the sixth floor, where Lord & Taylor ran, without a pretense of enthusiasm, a coffee shop known as the Bird Cage. Aside from its pale green wallpaper and a few gilt-flaked cages that contained some sedate birds, the coffee shop was undecorated to the point of shabbiness. That evening several women were scattered around the room's tiny, uninviting tables; my mother banged her hip as we edged our way around the corners of one and settled ourselves into the rickety garden-party chairs. We both stared moodily out into space as a heavy-ankled waitress shuffled over toward us. She had a pencil tucked behind one ear and her pad at the ready, as though she worked in a flourishing cocktail lounge. The waitress plunked down two stained menu cards and looked pointedly at her watch.

"Youse better rush it," she said. "Almost closing time."

"I thought the store closes at six," I said.

I had developed the habit, starting several years back, of mentally adding on adverbs whenever I said something to anyone—like stage directions from the director in myself to the actress in myself. I was always silently transposing my remarks into the third person in my head; writing in the desired tonal effect: "'I thought the store closes at six,' she said testily." The adverb I most favored in these silent addendums was *flatly*, especially when talking to my mother. I guess it came from reading so much, but it also derived from the radical detachment with which I tried to view my own existence.

"*We* close at five-thirty, dearie," she said.

It was quarter past.

"Nah, nah," my mother said.

This was the expression she used when she wished to smooth my feathers.

"I'd like some of the tea sandwiches," I said. "Tuna and egg. No meat, please."

"Coffee?"

The waitress had a pretty, weary mouth. She looked faintly Irish, and I began to wonder how she had ended up waiting on a disgruntled mother and daughter in Lord & Taylor on a Wednesday evening in New York City. Why wasn't she gathering speckled eggs on a farm in some misty village? I didn't want any coffee, but I suddenly wanted to please her, and I thought it would be more gracious to go along with her suggestion.

"Yes, please."

"Coffee for me, too," my mother said, "and a cheese Danish."

"Might not be any left," the waitress said. "Might be only cinnamon. But I'll check for you."

"That's very kind of you," my mother said.

"She must be tired," my mother said when the waitress had gone off.

"Yes," I said, full of sympathy. "She has such red hair."

We sat in the coffee shop until ten to six, the last to leave. Either the waitress had relented, or she had exaggerated to begin with. She hummed softly to herself as she wiped off the tables. As for us sitting there, what can I say but that the magic took hold? I was alone with my mother, and she was in a good mood;

besides, the chemistry of our relationship dictated that when I retreated, she advanced. She asked me questions, drawing me out as though I were a riveting guest at the Friday night dinner table. For a brief period I was the center of her attention. No one else had her but me, and my mother was all I wanted. By the time we left the Bird Cage, I wanted to remain there forever, in that setting of strangely outdoorsy furniture—like a deserted summer party. The rest of my life—school, siblings, anxieties—dimmed into inconsequence as I floated up above the world in a glistening bubble with my mother.

Outside Lord & Taylor the bubble burst. Everything went on as usual: the sky had turned black, and the buses roared down Fifth Avenue. Suddenly it seemed to me that I had, briefly but completely, lost track of who I was—a high school student in a plaid coat out shopping with her mother. For a moment, merged with my mother in the coffee shop, my dream of union come true, I had imagined myself going home to a variation of her life—a husband and children, phone calls in the morning, errands at Lamston's, theater tickets, and luncheons. It was disturbing how real it had seemed to me.

My mother craned her neck back and forth like a periscope, the way people do when they are searching for a taxi at rush hour in Manhattan.

"We could walk to Madison for the bus," she said.

But we both continued to stand there expectantly. I looked upward and noticed there were no stars in the sky—none that you could see behind the tall buildings—and then I remembered, like scattered parts reassembling, who and where I was: my father waiting for my mother, my brothers and sisters, the kids who didn't like me in Melamed, dour Lena, my periods that didn't come for months at a time and then poured out of me like angry streams, the details of my life stalking me.

"Here's a taxi at last," my mother said as a man puffing on a cigar got out of one almost at our feet. "What luck."

I wanted to walk away and off into the dusk. I hated the thought of going home. Everything felt so cramped.

"Nu?" my mother said. "Are you coming?"

How do you flee the unbearable when you are underage and afraid of being without your mother for more than a night? I stepped into the cab after her. My mother leaned over and gave the driver the address through the grimy plastic partition. She called him "driver," which made me cringe. I pressed my nose against the window and looked at the passengers in the bus that waited alongside us at the red light. Most of them looked straight ahead. The entire world was oblivious to me.

My mother leaned back in her seat. "It'll be all right, Hannah," she said, "you'll see," as though there had been a tragedy, someone shot in the back of the head right in front of us—his life trickling away.

I thought how odd, how impossible it was to comprehend that somewhere else the sun was just beginning to rise. It was hot there, and there were empty stretches of sand. Somewhere else again it was impossibly cold, below freezing, the footprints of furry animals animating silent expanses of snow. The idea of my own speck-ness in the universe soothed me. The taxi lurched forward, and I leaned back in my seat, letting my hand fall over my mother's gloved one.

* * *

My mother's sense of the practical often struck me as being applied exclusively to me and my siblings; it was on this score that I nursed my most serious grudge. As I saw it, she was quite capable of being anything but sensible, of throwing money to the winds when she felt like it. Her ideas—of value or wastefulness—were as erratic as her moods, and there were entire realms of merchandise on which she spent lavishly. Shoes, for some reason, were one of these; she usually bought several pairs at a time and didn't blanch at prices that seemed, from my perspective, beyond reason. I would make a point of going into her bedroom frequently to assess her plunder—noting the discreet price stickers on the boxes from Delman, boxes that said BETH LEVINE or DAVID EVINS or FERRAGAMO—storing up the information for future use. My opportunity for confronting her—enacted several times a winter over the course of a few years, as though each time I might succeed, finally, in shaming her, in catching her red-handed—usually presented itself on those evenings when she was getting ready to go to a charity dinner with my father. My parents went to fund raisers—for tiny, run-down yeshivas in Brooklyn and for architecturally up-to-the-minute medical complexes in Israel—a lot in those years, although my mother hated them. She claimed she had nothing to talk about with the other guests, and since my father was usually seated on the dais in some honorary capacity, she was often left to make conversation on her own during the dinner. Later on she would simply refuse to go to many of these events; my father, who relished the endless courses of food and the gossip, attended them by himself or with one of us. I know I admired my mother in those days for her failure to adapt, but I eventually came to view her professed social diffidence less as a becoming touch of modesty and more as a form of arrogance, a secret belief that she was better than the other wives—carefully groomed and flashily jeweled—whose company she was thrown into. Although I guess in her way she really was different if not better—vastly understated in her dress and somewhat unconventional in her opinions. It was hard to envision her fingering her pearls and discussing the advantages of Aspen over Vail. I could even feel sorry for her, having strained away from these symbols of the affluent life—no one in my family knew how to ski, and my parents didn't play golf or frequent vacation spots like Acapulco—only to be blithely associated with them all the same.

On one such evening I knocked on her bedroom door after first trying the knob.

"Who is it?" my mother yelled from the depths of her bathroom.

"It's me," I said loudly.

I refused to name myself on principle. I was intensely bothered by my mother's absent-minded habit of referring to me by one of my sister's names, and I took every opportunity to reassure myself that she recognized me by the sound of my voice, uniquely different from Lily's or Rachel's.

"Lily? Is that you?"

"No." I had bent down and was shouting through the keyhole. "It's one of your many Other Daughters."

"Hannah! Be right there," she said.

Seconds later I could hear the rusty, old-fashioned key—shaped exactly like the illustration under the word *clef* in my first French book—turn in the lock. My mother stood there in bra and underpants. She wore thin, plain nylon underpants and a bra that suggested, with its stiff underwiring and glinting array of back hooks, a more menacing purpose than its actual one.

"Come right in," she said, padding back toward her bed in bare feet. "My dress is all wrong. Maybe you can help me."

I had never outgrown the pleasure of watching my mother prepare for an evening out. When I was much younger, seven or eight, I had been entranced by the garters that dangled like four metallic tails from her girdle and by the way she first hooked her stockings over the garter button and then slipped the clasp deftly into place. By the time I was fourteen, a reader of my mother's copies of *Vogue* and *Harper's Bazaar*, I no longer mistook her rather spartan routines for dazzling preparations, but I still enjoyed watching the brisk, step-by-step manner in which she proceeded.

It varied little from time to time. She pulled on a paneled girdle and stockings—the latter eventually, to my regret, updated to the unintriguing convenience of pantyhose—and then stepped into a pair of pumps, usually brown or black silk, that had been chosen an hour earlier along with her dress. I sat on her bed and watched. The charity dinners took place in one clump in the winter, so the bedroom windows were usually closed, but the city sounded faintly in the background: an impatient driver honked; a siren blared; and a delivery boy from Lisconte's rattled his bicycle over a grating in the street. It was nice to be inside in the twilight hour, caught up in the aura of feminine bustle.

"What do you think?" my mother asked, nodding toward the black jersey dress spread on her bed. "I think I look like the caterer in it."

"I don't remember," I said. "Put it on for me."

My mother pulled it over her head cautiously. "My hair," she said.

"It's fine," I said. "Elegant."

"Really?"

She sounded delighted, then pulled it back off.

"It isn't too—"

"It's fine," I said.

I picked this moment to spring my trap.

"None of my friends' mothers spend a hundred and fifty dollars on shoes."

I followed her into the bathroom. Without her dress on and in her shoes and stockings, she looked like a thickened version of a chorus girl, someone with still-shapely legs who had once danced on top of tables at the Blue Angel, hoarsely belting out *Lieder*.

My mother peered into her lighted mirror and sighed. "Hopeless," she said, but I had the distinct feeling she didn't mind what she saw.

"Did you hear what I said? About your shoes?"

"I did," she said. "I'm glad you found something to complain about."

Her refusal to swallow the bait pleased me for some obscure reason—reminded me of who I was in reality, in the world outside of my head.

"You never buy me things," I said.

She had applied foundation from a small frosted-glass bottle, placing it in beige circles on either cheek, and on her forehead and chin. For a second, before she rubbed the circles in, she looked like the demurest of circus clowns. Her eyes shifted briefly toward me in the mirror and then back.

"Like what?"

She dabbed on two blobs of cream rouge and now rubbed these into her cheeks with quick, impatient strokes.

"You do everything so *hard*," I said. "You'll pull your skin that way. *Pat* it in."

I read the beauty columns in her magazines carefully and could enumerate most of the cosmetic companies in the country, obscure ones, too. I knew facts I had no use for: which eye cream was considered the best and which finishing powder; the right shade of pencil with which to darken graying eyebrows.

"You know so much," she said. "I mean it."

"Presents," I said. "Whenever my friend Sylvia mentions that she needs something, her mother goes out and buys it for her. She finds it on her bed when she comes home from school."

"Lucky Sylvia," my mother said.

She brushed eyeshadow in a taupe color on either lid, squinting downward so as not to get any of the powder onto her contact lenses.

"Damn!" She stamped her foot.

"What happened?"

My mother blinked rapidly and held her palm under her left eye. She pulled the lid to the left, and a tiny lens popped out. She stood a moment with the lens in her hand, looking at it, daring it to cause her further discomfort, then put it back in her eye.

"You need mascara," I said.

I liked the role of lady-in-waiting. It gave me an opportunity to act bossy in the guise of being helpful. My mother rummaged around a Lucite cube until she found her mascara wand, then combed it tentatively through her lashes.

"Do the bottom ones," I commanded. "They're important."

She leaned closer to the mirror and dutifully ran the wand over her sparse lower lashes. While she was shaping her eyebrows up and outward with a small brush, I studied my face in the mirrored bathroom wall alongside her. No matter how much I looked at myself, and I checked myself out tirelessly, I never got used to the arrangement of bones and features that comprised my face. Once I was away from my own reflection, I tended to compose a whole new set of features for myself—trading in my brown eyes for exotic green ones, my long mouth for a small, full *moue*—and I was always somewhat chagrined to find that my actual image in the mirror fell short, once again, of my imagination's best work.

"I look so *grim*," I said.

My mother was putting on perfume. All she had left to do was her dress and then lipstick after that. She was meeting my father at the Waldorf-Astoria; on evenings when he came home from work first, I couldn't hang around her, but I would go into their bedroom afterward and survey the signs they had left: a shoehorn lying on the carpet or a pair of stockings curled on the bed like two rosettes. The room had a startled look, like one of those vacated supper tables in a fifteenth-century Dutch still life, and it smelled of my father's spicy cologne. I would survey it, then go into the bathroom to try on a lipstick or simply to stare at myself.

"Do you like my looks?"

"Yes," my mother said.

"I don't," I said, following her out into the bedroom. She buckled a narrow platinum and diamond watch on her wrist.

"You're very striking. Everyone thinks so."

By "everyone" I assumed she meant the ladies who went to *shul*, and I hated the description of myself as "striking." It sounded suspiciously kindly.

"Do you think I'm beautiful?"

Why, oh why, didn't I have a mother who showered me with praise, who held deeply subjective opinions about my appearance and character? Her objectivity angered me, her inability to comprehend that to a mother—a good mother, like Sylvia's—a daughter wasn't relatively anything, wasn't to be compared to standards other than those of blind love.

"Sometimes," she said. "When you're not moody. I've never seen a girl whose looks it changes so much for the worse."

According to my mother my being "moody"—another of her favored words—altered my appearance in a Jekyll-and-Hyde way. One moment I was nice to look at, the next hideous to behold. I didn't quite believe that my sullenness could cast such a pall, but it made me self-conscious, and I reminded myself to lift the corners of my mouth when I was angry.

"Sylvia's father calls her 'little princess.'"

"I'll tell Daddy to call you 'little princess,' too," she said.

She was ready to go. It was only at leave-takings, however temporary, that she became even disingenuously magnanimous.

"Momma?"

I groaned. It was Eric. He liked sounding like one of the Little Rascals or the boy on "Lassie," pretending he had a cowlick and speaking with a twang.

"Momma, is you dressed?"

Eric squeaked in on his sneakers.

"You look nice," he said. "Benjamin's hogging the TV."

"Don't you have any homework to do?" my mother said.

"Good night," I said.

Rachel, I knew, was studying for a math test. She got uniformly high marks in school and would bend her head myopically over a textbook, chewing a pencil, for hours on end. Arthur was too young, and Lily and I were having one of our many fights, so there was no one to talk to. I wished I lived in a cozy frame house and could meet a crowd of friends at the Soda

Shoppe, the way they did on "The Patty Duke Show," or that I had a father I could have soul-searching conferences with, like Sally Field on "Gidget."

What I wished for most was to be older—elderly, in fact. Sixty seemed like a soothing age to me; my life would be mostly behind me, all choices made. I was fifteen years old, the youngest sophomore in my grade, and what I dreaded most at that moment in my life was the trip my class was scheduled to take the next day. School outings dissolved the regular schedule, showing up the leaders from the kids on the fringe. They made me deeply uneasy ever since the last bus trip I had gone on—to a protest rally in Washington, D.C. All the Jewish day schools in "the Greater New York area"—this was the phrase our principal had used—had decided to participate in the rally. I had wanted to stay home, and although my mother didn't object—she heartily shared my dislike of group sojourns—I was afraid it would look too obvious. Afterward I bitterly concluded that no one would have missed me anyway. I had no "partner" for the bus—all the other girls, including Sylvia, seemed to have planned for this months ahead of time. I ended up sitting in the front, next to Ruth Samuel. I cried steadily for the four hours that it took to get to Washington, although Ruth was pleasant enough. It was too degrading a judgment to be sitting in the seats behind the bus driver and near the teachers when all the popular kids were lumped in the back, giggling over *Playboy*. One of the reasons for this was that I had remained defiantly uninterested in boys while the rest of my classmates had become "boy crazy." It never occurred to me that I lagged behind them developmentally; I couldn't understand how anyone could get excited about the pimply or leering specimens of masculinity who sat boredly or overattentively in the same class as I did.

My mother was in her fur coat saying good night to Lily and Rachel. They clustered around her in the hall as though they might never see her again.

"'Bye," I said again. "I may stay home tomorrow."

"Fine," my mother said.

Her casualness should have made me happy but only made me feel more isolated. I couldn't figure out why she was so indifferent to attendance or to school matters generally. It undoubtedly had something to do with her anti-American stance. I thought of Sharon Levi, who at this very moment was probably discussing the trip excitedly on her Princess phone with some boy or other. I decided to wash my hair before Lily installed herself in the bathroom. It usually took me a good half-hour to wash my hair. I wore it long and parted in the middle, and Sharon Levi admired it. Once under the hot shower, with my trusty tube of Prell, I was free to pursue my fantasy: behind the white plastic curtain strewn with yellow flowers, I became an Only Child, a mixture of Sarah Crewe, Eloise, and Gidget. My mother had died when I was very young, and my doting father took me to the Plaza for breakfast on Sunday mornings. I had hardly any cuticles on my fingernails and blonde fuzz instead of black hairs on my legs. I wasn't, until the moment when Lily banged on the bathroom door, me.

FOUR

Maybe memory gets it all wrong, I don't know. I know that once I was little and now I am not. I am in my mid-twenties, although I'm told I look older: I think it has something to do with a lack of gleam in my eyes. There is no one to tell me what to do anymore, which leaves me with a lot of decisions on my hands and very little conviction that I am making the right ones, even about small things. I am on my way to the third floor of Bloomingdale's, unfettered by my mother's taste or Lena's prohibitive eye. A very old lady, her back curved over like a snail's, stands ahead of me on the escalator. She clutches at a pocketbook with one gnarled hand; the other rests on a cane. I notice a wedding band on her bent finger and imagine that she once had a loving husband named Sam. When the escalator levels off at the second floor, she stumbles, and I almost fall over her.

"Sorry," I say, "did I hurt you?"

"Oh, I don't think so," she says, dusting herself off like a piece of furniture. "You young people are light on your feet."

Her face is etched all over with fine lines, as though her skin has been caught under a butterfly net.

"These escalators," I say, "are difficult to maneuver. I hope you're all right."

"Yes," she says. "I don't come here often. I usually take the elevator."

Her blue eyes remind me of my grandmother's—so blue they are almost purple.

"Well, good-bye," I say. I am almost yelling.

"Good-bye," she says.

I want to stay by her side, but she moves off into the hectic, bazaarlike atmosphere of the second floor. On the third floor a man and woman are spraying everyone who steps off the escalator with large flacons of perfume. "Just in from Paris, ladies," the man says in a high, nasal voice. "You must try it—the smell of romance captured. It's just *sinful*." The man and the woman, who is a pencil-thin brunette, laugh gaily, as though they were standing on top of the Eiffel Tower, the breeze ruffling their hair, a shimmering city beneath them. Although they pretend to be a couple and the woman has her arm in his, the man is clearly homosexual. I wonder if the old lady will be sprayed by them and if she will think they are lovers.

Bloomingdale's always makes me lonely: all the choices, so many possible ways to look, everything requiring an output of energy, a core of solid conviction —*This gray sweatshirt is me*. Nothing I buy can't be bought or worn by thousands of other people. I wander into an alcove that has several layers of V-necked T-shirts displayed on a headless torso. I study the shelves of neatly folded shirts, debating whether to buy several of them in yellow, bright pink, and apricot and then stick them one on top of the other; this is how the torso wears them, and it looks wonderful. The black saleswoman behind the counter is wearing an ivory T-shirt and a necklace of ivory bells that tinkle when she moves.

"You're not going to believe this, but I just saw Warren Beatty go by," she says to me.

"Really?" I say. I've decided against the T-shirts.

"Isn't he gawjus? Some body he got on him."

"I know him," I say, which isn't true, but I am beginning to feel lost, without any sense that I make a dent anywhere.

"Yo-o kiddin'," she says, alert to my presence.

"I met him at a party," I say. "He isn't my type."

Her eyes widen.

"Give him to me, honey. I'll take him off you."

I want the saleswoman to appreciate me, my sense of discrimination rising above the tide of opinion, but I think she's convinced I'm nuts, passing up Warren Beatty, whom I've never met.

"This store is so hot," I say.

"Hot as hell," she says.

On the escalator going back down, I decide that what I really need is some new makeup, something to dispel the pallor of my existence.

The main floor mills with customers. Its huge island of cosmetic counters is dotted with women in pink or white smocks. From a distance they appear to speak authoritatively, like doctors, tapping on jars with their pens to emphasize a point. I move closer to the Ultima II counter and watch as a vivaciously made-up woman with gold flecks in her eyebrows leans over and rubs a cream into a customer's face. Her technique is nothing like my mother's; she uses wide, massaging strokes, and in the bright light her long scarlet nails flash.

"Like velvet," she says. "Your skin just drinks it up. Take a look." She steps back and folds her hands under her elbows, an irrefutable presence. The customer cocks her head in the small mirror she is holding. When she puts her chin down, the flesh around her jawline ripples.

"Lovely," she says.

After this I stop at a makeup counter that is advertising a free gift with purchase. A sweet-looking Japanese girl in a blue and white flowered kimono gives me a card from the basket she holds over one arm. Her basket also contains samples of the free gift—a vinyl envelope filled with miniature jars and compacts. The samples make me think of *The Borrowers*—one of Lily's favorite childhood books, about a pea-sized family who ingeniously adapt small, ordinary human objects, like thimbles, for their own use.

I am drawn to these merchandising come-ons for the same reason I enter sweepstakes: I like the idea of incentive for its own sake, of aimless proliferation. An urge overtakes me, and I fill out a card, only to find myself, in six weeks' time, the owner of a Zircon engagement ring. I received this ring, which sparkles like a real diamond, as one of several gifts when I entered a mail-order-house sweepstakes. To enter, I ordered a wooden foot massager and a roll of extra-strong adhesive tape from the catalogue. In return I was sent the ring, mounted in a velvet box; a plastic device for measuring pasta; and a booklet on how to make 300 different kinds of salad. I don't suppose I'll ever use any of these items, but their arrival in the mail, packed in auspicious brown cartons, made me feel momentarily less lonely, at the other end of someone's thoughts.

Another Japanese woman in a kimono stands behind a display containing several vials, like those in a lab, filled with colored liquids. Next to them is a larger vial filled with white blossoms; it is spare yet decorative, like a sushi platter.

"Have you tried our line?" she asks.

"Once," I say.

"You should," she says. "Shiseido is very serious."

"Oh," I say, putting my shoulder bag down on the counter.

"Japanese women are known for their beautiful skin."

She touches her own cheek promptingly.

"You do," I say ungrammatically.

"Your pores," she says. "Have you thought about trying to reduce them?"

She holds a mirror up to my nose. In its magnifying reflection my pores look like craters, the way Gulliver's must have looked to the Lilliputians.

"Are you using a tightening astringent?"

"Yes," I say.

I have enough bottles of toners and astringents to see me through the next decade, but I pick up one of the bottles on the counter and study the ingredients listed on its label.

"It doesn't seem to be working for you," she says.

Her slanted eyes are rimmed dramatically with blue and she speaks a perfect, if somewhat slowed-down, English.

"I guess not," I say.

Adam, the man who cuts my hair, once told me that during the Depression the sales of lipstick went up. He said it disdainfully, while snipping the hairs on the back of my neck, but I took the fact instantly to heart. It was easy for me to see how a new lipstick would offer solace.

The Japanese woman tips a bottle of pink lotion

onto a cotton ball and wipes it gently around my face.

"See?" she says.

She holds out the puff; it has turned gray.

"That's the dirt which has accumulated on your skin during the day. It must be removed to prevent the formation of blemishes and blackheads."

She intones this as though it were a complex mathematical solution to a problem she has been working on for years. I nod my head sagely, although it occurs to me that she has demonstrated nothing other than the fact that it is the end of the day and that I don't live on a clean, secluded island.

"It feels nice," I say.

She has made me feel very precarious, as though at any moment my face will burst into a riot of pimples.

"You will also need cleansing cream. And a clay mask to use once or twice a week."

Her tone has become firmer.

"I think I'll just take the astringent for now," I say.

"Okay," she says, shrugging. "But you really should come back so we can get your skin in shape. Will that be a charge? And you get a gift with your purchase today, so you'll be able to sample more of our products."

I hand the saleswoman my silver charge card.

She leans down and writes out the sales slip in a careful, round script. She is very attentive, as though the procedure were something she has just learned how to do. Keeping an eye on her, I pick up a tiny jar of eye cream and slip it into my jacket pocket. When she looks up and hands me a pen to sign my name, I smile at her.

FIVE

It is early Sunday afternoon and "Under My Thumb" plays on the stero in Eric's old room. The bedrooms in my parents' apartment continue to be referred to by name long after their occupants have gone. Although you wouldn't know it from his swagger, Eric was the last to go, a hold-out for the relative comforts of home —his narrow bed made up for him every morning by Lena and his laundry done by Ida—well after Benjamin and even Arthur had struck out for richer ore, their own ways of mining sustenance. He sits on a chair now, reclaiming the furniture, his fingers plucking at the guitar that lies across his lap. Having recently decided to get engaged, Eric has taken to mournfully inspecting the contents of his room every weekend—as though in them might lie a clue to the rashness of his romantic impulse. He is especially fond of his gleaming basketball trophies, which take up a bookcase shelf and have not been transported to the apartment he shares with a friend from high school; Eric is the only real athlete in the family, and it is an identity of which he is furtively proud.

Eric's room is cavernously still and neat, the way it was when he slept in it. The room has one long window that overlooks the rooftops of several townhouses nearby; direct light is cut off by the back of a large, official building that takes up a full block diagonally across the street. I slept in this room along with two of my brothers until I was eight and was disoriented by its state of permanent semidarkness. I had trouble falling alseep and woke up easily; I remember that I often mistook midnight for early morning. We went to bed very early then, without ado, which only added to my disorientation. It never occurred to Lena to ease the transition from wakefulness to sleep, to sit by our beds and tell us a story, or to sing to us: promptly at seven o'clock, teeth brushed and *Sh'ma* (the Hebrew version of nighttime prayers) rapidly recited, Benjamin, Eric, and I lay in our beds, sheets and blankets firmly pulled under our chins. "Good night," Lena said, and snapped off the light. We were plunged into darkness and separateness, abandoned to our own devices. Several times, after having been asleep for what I took to be the whole night, I went out to the hall and into a blaze of lights: my parents were still sitting in the living room downstairs with dinner guests. As a precaution against my getting up in confusion, Lena got in the habit of leaving the venetian blinds half open. "Stay in bed," she directed me. "Stay in bed until you see it's morning." My brothers, who slept heavily and were less afraid of Lena than I, giggled.

* * *

In the far corners of Eric's room are the same two beds with wooden headboards and frames that have been there for years; next to each of them is a small chest of drawers with a reading lamp. The only other place where I saw beds as utilitarian as the ones my mother selected was in a youth hostel in Paris. I had met up with Rachel there after spending a week with some cousins in London. Lily had chosen to stay home at the beach for the summer. I would think of her—slouched in a garden lounge, buried in one of her beloved and carefully chosen books—while I stood at a foreign intersection peering at a guidebook. I could see her clearly, knees forming a hill, the summer sun glancing in over the hedge that walled off our garden from the street, her chin tucked under in an attitude of total absorption. What would she be reading? Lily liked novels about large Catholic families and, for a brief period, ones about nurses. I knew she had always wanted to have red hair, and most of the nurses she read about were, unaccountably, auburn- or carrot-haired. She and Rachel also hunted the library shelves for teenage romances—eighteen-year-old girls who worried about being asked to the senior prom and about how to obtain the proper organdy or crinoline. I couldn't, in all consideration, understand this particular preference; neither Lily nor Rachel seemed interested in boys or clothes in their own lives. It was as though these vagaries of adolescence were given their due only in the guise of literary fancy, the way my brothers read adventure books.

I remember I spent much of my trip that summer—I had just turned sixteen—roaming in my head over the contents of my drawers, worrying about the clothing I had left behind. The clothing stood in for my mother, for all the many aspects of her. I missed her to the point of feeling disoriented without her presence to anchor me. There was a white T-shirt I longed for on an almost daily basis, as though it were an essential piece of my being. And, as I kept reminding Rachel, who suffered from no such obsessive accountings, I had left a very important belt at home! I ran over these small details endlessly in my head, like a tongue returning to an aching tooth, just to remind myself that the throbbing hadn't gone away.

I'm not sure how much of Europe I took in. I know I took in more with Rachel at my side than alone, for she tended to mute my sense of loss. After all, she lived in the same family I did, and managed to seem at home away from them. Why couldn't I feel similarly? "It doesn't matter," she would say in the mornings, with far more sisterly kindness than Lily ever displayed. "It'll all be there when you get back. Do you want to borrow a top of mine?"

At one point I wrote my mother an express letter asking her to send me a package of all the things I had forgotten to pack, although I was only intending to be away for six weeks. "I need my sunglasses," I wrote. "They're in my underwear drawer, on the right-hand side. And that black leather belt, the one I wear with everything." The sunglasses were cheap plastic, infinitely replaceable, and I don't think I wore the belt so much as eyed it a lot as a possibility when I got dressed in the morning.

My mother called that same week, on a Friday morning, at the apartment of a cousin Rachel and I were staying with in the Hague. Marta, an older woman renowned for her fine-boned beauty among my mother's mostly unbeautiful relatives, was sitting with us at breakfast. She treated my sister and me like real guests, something neither of us were much used to. She had carefully planned out our week's stay for us, and in between excursions to Amsterdam and the seashore at Scheveningen, we had long talks at coffee houses. Marta was one of the few members of my mother's large and extended family who was not Orthodox; I delighted in this fact as much as Rachel—whom I sometimes referred to as "Pious One"—feared it. As it turned out, Marta was careful not to upset any apple carts. She served us only dairy food in her home, which was not kosher, and delicately arranged for us to stay elsewhere for Shabbos.

At night, before she went to bed, she would undo her loosely pinned topknot and release her long silver-gray hair. After we had been there several days, she asked us if we would mind brushing out her hair, explaining that she sometimes had difficulty untangling the knots in back. Rachel took several swipes with Marta's embossed silver brush and then handed it to me; she seemed uncomfortable. There was something about our cousin's rapt enjoyment in her own pleasures that annoyed her, I think. I took the brush and ran it slowly through Marta's hair. She was humming to herself in a tremulous voice (another habit of hers that made Rachel flinch), and her hair smelled of seaweed. I stood behind the chair in which she had seated herself and brushed. For a moment I felt as though I were being given a taste of the childhood I had always wanted—a childhood out of a Renaissance painting, rich with shadings, thick-stroked, a Mother and Child surrounded by halos. Did I imagine the conspiratorial tinge to Marta's smile as she looked at me in the brass-edged oval mirror that hung over her bureau? Probably I did. For one thing, Rachel was still in the room; for another, I was always looking for signs of favoredness. Marta may have in fact inclined toward me, if only because I so uncritically accepted her, but she was far too sophisticated a hostess to want to give cause to sibling dissent.

We were eating that Friday morning, as we did every morning, at a table set with mauve linen mats. There were rolls and strawberry jam. The jam was kept in a ceramic pot with a little matching ladle. I loved that pot, and when I got back to New York I would look for one like it without success; it signified everything gracious to me.

"I hope my daughters are behaving."

Rachel and I could hear my mother's sliding, up-and-down voice very clearly from where we sat.

Marta laughed her light laugh. "Why, of course they are," she said. "I've never enjoyed myself more."

Both my mother and Marta were immigrants, but whereas my mother seemed obdurately European to me, Marta, who lived in Europe, seemed far more adaptive, more American. I cannot, for instance, remember the sound of her accent, although I'm sure it was at least as strong as my mother's.

Rachel went to the phone. I didn't want to talk to my mother. I felt furious at her for asking after us as though we were children, in need of a controlling force outside ourselves. I had, in the course of the week with Marta, gotten used to thinking of myself as a "young lady," a category I don't think my mother recognized.

"She wants to say hello to you."

Rachel looked happy. She, unlike my own treacherous self, still openly loved my mother better than Marta. My loyalty was the more intense for being furtively maintained. On the surface I had already switched allegiance and was envisioning what it would be like to stay on forever, eating almond cookies and going to movies in the late afternoon with the cultured citizens of the Hague.

"I hope you're enjoying yourself," my mother said. "All you seem to write about are your clothes."

"I love Marta," I said. "She's so *open*. And I don't write only about clothes. I described Versailles very well, I thought."

What I had actually written was this: *Versailles was expectably grand. I didn't notice any kings and queens, however. All the royalty have bit the dust. I don't like the French. Please send the stuff I mentioned in my last letter. It's very important. I miss you.* I thought it sophisticated of me to sound so unimpressed, old beyond my years.

"Forget about your T-shirts," my mother said. "Look around you. You may not get to Europe so soon again."

My mother always managed to make me feel both unappreciative and temperamentally unsuited to the act of appreciation at the same time. Why wouldn't I travel to Europe soon again if I wanted? Was it about to blow up? Was my father about to lose all his money? Why did she make every enterprise seem so dark, as if it were about to disappear? And why, with all this, did I feel so homesick? I had realized earlier on the trip—in Paris, where the French failed to welcome my halting conversational efforts with open arms—that I wasn't really all that curious. My emotional geography seemed unchanging no matter where I was. I had only to enter the youth hostel with Rachel and spot the recognizable thin-mattressed beds that we were supposed to sleep on to think with a clamorous love-hate of home. I kept conjuring up Lily, peacefully sticking to the familiar. On some level I think I recognized it as more problematic than that: Lily *couldn't* leave home or my mother; she couldn't even try to. Still, I envied her ability to see—and accept—her own limitations. I was forever testing mine, pretending I wasn't glued by the same adhesive to the same mother, and coming up short. Everyone else seemed to love to see new places, so I had to want to, too. Not that ours was a traveling family, in any case. My mother accompanied my father, mostly on business trips, without us, and the only one of us with a naturally adventurous soul was Benjamin. It was his guidebook, scored with arrows and zealous insructions—*Must see early in the day! Worth a second look!* written in his ledger-keeper's print—that Rachel and I carried with us along the streets of Paris.

He had been a tireless sightseer, it seemed, in the reported tradition of his German forebears. My mother had instilled in all of us a sense of her Frankfurt childhood as limber and nature-loving—passed in an atmosphere of great heartiness, a constant round of Shabbos walks and holiday outings with her siblings and father. I pictured them sallying through the lush German countryside, my mother and her brothers dressed in bright felt hats and leather suspenders—a page out of *Heidi*—her father clearing the brambles with his walking stick and all of them nimbly jumping across a rock stream. I wasn't entirely sure I believed in the portrait my mother had given us leave to create; the actual photographs she saved from that period showed a rather glum and uniformly bespectacled group lined up against the backdrop of some nameless horizon. These snapshots, in serious black and white, also revealed a father who looked far too cerebral for the role of spry mountain guide he was cast in. It seemed to me that my mother was more interested in showing us, her non-German children, up as namby-pambies—incapable of the sort of good sportsmanship that was taken for granted in her youth—than in realistic descriptions of what her childhood had actually been like. But Benjamin, who was fiercely competitive, vied with the image.

I, on the other hand, felt little desire and even less inclination to maintain such high standards of endurance. I was forever willing to take a break from sightseeing, forever suggesting to Rachel that we stop at a sidewalk cafe after we had merely circled the Arc de Triomphe or walked in the Tuileries. For some reason I was always hungry; I couldn't go for more than an hour or two without thinking about food, and Rachel wasn't much more resilient.

Privately I considered my leisured way the more subtle—a passive approach that allowed for observation of the intimate life of the people rather than the standard tourist's gaping and camera clicking. I hated the idea of rushing around at eight o'clock in the morning to catch some ancient fresco. At least this is how I explained my philosophy to Rachel as we settled at yet another table and ordered eggs with mayonnaise. Sipping on coffee and crème fraîche, which Rachel hated and kept ordering in the hope that it would turn out to be the sweet whipped cream it looked like, my sister and I talked about the things we always talked about. Rachel muttered about the heat and flapped at her face with a napkin; I took the opportunity to observe French mothers and their children. "They seem rather cold to their kids," I said to Rachel, "don't you think?" In truth, discovering gaps in other families—coming upon the fact that maternal examples of deprivation flourished in Paris as well as in my own home—interested me far more than exploring the picturesque kiosks winding along the Left Bank. Now that I was in Paris, where I knew Hemingway and Gertrude Stein had come to kick up their heels, all I could do was feel mired in the complexities of my own character, the same ones that weighed me down back home.

Later, while Rachel and I lingered over a bitter French version of lemonade in the still, hot air of the outdoor cafe, I wondered briefly what it would be like to set myself free. I would find a job as a waitress and live in a shabby but cozy room. My life would be full of character. Rachel pooh-poohed the idea. "You can barely do your own laundry now," she said, "much less cook for yourself. And you'd miss Ma within two minutes." She was right. At sixteen I had some of the attitudes of a ten-year-old and some of an old lady; I seesawed between utter dependence and a feeling of solitariness that verged on the bleak. I couldn't really see the glamour of striking out on my own, no matter how hard I tried to convince myself; I knew I hadn't the sort of blithe but sturdy spirit that would make getting up in the morning and arguing the price of a brioche with the woman at the corner *pâtisserie* an adventure. I tried to paint myself as Jean Seberg in *Breathless*—all cropped hair and *je m'en fou*-isms—but kept coming up with a deeper longing to be the shielded and chaperoned Leslie Caron of *Gigi*. It was a portrait of myself, once again, as somebody's adored daughter or granddaughter, with Hermione Gingold in the role of Marta, looking on with misty-eyed affection.

What I didn't like, it seems to me now, was just that feeling of foreignness people travel for. To me it felt unsafe. The most immediate symptom of this was that when traveling I felt acutely, uncomfortably conscious of my physical self—in a way even more extreme than I did at home. Throughout our trip I constantly and savagely applied Blush-On in closetlike train bathrooms and tiled restrooms as though I would drop off the edge of the continent without my two highly colored cheeks to lead the way before me.

"Rub it *in*," Rachel would say, sounding just like I did when overseeing my mother's makeup. "You look like you're in the circus."

We were on a train on the way to yet another spot in Holland. Rachel stared out the window contentedly, munching on some of the fragrant almond-dotted *speculaas* that Marta had packed for us. Around us were what seemed to be an entire population of blonde and blue-eyed women and children. It was midday, and there were few men on the train. The old doubt about who I was when I wasn't in a familiar place rose in me. I looked across at Rachel and wondered if I looked as pale and un-Dutch as she did. Rachel wore large blue-rimmed glasses, and her brown hair was pulled back from her forehead and along the sides in what my mother referred to fondly as a "half-ponytail." It was a hairstyle that I hated precisely because of its goody-goody effect, lacking either insouciance or fashion. I had been squinting for years rather than wear glasses all the time or tolerate the discomfort of contact lenses, and I sported a very "with it" multilevel cut. I had been assured by Sergio—the Italian prima donna of a hairdresser whom I then frequented, along with a bevy of Park Avenue matrons and one or two models—that its tiered effect flattered my face. Neither of my sisters had their hair fiddled with as much as I did. Rachel, it struck me anew in a wave of irritation as I sat across from her, was either beyond—or before—the lure of artifice. She might as well never have heard of cosmetics, for all she used them. There was something docile and childlike about her generally, as though the cranky stirrings of growing up female had skippped over her and left her in an earlier state of little-girl trustfulness. In that way she was a model older sister—from a parental point of view, at least. From a sisterly perspective, she was a let-down, setting an example of compliance that I couldn't follow unless I wanted to look prehistorically artless, as she did.

"You look," I said, "terrible."

Rachel eyed me with quiet fury from behind her thick lenses.

"Shut up," she said. "You can't get along with anyone."

Rachel was echoing what my mother said about me whenever I had a fight with Lily. Rachel and I didn't so much get along as not *not* get along. She tended to be accommodating unless riled, and then she struck back with a disquieting skill. I suppose it was because of her pacific disposition that my mother tended to put her, rather than Lily, "in charge" of my brothers when Lena had the day off. Unlike Lily, who scowled at the very idea of playing oldest, Rachel liked the responsibility. But I saw neither of my sisters as the genuine, heartfelt article. For one thing, I was convinced that they liked each other more than they liked me. It pained me that we couldn't be a happy group like the sisters in *Little Women*, or haunted by a mutual sense of *un*happiness, like the Brontës.

Of course, Lily and Rachel had been lumped together from the beginning, when they shared a sloping-ceilinged room at the top of our first summer house. It was an endearingly small room, outfitted in the palest of blue wallpapers, smelling of old wood. To get to it you had to go beyond a folding gate that closed off the second floor from the third, and up a rickety flight of stairs. There were one or two guest rooms that shared the hallway with my sisters' room and a large playroom at the far end, but no one ventured up there much at night. It was under the eaves, reading and giggling in their twin beds, that my sisters must have forged what appeared to be an exclusive bond. I was stuck by myself in a small room behind Lena's on the second floor; I disliked the room intensely and felt like a captive with Lena keeping guard next door. She would sit bolt upright in bed in her skimpy summer pajamas, her "baby dolls," reading paperback novels late into the night. The floor of my room was covered in a patterned linoleum that looked as if someone had strewn confetti, and it was always cold. Occasionally I would visit my sisters in their hideaway; I sat on one of their beds, usually Rachel's, and read a library book of my own. I liked anything that was sad, novels about orphans or children who had to go and live with cruel uncles; being not only an avid but also a very quick reader, I must have over time gone through every tragic children's book ever published. My favorite among the orphan literature was *Nobody's Girl* and its companion, *Nobody's Boy*; translated from the French, they surpassed anything I read before or after in the intensity of their desolation. My favorite among the cruel-uncle group was a book called *Phlippen's Palace*, which featured an intrepid band of siblings who ran away from the uncle who beat them and had to fend for themselves in New York City. Although my reading sessions in Lily and Rachel's room began well, they invariably ended badly: Eric would barge in and start a fight, or Lily and I would quarrel. We three girls wore the same style of cotton pajamas and closed-toe leather slippers; the latter were bought at Indian Walk, the Madison Avenue children's shoe store. All this matchingness should have spread harmony, but it seemed to pull us apart instead, leaving me out. I usually found myself descending tearfully to my room behind Lena's, vowing never to visit again.

* * *

As the train rumbled along, I checked my watch, a cheap imitation of a famous French style, and asked Rachel what time we were scheduled to arrive at our next destination, earmarked by Marta.

"Find out for yourself, you idiot."

The tide of Rachel's anger, as I knew from past experience, would not be stemmed for a while now. She had hardened her heart, like God had hardened Pharaoh's heart against the Jews. *Vayachbed libo*: it was one of the few expressions I remembered from the five books of the Torah that we studied in *chumash* class. I liked the concreteness of the phrase, the shape it gave to the obdurate quality of temperament that my sisters shared with my mother. My own feelings were flexible to the point of chaos; I couldn't rely on them, and I never believed in my own fury long enough to stand firm. The very fact that Rachel could choose to stay angry when I was the only person she knew on the whole train filled me with a kind of awe.

"I'm going to the bathroom," I announced. "My stomach hurts."

Rachel glanced at me witheringly; she could read beneath my deception without trying. I was planning another of my Blush-On sessions. It was a sign of my wish to please that I had lied about my intentions, as though the idea of my being unwell would melt her. It would take more than a stomachache to move her, however; I would have had to cough up blood at the very least, emerge from the bathroom green-gilled and staggering before Rachel would give up on her position.

I nodded at a friendly looking ticket collector, with whom I almost collided in the narrow aisle that led to the bathroom. I shoved the lock closed and then turned to study my face in the small, grimy mirror. I hated what I saw, the angles everywhere, the definitive jaw and chin, the adamant physiognomy that misled people into taking me for someone who knew her mind. I wished I were Dutch, that my eyes were wide, my skin rosy. I rummaged in my canvas bag, scuffed with dirt and ink marks, for my faithful tortoiseshell compact, embossed with a flowery *R* for Revlon. For a minute I floundered in a welter of tissues and tickets and other useless items. If I didn't have my Blush-On, I was lost.

Rachel looked up when I returned. "I don't know," she said, "who you think you're fooling."

I wasn't sure if she was referring to my cheekbones, daubed now with a violent pink, or my character. I said nothing.

As it turned out, I felt most at ease in one of our last stops, the tourist village of Marken. Everyone walked around in "native" costume, smiling. Everything seemed to be tinged a shade of orange by the sun reflecting off the water. I loved the windmills and the breeze that lifted my hair. Rachel and I were friends again; we stood at the water's edge and watched some far-off white sails bobbing. I nibbled on a chunk of freshly made Gouda that I had bought from a plump woman in native dress, who whittled it from a large, red-skinned wheel. Rachel, who generally protested my lack of adherence to childhood rules—the cheese in our house was kosher and bland, Swiss or Muenster—didn't say anything for once.

"Siamese *cat* of a girl," Mick Jagger hisses. I dance around Eric's room with Max, who is wearing red corduroy overalls and a red and white striped turtleneck. Max is four years old and has been trained by Eric to love the Rolling Stones; his favorite song is "Out of Time."

"This is such a sexy song," I say to Eric.

The guitar on his lap is burnished, glossy like the shine Lena used to put on my hair with her brusque shampoos. Eric may be the original homebody, but there is something about Sundays that draws me back, too, the magnet of self-definition pulling me back to the imposing stone building on the Upper East Side where I started.

"Stop it!" Max yells. Eric has picked him up and carries him over his head like a missile.

"Put him down," I say absently. "Don't make him so wild. What are you going to do with all your ties?"

The door to Eric's closet is open and displays an astonishing selection of ugly ties on its inside rack. The ties are either wide or striped in psychedelic colors and reflect the bad patches in my brother's—or the decade's—sartorial sense.

"Keep them. They might come back in fashion."

"You are my very favorite," I say to Max. "Do you know that?"

The only part about Sunday that I like is the morning; past twelve o'clock I begin to hate the day, the way in which it sags. I am not a naturally well-planned person and Sundays aren't good, I've come to think, for people with leanings toward the void; they remind me of the existential novels that made up the reading list in my ninth-grade French class—barren books with stark titles in which the main character stands around unfeelingly, lighting cigarettes.

"I'm thinking of going to a movie," I say to Eric.

"Heh, little sister, look what you've done," he says.

I hold Max against my knee.

"Give me a kiss," I say. "A dry kiss."

Max and I have a game we play in which we compete to see who can give the other the driest, least spit-ridden kiss—a wisp of a kiss. "Dry Kisses," we call it. It got started because Max doesn't like my father's wet-lipped kisses, the residue of saliva they leave on his cheek. He wipes the back of his hand across his mouth and leans over.

"It better be dry," I say.

Max giggles. It excites him no end to play this game —to plant a kiss without leaving any trace, any spoor of affection.

"I get two chances," he says, then gives me a feathery kiss, his lips barely brushing my cheek.

"My turn," I say and repeat his routine.

"That was a good one," he says, nodding his head in agreement with himself. Max wiggles off my lap and goes out of the room.

These days I find myself longing for what I never thought I'd long for: the overscheduled Sunday mornings of my childhood with their obligatory attendance along with Lily and Rachel at a musty music school on lower Broadway (Benjamin and Eric, being boys and therefore seen as less in need of the finishing touches of culture, were let off the hook after vehement protest). I took classes in piano and sight-singing, theory, ballet, and Israeli dancing. I was scared of the block the school was on, a block that was steeped in shadows even in brightest May, and I hated having to get up at a set time early Sunday morning as though it were a regular school day. I remember sitting at a folding table under a naked light bulb in the basement that served as the school's lounge. It was there I waited for my sisters, faintly sweaty in my clothes after a dance class in which I leaped around the room in a panicked imitation of grace. We usually were home by one or two o'clock, and there was something about the lassitude of the rest of the day, following upon the tightness of the mornings, that I especially liked.

No, if I wonder at anything, it is not that I have come to miss those music school mornings, but why none of the structure has stayed with me—why I float in the present as though time did not really exist, except as a means of sighting how far I have come from my childhood.

My mother has always been haunted by the wasting of time—minutes, even. "Time is money," she used to say to me when I talked too long on the phone, as though she were a departmental manager at Exxon and I a lazy employee. Perhaps I resist her attitude to the point of squandering my own hours in the present because it was once the only way open to me of defying her without bringing the house down. What I did fairly early on as a child, and still do now as an adult, is stall. I have only to be asked to be somewhere promptly, and the shadow of a barred window flickers across my inner vision. (When I came across the line "shades of the prison house begin to close upon the growing boy" in my college poetry anthology, I knew exactly how Wordsworth felt.) I *must* dawdle; it is an impulse toward freedom that cannot be resisted.

"Do you remember the first time we saw the Beatles on Ed Sullivan?" Eric asks, looking at a record he pulled out from the collection that stands on top of a chest of drawers.

"Lena let us stay up late to watch," I say. "I still love them. You know what happened last week? I thought I saw Ed Sullivan on the street. It was so odd—this little man scurried by me with his jaw stuck forward and no neck. Then I remembered that he's dead."

"I always liked George," Eric says. "A great guitar player. John was overrated, if you ask me."

With this remark, my brother leaves the room, as though to insure that his pronouncement on the relative merits of the Beatles will be the last word. I pick up the record—one of their earlier albums—and stare at the photo on the cover, at what were then four daringly mop-topped boys in tight pants and collarless jackets, and think how dated they look. It was Benjamin who had brought home the record *Meet the Beatles* a few days before their TV appearance, claiming to have read about them in the *Herald Tribune*. Benjamin was the avowed anti-populist among us, forever sticking up his nose at Eric and, to a lesser extent, at Arthur's delight in baseball cards and "The Three Stooges." He was capable, at the age of eleven or twelve, of referring to "the masses." Somehow the Beatles got by his filtering system, and I remember the six of us sitting spellbound as "She Was Just Seventeen" spun on the turntable, Arthur picking up on the excitement without quite understanding it. Even my mother came in to listen.

On Eric's desk, left behind with his ties and trophies, is a globe of the world that spins to demonstrate how the earth turns on its axis. The globe is mostly shaded in with blue for the waterways, and there are raised beige ridges to simulate mountain ranges. I like twirling it and watching the countries pass under my gaze. Small-scaled things have always comforted me—tiny replicas, the contraction of the world.

In reality, my grasp of even domestic geography is blurry. I must continually remind myself that west is to my left, east to my right. I tend not only to forget which state borders on which, but to confuse cities and states. It must be a kind of tone-deafness, an inability to read the music of the spheres. In my ear the notes are all jumbled: Michigan, for instance, sounds like a city to me, and New Jersey feels like one eternal suburb—how can New Jersey qualify as a serious state? And it was only recently, I must admit, that I realized with any certainty that Cincinnati is in Ohio. It didn't occur to me in a flash, exactly; what happened is that I must have been paying attention for once. I was staring at a borrowed tube of Head & Shoulders shampoo in a public shower, and there it was: *Made in U.S.A. by Procter & Gamble, Cincinnati, Ohio*.

In fifth grade I was assigned Kentucky as "my" state for a history project. I researched it exhaustively in Melamed's small but well-stocked library, reading about horse ranches and the Blue Ridge Mountains. I wrote out my report on blue-lined paper that I stapled to construction paper; the whole thing was punched with holes along the margin and then tied together with yarn. These were the aesthetic standards that everyone—except hopelessly left-out types like Ruth Samuel—adhered to. I remember I worked hard on tracing a cover of several magnificently tailed horses grazing, but when it came to handing the report in, I saw that Sylvia's cover far outshone mine. Her mother had helped her trace the outline of *her* state, Florida, with gold glitter; even the piece of yarn had flecks of glitter in it. Lena, muttering all the while about the unnecessary fuss, had helped me shade in my horses with different-colored crayons, but they appeared drab in comparison. To this day I feel as if I have a slightly embarrassed kinship with Kentucky, even though I still can't place it accurately on the map.

My mother comes into Eric's room with Max trotting after her. My nephew enjoys accompanying people—Eric, my mother, me—wherever they may go; he would make an excellent companion in old age.

"Do you have any plans?" she says.

It must be German, my mother's fear of leisure, her blind faith in a strict, all-encompassing regimen.

"No," I say. "It's Sunday."

She picks up Max. "*Knutch*," she says, which is either a rare German bow in the direction of child-love, like *schatzekind*, or one of her colorful handmade endearments, like "macaroni-man"; I've never bothered to find out which. "You're such a *knutch*, you are."

"Did you read the article about that horrible affair?"

The Sunday papers are full of details about a murder trial involving a romantic triangle at a glamorous beach colony.

"Yes," she says. "Terrible. I've never understood these affairs."

"What's that supposed to mean?"

"Aren't they worried about bumping into each other when they're out with the other one, the one they're not supposed to be with? All that time and energy spent on such *schmunzes*! What would keep me are problems of geography."

"I don't know what you mean," I say, although I do. *Schmunzes* is my mother's word for anything that doesn't make sense to her—divorce, love affairs, the raw access of passion, dramatized emotions. I tried once to look up the word in a German dictionary and couldn't find it, but it has a clarion ring, my mother's *schmunzes*!—a dismissive contempt far more potent than the English *nonsense*.

"Another of my wise remarks," my mother says, "wasted on you."

She is wearing a printed cotton house dress—what is known, in the terminology of department store catalogues, as a "model coat." It is the sort of minimally styled, snap-buttoned garment you would expect to find on a citizen of some chaste People's Republic or on the staff of a cleaning service. Oddly enough, my mother looks her best in these house dresses—soft, almost beautiful. It is as if the plainness of the dress accentuates and at the same time holds in check the many possibilities—the conflicting signals—that lie dormant in her character; her mercuriality is temporarily grounded. When I came home from school as a child and my mother was wearing one of her "model coats," she ceased to frighten me. Even now when she wears them, she seems more of a piece that she actually is: a mother, pure and simple, a cozy approximation of the loving mother I had in mind. Her bare legs under the coat are pale and shapely, but knobby with varicose veins.

"Eric seems moody," she says. "He's sitting in the kitchen and eating up all the leftover cake from Shabbos. How did you find him?"

Eric is my mother's golden-haired child, as much as she has one. While Benjamin embodies all the character traits she liked least in her own brothers and all she would like to have stomped out in the emerging characters of her own children, Eric is free of such associations. He is to this day the one of us my mother's heart throbs for, the lioness's alter ego.

"I don't know," I say. "Fine. Maybe he's just hungry. He was playing records minutes ago. This family! Something's always wrong!"

"Of course," my mother says. "It's all my fault."

"You don't believe that in the least," I say, and my mother smiles at me, an unruffled smile.

Max, who is devoted to my mother, senses a fight coming. "Stop being mean," he says, pushing me slightly.

"Only if you be mean instead," I say, catching at his hands.

"Soon enough," my mother says.

Eric stands framed in the doorway and curls his hands up one before the other, then trumpets through them, "Make way for the groom."

Everyone laughs.

"Play another record," Max says.

"Please," my brother commands.

"Please," Max says, parrotlike.

My brother pulls an album from his densely packed collection, his fingers gravitating as if by instinct to the one he has in mind. On it cover is a giant birthday cake, dripping with white, pink, and green frosting, alight with candles. He carefully blows some dust off the disc, then holds it out to Max.

"Now you blow."

Max puffs out his cheeks, and I am suddenly reminded of the way God is portrayed in children's Bible stories, grandly blowing out the weather—clouds and lightning, the moon and the sun—through his pursed mouth.

"You spit on my record, you my enemy," Eric says, mock-threateningly.

"You cain't ahl-ways git what you wa-hant," Mick Jagger sounds from my brother's large and expensive-looking speakers, his voice amplified to an ominously breathy depth.

"This music you listen to," my mother says. "No wonder you never want to do anything. None of you has inherited my *joie de vivre*. What a pity."

I bristle at this mention of one of my mother's favorite themes, one of her many packets of convenient misinformation: she believes that all six of her children have unaccountably been cursed at birth with depressed genes. I can even envision these genes as she sees them—swimming inside us, gray little blobs of life, weary before the day has begun.

"You can't inherit *joie de vivre*," I say. "And I was probably a cheerful baby when I first emerged."

"But it was beaten out of you," my mother says. "We all know that."

I glare at her. What makes me so angry is that there is no way to make my mother run for cover. Whatever zingers of blame or accusation I throw at her are mocked into innocuousness—stale jokes aimed at the balcony. She is an ingenious self-preserver, my mother, whistling her way out of all darknesses, steering clear of the rubble.

"No one listens to this music all day, Ma," Eric says, "unless they're getting paid to."

"Oh," she says, "really?"

My brother has always taken a reasonable approach to the exaggerations and caprices of my mother's style. I envy him this ability, although her notions of cause and effect—in her children and in the world at large—don't strike me as being susceptible to the light of reason.

"*You* even like it sometimes," Eric says.

The music my mother likes, that she will actually stop and listen to, is in fact exactly the kind of music Eric and I call "low energy"—Neil Young's wistful, immobilizing songs or the Phil Ochs ballads Arthur used to replay endlessly. She knows the opening stanza of "Heart of Gold" by heart.

On any given evening for a period of several months after Phil Ochs committed suicide, Arthur could be found lying on what was then his bed in Eric's room, hands behind his head, listening to some antiwar dirge or other. Arthur was too young to have been aware of

Ochs in his heyday, but I doubt it was the sixties' protest element that caught my brother's interest in the first place. I think it had more to do with the sad, twangy sound of Och's songs than with any particular sentiment they expressed. Arthur read a biography of Ochs, which he continued to talk about long after he had finished it, as though new ideas might occur to him at any moment. He tried to get me interested, and I obliged by skimming the biography, one of those hastily assembled "I remember Phil" books where all the incidental people—his high school principal, a guy who lived down the block from him when he was four—spoke up, and all the crucial onlookers—his wife and close friends—remained silent. I remember we had a heated argument about the merits of Ochs compared to Bob Dylan, and Arthur referred to Dylan contemptuously as a "survivor." But one evening when I came into his room, he seemed mysteriously to have dropped the subject.

"I've studied the case," Arthur said.

In those days Arthur was still clean-shaven, and he had a nice, well-defined jaw. Later on, when he grew a beard, it became hard to discern that he was good-looking.

"The clues," he said, "were there from the start."

Arthur was speaking loudly because he had replaced Phil Ochs with the Grateful Dead, at high volume.

"I see," I said.

"Nothing could have saved him."

"What about his family?" I thought I had read that Ochs had been close to a sister.

"Too late. Didn't come through soon enough."

Arthur's curiosity is piqued almost exclusively by the morbid, like an onlooker at a car accident. He is more interested in legacies—especially if they are tragic—than in the histories that precede them. He digs up the oddest people this way, and the books he collects are a compendium of thwarted lives—painters who stopped painting and psychiatrists who went crazy. It is as if he finds something innately suspicious about people who manage to stay afloat, as if those who drown—the Phil Ochses rather than the Bob Dylans—are on to something.

The venetian blinds rattle against the window in Eric's room.

"You were going to clear out your drawers," my mother says. "Unless, of course, you're too busy. Or tired."

"What are you talking about?" Eric says. "I'm a ball of fire."

"Ball of fire," Max repeats, giggling, looking at my brother adoringly.

When I was younger, it seemed to me that Sunday afternoons—preceded by the routine inaction of Shabbos and the structured schedule of Sunday mornings, followed by school on Monday morning—stretched on forever, in a relative lack of form. I could never believe they would turn into evening, then night, and then into the next day. On Sundays I got to wear my beloved Danskins—beloved because they were what Sharon Levi, the girl in my class I then wished most to be, wore. The Danskins consisted of stretch pants in a faintly itchy material. They came in purposeful shades like navy, purple, and maroon (I learned to refer to these colores as "plum" and "mauve" from Sharon, but Lena and my mother continued to call them by their crayon-box names) and could be bought with matching striped tops. Even at the age of eleven or twelve, I had the protuberant belly that much younger children often have; I remember the elastic waistband of my Danskin pants digging into my flesh. The truth was that I felt far more comfortable in the wool or corduroy pants that my sisters wore, but I refused to acknowledge this.

These days Sundays remind me only of other Sundays—the Sundays that were and the Sundays still to be—although I have a tendency to treat the whole day as ahistorical, out of time. It has occurred to me that it may be *The New York Times*, an apparition of adulthood, that gives me this sense—bulging every week with sections on places I have never been to and reviews of movies and plays and exhibits I promise myself to see but rarely do.

If, as it seems you can never catch up, why not pretend you can begin anywhere? Why not arrange to be suctioned back into the womb and come out a conqueror?

One Sunday I pore over an article about an inn filled with flowers and polished walnut in the unfrequented alps of Italy. Italy is a country I have not been to even at its most overtouristed—the obligatory pilgrimages to Rome, Florence, and Venice. It is almost embarrassing to have arrived in my mid-twenties from a background of no visible hardship and not to have seen Italy. "Italy!" people say. "How can you skip Italy? How is it possible *you* haven't been to Italy?"

What I would like to say in answer but don't is this: "And how can *you* leave home? How can you go anywhere? How do you know what to pack and what to leave behind? How can you be sure there will be anyone to come back to—that they will take you in again and remember you, much less love you?" As I have grown older, I have grown more scared. Rachel is married and no longer available to calm me down when I forget my favorite item of clothing, and Blush-

On won't suffice in a pinch when I am feeling lost. But there are things I have learned to pretend, constrictions that are passed off as choices—as willed eccentricities—a preferred mode of being. I have learned, in short, not to say, "Help me. I am broken in pieces." Is there anyone who would believe me if I explained that I know Italy in my bones? I see myself in a small, elegant dining room, airy with fronds, in an inn near Tuscany, sipping espresso. It is clear I am the sort of visitor who knows Italy well, who finds attractions off the regular track.

Another Sunday I get up late and read an article about the Scottish Highlands; I see myself stopping in a pub after a day's walk, blowing into the froth on my glass of beer, pulling out a book of verse—Robert Burns, perhaps. In my mind I am always traveling alone, and I resemble myself as I am—sitting in a nightgown and robe at the eggy remains of breakfast, though it is well into the afternoon—not at all. I am, in these flights, parentless—middle-aged and brisk, a bit broad in the hips but not fat, with something impersonal in my character that invites the confessions but not the questions of other travelers. I don't quite know where I picked up this image or why I should wish to be so much older than I am when the rest of the world wants to remain young. I do know there is an aspect to it that I find infinitely peaceful.

Across Eric's room the outline of my mother's figure recedes beneath the smock, except for her chest, which is full and slopes gently outward. In the room there are the four of us and a clock, ticking, and for a moment—no longer than several seconds—I am both in the room and outside it, looking at Eric, my mother, Max, and me. It seems as if we compose a *tableau vivant* and that we are on the edge of something wonderful.

My mother yawns, her mouth wide open. I always expect her to lick her chops afterward, a contented lioness. There is something primitive and fierce about my mother's yawns, just as there is something primitive and fierce about her love of raw chopped meat. I used to watch, mesmerized, when she came into the kitchen while Louisa was preparing meatballs and scooped out a bright red mound for herself from the mixing bowl.

"Can't you cover your mouth?" I say.

It has annoyed me for years that my mother sidesteps her own injunctions. On Friday nights, the one night of the week when the six of us used to eat in the dining room with my parents instead of in the kitchen under Lena's aegis, we were badgered about table manners. Benjamin was ritually accused of chewing with his mouth open, Eric of smacking his lips when he ate, and I of failing to keep my elbows off the table. Although I regularly pointed out to my mother that my father slurped his soup, she wasn't deterred, just as she didn't seem to see anything contradictory in her habit of picking the crumbs off the tablecloth with her index finger and then popping them into her mouth.

"Gotta go, Ma," Eric says.

"Me, too," I say, but I don't move.

"Me, *too*," Max says. "Where's my Mommy?"

"Margot!" my father roars from downstairs.

"Com—ing," my mother yells.

"Can't he come and get you when he wants you?" I ask. These questions are nothing more than spasms of irritation, like stomach cramps, and no one gives them the benefit of an answer. My father has never walked a block if he can take a taxi, and he's certainly not about to become a climber of steps in his later years.

My mother takes Max by the hand; I hear her discussing flavors of ice cream with him as they go downstairs. Eric slips on a leather jacket.

"Is that *red*?" I ask, as though I disbelieve the evidence of my senses.

"No, black," Eric says. "You're color blind, know that? You must have trouble crossing streets. Like it?"

"I think it's vulgar," I say, sounding like Emily Post.

"Jealous?"

"Please," I say, as though pained by the suggestion. "It's just that I think it's misleading."

But do I really care that Eric dresses like a daredevil and is the original homebody underneath his clothes? I *must* be jealous; alone of us, Eric has always worn what he wants, in spite of my mother's protests that he has "Puerto Rican taste." Benjamin, by contrast, wasn't allowed to deviate so much as an inch from what my mother deemed proper, even in his high school years. When he grew his sideburns long in sophomore year, in imitation of his classmates, she repeatedly mocked him for looking feminine, like a "homo," until he shaved them off. As a result he now dresses like an old man, a habitué of library reading rooms.

"See you," Eric says.

"Off to see your true love?"

My brother grins. When he smiles like that, I can see his appeal, his success at vaulting across even my mother's barriers.

"Off to play some ball. With da guys."

Linda, his fiancée, is an extremely accommodating girl. She seems to spend most of her time waiting for Eric to show up after he's done something else first. He walks out the door with his bowlegged rancher's gait, and then I am alone. I get up and wander around his room. All of the objects Eric has left behind seem entombed. I stop in front of the full-length mirror that hangs on the outside of his bathroom door and put my face up close to it.

"You," I say out loud.

A flicker of dust settles on my sweatshirt, and I watch out of the corner of my eye as it disappears.

SIX

If your heart is broken early enough, do you begin to mistake pain for love? Do all attachments become inextricably linked with submission? Or do you, perhaps, learn to turn your back on the very idea of attachment—fraught with now-or-neverness, each casual leavetaking suspected of being the last? There are professionals who can be hired, at great cost, to disprove the infallibility of this sort of damage; they talk about *nurturing* and *ego strength* and *reparenting*. It would be nice to think they were correct in their optimism or, at the least, devoted to the act of reparation. Like the psychiatrist who sums up James Stewart's prognosis in *Vertigo*: "You're suffering from severe melancholia and a guilt complex," he says briskly but not without compassion. "It will take a year to cure." The audience when I saw the movie howled at this, although I trust the line is meant seriously. I laughed, too—at the neatness of it, like a well-ironed piece of laundry—but I envied James Stewart his white-coated doctor.

I have never gone to a psychiatrist who said anything nearly as definite on my behalf. Over the years I seem to have seen only bearded but weak-kneed followers in the footsteps of Freud. I noticed that one of them, Dr. Blue ("Blue?" my mother said. "Blue? That must be Blum. Another self-hating Jew. Ask him if his father changed his name or if he did"), had wet hands when he extended one to wish me good-bye the last time I saw him. Outside his office, on the hall table, some flowers were dying in a vase, and I wiped my hands down the sides of my jacket. My mother's hands were always dry. How could I be helped to escape her influence by a doctor who was far more tentative than she was, so eager to prove himself in the world that his palms perspired and he dodged his own name? I was to be stuck forever, immured behind unbreachable walls, my mother's dominion stretching on as far as I could see. Beyond it I knew was the world, what I needed in order to survive, but how was I to get to it? Dr. Blue had tried, but his voice came to me as a far-off echo, patient and sympathetic. The voice I carried inside me had many years—all the crucial ones—over Dr. Blue; it spoke a different language, a language of deflation and absence, reminding me of a Dr. Blue who was a Dr. Blum in disguise.

"You always pick at your scabs," Lily says. "You never let a scar grow over things."

She says this to me in a corner booth in a coffee shop on Amsterdam Avenue. The coffee shop is run by Greeks who yell a lot but seem united among themselves. In our adult lives Lily and I have formed a delicate alliance, frequently jostled by disputes and huffy silences, but sustained by the fact that we both have long memories. It is early December; there are chains of red and green tinsel looped around the coat stands, and a SEASON'S GREETINGS sign in red and green glitter hangs behind the cashier's stool. The tinsel looks tired already, weary of having to sparkle.

"Maybe," I say and duck so deep into my coffee cup that the tip of my nose gets wet.

"It's too cold," Lily says.

Outside the panes of the coffee shop snow falls at a slant, building up a frosty crust. I slithered here in a pair of sneakers, having failed to open the blinds before going out. For as far back as I can remember, I have never wanted to get up in the morning. Sometimes it seems to me that I swim up from sleep rather than simply waking, and I tend to keep my morning atmosphere grottolike—no TV anchorwomen smiling cheerfully at me or radio announcers breaking in with the latest traffic conditions between songs.

"I forgot my gloves," I say. "I didn't want to be late."

A thin, dark waiter bangs a plate of eggs, sunny side up, on the table in front of me. He pulls out a pad from his pocket, scribbles, and tears out a bill with amazing speed.

"They broke the yolk," I say to Lily. "I hate when the yolk spreads over the white."

"It tastes the same," she says, biting into her toasted bran muffin.

I order fried eggs not so much because I like the way they taste but because I love the way they look—two glistening circles of yellow in a sea of white. There is something about the way the yolks rise up slightly from their viscous surrounding that strikes me as being nearly perfect.

It is eight-thirty on a Tuesday morning. Lily, who is a naturally early riser, was waiting for me when I arrived. I had planned to talk to her about the usual things—how crappy I feel, does she remember this or that incident from our childhood that would explain why I feel the way I do—but there is a quality to the hour of our meeting that is not conducive to rummaging around in ancient baggage. Everyone in the booths around us seems intent on the day ahead, propping newspapers against their cups or having low-voiced conversations.

"I'd check on that if I were you," says a man in the booth behind us, his voice carrying clearly in the lull in our conversation. "There's no use going directly to the source until we have our facts straight."

I turn my head to catch sight of the speaker. He sounds so earnest and responsible, so middle management. Briefly I wonder why he hasn't risen further in his company. Why is he meeting in this place instead of at an elegant business breakfast at the Plaza or the Regency? The man's face has that bluish hue that heavily bearded men have even right after shaving; the cuffs of his shirt are too long, trailing over his wrists.

"Don't you set an alarm?" Lily asks. "You always resist doing things the routine way—like other people do them."

She is wearing a knitted vest over a sweater. The effect is pleasantly bulky, although the colors Lily likes—bright greens, purples, pinks—always remind me of an ethnic parade.

"Of course I do," I say, although I don't.

I can see this is not going to be one of our more amiable times.

"I wish it were last week," I say.

"Why?" Lily asks. "What was so great?"

"It was warmer," I say. "You didn't have to bundle up."

The moment the winter starts in earnest, I dream of beaches, of turning brown and grizzled in the sun.

Once, several years ago, I went to a Caribbean island with a college friend of mine for a week's vacation and considered staying on, marrying the waiter who had proposed to me in halting English. I saw myself settled under a palm tree in late afternoon, my toffee-colored children playing in the sand around me. All vestiges of my past—family, faith, friends—banished in one radical gesture. How free I'd be! I couldn't really have been serious, but I thought I was then. All that had been stopping me, I announced to my friend when we returned home, was the waiter himself. He was, I had decided, too eager. Who knew what schemes lay behind his apparent ardor?

I had met the waiter at the hotel bar on the second night of our trip. My friend, Laura, was mournfully examining her sunburned arms, and I had just ordered a round of drinks when two cats slunk in. I shrank in my chair.

"Do you think they wandered in from outside?" I asked Laura nervously. "They look like strays."

"No, they must belong to someone here," Laura said. "Those are definitely house cats."

I looked at her across the rattan table and thought how nice and reassuring she had seemed at home, where I didn't have to live with her.

I kept darting glances at the cats, willing them to stay away from me, when the slim, dark-eyed man who brought us our drinks came to my rescue.

"Me take care," he said. "No afraid." With this he

picked the cats up by the scruff of their necks and disappeared with them. He returned, beaming.

"Thank you," I said. *"Gracias."*

Laura hissed at me that it was the wrong language, but the waiter seemed to understand.

"My name Philippe," he said. "You?"

I told him my name, which he mispronounced with great joy. "Kana," he said. "Kana, I like. More drink?"

I left an uncharacteristically lavish tip that night and every night thereafter. On the last evening of our stay, when I told him we'd be leaving early the next morning, his face fell.

"You stay?" he asked. "With me."

I laughed, embarrassed, even though I was alone at the table at that moment.

"Bring drink," he said. "Maybe Kana stay. Be my wife."

I had begun to like the way he exoticized my name, and while he was away filling my usual order of a piña colada or a Tom Collins (Laura had convinced me that these were the only drinks to have in the tropics), I had a vision of myself as Island Girl—Rima in *Green Mansions*. I had never cared for the book when we read it in junior high school—all the rapturous nature description had bored me—but I liked the movie version with Audrey Hepburn.

Laura returned from the bathroom, and I reported the news to her. "Philippe wants to marry me," I said. "What do you think?"

"You must be kidding," she said.

I noticed that her nose was peeling badly, and suddenly, momentarily, I hated Laura. She was wound up in orderly habits to the same extent that I tried to resist them—unpacking immediately upon arrival, confirming our plane reservations exactly three days ahead of time as requested by the airline, ordering the same healthy lunch every day, making sure we saw the sights. While this made her an excellent travel companion, she was hardly the person to look to for advice on so heedless an impulse.

"I'm not," I said. "I like him."

Laura snorted. "Because you know him so well. He may have a wife already. Or two. They get married young here." She made me sound like Philippe's grandmother. "And what would you *do* here?"

Her practical questions disrupted my idyll—based, after all, on little more than the politest of service relationships—but I refused to let on. "Not everyone," I said, "has your high tolerance for routine. Ever heard of Gauguin?"

"Excuse me," Laura said. "I've got a few last-minute things to do in the room."

Philippe returned carrying two drinks on a tray high over his shoulder. "Friend gone?" he said.

For a moment I thought he was going to sit down with me. "Yes," I said a bit frostily.

"Take one away?" he asked.

"No," I said. I drank two piña coladas while Philippe looked on, sadly. I avoided his gaze as I stood up and said good night.

"Good-bye, Miz Kana," he said, dropping his former familiarity.

"See you next year," I said.

"Yes," he said, his hands clasped behind his back. He was sad or indifferent—I couldn't tell which.

On my way out of the bar I turned around and saw Philippe laughing his gentle, gap-toothed laugh with another guest, a young woman seated by herself.

* * *

Lily pushes away her cup and saucer. The surface of the coffee shop table is scratched and dented, the vinyl flaking off in places. Her cheeks are ruddy from the cold, but she barely acquires a tan even in high summer, so I don't air my tropical longings on her.

"Do you want anything else?" she asks. "I'm in a slight rush. Sorry."

"That's okay," I say. "I'll go home and kill myself."

She ignores this and takes out her wallet. I can see from where I sit that the interior of Lily's bag is formidably neat. There's a packet of Kleenex in a leather case; glasses; keys; a tube of Chapstick, some mascara, face powder, and a compact that looks like it contains rouge, all zipped inside a transparent plastic clutch; a ball point pen; and an appointment book. Not the mess of paper, scrunched-up tissues, and loose makeup that my bag always is. I keep trying different-sized bags in the hope that either extreme—capaciousness or diminutiveness—will force me to organize. Having recently abandoned the saddlebag that I lugged around like a portable home, I now have a petite, ladylike curve of black leather, which I fill to bursting.

"How's work going?" Lily asks, by way of politeness.

"I'm thinking of leaving," I say, scraping up the last of my home fries. I've been at this job for four months.

"You're always thinking of leaving," she says.

"Except when I should."

"That's a different problem, isn't it?"

Lily discriminates between issues very well, refusing to lump everything together the way I do. What I am referring to is the fact that I have no trouble forsaking professional opportunity; it is people I can't let go of. The most vivid image I have of myself is of a person standing in other people's doorways, hugging the threshold, unable to leave.

"But you like what you do there," she adds, reaching for her coat, a cherry-red loden with toggles. "Stick with it."

"When did you get *that*?" I ask. "Is it new?"

"Don't you like it?"

"It looks warm. Sort of Bavarian."

Lily frowns.

"But it suits you, in a way."

Both Lily and Rachel demonstrate aspects of my mother's rules of good taste—legislated in childhood without consulting us—in their adult wardrobes. Although my mother shudders at my oldest sister's palette, there is a naive, folksy quality to Lily's choice of clothing that reflects the deliberate antisophistication of the clothes we wore while growing up. My mother loved wide hip sashes and dotted Swiss, smocking and corduroy jumpers—anything that spoke of the European rather than American influence and, even more important, of the girlish. Once, when she was especially pleased with the way an outgrown dress of Lily's looked on me when I tried it on—a gray knit with white buttons scattered across the front—she said happily, "You look just like a French orphan!" Nowadays my mother is disconcerted by Rachel's habit of allowing Max to pick his own clothes. Ella, who is too young to clamor in other regards, gets to decide how many barrettes she wears in her hair. My sister lets her wear three or four at a time, to my mother's disgust.

"But the children have no idea!" my mother says.

"Ella looks terrible in those *tsatskes*. Like a slum child! Take her for a haircut."

"She likes her hair long, Ma," Rachel says calmly.

"This is America," I say when my mother repeats her objections to me on the phone. "Children have a voice here. Unlike your own."

"Look who I started up with," my mothers says.

"Why didn't you ask us what *we* liked?"

"You were the best-dressed children in the neighborhood," my mother says heatedly. "Everyone thought so."

For a second I feel sorry for her, so sure of her opinions yet capable on occasion of being stung to their defense.

"I hated those short bangs we all had," I say. "They made us look retarded."

My mother, who should have devoted her passion for arranging in multiples to a cause more abstract than the maternal, has always warmed to the concept of uniformity—of applying one principle collectively. Nothing brings out the blood in her like having to make travel arrangements for a platoon of guests in the middle of a snowstorm with no taxis running. Lists excite her, drawing up maps, the creating of a complexly delineated order. The notion of arrangements seems to suit something in her nature—the desire to impose without the inclination to get involved, perhaps. If mothers were merely arrangers, she would have made a marvelous one. That not being the case, she would have made a good Communist or, as I feared for a while she actually had been, a good Nazi.

When we were all still quite young—Lily could have been no more than seven or eight, and Arthur had just been born—my mother hired a hairdresser from Michael's, the leading children's salon on Madison Avenue, to come and cut our hair at home every two months. This must have been the easiest money Daniel ever made, for there was no struggling, no pouting about styles such as he must have been used to from the children who were brought to his shop. There were only two types of haircuts—one for the girls and one for the boys. Lena watched to make sure no one protested. "Such good, unfussy children," Daniel would say, stroking our hair. He showered us with lollipops in gratitude.

"They were the fashion then," my mother says.

"So were crewcuts," I say, "and the boys didn't have them."

"Because they were hideous, as everyone realizes now. I was ahead of my time."

"I always wanted saddle shoes," I say.

"Didn't you get them?"

"By then it was too late," I say.

"*Nebbish,*" my mother says.

"I was," I say.

"And to think you survived," she says.

"Barely," I say. "And Ella looks cute in barettes."

"Look whose opinion I'm asking," she says, signaling the end of the conversation.

I finally got saddle shoes when I was about fifteen or sixteen, right after Lily did; we both had been beseeching for years. I loved the black-and whiteness of them and the slow deterioration of the white half into gray, like dirtied snow. Then Lena, who kept a whole collection of shoe brushes and jars of Meltonian cream in a wooden box beside the toilet, would polish them, and there'd be a fresh, cakey layer of white to scuff all over again. It occurs to me now that I coveted saddle shoes because they were the kind of thing that American kids of a certain age and wholesomeness were supposed to wear. They made me think of climbing apple trees, which I had never done in my life, and of a certain slapdash attitude toward the precepts of adults.

In reality I and my siblings aged young; anxiety and doubt, an awareness of the cruelty of the world—the world as it began at home—beset us before they ideally might have, and we were anything but careless of authority; we were too cowed for that. For a time when I was twelve or thirteen, it seemed to me that the clue to my mother's more fearsome aspects, her coolly punitive approach to all of us—whether it was in the form of verbal slashes, digging her nails into our arms, or slapping one of us in the face (Benjamin, especially: it was to him that she prefaced her slaps with the graphic warning, "You'll feel my five fingers in your face")—rested somewhere in her German past. After I learned about the Nazis in detail at Melamed, I decided that my mother had been Ilse Koch, chief female S.S. officer at Auschwitz, before she married my father. It was an awesome secret to have to bear about your own mother, and I thought I'd check with her before I let my father in on it.

"Were you?" I asked her, convinced that this woman who bore me was really a blood enemy, a hater of the very race I belonged to and in whose most particularistic traditions I was being reared.

"Of course," she answered in her bemused way. "Don't you know? I was the first Jewish Nazi."

I asked her several more times after that, and she always answered with the same mocking smile, never denying the possibility. But there was something about my need to come to her with my discovery, about the very fact that she was not horrified by my suspicions, that made me keep this exposure of her true identity to myself. As I grew older, I realized how ludicrous this "explanation" was, but I look back on it as a measure of the lengths I went to try and make sense of her arbitrary cruelties.

I got my images of the world—the world as it might be—out of books; the saddle shoes were lifted from a novel about a plump tomboy, Rowena Carey, who was forever licking the last of her mother's cookie dough and causing good-humored neighbors to shake their heads at her escapades. I believed fervently that if I only implemented the details of a life I longed for, the rest was sure to follow. If I wore saddle shoes, for instance, my mother would miraculously start baking cookies; we would no longer live in the city but in a frame house on a tree-lined street; and my father would metamorphose from a remote businessman into the town's soft-hearted doctor, like Rowena's father. This wishful effort at transformation persisted for many years, and I never failed to be caught by surprise at the realization that it didn't work—that I and my family remained, unacceptably, who we were.

Lily picks up the bill. The coffee shop is nearly empty by now, except for several lone men, none of them in business suits, and an elderly woman with a thin, patrician neck, who sits wedged over near the window in one of the front booths. The cold seems to have seeped in from the outside.

"What's my half?" I ask.

In my family we are very proper about money, even minute amounts. No one indulges in expansive gestures, although I tend to be more nit-picking than my sisters. Benjamin is probably the worst in this regard; he is implacably stingy. But we are all conscious about boundaries, even more conscious that we are the children of rich parents rather than rich in ourselves. The only one of us who even tries to step out of this role is Eric; he buys generous presents when he remembers and is an inveterate taxi taker. Arthur, like Benjamin, knows the New York subway system by heart, but in his case it has less to do with a penny-pinching attitude than with his innate ascetic tendencies.

"It's on me," Lily says.

"I'll leave the tip, then," I say.

"Fine," she says.

"I wish I had a nurse," I say on our way to the cash register. "Someone to make sure my gloves are in my pocket and that I get to work on time."

"You hated Lena," Lily says.

"A nice nurse," I say. "Not a terror like Lena."

The girl at the register is wearing a cross, and her long, vermilion nails click when she hands Lily the change.

"Hannah," my sister says, and I can tell that she is impatient to move on. "Stop living in the past. There are plenty of people with unhappy childhoods who get over them."

"Oh, I see you're in your make-the-most-of-it mood today," I say. "You should have warned me."

I feel suddenly, unaccountably, bitter—stranded in my mourning. When Lily joins me there, unlike today, I am consoled by the twinning of recollection; I hold on to the raft of her suffering, the small memories that still rankle. ("Ma never liked my looks," she says on those occasions, while I murmur soothingly. "She thought I took after Daddy's family. She used to tell me I had 'cow eyes,' do you remember? She thought that was cute!") But now I begin to feel a twinge of unsureness: was it all so dark the way I have it? Or do I exaggerate out of some horrible need to duck responsibility for anything I do in the present, as though I have only to point backward and thereby rest my case? My mother's mocking words on this subject echo within me, furthering my doubts: "Aren't even you bored with it by now? All of this is ancient history! You could have been starving!"

"Starving, shmarving!" I am yelling at her now in my head, at the place inside my cranium where my mother reigns still. "No one we knew lacked for money! And there are other kinds of deprivation! What about too little attention? Not enough hugs? Jeers instead of encouragement?"

I think of Lena trying to teach Arthur to ride a bike on the street outside the beach house. He was ten years old, a quiet shadow of Eric; the kids hitting a baseball in the street stopped to watch as he wobbled on the midget-sized two-wheeler, his long legs ridiculously folded over. Lena held the seat from behind with her tanned, muscular arms. "Ten years old and still can't ride a bike," Lena said. "Shame on you." Arthur made it down the street, the kids hooting and cheering. After that he got off the bike, ignoring Lena's loud protests of "Coward! Do it again, or you'll never learn!" He went inside the house with what I, watching from behind the front door, took to be a certain intact shred of dignity.

Lily pulls on a pair of gloves and winds a blue and yellow checked scarf around her collar.

"Cheer up," my sister says. "Aren't you wearing gloves?"

"I told you," I say. "I forgot them."

There is a note of victory in my voice, as though I've proven something. Perhaps it is not only the healer, like the doctor in *Vertigo*, who must be gifted, but the person who is to be healed. Often I think that

Lily wants to be healed in a way that I don't, that I prefer to lance my wounds. Take Franklin Roosevelt, for instance, choosing to be photographed from the waist up so that he appeared to be just like any other president sitting. In his situation, I would have opted for close-ups of the wheelchair. Although this may have to do with an inclination on my part to try for sympathy rather than admiration, I don't think that's all there is to it. It has also to do with what I believe: that scars never completely fade. The line of breakage, like a strand of hair, will always show up on film.

"Buy a pair," Lily says, "unless you prefer to grieve over the fact that if you had had a mother who clipped mittens to your snowsuit you would not now be gloveless."

"I do," I say, smiling.

We are at the door. Ahead of me is the subway and my tiny, overheated office. Lily has taken a leave of absence from the university where she teaches and is trying to finish her doctorate on Flemish still lifes. I picture her in the library peering knowledgeably at scenes of village burghers enjoying a smoke or at the precisely rendered leftovers of a meal—a torn loaf of bread, an orange rind curled upon a plate next to a cluster of grapes.

"Are you going uptown?" I ask, hoping for company on the way to the subway.

"No, I'm going to read at home. I've got a pile of articles."

"The life," I say.

"Yeah," Lily says, "and you toil in a coal mine."

I hold my bag against me, and the beeper that connects to my phone answering machine goes off. I pay an inordinate amount of attention to the phone. I check in for messages constantly, as though one day I will receive a magical summons. My mother, who calls in erratic bursts punctuated by long periods of silence, notices how often I update my message, trying to make it ever more alluring. "Very sexy," she says. "Who were you expecting? It's only your old mother. Should I sing you a song?" Besides her, there are several regular callers and a lot of hang-ups.

The old woman who has been staring out the window turns and yells from her booth. "Are you a doctor? I hate doctors! They killed my husband!"

"'Bye, Hannah," Lily says at the corner. "Things could be worse. You could be crazy, like that old woman."

"Crazy might be better," I say. "Lily, if I went crazy, completely crazy, I could get better. Like being reborn."

"Maybe," Lily says ruminatively, as though she's considered it herself.

The light changes.

"I'm going to be late," I say. "'Bye."

"If you run," she says, "you can still make the light."

The snow sticks to my hair, and as I am going down the subway stairs I notice a bright pink wad of gum stuck to the underside of my sneaker. I wonder what I'll eat for lunch. I think I am happiest when eating. The very sight of dessert, even after a big meal, brings on in me a sublime and undoubtedly infantile state of contentment. Could it be that it is only those rare adults with perfect childhoods behind them who have a reasonable attitude toward food—who don't mistake the pangs of hunger for the wolf call of starvation, who don't confuse gratification with excess? The train, when it comes, isn't very crowded, but I stand and read the ads until my stop.

SEVEN

Even so, what happened before never explains what comes later. There is the childhood in question, and then there is the particular child who becomes an adult. Why am I fixated and Benjamin, for instance, is not? "You gotta play with the little hurts," Benjamin says in the present, quoting football coach Vince Lombardi, one of his favorite sources of wisdom. My brother wouldn't begin to survive on a football field, but about the emotional life he is a Darwinian: you survive, or you don't. My memories aren't Benjamin's; they won't let go—they lead me straight back to the womb. One day, I imagine, they will invent the proper antidotal pill—"to be taken three times a day, against remembering"—but meanwhile I shove and hack at my memories only to find myself subservient. *You are stuck with us*, they say. *Try getting friendly.*

When I cried as a child, my mother said, "Your

tears don't move me," so I never cry now in psychiatrists' offices, although there is always the gentle inducement of a box of tissues. But does one explain the other? There are those experiences for which no explanation will suffice, and I often wonder if I place too much faith in them.

It was Lena, not my mother, who took physical care of us. My mother took over only on Thursdays, Lena's day off, and then only when Ida or Louisa couldn't. Even my mother's pendulum ways—swinging away from, now toward me, wanting me, rejecting me—could not diminish my excitement when she gave me a bath or sat by my bed. She was crowned by a halo, a yearned-for presence. If it was not reliable enough to be real love, it was something to hold on to all the same, distinct from Lena's professional ministrations—what real love would look like when it came.

Present time depends for its power on our acquiescence, our relinquishing of the past. If I believe only in the present which is the past, will the present which is the present fade into nothingness?

I am six or seven years old. I am standing with one leg on the gray and white checkerboard tile floor and the other leg up on the toilet seat. Lena is cutting my toenails, a weekly procedure that is part of Friday afternoon. Lena's hands are strong; she doesn't resort to clippers but uses regular nail scissors. We don't talk, and I watch closely as the curved, papery shells fall into the wastepaper basket that Lena has placed directly under the toilet. I am tempted to collect these clippings and store them; when she isn't looking, I pick up a piece of nail that has fallen to the side of the basket and put it in my mouth, where I chew on it, like an anteater.

Before Lena cuts my nails, she washes my hair in the bathtub. She uses Breck shampoo and rubs my hair into a sudsy pinnacle. Her shampoos are too hard; I concentrate on the clear, piney smell of the shampoo and the squishy sound the soap makes in my wet hair. Lena uses a metal spray attachment to rinse my hair. I like to watch her as she screws the attachment into the nozzle, the decisiveness with which she fits one part into the other. Then she turns the faucet back on, running the water first on her hand, the way mothers test warmed milk bottles on the inside of their wrists.

"It's not too cold?"

"No," I say. "Lena?"

"What?"

Lena doesn't like to talk, not the way Louisa does. On Thursdays, in the late afternoon, I often sit on the kitchen stool and watch Louisa make meatballs: she cracks a raw egg on the side of the big mixing bowl, then kneads the egg into the chopped meat along with some bread crusts, onions, and spices. I listen to her retell me the stories of her life—stories whose sadness she passes over lightly, as though they are misfortunes in a folk song—the stepmother who switched her legs with fresh-cut branches, the baby she lost, her husband, George, and how he is about food.

"Never seen a man so particular 'bout what he puts in his mouth," she says. "And do he get *mad*!"

She throws her head back and laughs. Louisa's laugh begins high and descends from there like a cascade—or something wilder. She seems to laugh about everything, which is the opposite of Lena. I feel safer around Louisa than I do with Lena, whose skin is the same color as mine.

Louisa wets her hands first to prevent sticking, then

rolls pieces of meat in her pink palms, shaping them into small balls. She plops each one into a sizzling pan of oil as soon as she is done with it. I always think she will burn herself, but she never does.

"Spell *Mississippi* for me," I say.

"Easy," she says, stepping back from the pan as the oil jumps. "Don't you remember?"

"Tell me again, please."

"Em, ah," she begins, pausing briefly, "crooked-letter, crooked-letter, ah . . ." Here she pauses again, then quickens the pace. ". . . Crooked-letter, crooked-letter, ah, hunchback, hunchback, ah."

I love her singsong, the way the familiar alphabet is transformed into wizened little people.

"Louisa," I say, "do you have any children?"

"Now, you know the answer to that," she says. "I done told you I lost my baby. Couldn't have no more."

I deliberate for a second or two, wondering what it would be like to eat dinner every night with George. I've talked to him a few times on the phone when he's called for Louisa, and his voice is so deep it scares me. Then I remember that Louisa has told me her apartment is decorated all in pink, even the bathroom.

"*I'll* be your child," I say.

Louisa, who is running water into the bowl, makes a sound somewhere between a laugh and a snort.

"Lordy, Hannah," she says, "you *got* a mother."

"I know," I say. "But you can be mine."

"I's too tired for all that," she says. "Besides, what you gonna do in Harlem without your sistuhs and brothuhs?"

She is peeling cucumbers now for the salad. I can't decide whether she wants me or not.

"You gotta be glad, girl, for what you all got. This pretty home."

I put my arms around her waist. Louisa is proud of

her waist; set against the amplitude of her hips, it's almost tiny.

Lena frowns at Louisa's ceaseless conversation. "Yap, yap, yap," she says, flapping her fingers in imitation.

"What's your favorite food?" I ask her as she pulls the stopper. I like to let the water run out between my legs.

"Ach, I don't know," she says. "Okay, out."

I step over the ledge of the tub and into a large, rough towel, which she wraps around me. "You want to know mine?"

Lena takes another, smaller towel and flicks my hair with it.

"Ouch," I say.

"Stand still then," she says.

"I am," I say, but lamely.

I am afraid of Lena, of her strong hands.

"Cake," I say.

"What?"

She is combing out my hair; when the teeth of the comb get caught in a knot, Lena tugs harder: she doesn't like to be resisted. The comb is tortoiseshell, and it is printed with the name KENT OF LONDON in small gold lettering.

"I love cake," I say.

"Hm," she says, pushing the comb through my hair, like a rudder, to make a part.

"It's very straight," I say, peeking in the mirror.

Lena's parts are ruler-straight—unlike the ones my mother and Louisa make on her day off, when the whiteness of my scalp peeks through in an uneven squiggle.

"Um huh," she says.

* * *

Lena loved Eric the most and because of this she spanked him the most. She spanked all of us, and sometimes she pulled our hair, and Benjamin she kicked when she got really angry, but Eric she seemed to want to caress with discipline.

I stand in a doorway and watch as she pulls him over her knee, his blondish head of curls dangling. I hold my breath when she pulls down his underpants and exposes his round, little boy's buttocks. They are smooth, small enough to cup in a hand.

"I told you I'd spank your bottom," she says. "Fresh boy."

Is Eric whimpering? Crying? Is he silent? Memory is a kind of condemnation, forgetfulness a kind of reprieve.

I stand in the doorway and titter. Am I nervous? Excited? Scared?

Lena brings her hand down—once, twice—on my brother's bottom, reddening it slightly.

"You won't talk back to me anymore. Any of you. Benjamin either."

The door behind which I am standing is only slightly ajar. I don't think Lena knows I'm there, but I'm sure Eric does. My bottom pulsates with his, yet by watching, it is I who administer the spanking to him.

"What about Benjamin?"

"He'll get his next," Lena says.

Where is my mother? Does she condone this? Does she know? Would she think Lena was bad if she knew?

Now Lena takes up a brush that lies next to her on the bed. Another KENT OF LONDON appears on its handle. The brush is oval-shaped, of sturdy, light-colored wood; it is meant to brush hair with. She slaps the back of the Kent brush across the middle of Eric's orbed exposedness: once, twice, many times. Eric begins to bawl, and I am so excited, I feel a wetness in my underpants.

At some point Lena lets Eric up. "There," she says. "And next time it'll be all of you, down the line."

Before Eric pulls up his underpants, I get a glimpse of him—red-assed, like a baboon.

I don't claim to understand the intricate process whereby the unbearable is made bearable, whereby imagination runs off with reality, like the dish running away with the spoon. The easiest way to be a victim is to align yourself with the victimizer, to create pleasure out of the pain. I do know that by the time I was ten, my imagination had thrown up its defenses, had successfully intervened between me and Lena's spankings. I was spanked, too, but the role I cast myself in was a voyeuristic one, a witness at the scene of humiliation.

At some point, I must have been nine or ten, I began looking up the verb *spank* in the dictionary because the act of seeing the word in print and the details of its definition gave me great excitement. At around the same time I also began having a recurring dream in which I spanked a little boy, my son, and then threw him out the window. As an adult I can't see a brush lying harmlessly on a chest of drawers without immediately flashing back, like a cut in a movie, to this scene; I am Lena, and I am Eric. It is all in slow motion, almost lyrical, the way it surely wasn't then: Eric, his underpants in a white puddle around his ankles, lies across Lena's lap; the softness of his bottom is almost palpable, and it is about to feel the flat blow of her hand or the more neutral sting of a brush. Does Lena rub his bottom between spanks, caressing it before the assault? I strain forward to see, but somewhere my urge to transform intercedes—pain and humiliation converted, by who knows what manner of ingenuity, to a wetness in my pants.

In the bathroom with the gray and white floor, I sit on the toilet, my stalky legs dangling. I hate my legs; they remind me of a seagull's, the way they refuse to bulge at the calves, growing undeviatingly straight. One of them is thinner than the other, and for a year I have to wear a corrective heel in one shoe. I wish I had Lily's legs, trim-ankled and curvaceous, or even Rachel's sturdy-looking limbs.

At what age did I begin my fierce self-judgments, seeking to expel all flaws? I giggle at the bossy Queen in *Alice in Wonderland*, who demands, "Off with her head!" But inside *my* head—although this is not something I admit to—I think she is perfectly right, her murderously intolerant instincts a match for my own.

Somewhere in the future, mortified by the comments of some boys in my class, I will send away for a pamphlet called "Skinny Legs." I spotted it in the same box with one on "Fat Calves" in the pages of small-print ads at the back of a movie magazine. The pamphlet, when it arrived in a plain gray envelope, was printed on cheap paper. On its cover was a grainy, disappointingly black and white photograph of a dated-looking woman in a two-piece bathing suit, modeling a pair of distinctively pudgy legs. It included a bunch of intricate exercises and some suggestions on foods to eat that would stick to our legs. I remember that I felt gypped, but expectantly so. I was, after all, a faithful consumer of small, miracle-promising products and had ordered a bottle of tooth-whitening liquid from a similar advertisement not too long before. Following the directions, I had applied the polish with the tiny brush it thoughtfully came with, hoping that my teeth would suddenly but discreetly gleam. What happened was that the liquid stuck to my teeth in resinous clumps, and the starkness of it made my own color look even more blighted. While waiting for it to dry, I kept grimacing in front of the mirror, trying on brief, stretched-out hints of a smile to see if the effect could pass for natural, then cocking my head and baring my teeth savagely, the way Angie Dickinson did. Would my mother or Eric notice and make some horrible comment? I needn't have worried; as it dried, the polish began to peel away and I soon went to work scraping the rest of it off. I consigned the bottle to the far reaches of my desk drawer, where the "Skinny Legs" pamphlet eventually joined it.

I count the checkered tiles in horizontal rows until they begin to merge with each other. In the side of the porcelain sink, traced with fine cracks, I discern a fleeting shadow of myself sitting on the toilet. It takes me a long time when I have to make "push" and not "wee wee." Lena has given them these names, and I wonder now if I strained so because I took its meaning—*push*—literally. Sometimes after Benjamin or Arthur has been in the bathroom, Lena will wrinkle her fine bridged nose in distaste. "What a stink!" she says, and I think, protectively, of my own smells. I will keep them inside, away from Lena.

I put my chin in my hand and sink further into the seat, feeling something coming. I push the pressure upward, staving it off, and look at the dark hairs along my legs. I am six or seven and the world is up too close, like a fly under a magnifying glass. Everything looks obscenely clear to me, distinct: two turds float in the bowl, mottled brown against the water. I stare at them mournfully between the valley of my thighs. Once you start not letting go of things, there is so much not to let go of. You could die letting go. Who's to say I won't one day dissolve into smelly pieces and fall into the toilet after them? I stand up and pull the paper roll, imagining myself gurgling down the hole, ending up in a cave of stink.

Someone bangs on the bathroom door. "Supper," Lena says. "Hurry up."

I give the contents of the bowl another lingering glance and then I flush them down. All gone. Downstairs in the kitchen there is fried fish, potatoes, and spinach, ice cream for dessert—the same every Wednesday without fail. My father comes in to say hello and inclines his cheek for my sisters and I to kiss.

"There'll be no food for me," he says.

Lily laughs uproariously.

It is a few minutes past six on the big kitchen clock. My father's cheek smells minty, like the sloping lawn in front of our summer house. I sit between Benjamin and Eric along the counter. Eric is wearing pajamas illustrated with little Donald Ducks standing at the ready—forever about to bang the little gold drums that hang from their necks. Lena cuts my fish; she always cuts my food, but she seems to do it more sweetly while my father is around. When he leaves the kitchen, I wonder how he makes "push," and if his is smelly, too. The image of my father sitting on the toilet is slightly terrifying, but there is something about it I like. I picture a steaming pile of feces on the floor—his? mine?—and it makes me feel brave.

On the edge of a bed against the wall, in a room in the summer house, I am sitting between Lily and Rachel. We have been propped close to each other, like toy soldiers on a shelf. The three of us are bathed and in pajamas, although Lily is already six or seven. It is late in the afternoon, not yet evening, but Lena likes to finish off the day. Outside our house there are children playing football; I can hear the dull thud of the ball as it is kicked. I am too little to compare myself to these —or any—children, so I don't envy them. It is only when I am old enough to visit other people's houses that I realize how iron-clad our childhood is. My mother stands in the doorway. She is wearing a deep blue shirtwaist cinched with a wide leather belt, the sort of dress that goes with medium-heeled pumps and the rosy beige stockings women wore in the fifties.

"Don't fidget so, Lily," my mother says.

Her hair is dark and short, and the lipstick on her thin mouth is a slashing color. Somewhere along the line, before I am born, my mother has shifted into an American image. Only her thick eyebrows, in a period of pruned ones, suggest an obtrusive factor—a will of her own or the incomplete grasp of a foreigner.

Rachel takes my hand, readying herself for the pose of older sister.

"That's nice," Lena says.

My mother bends slightly and clicks the tiny camera she holds in front of one eye.

"Baby," I say, meaning the camera.

In the second before my mother took the photograph, I must have leaned forward, ahead of Lily and Rachel, and held up three fingers to demonstrate my age. I found the snapshot not too long ago in the drawer of a little-used wicker desk out at the beach house. It is one of what are only a handful of my mother's informal attempts to catch the spirit of our growing up. Most of the family photographs were more official, the work of a professional—a woman who came once a summer with a lumpy bag of film and elaborate tripods. My three fingers look like a splayed victory sign, and my mother's dress, which is not in that picture, would have shown up black: there is no evidence for what we feel to have been the truth, no documentation we can point to. Who, for instance, is that defiant toddler in the photo? And why don't I remember being her?

Besides Lena and my mother and my father, I was afraid of Lily. Lily rarely took my hand, too sullen for photogenic gestures. Throughout my childhood she minded my presence, even if she tried not to.

She pulls my hair and I scratch the inside of her arms. Our discord is constant, but it only bothers my mother when it becomes noisy and threatens to wake my father from his Shabbos afternoon nap. At these times she slams out of her bedroom, nightgown flying.

"Stop it!" she yells. "Stop it this instant!"

"Lily started it," I say.

I am always crying, and Lily is always withdrawn, moated by moodiness.

"Liar," she says.

"I don't care," my mother says. "You have bad characters, both of you."

"No, I don't," Lily says.

"You're the eldest," my mother says. "Can't you act like it?"

"She doesn't listen," Lily says. "She doesn't stick to the rules."

Lily and I have been playing Plumfield, a game of our own devising, based loosely on the boarding school that Joe and Professor Bhaer run in *Little Men*.

"You keep changing the rules," I say, hiccuping.

This is true: Lily can't decide whether she and I are the headmistress and assistant headmistress, respectively, of a kindly orphanage, providers of love to lonely boys, or whether we are the tyrannical heads of a reform school, swooping down in violent rampages upon our dolls. I prefer the latter version, although it deviates sharply from the original Louisa May Alcott model. It gives me the opportunity to mete out brutal spankings and to pull the long carrot-colored hair on my favorite doll. I love screaming, "Behave yourself!" and "You'll be sorry!" I think Lily enjoys this version more, too, but she also likes to pretend that she is Professor Bhaer and I am Jo; at these times we sing good-night songs to the dolls and give them gentle haircuts.

My mother turns to me. "She's the oldest."

Lily glares at me from behind my mother.

"Tell her to be nice to me."

"I won't," Lily says. "You're spoiled."

"You are."

It is usually around now, when the fight shows no sign of dying and every sign of rekindling, that my mother has enough.

"You're both bitches. You deserve each other. Don't play with each other if you can't keep peace!"

Rachel, The Pacifist, is off somewhere, untainted by the bellicosity that marks Lily and me.

But there were other moments, too, on other Shabbos afternoons. Less dramatic but no less intense, they attested to a different form of "deserving," a happier mating. My mother seemed to encourage these not at all, as though she feared that even the most tentative of intimacies between the two of us would incite a movement against, or away from, her. And in a sense she was right, for no sooner did Lily and I like each other than we began to test the waters of a mutual sense of frustration, taking courage from each other's confessions of negative feelings.

"Lily?"

"What?"

Lily speaks to me in a determinedly curt tone, as though it would be a betrayal of her principles to sound amicable.

"I can't spread it," I say, waving the plastic knife around. "It's too gobby."

She looks up, alarmed, from her task of setting out paper plates and plastic utensils.

"Let me do it," Lily says.

She takes the two chocolate halves of the sandwich cookie away from me cautiously.

"They're not gold," I say, forgetting for a moment that we are supposed to be poor.

Lily wipes her hands on one of Louisa's old aprons, which she has tied over her smock. Once my sister gets into the spirit of the game, there's no stopping her.

"You have to be careful," she says, "or you'll break the whole thing. This cake has got to last us the week. And Polly's been sick, and the doctor says Tom's got to eat well or he won't grow up strong."

Polly and Tom are our imaginary brother and sister, names we have chosen for their simple, country ring—like "Mum" and "Papa," which is how we address our saintly but dead parents. Lily and I are sitting on the floor, preparing "dinner" for the family of four for whom we, as oldest, are responsible. Poorhouse, as this game is called, to differentiate it from Plumfield, is the closest Lily and I come to sisterly bliss; there is something about the minimalist ethos of the game that appeals greatly to both of us. Rachel, never much drawn to Lily's and my fantasy-ridden enactments, prefers to play board games—Sorry or Scrabble or Clue—with Benjamin in the boys' room while we dress up in my mother's discarded smocks and tie kerchiefs under our chins. I don't quite know why these kerchiefs were featured, but I can see us in them, admiring each other's raggedy appearance in front of the mirror.

The high point of Poorhouse consists of an activity that Lily calls "stretching the supplies." Having begged a handful of cookies and a half-bottle of juice from Lena, we manage to feed Polly, Tom, Meg (Lily), and Dot (me) for months by ingeniously transforming each sandwich cookie—a kosher version of Hydrox called Smokey Bear—into a "cake." Lily is more adept than I am at scraping the vanilla filling off the halves, clamping the two together, and then spreading the "frosting" on top of them, although she usually lets me try first.

"Meg?"

"Yes, Dot?"

Lily speaks more sweetly to me when I am Dot.

"There's no more soap. You think we can borrow a bar from our neighbor?"

"Guess so. Otherwise we'll have to go without bathing for a while, and you know how much Mum would've hated that."

Lily hums as she smooths the thin white paste over the hard cookie surface.

"Did you sew up the hole in Tom's overalls?"

"Yes, Meg," I say, envisioning myself as sooty but nimble-fingered. "And I ironed them, too."

The nice part of Poorhouse is that I can pretend to have all sorts of skills I don't have—a level of competence that is the more delightful to fake because there is no call to aspire to the real thing in my own life.

"You're such a help, Dot," Lily says.

There is a moment of silence as we contemplate our happy life of impoverishment.

"Lily?"

"Um."

"Don't you have Daddy's eyes?"

I know enough to start small, to creep upon Lily so she doesn't suspect the torrent I'm about to unleash.

"Sort of."

"They're so peensy, like mice eyes."

"And pink," Lily says.

We both laugh, and I am emboldened.

"I can't stand Lena."

"Yeah," she says, not willing to commit herself.

"How about you?"

"I don't know."

I seat Polly in front of a paper plate while Lily reties her kerchief. The doll is wearing a flowered dress with a drooping hem.

"She's so mean."

"Not always," Lily says.

"But mostly. Don't you think she's mostly mean?"

"Mostly."

I am about to move on to our mother—the true object of my probings—when the door crashes open. Rachel and Benjamin stand behind it with their arms extended and their eyes closed, like sleepwalkers.

"Get out!" I yell. "You're ruining the game."

"Is . . . this . . . the Poorhouse?" Benjamin drones in what is meant to be a ghostly voice.

"We're finished anyway," Lily says.

"It's about *time*," Rachel says, dropping her arms.

"It's not over," I say, but Lily is already putting the dolls away.

And then there were interludes of nearly perfect harmony, my fantasies seemingly meshed with Lily's. When Lily practices piano, in a robe and pajamas, I am fascinated by the strange glistening around her knuckles—the way the light seems to bounce off them. Lily's fingers are spatular, like my father's—"oily fingers," I call them—and she thumps the keys earnestly. Her repertoire is one of standard, easy classics—Mozart minuets and Beethoven sonatinas—but her favorite piece is a merry Jewish melody, "Der Rebbe Elimelech." The reason Lily loves this song is because she has a crush on Theodore Bikel, whose recording of "Der Rebbe Elimelech" she listens to whenever she thinks no one is around. *Theodore Bikel Sings Jewish Folk Songs* is one of about ten records in our joint collection, all of them chosen by my mother for their spiritually uplifting value. For this song, full of B flats and F sharps, she moves deep inside the keyboard, almost standing on her fingers. She plays it, signaling the conclusion of her practicing, with greater verve than she plays anything else. I lean against the blond upright Knabe and listen to the Yiddish words that Lily has learned and sings under her breath, accompanying the staccato tinkle of the tune: *"Az der Rebbe Elimelech iz gevoren zeyer frailich, iz gevoren zeyer frailich, Elimelech."* I forget to tell her that her fingers are oily, and she forgets to tell me to leave her alone. There is a drawing of a plump little *rebbe* dancing on his toes, sidelocks askew, in the right-hand corner of the page. Long after Lily stopped playing the piano, she returned to this song. At some point her fingers stopped looking oily to me, and it is by such small shifts that I look back and measure the passing of time.

There are so many mysteries—the mundane mysteries of households—taken for granted by everyone except me, for whom they are urgent.

Does Lily get lost in my visions, my glimpses of sentiment? Does she paint herself into a gable-roofed village out of Sholom Alecheim, two sisters sweeping the hearth, the way I do? Or does she play "Der Rebbe Elimelech" while ignoring me and dreaming of her beloved Bikel? Is that why she seemed not to mind as I stood practically on top of her?

And what did Lena do in her room once she was finished with the day? What, exactly, was she rushing toward other than the absence of us, her "charges?" The freedom to sit in a chair and smoke cigarettes? To watch an hour or two of television?

Also, why am I wearing the same pair of pajamas in every frame of my memory?

Where is my father?

When Lena invites Eric into bed to snuggle with her as she watches a TV program, does she pretend he is a grown man or does she like him because he's not grown, young enough to spank?

Why didn't anyone intervene, save me from falling off cliffs in my dreams?

The odd thing is that I am tugged equally by the unimportant holes as by the important ones. Perhaps all synapses feel the same to the brain.

Those pajamas, the faded pink cotton ones, feel better than wearing nothing. They smell of ironing and bleach when I first put them on; after several days they begin to smell faintly of skin. The laundress, Ida, doesn't smell like my pajamas, although I think she should. Her skin, dark brown like Louisa's, has a stronger smell than Lena's. Ida wears a gray and white wig plopped on top of her own grizzly hair, like a hat.

"It looks like a sheep," I tell her.

Ida laughs softly, her pink tongue sliding into the slot between her front teeth.

"Jesus lead the little children," she says.

Ida pronounces words more clearly than Louisa, but she is cooler, a buffer state rather than a warm zone. I never hug Ida—she is too thin, for one thing—but I talk to her about serious things, Moses and Jesus. Ida reads her Bible a lot, forming the words silently with her mouth. The New Testament is a thick book with a cover that looks but doesn't smell like leather; its pages are tissue thin and hemmed with gold. Her initials, I.B., are stamped into the lower right-hand corner, and I like to run my finger over the imprint, to feel the slight dip it makes.

"The *B* is for Brown, right? Ida Brown," I say.

I am sitting on the dryer in the tiny laundry room behind the kitchen, where Ida works. The window in the room is always darkened by dirt, and I like to watch Ida push the steaming iron back and forth along the board. As she navigates its silver tip in and out of collars and around pants zippers, the bone in her arm stands out.

"Yep," she says, "that's my name."

Ida cracks her chewing gum, scrunching the corner of her mouth down on the grayish wad that appears intermittently and then disappears inside the wet tunnel of her mouth.

"Are you religious?"

I can't fit Ida's love of chewing gum together with her being so pious, especially the way she cracks it.

"Are your Mommy and Daddy religious?"

"Yes," I say, wondering how she can ask such an obvious thing.

"Well then," she says, as though that answered it.

The iron gives out a sound like a sigh as Ida lifts it and places it back down on another spot on a white damask tablecloth.

"I'm religious, too," I say, just in case this point is in doubt. "But I don't read the same Bible you do."

"That's all right," Ida says, unperturbed.

She stands the iron up on the board and lifts the tablecloth, folding it lengthwise along the crease she has just ironed into it. Ida's creases, razor sharp, show up everywhere: in the sleeves of my father's glossy shirts, in my mother's linen napkins, in the stiff uniforms she irons for Louisa and herself.

"Can I look at your Bible?"

"If your hands are clean," Ida says.

She takes another piece of wash from the plastic laundry basket. It is damp and wrinkled when she unrolls it but will soon be turned into a smooth expanse of white, like the tablecloth. I jump off the dryer and retrieve Ida's book from the top of the washing machine. I turn its pages, which remind me of the paper in the airmail pads my mother uses. The names —Paul, Matthew, Luke—are what I notice first; they stand out from the tight print because they're capitalized and because they're different from the names on the English side of the *chumash* we read in *shul*.

"I like your names better," I say. "I'm going to call my sons Matthew and Peter."

"Those Hebrew names are beautiful," Ida says. "The kings, David and Solomon."

"It's so fancy," I say admiringly, rubbing the strip of crimson ribbon that is sewn into the Bible's binding.

"You're going to lose my place," Ida says, as though I already have.

"I *won't*."

"Huffy Hannah," Ida says. "Blow the house down."

"My ankles hurt me," I say.

Ida laughs, not ungenially.

"You're an old lady," she says.

"I am not."

There really is something wrong with my ankles, a slight weakness in the bone because of the disparity between my legs. Sometimes Ida even rubs them with witch hazel. But she is right; by the age of nine or ten, I have an assortment of geriatric ailments, including constipation. For a while I drink a glass of prune juice in the morning, along with my cereal, the way the guests did in the hotel we went to once or twice in the mountains. Eric claims the juice looks like push and that's why it works.

The gravity of being a child in that family! Did Ida understand it, or did she merely indulge an easy stereotype—the poor little rich girl? To people without money, all other griefs run a distant second, and even craziness can seem like a luxury.

On a Friday night in the middle of winter, the curtains are drawn, and Ida's snowy tablecloth, not yet spotted with gravy or wine, rests under settings of china and silver. I am eight or nine, wearing a black velvet jumper that belonged first to Lily and then to Rachel, and when Ida comes in to take the jellied *putscha* away, I say hello to her shyly, as though we recognize each other fully only in informal surroundings. I pick up my soup spoon and cup the flames from the silver Shabbos candlesticks, which stand high above us in the center of the table; two blurred points of blue-yellow light dance in the curve of the spoon. When I tilt it further, a mirror to catch whatever I please, my father's face comes into view; he is peering over his glasses at a guest.

"I didn't catch your name," my cousin Beatrice says loudly to the woman sitting next to her.

"Dora," the woman says, "Dora Fischer."

"Call me Bea," my cousin says, conferring intimacy upon a perfect stranger. Her bracelets rattle welcomingly when she puts a pudgy wrist forward to shake the woman's hand.

"Very pleased to meet you," Dora Fischer says.

"I'm Walter's cousin," Beatrice says. Her tone is strident, and it is hard to tell if she characterizes herself this way out of pride or chagrin.

"That's wonderful," Dora says. "Have you ever been to Israel?"

"Oh, several times," Beatrice says, "several times. Once with the children here."

"And you are the oldest?" The guest my father has been talking to addresses this question to Benjamin.

"No," Benjamin says, "Lily is."

"So many children!" Dora Fischer says. "How do you do it?"

Across the table, as if to emphasize the enormity of the situation, Eric knocks over his water glass. The water spreads across the tablecloth in a large, colorless circle.

"You klutz!" Rachel says. "My sleeves are all wet."

Lena sets down a bowl of soup on my plate and whispers something in my ear. The soup, a dark yellow, has stands of parsley floating in it and two of Louisa's small, springy matzo balls.

"What?"

"I said to use your napkin," Lena whispers dramatically, as though she were telling me a state secret. "You're such a mess pot."

"I doubt it," my father says to Dora Fischer's husband. "Americans are too naive."

"That depends, Dad," Benjamin says.

"No one's asking you," I think but don't say.

"Schrecklich," my father says, shaking his head

woefully at some pronouncement. "Margot, did you hear that?"

"How long did you say you were staying?" my mother is asking.

"A week," Dora Fischer says. "My husband's here for business, and then we go back."

"I've never been able to do my own nails," Beatrice says to Lily. "Although dark polish isn't in anymore."

"Really?" Lily says.

"I bite my nails," Rachel says. "But Hannah doesn't."

My father bangs on the table, a cufflink gleaming at the end of his sleeve.

"Have you seen the Yves St. Laurents?" Beatrice asks loudly.

My mother shakes her head, as if quieting an unruly child.

"And now," my father begins, "if the women can refrain from . . ."

Up toward the ceiling a chandelier pendant swings lightly, imagining a breeze. Reflecting the flames of the Shabbos candles, its facets sparkle with color—orange, yellow, blue, and green. Once every few months Ida climbs on a small ladder with a pail and cleans the chandelier with soap and water. She is the stem upon which we flower.

". . . tell us about this week's *parsha*," my father says.

Benjamin slides his chair back on the carpet and stands up. He is good at his appointed task; he pulls on his lower lip and adjusts his glasses like a professor, ostentatiously studious. Every Friday night Benjamin is called upon to trot out his erudition with an entertaining tidbit from the weekly portion of the Torah that will be read in *shul* the next day. All the *parshas* run together in my mind, narratives involving flocks and shepherds, dispersals and betrayals, redemptions and abandonments. There are too many Big Themes, but Benjamin is able not only to remember which theme is exemplified in each portion but also to make it sound more diverting than it really is.

"There is a question," my brother says in his best pedantic singsong, "in this week's *parsha* about the distribution . . ."

"Der Junge hat einen guten Kopf," Mr. Fischer says, nodding his head approvingly.

The fierce loyalty of the German immigrants, refugees still looking back with longing, who visit my parents! Their German flows over us, a rocky stream, emphatic even at its most casual. It is unclear whether my siblings and I are or aren't meant to navigate this guttural language my parents speak with each other and their friends. Lily, who along with Rachel understands German the best, rolls her eyes as if beseeching the heavens at Mr. Fischer's words of praise for Benjamin.

I look at Mr. Fischer and wonder if he mistakes us for a happy family. Of course, it is unlikely that he speculates—on this matter, at least—at all. He is a successful businessman, a variation on the guest my father brings home to Friday night dinners and Shabbos lunches week in and week out—men with tight eyes that don't give anything away. What they seem to have in common with my father is an abiding pragmatism, a belief that ruminations of the sort I indulge in don't pay.

Eric talks softly to Rachel.

"Ssh," my mother says.

Beatrice holds up her hands and studies them, as though considering an exchange for a different pair.

"But Rashi," Benjamin is saying, "doesn't agree with *tosfos* here."

Mr. Fischer's eyes are closed; he is either concentrating deeply or fast asleep.

I get up from the table and go through the swinging door that connects the dining room to the kitchen. It is warm and bright inside. A platter of cut-up roast chicken sits on the kitchen table next to a bowl of rice, waiting to be served. Lena is reading the *Post* at one end, and Ida is laughing with Louisa at the other.

"Five hundred," she says. "He lost five hundred at one sitting, the big damn fool."

"He don' look out, he headed for the po' house," Louisa says.

I stand there until Ida looks up.

"Pretty dress," she says.

"Thank you," I say. "It was Lily's."

"Still looks good to me," Louisa says.

"What are you talking about?"

"Oh, just things." Ida says. "Folks we know."

Lena rattles the pages of the paper, as if to imply her greater curiosity about the folks Ida and Louisa *don't* know.

"It's so boring inside," I say.

"Ain't they almost done?" Louisa says. "This food gonna be ice cold."

"Benjamin can talk *forever*," I say.

Ida picks at her uniform; Louisa yawns and looks at me.

"Girl, I'm tired," she says. "I'm too old to be workin' like this."

"You always say that," I say.

Louisa seems ageless to me, her shiny brown skin as unlined as mine. She has been threatening to quit for as long as I've known her.

"Black people don't near rest enough," Ida says.

Lena looks up but says nothing. Ida doesn't tolerate her sniffs of contempt the way Louisa does. Suddenly it seems to me that they are all waiting for me to leave.

"See you," I say. "I've gotta go to the bathroom."

Sitting on the toilet in the flowery guest bathroom, I picture to myself what Mr. Fischer must look like on the toilet—his wide, hairy thighs and a small red penis, the size of the one I remember on Eric when he was little. I try and place him in a bed, holding Mrs. Fischer, the two of them naked. It eludes me—as unfathomable as the lives of Ida and Louisa when I'm not there.

EIGHT

The scenes we glimpse too early to make sense of generate a life of their own, an angry whirring in the head, like a top; they precede us into the present and are a fair indicator of what we will always fear—or be riveted by. "Long-term memory is pretty much permanent," a scientist who has studied the subject says in *The New York Times*. "It is below your level of awareness and it may well last forever." *The New York Times* was delivered in the morning by one of the doormen and placed on the dining room table next to my father's breakfast well before I, Hannah Lehmann, could read, and I know scientists are supposed to be impartial folk. No one, in short, has it in for me but my memory. Who can pinpoint its presumptions—why terror creates a stir, alarming the nervous system in some immutable way, while ordinary experience leaves no mark? Once you have been besieged, required to take in more innuendo than your receptors can handle —*I am not loved; this is all wrong*—there is no going back to the blitheness of recall by which most people live. The opposite of terror is blandness—a snub-nosed girl from Dayton, Ohio, who regards her family with the same lack of guile with which she regards the sky when it is blue.

Behind the gold bars of our apartment on the Upper East Side, the inmates go crazy: a relative madness, worse than some, better than others. My cousin Beatrice stands at the bottom of the curving staircase and says, "I shall scream, Margot." My mother's face is set in grim lines. I am watching through the banister, and I am amazed by the calm air with which Beatrice announces this violation of decorum. "I shall," she repeats as if on a dare, and now she opens her mouth and screams *(it may well last forever)*—a shrill, theatrical noise that leaves no echo when she stops.

Beatrice is very fat, and in the lingerie department where we are buying her a fancy lilac robe, size 18, to wear in the hospital, my mother explains that Beatrice has no will. "She never did," my mother says. "Peach? Or lilac? I think she looks better in lilac with that white skin of hers. Ever since I've known her, she's been unable to control herself." I picture my cousin in a hospital ward full of people who scream arbitrarily. I am not sure what my mother means when she says Beatrice lacks will, but I wonder if it is something catching, like measles. I decide that it must have to do with her being fat, the way her flesh seems to drip off her neck and wrists like wax. My mother says that Beatrice is very smart, that she could have been anything, but this only makes the discrepancy seem more tragic to me. When Beatrice gets out of the hospital, she comes to dinner on Friday nights like she did before.

There are details I noted but obscured, even then. Behind the banister my hair smelled of Breck shampoo—Lena's shampoo—and I understand more than I say or even know I know. Beatrice wants my mother to notice her, and my father even more. She is grown up; she is too old to be an orphan, but she wants my parents to care for her like parents. She will agitate them into concern; it is a pattern that she is setting, although at the time I only admired her for her lack of fear. I didn't yet realize that she was pointing the way, trying to jolt my parents out of their immunity by releasing the virus of her distress. What she underrates is their high tolerance, the ever-multiplying antibodies of their indifference.

After Beatrice screams, my mother says: "Are you done."

Her coolness is stunning. I blank out the implications of heartlessness; she is my mother, after all.

My father bursts out of his study, rocketed by fury at this disturbance of his evening. In the background, on his KLH radio set to the classical station, violins melt into each other.

"I won't stand for this!"

His spit sprays out, fireworks of disdain; I can see the droplets from where I watch.

"Leave me alone!" Beatrice yells.

Her skin looks clammy, almost yellow in its pallor, and her chestnut hair, which my mother asserts she never washes, has begun to topple from the loose French knot she wears it in.

"Take it easy," my mother says. "Save your hysterics."

In bed that night I am afraid to fall asleep, the beginning of a disorder. My parents will never be able to protect me from themselves. How can they know it is *they* I need protection from? They are granite, imperturbable.

I no longer sleep in a room with Benjamin and Eric, but my sisters are scant solace. Did they see what I saw? What did Beatrice do next? Did she hold her ground and scream some more? Who called the hospital? And if I asked them these questions, and they answered, would that avail? Why is it that we get our first taste of isolation within families?

In her narrow bed Rachel sleeps, her breathing soft and even, her blanket kicked off. Lily lies on her back, but there is something about the way her head is angled that makes me think her eyes are open.

"Lily?"

She doesn't answer.

"Lily," I whisper more loudly.

"Ssh," she says.

"Are you awake?"

I hear the rustle of a sheet as she turns in her bed.

"Not really."

"Lily, I'm scared."

I am too old to believe in monsters, but I do anyway. There is someone crouched behind the closet door who will kill me as soon as Lily falls asleep. The murderer is in the house.

"Don't be," she whispers.

"I am, though."

Lily sits up in bed.

"Of what?"

"The murderer," I say.

Lily lies back down, as though the answer is too boring to stay up for.

"Where?"

"Here."

"*Where* here?"

She yawns for what seems like a whole minute, and I feel a responsive tickle in my throat.

"In this room."

"Don't be nuts. We would've seen him."

"Lily?"

"I'm going to sleep," she says.

"What's wrong with Beatrice?"

"I don't know," she says.

Her voice is fading, pulling away from me.

"She's not mine," she mumbles.

"Who?" My own voice is pitched high with tension, as though Lily were withholding a vital piece of information.

"No," she says, "I didn't."

Lily's words are slowed down and spoken on a scale lower than usual—like a record played at the wrong speed.

"Are you dreaming?"

In answer there is only silence and, if I listen hard, two sets of breathing. I climb out of bed and open the bathroom door a crack, reaching a hand in before me for the light switch. In the seconds before I locate the switch and flick it on, I feel the skin on the back of my neck prickle with fear. If I turn around, the murderer will see me. If I can only control myself and not look behind me, then I am safe—unlike Lot's wife, whose plight I have learned about recently in school. The bathroom, exposed to the light, looks ordinary, and the faucets on the sink are cold to my touch. I turn them both on, just to check, and when I turn them off

I tap each one five times, counting 1-2-3-4-5 dutifully in my head.

Do the faucets know what has happened a few hours ago in this very house? If I tap them each five times, the murderer will leave me alone and Beatrice will be under control. My parents won't murder her for screaming and disturbing them in the middle of their evening. I turn off the lights and go out into the hall, where there is a desk lamp left on. The antique wall clock ticks steadily, and the door to my parents' bedroom, when I try it, is locked. Everything is quiet, even the air that looms beyond the stairs.

"Go away," I say, but my lips don't move.

"Stop it," I say, my brain talking to my brain.

Terrible things always happen in the middle of ordinary things, in the middle of a night like any other. In the air that looms beyond the stairs, I can make out a faint shuffling noise—what I am sure is the sound of Beatrice's corpse being dragged away in a burlap sack. I want to wake my mother up and ask her if she loves me, if I love her. But I can't because she never forgets to turn the key in the lock when she and my father go to bed, even though I always check. I know what my parents look like asleep anyway, from the glimpses I've managed to catch: my mother sleeps with her mouth slightly open, like a fish, and my father sleeps on his side, his back massive as a whale's. His slippers, round-toed leather ones from England, stand at the foot of his bed. My mother says he is cozy to sleep next to, but she is also fond of saying, "At night all cats are gray," so I deduce a certain impersonality in her preferences. When I creep back into my own bed, I pull the sheet and blanket over my head, making a canopy. Right before I fall asleep, there is a wetness on my pillow, and I realize my head is leaking.

* * *

Perhaps the subtler the terror, the worse it is for children in this respect: It allows for so much filling-in of the contours. When I think of Beatrice going crazy and getting better and going crazy again, I see a lonely black dot in the middle of whiteness. There is, after all, no blood, no flashing of knives; nothing looks any different after Beatrice has screamed. In response to so much subtlety, I go from being an uneasy sleeper to a full-scale insomniac, in need of sleeping pills. And it is, too, from somewhere around this time that I date the awakening of my impulse to disappear from the scene of my life—what I recognize years later, while sitting on the beach playing with my niece, as a chronic but undramatic wish to die.

My father shouted louder than anyone else: he is a red crayon scrawled every which way across a sheet of paper until it is all covered. I cannot remember ever having been in love with him, the way very young girls are reputed to be. It was, I suppose, a sort of pride—a determination not to be unduly wistful. My father scared me because of his remove and because of the violence that hung in the air around him. When it broke, prodded usually by unnecessary noise coming from someone beside himself—a dispute that was taking place among us while he was reading his slender, incisive newspapers (*The Wall Street Journal* or *Barron's* or, like a female in an all-male club, the blushing pink *Financial Times*)—its effect was more impending than actual. The signs of his rage, the way he bellowed and blew, never failed to electrify me. Would he go beyond all bounds this time?

"When he's mad," my mother explains, "Daddy sees red."

"Like a bull," I say.

Behind my cowering, I imagine myself spearing my father between the eyes, toppling him to his knees like some great beast.

It must be somewhere in the past on a Tuesday evening, not yet spring, that my father stands in the foyer outside his study, hands on his hips, his belly protruding before him like a round hill.

"What's all this *Geschrei*?"

In my memory German is the language of alarm: *Someone is done for.*

"Benjamin! Lily! Rachel! Hannah! Come down at once!"

The four of us slide downward along the banister, meekly in file, the same way we line up for the photographer.

"Whose fault is this?"

We stand in front of him, and no one says anything. I cut his lowered head off with one swipe of my sword and raise the bloody mess before a cheering crowd.

"The girls always want to watch what they want on TV," Benjamin says.

"That's not true," Rachel says. "You watched 'The Hardy Boys.'"

"*Shlock!*" my father says.

Who is he calling an idiot this time?

"Television's crap," he blares, spittle drooling from his lips. "No, it's not," Benjamin says. "It's got a lot of important things on it."

"Don't argue," my father yells, shoving Benjamin forward like a crate.

My father's lips are thick. He loves to eat, and when

My father's lips are thick. He loves to eat, and when he smiles, they stretch around his nicotine-stained teeth unconvincingly.

"He looks like a gangster when he smiles," I tell my mother, part of my unwavering campaign to woo her away from him.

"Yah?" she asks.

I rejoice at having piqued her curiosity about something she has always taken for granted.

"Like he's trying to fool you," I add.

"Maybe," she says musingly.

Spurred on, I go too far. It is mysterious to me, what my mother will or will not allow me to air. "I don't understand why you married him."

"It's none of your business," she snaps.

"But I don't like him."

"He's *your* blood," my mother says, as though I were somehow more responsible for her choice than she is.

"No, he's not," I say.

Who decreed genealogy to be inviolable? What if I don't wish to inherit the lineage available to me, the character traits and bulbous features that have marked generations of Lehmanns? Why hasn't anyone asked *me*?

"Pick another father next time around," my mother says. "One more to your liking."

I have this conversation or one very much like it with my mother at regular intervals over the years; it always takes place in the kitchen, and at some point there is a tea kettle that begins to whistle, like a soft but insistent scream. My mother has prepared a nightly tray of tea for my father—a thermos and two glasses—for as long as she has been expressing her morbid theories about the dictates of heredity.

"Jews are too old," she says on one of these occasions, rescuing the kettle from its hysteria. "They have tired genes."

Although this claim doesn't jibe with anything I have picked up in biology class, I am drawn to the picturesque quality of my mother's theories, their poetic authority. Besides, much as I would deny it, I have never quite given up on her as the source of my knowledge of the world. I think of the pallid coloring of the people I know—Jews all—and their lack of interest in the outdoors; none of my friends go camping or have fathers who sail. Perhaps my mother is right, and I sit so much, as opposed to striding around, because I am historically exhausted.

"That's ridiculous," I say. "You don't know anything."

My mother presses the spout open on the teakettle and pours the steaming water over several tea bags, whose strings dangle over the rim of a green china pot. The glasses she then fills, which have been specially ordered from a European firm, are treated so that the handles remain cool even when the tea is boiling.

"There isn't enough fresh blood," she says, persisting. "Not like the *goyim*, who can marry anyone."

"You sound like Hitler," I say.

There is a part of me that, even in adulthood, still believes my mother secretly subscribes to the Aryan doctrines that led to her having to escape from her native land. It doesn't help, of course, that she remembers one of the Nazi songs that was in the air before her family left Germany and has chanted its lyrics to me with a relish that, as I have pointed out to her, borders on the insane.

"*Natürlich,*" she says.

Her bare feet clap against the soles of her slippers as she goes to the refrigerator and takes out a carton of milk, sniffing it first.

"I love dairy products," she announces.

"You don't have to inhale it," I say.

"I could drink milk all day,"she says.

"I can't bear your exaggerations."

The walls of the kitchen are covered in a pattern that looks like colorful graph paper. Other than that, everything is white and metallic, like a lab; there are few homey touches of the kind I see featured in the women's magazines—no dotted Swiss curtains sweetly looped back or cute little plants lined up on the window sill.

Arthur lopes into the kitchen soundlessly, on the balls of his feet.

"R-r-uff, r-ruff," he says to me.

"Very lifelike," I say.

"Thought you needed a friendly dog to keep you company," he says.

Arthur is the only member of the family who likes animals. The rest of us have responses ranging from fear to slight distaste. My mother has passed on her hatred of cats to me ("such useless creatures," she says), and Benjamin crosses the street when he spots large dogs. As a concession, Arthur has been permitted to house a series of small, quiet pets in his room—chameleons and gerbils, turtles and goldfish. He seems to have a marked fondness for rodents, although he is absent-minded about their care, neglecting to clean the cage or leave them food. It is my mother who usually looks after them when the smell gets too strong, and once she had to rescue a couple of newborn gerbils from *their* mother, who had already eaten two; Arthur didn't even notice they were missing until he heard my mother's shrieks.

"Would you like some cookies?"

"Thanks, Ma," Arthur says. "What d'you have?"

"There aren't any," I say. "I checked."

"Did you look under the cabinet, where the big pots are?" my mother asks. "Lena probably hid them there."

"Why?" Arthur asks.

"So Dad won't find them."

"He's fat anyway," I say.

"Have a cookie," my mother says, holding out a plastic container. "It'll calm your nerves."

I bite down on one of Louisa's refined cookies, the only kind she bakes, hazelnut crescents dusted with sugar. It tastes crumbly rather than sweet, dryly familiar. Arthur grins at me, and when I stare back at him glumly, he stretches his smile even further and freezes it.

"You have yellow teeth," I say. "Like a zebra."

Under the fluorescent lights of the kitchen in which I grew up, I notice the way the veins in my mother's hands knot up when she is in repose, like used thread. Will I always find it impossible to connect her with the fact of mortality, with the certainty of her veins giving out before mine? Without my mother, who will cut up the world into bite-sized pieces for me?

In my own apartment I keep an unremitting supply of chocoloate cookies, but I catch myself stashing them behind bowls, hiding them from myself. Can it be that we come into our own only to realize that we are deformed, as well as formed, by what precedes us? I am imprinted, now and forever, like a duckling, by the wrong mother duck; a downy ball, I follow steadfastly at her heels although the direction leads astray.

NINE

The intense privacy of the life lived in families, the obsessions that get spawned! Ours was an attempt at a system: everything got hidden, and everything got lost. In the space under my bed, long after the age at which most children feel the need to bury their homely treasures, I stored things—a package of much-coveted Pepperidge Farm cookies that I bought on my way home from Melamed, safe from Eric's view; library books I had forgotten to return; a new pair of shoes that Lily would be jealous of if she saw. There were too many of us and too little of—of what? Money, I felt, even before I knew it, wasn't the issue, the way it was in *Little Women* or *Five Little Peppers*. What was missing was less clear-cut but no less impoverishing: some allowance for the spill of our personalities, the clamor of distinctive selves—a turf for each of us to stake out, mess up, tack drawings to the walls of, declare *Mine*. When I saw the rooms of friends, I became conscious of a difference, the voice they had been given in the choice of a ruffled bedspread, a white and gold desk. But it is not until I am grown up, when I will have friends with children of their own, that I am struck by the thought that what was absent from the rooms my siblings and I slept in was, simply, us.

We had an upstairs and a downstairs but only three children's rooms. My mother, who prided herself on ignoring the American model, didn't understand the need for separate rooms.

"You'd only get lonely," she said by way of explanation.

"But I wouldn't," I said, having broached the idea.

"I always wanted someone to sleep with when I was a child," she said.

"But I see them all the *time*," I said.

My mother's faith in the value of our keeping each other company at night serenely overlooked the fact of our relief at being free of each other's company. I never snuggled in Lily's or Rachel's bed the way Hayley Mills did when she discovered that she had an identical twin in the movie *The Parent Trap*. Lily would turn toward the wall with a book, her back to Rachel and me, the minute she got under the covers. Rachel's attitude was a bit more civil; she was willing to talk, but there were no eruptions of affection beyond that. Of course, this sleeping arrangement was a great improvement over the prior one that my mother had concocted—putting me together with Benjamin and Eric. I'm not sure at what point my brothers ceased tolerating my presence and began actively to torment me. I cried too much, for one thing, and my crying had a strange, nasal whine to it that they delighted in copying.

"Hey, Eric," Benjamin would say out of the darkness. "Pss."

"Yeah," Eric answered sleepily.

Unlike me, my younger brother dropped off in seconds, going from a wide-awake state to deepest slumber without any intervening terrors. Both Benjamin and Eric wore baseball pajamas, with YANKEES or DODGERS scrawled across them in glued-on letters. Benjamin took his glasses off only after he got into bed. He had the same frame for years—the bottom half was clear and the top half was black or brown. The clear part of the frame would yellow slightly with the passage of months; the glasses, because they made no attempt at style, gave Benjamin the look of a boy who you could expect to be picked on by his tougher peers, like Piggy in *Lord of the Flies*.

"How do you think Koufax will play?"

"Great," Eric said. "He's been playing great."

My brothers, including Arthur when he was old enough, followed baseball with competitive zeal—testing each other on batting averages and team ratings and on who had been voted "Most Promising Rookie of the Year" in the years before they were born. It was their version of world history; they referred other events of the time to it rather than the other way around. Benjamin had an astonishing memory for the facts and numbers, but it was Eric who played the best when they got dressed up in their pin-striped flannel uniforms and visored caps and went out to the fields in Central Park.

"Charlie's getting us tickets."

I listened from my bed in the corner opposite Eric's with undue vigilance, like an interpreter who wasn't needed but could be called on at a moment's notice to rattle off a perfect translation. My brothers' interest in baseball and their constant trading of baseball cards from huge decks, which they shuffled and eyed admiringly, made little sense to me; it seemed like yet another information-stuffed subject, the purpose of which I couldn't glean, like the lists of abbreviations I would later have trouble learning for science class. What was the point of memorizing H_2O and Fe when the words they stood for were so much more descriptive—*water*, which glistened, resembling tears, or *iron*, which rusted but still wouldn't bend? I disliked anything—like dividing one stream of numbers into another stream—that stood only for the thing itself. I was intrigued, it has since occurred to me, exclusively by those pieces of knowledge that I could translate into feelings: what went on elsewhere as it reflected what went on in me. History, for instance, was all right; the wives of the presidents, bustling Abigail Adams and unhappy Mary Todd Lincoln, stirred me enough so that I could make room in my mind for the events that swirled around them—the Alien and Sedition Acts and the Civil War.

"Front row seats," Benjamin went on, trying to keep Eric awake. "Charlie has connections."

"Charlie's great," Eric mumbled, "real great."

Charlie was Lena's boyfriend—the only one she had or the only one she was willing to display. When he disappeared, there were no more. Charlie was muscular, and he looked younger than Lena. His hair was cut close to his scalp, like freshly mowed grass, and his eyes rolled in their sockets like bright blue marbles; there didn't seem to be anything in back of them, no fleeting thoughts. Charlie's father was a retired policeman, and my brothers loved this as well as everything else about him. What he himself did—or whether he simply lived in his father's small brick house, on top of other small brick houses in the shabby, year-round section of our summer community, waiting for Lena and my brothers to return to the beach each summer—remained a mystery.

"Hey, Eric, d'you think Charlie has other girlfriends besides Lena?"

"Nah," Eric said, "he loves just her."

During the winter, when they saw Charlie less, my brothers talked about him a lot—as though to assure themselves that he was part of their lives, independent of Lena's romantic whims. It was hard for me to conceive of Lena, with her taut forearms and laconic replies, as anybody's girlfriend. But Charlie seemed to treat her as one; on Lena's day off during the summers he would accompany her to various beaches, and sometimes the two of them would take my three brothers on trips to Playland or Jones Beach. In the winter months he dropped out of sight, but toward the spring he started to appear again, looking gussied up and out of place when he arrived at my parents' apartment to pick up Lena. I never heard Lena giggle around Charlie, which was what I knew girlfriends did when they were around the boys they loved. I think Benjamin had his doubts, too, but Eric remained loyal to the image.

"She looks pretty good in a bathing suit," Benjamin said, as if to convince himself.

"I *know*. If he marries her, we'll be related."

"No we won't," Benjamin said, always a stickler for detail.

"Well, almost."

"I told him Koufax doesn't play on Yom Kippur," Benjamin said, "that he's really Jewish."

"Like us," Eric said.

"Charlie said, 'The guy's got principles.'"

"You told me already," Eric said.

"'You got to respect a guy with principles,' Charlie said."

"Hey, Benjy, I bet Sandy and Charlie would be best friends if they knew each other," Eric declared.

"You know what?" Benjamin said. "I think you're right."

As the two of them rambled on about the wondrous meeting of souls that would take place between the two men they adored—Sandy Koufax and Charlie Donovan—I began to sniffle. I squeezed my eyes tight against the urge to cry, but it didn't help. I was feeling lonely. I wished I had different brothers; but more than that, I knew exactly which ones I wanted: Robbie, Chip, and Ernie from "My Three Sons." I loved the genially masculine atmosphere of the program—the perennial twinkle in Fred MacMurray's fatherly eye, the fussy Uncle Charlie, who was a softie under all his harrumphings, and the way the three brothers always stood around with their hands in their pockets, worrying about each other. Would Ernie, the littlest brother, make friends at his new school? Would Chip find a date for the prom? The oldest brother, Robbie, was, admittedly, married—to a dimpled girl with a perfect blonde pageboy—but I could still see myself as the wedge to fill the gap in the show's heart: "My Three Sons and My Daughter." I would be Robbie, Chip, and Ernie's cute, fussed-over little sister—an afterthought and all the more precious for it.

"N-n-n-y-e-h."

My crying sounded out of the darkness like a lamb's bleating.

"There she goes," Benjamin said.

"Shut up," I said.

"N-n-n-y-e-h," went Eric.

Before going to bed I had scribbled across two pages of my Hebrew notebook: *I hate everyone in this house.*

"Maybe we should throw some cold water on her," Benjamin said.

"How come you cry like that?" Eric asked, trying to be kind.

"N-n-n-y-e-h," Benjamin said.

My brothers weren't entirely wrong in finding my crying so laughable; it had an odd, strangled sound to it, like sobs that got pinched through the nose instead of being released through the mouth. I'm not sure why I cried this way or that another, more compassionate set of brothers—the ones from "My Three Sons"—wouldn't have found these same noises heart-rending.

Sometimes after Eric fell asleep, Benjamin would warily talk to me. But mostly he lapsed into deep, even breathing within moments of Eric, and in the quiet darkness I stopped crying; there was no one to hear me, even if only to make fun of me. I would watch the shadows of passing cars flit across the ceiling, barred by the slats of the vertical blind, and follow them as they fell off the edge of the ceiling and into nothingness. The thought of disappearing from my room, like the shadows, soothed me, and eventually I, too, fell asleep.

In her tiny room behind the kitchen in my parents' apartment, Lena keeps a set of scrapbooks in graduated sizes. They are stacked on a shelf under her writing table, and when I was very little, I used to confuse the scrapbooks, which had vinyl covers in a leopard print, with the tigers in *Little Black Sambo*. I believed that Lena, whom I saw as inherently violent, had shot a jungle beast expressly to provide a leopard skin for her albums. I took it for granted when I was younger that she should bother to paste snapshots of my brothers and sisters and me, positioning them carefully inside the four triangular stickers that designated each photograph's place. We look to be a happy bunch, grinning forcefully into the camera. (There is no evidence for what we feel to have been the truth.) Here I am, tanned and shiny-haired, bent over a miniature golf club, ready to tap the ball into the hole. It didn't strike me as strange back then that the same woman who spanked us too hard and too often and who, when enraged, kicked Benjamin into obedience, should also want to remember us—to commemorate insignificant outings, like a doting grandparent. It seems a puzzle to me now, though—her wish to suspend the time she spent with us—when she always seemed so eager to speed up our bedtime and get us out of the way. In one of the scrapbooks, there is a photograph of Lena in a bright red two-piece bathing suit, standing tall next to an enormous stuffed fish. Charlie is standing on the other side, smiling proudly, like a father; to his right, lined up in size order the way we used to do for fire drills in school, are my three brothers.

Not too long ago I had a conversation with Eric in which he told me that Charlie, in the years he courted Lena, made up for all the things my father didn't do.

"He took us to all those baseball games," Eric says, his eyes wide, as though he were recounting a miracle. "Dad never took us anywhere."

"But what did he *do*?" I ask.

If you talk about the past relentlessly enough, will that rectify it? Or are the grievances of childhood inconsolable?

"I never knew," Eric says, laughing. "I think he did something connected to the Mob. Delivered dispossess notices. Who cares?"

"Was he dumb? He looked dumb," I say.

"I don't know," Eric says. "I guess so. He was nice. Real nice."

We are talking in my apartment, where I have served my brother a gin and tonic on a laminated cork coaster. It looks like the sort of thing I might have won in a sweepstakes, but I actually went out and bought a set of coasters at Woolworth's when I first moved in. As it turns out, I entertain very little.

"Nice place you've got here," Eric says, sweeping his glass before him. My brother says this every time he comes to my apartment, as though he's on a perennial first date.

"Can I get you another drink?"

"Thanks," he says, "I'm fine."

We are adults now, or old enough to be adults. Eric no longer ignores me like he used to do in the room we shared, and I cry less often, hardly at all in his presence. In my head, though, I am still arguing with Eric about miniature golf scores, the way he cheats when tallying up his penalities on the scorecard. Rachel thought he cheated too, but Lena always came to his defense. (We played in the most wilting of August heats, with a great rustle of competitiveness, as though it weren't miniature golf we were playing—with its stingy bits of fake turf and over-familiar obstacles in the form of wishing wells and schoolhouses—but something exciting, for real stakes.) In my head I am still living in the past: standing on the little putting green in Playland, under a broiling sun, without breasts or pubic hair, sent off by my mother to play endless rounds with my siblings, Lena in charge.

It must be said, however, that at some point on the curve that brings us to the present, Charlie and Lena stopped seeing each other. Eric must have been about fifteen. I don't know what he did with this fact, but it is easy to read back into the event now and say that Eric sticks close to home—that he connects to the world on a narrow rather than wide scale—because Charlie stopped taking him to baseball games. Too easy, I guess. It is simpler and less speculative to note that after Charlie, Lena ceased having beaux. She continued with her scrapbooks, just as she continued with her collection of miniature perfume bottles. I asked her once, a few years ago, what kind of fish she and Charlie had posed with. She said without hesitation, knowing immediately which photo I meant, that it had been a marlin. For some reason, her instant recall of that detail made me wonder if she thought of the six of us, grown distant from her now, as her own.

Every family has an inside lining—a secret history of idiosyncracy to which only members are privy. But there are questions that, even if answerable years later, don't avail, not now and not then, barring entry to members as well.

Why, for instance, on a chilly March Sunday afternoon—I must have been nine or ten—was my father's anger flagged by the smallest of annoyances: one misplaced pencil, a classic yellow Eberhard Faber No. 2? (To be replaced in later years by a more esoteric brand, with extra-black lead.) He had just returned from the weekly Men's Club breakfast in *shul*, featuring some minor politician as guest speaker. My father went for the food, although he could have had approximately the same at home: orange juice, coffee, scrambled eggs, and Danish. But no, he must have gone for the bustling atmosphere *around* the food: the steaming pots of strong coffee served by women in frosted bouffant hairdos and full makeup—the members of the Ladies' Club, which my mother joined but did not participate in; the camaraderie of other men, affluent and jovial; the gossip that might prove lucrative.

Although he had a whole bunch of exquisitely sharpened pencils, ten or twelve lined up in a row next to a stack of memo pads on his desk, the house was turned upside down upon the discovery of this missing implement.

Why? An indiscernible loss—to us, to someone else, but not to him. What, I now wonder, precipitated such obsessive attachment to an object so wholly replaceable? Perhaps it was nothing other than that, for a moment, when my father first entered the apartment and shook the chill off his black overcoat—an English blend, soft to the touch, from Tripler's—he resented the indelibility of his choices, the circumscription of the life he had chosen and to which he was now condemned. There it was, once again: my mother, in one of her innumerable faded housecoats, helping him off with his cashmere scarf, which she had tucked inside his coat collar two hours earlier while he stood passively by like a mannequin; and all of us scattered about, out of immediate view but taking up the air—a profusion of children, indicating a certain lack of control.

And yet, it is more likely that this eruption had its roots in something deeper—some trauma in my father's own past. What scenes did *he* witness, what arbitrary tyrannies did his own father impose? Once upon a time even my father was a little boy, the apple of a rapacious parent's eye. When I think of my grandfather—Opa, as we called him—I think of an unexplored lead, a darkening of the picture. Every family has its hit man, the one who doesn't look back. By the time I knew my grandfather, he was a successful patriarch, ennobled by age; he could be found in his den of a Shabbos afternoon, surrounded by volumes of Jewish learning, his *seforim*. Damages incurred along the way had long fallen off him, like leaves off a tree, attesting to the thick bark of his endurance.

At my grandfather's unveiling, which will take place a decade or so after the missing-pencil crisis, there is a long ride to the grave site during which we children are silent, and my father speaks in short German bursts to my mother, mainly questions about the arrangements.

"Rabbi Ziegler knows to be there at ten o'clock *sharp*?"

My father's face is creased with anxiety; he holds tightly to the leather handle above and to the side of the seat, his two legs sticking out stiffy, as though they have no joints with which to bend. Rabbi Ziegler is a fixture from my childhood, although he would never recognize me out of context—away from the family gatherings at which he sees me, dressed up in patent leather pumps and stockings that sag into rings of nylon around my ankles. He is known to be a *godol*, a luminary, singled out for his grasp of the Talmud. It is important to my father that Rabbi Ziegler come on time since he is giving one of the eulogies, but he is notorious for holding up the weddings and other ceremonies at which he officiates. He is spoken of by my parents in respectful, if slightly irritated, tones but to me he appears interchangeable with the other, less august rabbis they know—a hunched, white-bearded man with glasses and a stern, triple-chinned wife.

"Don't worry, *mein Lieber*," my mother says. "Everyone was told that the service will start promptly. Beatrice is bringing Tante Erda."

"Does the driver know where he's going?"

"Yes," my mother says. "He has written instructions."

Since Willy's death a few years ago, my father has tried a variety of chauffeurs, none of whom last long, all of whom fail to transcend anonymity. The driver behind the wheel of the hired limousine scratches the sandy-colored hair on the back of his neck. He has a name, something Irish, but no one remembers what it is.

"Ask him," my father says, "why it's taking so long."

My mother leans forward. "Driver?"

"Yes, ma'am?"

He looks at her through the rearview mirror, sunglasses shielding his eyes. It is impossible to tell what he's thinking.

"Will we be there soon? My husband would like to know."

"Only twenty more minutes, sir," the driver says loudly.

"Thank you, Bill," my mother says.

"That's not his name," Benjamin mutters.

"What is it, then?"

My father looks annoyed, as though his fiefdom—my mother—has been intruded on.

"I'm not sure what it is, but I know it isn't Bill," Benjamin says.

"Try Sam," Eric says.

"Oh, yah?" my mother says. "Is it Sam?"

"This is stupid," Lily says. "He can hear, you know."

Squashed next to Arthur, I look out a gray-tinted glass window as we near the cemetery in Queens. The chauffeur glides the long car past two-family houses set back from small front yards. There is an inflatable swimming pool that takes up most of the plot of one of them, filled with water that looks turquoise. On another lawn a pair of swings and an aluminum slide glint in the sun. There are no children in sight, and I wonder if there are wondrously average children inside the houses, born to conscientious middle-class parents, purveyors of almost-luxuries. The car stops at a light, and I notice an upside-down doll carriage on the dried grass in front of a house at the end of the street. Do the parents of the little girl whose toy this must be talk of love and loss on their way to sad occasions? Surely they arrive by subway and wave handkerchiefs, blow their noses and cry, speak sepulchrally of "the deceased."

"Ich bin müde," my father says. *"Sehr müde."*

My mother pats my father's hand, then covers it with her own.

"Daddy's tired," she says to no one in particular.

I do not say, "But is he *sad*?" Both my parents share what I think of as a displaced concern with logistics in times of stress; matters of timing and scheduling take precedence over feelings. My own feelings on such occasions are limited in the extreme and it seems to me, erroneously or not, that this has something to do with the rarefied milieu into which I was born. The dark side of urbanity and wealth is the exemption it provides from the normative—those small, affecting touches middle-class life abounds in: a makeshift kiddie pool or miniplayground, a brick barbecue pit in the backyard. There is something to be said for suburban conformity, for neighbors who watch television—the light flickering through screen doors and ground-floor windows, the rhythmic eruption of canned laughter as the same situation comedy plays from house to house.

What I am mainly thinking about is the disruption in my weekend this outing has caused. I have never liked Opa, my father's father, and would prefer to be at the beach on this stifling August Sunday. I never sat on my grandfather's knee or played with his goatee.

The image is sweet and American but has nothing to do with the fierce Russian Jew who sat in an ornate chair—a throne—at the head of his dining room table, lifting his head from the soup to ask me if I knew the derivation of my Hebrew name. Nothing comes from nothing, I tell myself. But why am I not loyal to the memory, even if it isn't the right memory? The grandfather I would have wanted was one who built model ships and smoked pipes, puffing gently—another image gleaned from the children's books I read one after the other.

"Remember to stand straight," my mother whispers to my father as they get out of the car.

We are not dressed in black; although I would like to look like Anna Magnani, there is no specific call for this kind of theater in Jewish law. What is called for at Orthodox funerals and unveilings is an extension of the usual ritualization: customs within conventions within laws, reducing the grasp of mere, God-ordained individuals. Everything is unexotically on the inside—where I am lacking.

"Imagine," my mother whispers to me. "All that life, and now he's dust. It happens so quickly, as though he never existed."

The women stand a ways off as a small group of men crowd near the memorial stone. The stone rises at a slight angle, like a jaunty sail, from the plot of grass. I try to envision my grandfather's body in the plain pine box that was lowered into a fresh brown hole in the earth exactly a year ago. I picture him lying in state, dressed in one of the gray or navy blue suits he wore on Shabbos, his eyes closed, in a temporary slumber. I wonder if it is cramped inside the box, and just as I think this, I remember what my mother has said.

"How *much* dust?" I ask my mother.

Knowing her taste for the mordant detail, I expect

her to give me an exact estimate. Is the dust that was Opa scattered in the box, or is it heaped together in a neat pile, an isosceles triangle? Are there bones, too, ancient and white, anonymous bones that don't imply the kind of man my grandfather was?

My mother shakes her head and taps her finger over her lips the way she used to do when I sat next to her in the front row of *shul* and talked too much.

Someone, a black-suited rabbi, is going on about the sharpness of my grandfather's mind and his generosity to the less fortunate, his commitment to his religion.

". . . and, above all, a good Jew, a *shomer mitzvot*. As he rose in the world, he didn't, as so many other have done, abandon the faith that had sustained him: *Yiddishkeit*."

My father nods, his hands clasped across his chest.

My neck feels sweaty, and I watch as several beads of perspiration run down from under the rabbi's hat and sit, trembling, above his jaw.

"Do you ever think of him?" Lily whispers.

"No," I whisper back.

"I do," she says.

"That's nice," I say.

"Do you think Dad misses him?"

"I don't know," I say.

A small breeze stirs, like a lapping of water, and the ceremony is over. My grandfather had a strange slant to his eyes, like a Mongol conqueror's—who knew where he began? He seemed to be unencumbered by the baggage of sentiment, unfettered by ties of guilt. His brothers had been left behind in Russia, and more than one of his daughters were made to marry for his good rather than theirs. No one has mentioned anything about the edge of brutality that distinguished him from the softer sort of religious Jew, but those who suffered its consequences aren't talking.

History belongs, at last call, to the strong—those who have forgone the niceties, whose versions of life have grown the thickest skins. There are always things, even in the most conspicuously open of accounts, that must not be said.

"Margot!"

A decade or so earlier, my father steps out of his study—a room sacrosanct, preserved for him, like the chair at the head of the oval dining room table.

"Yah, Valter?"

"Has one of the children taken my pencil?"

We are always "one of the children," as though to individualize us would be to concede a respect he does not feel.

"What pencil?"

My mother rises from her chair.

"My pencil," my father repeats. "I can't find it."

"Can't you use another one? For now?"

My mother appeals to the rational mode that is supposed to be one of his distinguishing characteristics. "Your father is so lucid," she often says, when pressed by me to enumerate his good qualities. "He never lets emotions get in the way."

"No!"

"Valter, don't yell."

Even the strong can get bent out of shape when they are being formed. My father, who was supposed to have been a brilliant student, was yanked out of school at the age of sixteen to go into business. Rage has wily substitutions with which to assuage itself—a pencil instead of a father.

"Check with the children."

"Fine, I'll check with the children," my mother

says, her thin mouth tightening so that it almost disappears.

"What does it look like?" Eric adopts his official cooperative tone.

"Like any other pencil," my mother says.

"You should know," Benjamin says. "You sharpen them for him."

It is Eric's self-appointed task to keep my father's pencils in perfect pointillist condition. On Sunday mornings he gathers them up and grinds them through the round-bellied manual sharpener that stands on a shelf in the study closet, which smells of mothballs. Benjamin disapproves of this service, happily undertaken though it is.

"I don't mind," Eric says. "Besides, he doesn't know how to do it himself."

"That's the problem," Benjamin says. "He tries to get everyone to do things for him. You act like his valet."

Neither of my brothers was wrong: my father adored being waited on, and was waited on daily, at home and at the office, more than most people manage to arrange for in a lifetime. My mother set the pattern for the rest of us by enabling my father to remain helpless when it came to basic skills like boiling water or sharpening pencils, but my father had a shrewd sense of his own about who was or wasn't likely to cater to his needs in a particular instance. I think Benjamin was half jealous that he hadn't been asked to do this job and was thereby denied the opportunity to refuse.

"I think I saw it," Rachel volunteers. "In the boys' room."

"My pencil," Arthur says.

He is no more than five, and he doesn't understand what is at stake. For the past year he has been busily drawing pictures, always in pencil rather than crayon, full of round, breastlike objects and careful curlicues of hair. My mother says they remind her of Picasso.

"What color is it?" Eric says.

"My pencil," Arthur says. "I want it."

"You can keep it," Lily says. "We just want to see it."

We are standing around the upstairs hall, huddled about my mother as though an accident has happened.

"Arthur," my mother says. "Can I see your nice pencil for just a second?" She speaks in a soft wheedling voice.

Arthur trots down the hall and returns with a jagged green stub, the top half of a broken pencil.

"Nope," Eric says.

"I'm drawing France," Arthur says. "And Europe. The whole world."

"France *is* in Europe," Lily says.

"Big deal," I say.

"Well, that about wraps it up," Benjamin says. "Court's adjourned."

"Can't you talk like a normal person ever?" Eric says, flaring up suddenly. "You sound like such an idiot."

Benjamin blinks rapidly several times; his eyes behind his glasses are the color of stone.

"What a beautiful pencil," my mother is saying to Arthur. "That's the best pencil I ever saw."

Arthur smiles and waves his pencil in the air triumphantly.

"Just because you have the vocabulary of a retard," Benjamin says.

"Boys, boys," my mother says, but she makes no move to stop their fighting.

"Yeah, and if you're such a big shot, how come you

can't do anything?" Eric says. "I can beat you in basketball *and* baseball."

"Here, give me that," Benjamin says, grabbing the pencil out of Arthur's hand.

"Can't you stop?" Rachel says.

Arthur begins to cry.

"Look what you've done," Lily says.

"Bully," my mother says, darting a fierce glance at Benjamin. "I hate bullies."

Eric snickers.

"And you, too," she says.

My mother leans down and gives Arthur a kiss. There is the softest of sounds, like a puff, as she presses her lips against his cheek. When I look up, I notice that my brothers and sisters are watching, too.

TEN

“She still does it,” I say to Lily years later.

“Does what?” Lily asks drowsily, not bothering to lift her head.

We are sitting in the garden of the summer house, behind tall hedges.

“Divides and conquers. Like a warrior.”

“Who?” Lily says. “What?”

“Ma. Us.”

The house is empty except for my sister and me. We have arranged to come out here for the day, midweek. There is a slight pall in the air that afternoons in late summer often seem to have, as though the sun has lost its glow. When I first saw this house, the second one my parents bought, I remember it occurring to me that we were rich. I was ten or so at the time, and I'm sure I must have had some inkling of this fact before, if only at the peripheries of my mind. But it had never been so boldly come upon before; looking around at the expanse of garden and the generous if boxy pool built up from the ground (a regrettable detail, since my ideal pool was the sunken, kidney-shaped one I saw on television shows, or the one I saw later on in *The Graduate*—the mammoth rectangle of a pool Dustin Hoffman stood on the bottom of in full scuba regalia), I no longer sensed my family's wealth as a misty, reticent condition. What the house—loftier in intention if not in scale than our first, solid-brick house—evoked in me was exactly the sort of feeling my mother had been trying to discourage: a thrill of ownership, an awed perception of what my father's money could buy. *A house, and not even the house we lived in all the time, with a swimming pool!*

"Oh, that," Lily says. "We can't talk about that again."

In a nearby backyard someone is playing a radio station on which the DJ keeps joyously referring to "your kind of music, all the time."

"'Oh that,' she says," I say.

"Sunshine on my shoulders make me cr-ah-ha-yee," John Denver's crooning floats over the hedge.

"You don't have to react to it like a maniac."

"But I do," I say. "She's still doing it like she used to. She always talks about how important it is that we all get along, but she doesn't really want us to. God, this guy must be deaf."

I am thinking of the way my mother seemed to promote a degree of dissension between us children so that, united, we wouldn't turn on her. That would have explained the strange tentativeness of our sibling relationships, their intermittent quality. We paired off—Lily and Rachel, Eric and Arthur, Benjamin and Rachel, Lily and me, Eric and Benjamin—but we never seemed to link up in one chain, however wobbly.

We never seemed to realize that we were all caught in the same web.

"Sunshine make me haa-pee . . ."

"Such a pretty song," Lily says, as though she's eighty years old and has just tuned in.

"None of us really liked each other."

"Liked?" Lily says. "None of us is dead."

"I'm talking about the past. When we were young."

"Oh."

Lily's legs, a gleaming white, are stretched out on the lounge chair. Two of the chair's strips of webbing hang down toward the ground like limp orange ribbons. In the chair I sit on there is a corresponding hole in the fabric, and I have arranged my body carefully around it.

"Although," I add, "I don't think it's changed all that much. There's so little love lost between any of us."

"Speak for yourself," Lily says.

"I am," I say stiffly.

But I'm not. What if I think I'm speaking the dark truth for all of us, for our family as a whole, and I'm only speaking for my view of us? What happens if the people you want to save—to rescue for normalcy—don't want the scenario you're offering?

"Do you think everyone's family is nuts?" Just posing the question seems to add a melancholy purposefulness to the conversation.

"Probably," Lily says.

A sparrow hops near the side of the pool, and in the bushes behind us the cicadas hum loudly.

"These chairs," I say, "have been rotting for years. They've been here as long as we've been here."

"Ma doesn't use them enough to notice," Lily says.

"But other people do," I say. "They're used all the time."

"It doesn't bother her," my sister says, shrugging.

"Do you think it's their wings that make so much noise? They seem to get louder every summer. Did you know that cicadas die right after they reproduce?"

"Not a bad idea," Lily says. The ice cubes in her glass tinkle as she lifts it to her mouth. We could be characters in a sad, leisurely play by Chekhov, in mourning for our lives.

"And Lily," I say, although there is no one else I could possibly be talking to, "you were never a good sister."

"Not that again."

"Well, you weren't," I say, undeterred. "Not like a real oldest."

"Oldest," Lily says, mocking my emphasis. "What's an oldest? And maybe I didn't *want* to be the oldest."

"Well, you didn't act like one."

From across the street a neighbor, a bearded man I haven't said more than hello to in all the years we've been here, revs up the motor on one of his three cars. He spends hours on them, buffing their shine and tinkering with their insides in his driveway.

"I had as many problems as you did," Lily says, raising her voice. "I had the same mother, lest you've forgotten."

I pick up my sister's glass. Holding its cold plane against my cheek, I admire my legs, time-consumingly tanned to a light gold. I wonder how quickly they'll fade to their usual pallor—the same as Lily's—and why I bother with these small, unredeeming transformations. In the distance, a lawn mower drills.

"Did you say something?"

"No," Lily says.

"Uch," I say, "now I have to pull it out of you."

"I said I didn't say anything," she says. "Stop griping."

I close my eyes and briefly ponder the horrors of my personality: I am a griping mollusk, complaining as I cling. No wonder Lily doesn't demonstrate her love for me. Shall I bother to explain to her that my gripes cover my fears, that I have to be persuaded to see the world as other than lupine? And would she understand that I bare my fangs only in self-defense?

Lily is standing now, a hand shading her eyes.

"What are you looking at?"

I try to ask the question gently. My head is tilted back against the chair, and my sister comes into view only if I make an effort. She looks lonely standing in the middle of the garden with the sun going down over the hedges behind her.

"Nothing," Lily says.

"I should have moved away years ago. Instead, I'm still here, where I started."

"Maybe you couldn't," she says.

There is the shrill ring of the ice cream truck as it passes up and down the street, and I think to myself how everything seems to get more instead of less jarring as I get older, how the coming of the Good Humor man used to be announced with a decorous jingling of bells.

"You know, you don't have to come here," Lily says, turning toward me. She announces this as though she's been considering my situation and has come up with the only reasonable solution.

"But I have nowhere else to go. Not in the summer. I suppose I could sweat in the city. You have a husband, at least."

"What does that solve?"

My sister seems outraged that I think of marriage as any sort of mitigation—as clearance from the past.

"Groo-oovin' . . . on a Sunday afternoon . . . couldn't get away too soon," blares the radio. My sister and I listen in silence to the rest of the song, and when it's finished, there is an overamplified commercial for Coppertone tanning butter.

"This time of year everything seems so over," Lily says, starting up the conversation again. "It's sort of sad and sort of nice. I think I still feel that way from school, that fall means the beginning of everything, new classes, new clothes. Don't you?"

A shadow falls across my feet, and I notice that my toenails need cutting. I have read in a magazine recently that overgrown toenails are a sign of neurosis; Marilyn Monroe was supposed to have had them.

"I hate it when the summer begins," I say. "I always think, Not again. But I hate it even more when it ends."

"Don't hate so much," Lily says, simple as that.

That water in the pool glows pink and yellow. The surface closest to our end, near the large tree, is flecked with twigs and several dead bugs.

"Other people are happy," I say, sighing. "I know they are."

"They probably say the same thing about you," Lily says.

Seconds later a plane thunders by, ominously low in the sky. The angle from which I watch it pass makes it appear to be barely clearing the top of my sister's head.

"And who but our family buys a summer house on top of a major airport, just because there happens to be a *shul* nearby?" I yell over the roar of the plane. "Everyone else is in the Hamptons."

"Stop complaining!" Lily says. "Go to the Hamptons—you have friends there. They'll take you in."

"I'm not a dog," I say.

"Get up!" she says. "Do something constructive! Go for a swim!"

I sit up in the chair, which creaks beneath me.

"The water's probably very cold," I say. "Do you think I can still get a tan this time of day? Or is it too late already?" I peer anxiously into the sky.

Lily pats her legs. "I don't know why you'd want to get any darker," she says. "It makes you look hard. *I'm* going running."

The phone rings in the house. She walks quickly toward it.

"How much thinner do you want to be?" I yell after her.

The screen door slams, and when I get up, the garden is suddenly full of long shadows, displacing the last of the sun. Or maybe it just looks like this to me. Maybe someone else would notice only the way the shadows, like brushes dipped in yellow paint, are rimmed with light.

"The past is nothing," says a narrow-featured magazine editor, a character in a movie.

The movie is French, the character is not meant to be endearing—he is a thin-lipped intellectual who makes this pronouncement in the middle of a dinner celebrating the wedding of his sister—but still I feel a pang. There is some truth to it, in the abstract, but it is beside the point in the specific.

The past is everything: it is all I have that is unique to me, that keeps me separate. Next to the lineup of pencils on my father's desk, for instance, was that stack of memo pads—plain white, ranging in size from the very small to the merely small. He made what were referred to as his "notes" on them, incessant reminders to himself about everything from the trivial to the significant. These notes would be gone over later with my mother, on Sunday afternoons around three or four o'clock, the two of them sitting at the dining room table.

"Yah?" My mother looks up when I intrude soundlessly through the swinging door that connects the kitchen and dining room.

"I have to talk to you," I say.

Early on I adopted this urgent tone, like a buzzer: *I require attention*. My father never thinks I require attention; he wants it all for himself. And then there are all the other kids. How else to indicate my wish to be noticed other than by a jiggling of my mother's nerves?

"What about?"

She says it not unkindly, but there is too much to pull her away from. The papered welter of my parents' life together surrounds her: dinner invitations, funeral notices, and wedding announcements lie scattered in piles across the table.

"Not now," my father says, turning his head only slightly toward me, silently commanding me to step back. "Can't you see we're busy?"

"It's important," I say to my mother.

My father picks up a half-filled glass of tea from a small, round tray. On the tray is another glass, emptied except for a few leaves of tea on the bottom. He sips from the glass, looking at the wall across the room, away from me.

"I'll be up soon," my mother says.

The floor-length curtains hang in neat, clean folds along the windows. Behind them is a world where people do things differently, better or worse, creating what will become, in turn, entirely other sorts of pasts. The only link I will have with these people is one I or they choose to forge; either way, it will be deliberate. My mother and my father, hunched over their papers like two strategic advisers, are not of my choosing. This fact never ceases to daze me.

"I might be gone by then," I say.

My father sets his tea down and looks irritated.

"She'll be up," he says.

His voice is impatient and loud.

"I'm going," I say.

The dining room is warm, and every few seconds the radiator hisses. I want to stay with them, to find out who is marrying at the Pierre and who at the Plaza, which weddings they will both agree on the necessity for attending, which my mother would prefer to skip. My parents' acquaintances have uniformly older children, separated by enough years from me and my brothers and sisters to make them seem members of another generation. In their plans I hope to catch a peek at my future, an image for my own life, a certain level of wealth and class taken for granted along with other prerequisites: the right husband under the *chuppa* (a lawyer or businessman of solid disposition and unsurprising family); bridesmaids fittingly accoutered in gentle colors from Bendel's or Bergdorf Goodman's; mothers who wear deep beige foundations the thickness of which disguises the actual state of their skins; and fathers who show their love—or, at the least, their responsibility—by balking at no expense, not the food or the flowers or the hot intrusion of klieg lights for the movie.

But nothing is this simple, really. What happens after the wedding is over and all the guests have gone and the hotel ballroom is dark for the night and everything is empty and there you are with your new husband? I feel lonely just considering it in my mid-teens. It is this sense of loneliness I try to conceal by seeing marriage through other people's eyes—Lydia Blumfeld, for instance, who sits near my mother in *shul*, whose hair is shiny and black. She is engaged to be married; her crisp brown clothes speak of conviction. Lydia is only a couple of years older than Lily, but she seems never to have had a childhood, to have been bred instead for this role of young-woman-about-to-be-married—an almost pious identity. "Miss Demure," my sisters call her. "Did you like Miss Demure's new Golo boots?" they will ask each other at lunch after *shul*, like poor relatives or housemaids. There is one hitch: Lydia is not really pretty. Still, I would like to be her—the surety of it, the confinedness.

How everything goes back to origins! I have the distinct feeling, as I climb the stairs to my room, that mine are all wrong, my untiring efforts at normalization come to naught. When I graduated sixth grade, for instance, I went around with an autograph book as everyone else at Melamed did, although my sisters before me had not succumbed to this inane tradition. It was important to fold down the inscribed pages in the autograph book in a specific, artful fashion and not to have too many empty pages. All this I managed, but what could I do about Arthur, who wrote in large and scrambled print letters, *Six caps are blue / One of them are you,* instead of something normal like, *Remember Grant / Remember Lee / But best of all / Remember me?* Or about Sylvia's taking the opportunity of assuring me, *in my autograph book,* that yes, she did like Sharon Levi very much, and she hoped we'd be friends in the fall? Beyond the desk in my room, the sky is dark; it is almost night. Downstairs my parents, who are strange, who are not Lydia Blumfeld's parents, and who have therefore insured that I am not Lydia, continue to sift and plan: funeral notices, theater parties, small dinners at people's homes. Social life. And underneath it nothing but a cold wind, the future that falls out of my grasp even now, as I dab at a pimple on my chin in the bathroom—vehemently, as though it alone stands in my way.

ELEVEN

How we conspire against ourselves! The roads that led away from self-acceptance—my joining up with the irascible Queen, decapitating the hapless Alice in me—also led toward ceaseless glorification of anyone who was not me.

Rita Katz, in the ninth grade of Melamed just like me, couldn't be more different. She leads the Israeli-dance club, curvaceous legs flying, with a theatrical and self-observing grace. I watch her practicing the steps with the other girls in the group and feel something beyond envy at the way she bossily demonstrates a twirl, brings her thin arms together flutteringly, like a bird. She wears her long-sleeved black leotard under her skirt to class so no one can forget she is a dancer.

I am young for my grade—the youngest, except for Judith Kaplan, who shares my birthday. Judith wears her hair in a prim bun skewered with bobby pins, and her bangs stop in the middle of her forehead, like mine used to when I was three. Judith Kaplan and the penniless Ruth Samuel are unfashionable birds of a feather, flocking by some fatal serendipity to none other than me, hobbling me by association; I will never fly, bring my arms together flutteringly, like Rita Katz. When I move, I am conscious of all my limbs, my skinny and uneven legs, and wish I never had to get up and present my history project in front of the class. Why can't adolescence be passed in a chair, sitting down, with no one to look at you and see your ungainliness on display? Adolescence is cruel to girls who aren't girls like Rita Katz—nubile, coherent, and coy.

When I get up to present my history project, my feet, which are narrow and high-arched—the feet of a dancer, if only I hadn't stood in the back of the class in music school all those years, if only I didn't sweat with embarrassment whenever we performed on parents' Sunday, if only I wasn't so afraid of shining, of being called a "big shot" by Lily or Rachel—land on the floor heavily; they clunk. I am thin, but my embarrassment settles its weight on me like extra flesh, and I don't think any of the boys realize that I have a nice figure. My subject is the Salem witch trials. I have read an advanced orange paperback on the topic by a British historian with a double last name; I quote extensively from his orotund views, hoping that Jonathan Brill will admire my appreciation of the language from the back row, where he flirts with Anita Schoen.

Jonathan Brill has very light blue eyes and dusky skin. He is not a classically good student—I am not, either—but he seems to have passions of his own: antiquity and politics. Jonathan, an exception to the rule of my indifference to boys, interests me from the freshman year of high school right through the senior trip, which I don't go on and which is reported to be an orgy. Jonathan plays with Anita's large breasts practically right under my nose, but I keep believing he has only to be awakened to a more just ardor—like Blanche DuBois believed about Stanley Kowalski in *A Streetcar Named Desire*. Once, in our junior year, I walk with him in Central Park, and he kisses me gently while we are standing on a rock. Jonathan's lips are puffy and soft; his mouth reminds me of the round, O-shaped mouths that Mrs. Lederer, the music teacher, gives to the faces she draws on posters advertising chorus tryouts.

For weeks after Jonathan kisses me, I hoist my breasts forward and make what I consider to be challenging remarks in his presence. When he fails to respond, I write him a deeply aggrieved note: *And when we bump into each other, years from now, among the Sumerian vases, I hope you remember that I tried, in my way, to love you.* Jonathan had told me that the Sumerian section of the Metropolitan Museum was his favorite; he had taken me there on the same day of the kiss, and I had tried to appear consumed with interest as he explained the uses of the various shards and relics encased in glass.

I threw him the note, having first folded it carefully into eighths, in the middle of Jewish History. I hated hearing about the endless persecutions, and I found our history textbook, imported from Israel, drab beyond compare—the paper was yellowed and roughhewn, unlike our English books, and there weren't enough illustrations to occupy me when my attention strayed. How many times could I study the same tiny black and white reproductions of a long-ago *menorah* or the caves at Masada where the Maccabees were reputed to have hidden? Someone giggled when the note landed, probably Anita, but it lay on the floor a while before Jonathan picked it up. I burned inside while he read it, picturing an eruption, a scene worthy of *Romeo and Juliet*: Rabbi Scharf, droning on about the reign of some corrupt Babylonian despot as he picked at his sallow skin, would be startled out of his usual torpor. The light flashed off Jonathan's glasses as he bent down to read the note a second time, but nothing happened. He didn't even look at me when he was done. All the effect my declaration had was to make Jonathan slightly wary around me afterward, as if I had proved to be an odd, troublesome girl—someone to sidestep, like Judith or Ruth.

There are people who let go easily of what's gone before, who allow the rawness of the past to grow a skin, heal over; I know this without understanding it. As children, these people definitely do not save tissues stiff with snot or dog-eared memo pads or cracked pocket mirrors or small plastic combs with teeth missing. With what vigilance I saved all these things! Throwing nothing away starts early. The less I threw away, the more attestation I had that I existed; everything was evidence that I displaced volume somewhere, that I wasn't just an important figment in my own snarling imagination. Oh, but it is true: to everyone else, to my mother and most of all my father, I am secondary, peripheral to the vision in which they occupy center place. And what am I to my three brothers and two sisters but something even worse? What they mean to me I suppose I must mean to them: another. Another of the too many claimants, a multiple of the needs and wants they feel inside themselves.

Rita Katz has only one sister, Barbara, and a mother to whom she is everything. Rita is in the other of the two classes that comprise each grade at Melamed, so our paths converge less than they might have—at lunch and gym, in extracurricular activities that are scheduled at the same time. Once, the design of our high school lives throws us together, and I am invited to spend the night at Rita's house. Rita is what's known as a "grind"; she gets good marks in everything not necessarily because of an abundance of brains—Jonathan Brill, who fails most subjects, is clearly smarter—but because she applies herself indiscriminately. I am an erratic student, not the type to press down before tests, so I am rarely included in cramming groups. There is one subject, however, that I come in handy for. The night before the final exam in the advanced placement section of English, in our junior year, I find myself holed up in Rita's bedroom going over the plots of *Wuthering Heights* and "The Diamond as Big as the Ritz."

Rita doesn't understand character development. She tries to study English the way I study math, figuring out answers without understanding the process. I patiently explain Heathcliff's psychology—revenge being a motive that seems singularly logical to me, I make Heathcliff sound like the most amicable of creatures—while Rita takes notes in her neat handwriting, drawing diagrams replete with arrows pointing to A, B, and C. By the time she gets done mapping out the story of *Wuthering Heights*, it looks like an explanation of something combustible, a steam engine or poison gas.

"Do you think I have it down?"

Rita takes a cookie out of the Pepperidge Farm bag that lies near our feet and munches on it with her front teeth, like a rabbit.

"I think so," I say, looking into her close-set blue eyes. "Try and think of them as people you know."

Rita's eyes are carefully made up with white eyeshadow and black liner and some sparkly stuff around the outer corners. She replicates this exact plumage every day, along with light pink lipstick and a bisque-colored pancake makeup that gives her an exotic, harem-girl look. Under the makeup her skin has a sheen, and her pores are larger than mine.

"All those Catherines mix me up," she says, yawning. "I hope there aren't too many questions on them."

"Just remember what I told you," I say. "It's about passion. Remember Mr. Tepler was talking about the way in which the love the two characters feel for each other can be seen as anarchic—a danger to the society that they live in?"

"I don't think I was paying attention," Rita says. She taps a finger on one of her front teeth. "I better write that part down. What was it you said about anarchy? Hannah, you know, you're really good at this."

"I like it," I say, pulling at the strands in the deep-pile carpeting we are sitting on as though they were blades of grass.

The carpeting covers the entire apartment, like a speckled turquoise meadow. There is no separation from one room to the next; it flows through the living room and small, square dining room, on into the bedrooms and bathrooms. The carpet feels coarse when I touch it, like rope, but there is something lush about it all the same.

"These are great cookies," I say, while Rita checks her notes.

"Nassau?" she says. "They're my favorite kind. The peanut butter and chocolate are so good together."

"I don't think I've ever had them," I say, sniffing the inside of the empty bag appreciatively.

Rita lifts her head. "Really? That's amazing."

"I've got to tell my mother to buy them."

I would also like to tell my mother to throw out her rugs and bare floors and close-piled, neutral carpeting

—to replace her entire decorative scheme with Mrs. Katz's.

Rita musingly probes the skin over her right cheek with well-shaped fingernails.

"Shit, I'm getting bumpy again. I've never been in your house, have I?"

"I don't think so," I say. "But you can come."

"We should be friends," she says expansively. "I could show you how to do your eyes if you like."

"But they're not the same color as yours," I say, as if this tiny fact were the single impediment to a fast friendship.

"I'd use lilac," Rita says confidently. "Even a little green. Want some more cookies?"

"Yes," I say, "if you have them."

"My mom keeps loads," she says. "Lemon Nut Crunch for Barbara and Nassau for me."

On her way out of the room, Rita pauses in the doorway. Her hip-long, light brown hair frames her small face, and beyond her, in the carpeted bathroom, someone is taking a shower.

"Barbara," she says, grimacing. "She's always washing her hair. Always."

"I know what you mean," I say.

"Hannah," she says, "can I ask you something?"

"Sure."

What are friends for, especially brand-new ones, if not confidences?

"You've really never had these cookies before?"

Wouldn't I have remembered the compact, seashell shape of Nassau cookies—their ridged, peanut-butter-flavored outside and the thin center of bittersweet chocolate? And don't I love the way they are stacked sweetly in the bag, five to each fluted paper cup, separated by a thoughtful piece of cardboard one row from the next?

"Oh, I've had others," I say. "But not *these*. My mother doesn't buy Pepperidge Farm that much."

The things that can't be said, right from the start, even to new friends, condemning me to the spiral of my own life—the curlicues that won't fit into Rita Katz's existence: that I like these cookies specifically because I have eaten them in an apartment not my own, caught up, if only for one evening, in the routines of a different family? That I like Pepperidge Farm cookies in general because I like the television commercial for them, with the gravelly voiced old man reassuring one and all that "Pepperidge Farm remembers," allowing me to imagine my very own thick-waisted, smiling, American grandmother baking me up a batch of warm cookies at an old, potbellied stove? That I am forced to hide cookies under my bed so Eric won't wolf them down first and that someone, Benjamin or Rachel, has claimed that Pepperidge Farm cookies aren't really kosher, after I convinced my mother to order them from Lisconte's? So that although there is nothing absolutely wrong, kosherwise, about Pepperidge Farm cookies, there is nothing absolutely right about them, either, and now I have to be doubly careful?

"I thought," Rita says, "your family's supposed to be rich."

"Not really," I say.

Is there any hope that Rita would understand if I said what I'm thinking, which is this: Rich is in the eye of the beholder. And rich to me, Hannah Lehmann, is Rita Katz and an apartment in Astoria, Queens, just like this one.

"Oh, come on," Rita says. Her voice has gone hard, like a much older woman's. "Your father's a millionaire. Everyone knows that."

Does Rita's mother, who served me salty Southern-fried chicken for dinner, know it? Is she the one who really knows it?

"Maybe," I say. "My father doesn't talk much about business." And then I add with a false chuckle, "For the longest time I thought he sold chairs."

"Chairs? Is that true?"

She leans against the doorway, twining a strand of hair around her finger, checking it for split ends and then moving on to another strand. I am sitting straight-backed on Rita's bed. There is nothing funny about any of this. It is clear to me that she and I will never be friends. We might pretend a while longer, but it is not to be. I feel relieved, as if there is no longer any need to strain at similarity, as if now all I need do is identify the many points of divergence.

"That's what he told me when I asked. It was supposed to be cute. Chairs . . . Shares."

"I don't get it," Rita says.

"He works on Wall Street."

Is it cute that I believed that my father sold chairs —rickety four-legged things to sit on—well after the age that it could be considered cute not to know what your father did for a living?

"That's what I thought," she says. "And that you have a chauffeur . . . and lots of maids."

"Three," I say, leaving out Mrs. Rausch, who comes to do the sewing once every few weeks. I also leave out this piece of information: I still have very little idea, or even image, of what my father does, my curiosity permanently waylaid.

Later that same evening Rita, her sister Barbara, and I watch "Bewitched." There is a TV in the bedroom the two sisters share, and I don't bother to explain that in my house there is only one television aside from the little Sony in Lena's room, or that I rarely watch on week nights. (From Friday night to Saturday night, the whole of Shabbos, the television set in our religiously exacting house is *muksah*—forbidden to so much as touch, off-limits.) Rita sits, her legs folded under her, Indian chief fashion, with a towel wrapped around her freshly shampooed hair. Barbara, who barely speaks to either of us all evening, sets her hair while she watches the show. This she does with amazing speed and dexterity, picking a mesh roller from the pink vinyl bag in front of her and clamping a pin between her teeth, then winding the roller in her hair and securing it with the pin—all without taking her eyes off the screen. She could be a blind person setting her hair. I try to sit the way Rita does, but after a while my legs begin to hurt, and I stretch them straight out in front of me, like an old lady. During a commercial Barbara says that she likes my robe, but otherwise we seem to sit in a trance until the show returns.

I had never seen "Bewitched" before, and I immediately loved its premise. I loved the way Samantha wiggled her uptilted nose, messing things up and then putting them unflappably right again. Although her husband, Darin, frequently got upset or worried, she never did. Samantha was always resourceful, and her smooth blonde flip always stayed in place. Darin and she had a button-nosed little daughter named Tabitha (I decided on the spot that this would be what I would name my own daughter), and Darin worked in advertising, for a furrow-browed, perpetually anxious man named Larry Tate. The fact that Samantha was supposed to be a witch—hence her magic-working nose—only made the rest of the show's realism seem like a brilliantly heightened effect. The car in the driveway, the refrigerator in the kitchen—everything became riveting, no matter how normal-seeming, because it was capable of sudden transformation under Samantha's spell. Nothing was doomed to remain as it was, forever itself.

The fact I keep coming up against, so constant in its truthfulness that it feels like something inanimate, a cup or an armchair, is this: *I* am doomed to be me. The silky wisps of underwear lying in a careless heap in a corner of Rita's bedroom—bits of pink bras and lacy smidgens of blue bikinis, the most delicate underwear I have ever laid eyes on—belonged, by some bewildering category of rightness, to a different girl than me, a size three. It seems that I have not been put in this world to have such underwear; it presupposes a different set of circumstances than the ones that hedged me in, my abstemious sisters and my wayward mother, who didn't understand the purpose of frivolous detours from so basic a requirement as underwear. What I understand—now if not then—is that it is relatively useless to go against such massed pseudologic, the family mode that says *plain white cotton briefs* instead of *lacy blue bikinis*, this way and not that. Planted and watered in me early, like the hardiest and least succulent of cactus I can defy but not uproot such flourishing illogic.

What you get left with, years later, are the tics of survival. A fully matured specimen, I stand in the small dressing room of a lingerie store on upper Broadway and look at my reflection in a blue-tinted mirror with a crack in it. The chronology of my body doesn't coincide with the image inside my head, where my chest still resembles my brothers' and the crack between my legs hasn't sprouted a bush of hair. A piece of flowered fabric, hideously bright, is gathered on curtain rods across the doorway, barely separating my semi-nakedness from the bustle outside.

"Ya like it? We sell loads of that style. Can't get enough of them."

The Spanish salesgirl looks at me impassively, cracking a piece of gum, her breasts enormous. She has informed me that it is against the law to try on underpants, but that her boss—she pronounces it like two separate words, "baw-us"—doesn't care.

"I'm not sure how well they fit. Do they shrink a lot?"

I snap the hip band of the bikini underpants, a white frill with a pale blue ribbon running through it. The underpants are tagged with a photograph of the woman who created them: Olga, her name is. Can Olga make me look like Rita Katz? Can she collapse the years in between, the years in which I've continued to be me, and make me be Rita of ten years ago, long brown hair and a dancer?

"Ya should wash them by hand," the salesgirl says. Then, cocking her head to the side, she adds, "Maybe ya could take them a size bigger. Let me check."

She pulls the curtain closed after her, and I can hear her laughing with another salesgirl outside. I tug at the curtain to insure myself privacy, and then I turn to observe myself in profile. I let out my stomach, which I have been tensing in for my own pride—for the salesgirl; it sags now over the rim of the underpants. I catch myself in the mirror, in bra and tiny bikini, white, fleshy, too much of me, a would-be Rita. Oh, I am doomed. *Off with her head.*

The salesgirl extends her hand through the curtain—a small hand, multiringed, at the end of an arm covered with long black hairs—and dangles a pair from behind it, as though I were in purdah.

"Here," she says. "Size six. Pink is all I have it in."

"Thanks," I say loudly. "Just a second. Can I show them to you?"

"Shu-wah."

She speaks in a rapid-fire volley of Spanish to someone outside, and for a second I imagine myself galloping out from the dingy dressing room to stun the collected salesgirls, a spangled circus performer seated on a majestic white horse, rising out of my Olga panties.

"Okay," I say, my stomach sucked in again.

The salesgirl pulls open the curtain and says, "It fits fine. Defunutly so."

She is not even looking at me. She is tired of my attempts to involve her in my purchase, to make her into an interested party, a mother or a sister.

"I wonder if the smaller size is more the way it's supposed to fit."

This pair is as tiny as the pair I tried on earlier, but I am convinced there must be some indecipherable difference in the way it clings. What I am hoping for is a clear signal that Olga had precisely me in mind when she designed this pair of "panties." How can I buy "panties" when I am still thinking: *underpants*?

"Well, you decide," she says, shifting her weight. "I'll be outside."

"Thanks for your help," I say. "I think I'll probably take the larger size."

She departs through the curtain, like a fortuneteller, leaving a fruity whiff of perfume. I take a final look at myself in my scrap of loincloth, barefoot on a floor in a store I have never been in before and will never—now that I've revealed myself as a hopeless obsessive, a bag lady in the making—be able to return to. Oh, why can't I be Maria in *West Side Story*, lightheartedly trying on dresses, singing "I Feel Pretty"? In a corner of my brain, like an inset of someone doing sign language on one of those programs televised for the deaf, Lena speaks to me out of a box. "Floozie," she says. Exactly the sort of comment she might make if she saw me and if she knew the word.

How is it that Rita Katz has been married and divorced and remarried in the space of time in which I have stopped barely knowing her? Why has she moved ahead, forged and dropped connections, with such alacrity? She has ceased to be real, flesh and blood, like me; she has become dipped in the mortar of memory instead—a symbol. I know of her life beyond Melamed in that amorphous, grapevining way we learn about the adulthoods of people we knew in high school. Her first husband was a basketball player from Benjamin's class, a perky-featured boy with a shock of hair that kept falling into his eyes. They must have looked good together.

And it is again years later, a night right before the first snow of the winter, that I have a dream in which I explain to Rita the mistake she's been making in her eye makeup. Gently, but with the firmness of a professional, I point out that the white shade she's been using as a highlighter is too raucous. "Pale pink or yellow would be so much more flattering," I say, "right beneath your brow, on the bone."

How gratefully she listens, as though I were a famous makeup artist appearing on a talk show and she were one of the women brought up from the audience to reap the benefit of my expertise. "I should have been doing that all along," she says. "It takes me seven and a half minutes to apply my makeup."

"But it should only take five and a half," I say.

These numbers float through my dream like the

doodles in a Miró painting, cheerful punctuation marks shaping the flux of my emotions. In my dream it seems to me that Rita has admired me all along without my knowing it. But when I wake up, I feel terribly sad, as though an idea of order—of everything making sense—had been somewhere within my grasp only to be lost forever.

TWELVE

If the past really is nothing, then the present must add up to nothing as well. The cars going through Central Park at this very moment, their taillights like cigarette embers—stabs of red-orange in the dark—are really rusting pieces of machinery, abandoned to a junk heap, and the passengers within them are deluded into believing that they really exist, that they warm the seats on which they sit, traveling into more of the present-about-to-become-the-past. But is there a person alive who can seriously take in—other than as an abstraction, a theoretical construct, like the existentialism pondered by the cigarette-smoking heroes of French novels—the idea of being a drop in the universal ocean?

I, for instance, can't stand the idea that Jonathan Brill has disappeared without a trace; I hear nothing of his life other than a rumor that he has gone to study history in Germany with a non-Jewish girlfriend. This rumor rests in my head for a long time until it takes on the appearance of fact: I can see Jonathan striding purposely through the University of Heidelberg, slim-hipped, on his way to meet his non-Jewish girlfriend, Sigrid. Instead of falling asleep in class, as he used to do at Melamed, Jonathan is now a respected scholar.

So it is five or six years after I have passed him a declaration of love in Jewish history class, years later but not in a dream, that I call Jonathan's parents one night. I look up their number in the phone book and find it under ELIAS BRILL. The phone rings several times before it is picked up somewhere in Riverdale, where Jonathan used to live before he stepped out of my line of sight. I imagine the apartment while the phone rings, small but conscientiously furnished, with low-slung chairs and an artistic sculpture or two—a piece of driftwood hinting at the shape of a bird, a chunk of stone meant to suggest the Tablets of the Law. I remember that Jonathan liked his mother, and that when she came to school one day to hear him debate in a special assembly, she wore a mink hat, which she kept on with her dress. Why, then, as the phone rings, am I sure that Mr. Brill, whom Jonathan despised, will be the one to pick it up? Somewhere in a tall, modern building on Henry Hudson Parkway, in a two-bedroom unit, Jonathan's father folds the paper that he is reading in front of the TV, which is turned down to a soft murmur of voices.

"Hallo?" His accent is heavy, and he sounds more than cautious—reluctant.

"Mr. Brill?"

"Who dot iss spicking?"

"Hannah. Hannah Lehmann. Mr. Brill?"

"Hm? Who iss?"

"This is Hannah Lehmann, Mr. Brill. I'm a friend of Jonathan's. I used to be in his class."

Something seems to click in Mr. Brill's head, a faint tapping in the storehouse of his brain. He, too, in his living room in Riverdale, must have memories—a past to be nudged out of somnolence.

"Lehmann," he says. "Lehmann. Yah, you were in his class? Your father iss Lehmann from Vall Street?"

"Yes," I say. "At Melamed."

"Just a minute, pliz," Mr. Brill says and puts down the receiver with a great clanking.

He goes off—to the bathroom, I guess, or to turn off the flame under a teakettle. Does it disturb him, make him impossibly sad, to hear from someone who knew Jonathan while he was still a boy to be shaped and controlled by the fixed opinions of a father? And why do I think that something has happened to Mrs. Brill, that she has collapsed under the strain of living with Mr. Brill and is now dead or institutionalized?

I hear a door being closed in the background and then the phone being picked up; Mr. Brill breathes heavily on the other end. "Hallo, sorry for the interruption."

"That's okay," I say. "I was wondering how Jonathan is."

"My zohn," he says. "You know I have two zohns. Jonathan's brother, Richard, too."

He says this sternly, as though I have made a grave error in asking about the fate of one without the other.

"I knew that," I say, "but I didn't know Richard. Only Jonathan."

"Yah," he says, "I understand vot you say. Richard iss a lawyer." The acrid note in his voice is momentarily warmed by a sound of pride.

"That's nice," I say, hoping I sound sufficiently impressed. "What's Jonathan doing?"

Mr. Brill's voice returned abruptly to what seems to be its characteristic bitterness. "He's fine."

There is a short silence, and then I try once again, although I'm not sure anymore what I'm trying to find out all these years later. Suddenly it seems to me that it's not Jonathan's fate I'm curious about but Mr. Brill's—the secret of *his* life, what it is that he finds bearable, what it is that keeps him from opening the window and jumping onto the parkway, between the cars with their MD license plates.

"Is he studying?"

"Yah. He alvays likes to study."

"Is he here?"

"No, he's away. In Germany. He studies there. I don't know vy he likes to study there."

There is an almost audible shrug in Mr. Brill's voice. Why would a Jew, the son of a concentration camp survivor no less, want to live among non-Jews, Germans no less? And why do I taunt him with questions about this no-good, lost-to-history son when there is another son to focus on while sipping tea after dinner—a son who lives nearby and is a lawyer?

And then, out of the blue, Mr. Brill says, "I think I remember you. I remember all of Jonathan's friends."

At a loss for what to say, I say nothing.

"He come back home soon," Mr. Brill says. "I tell him you call."

"I'd appreciate that," I say. "I just wanted to see how he is."

"He come back home soon," Mr. Brill says again.

If wishes were supreme, then Jonathan would ring the bell this minute and undo his father's corset of grief, let him breathe freely again. But how rarely our wishes coincide with what actually happens, with other people's impulses. A son who chooses, mockingly, to embrace the country of his father's nightmares is no more the repository of his father's wish than the boy who sat in the back of the class in Melamed was the repository of mine.

"Well," I say, "thank you very much. I hope I didn't disturb you."

Mr. Brill coughs into the phone. "Excuse me. No, you didn't disturb me. Not at all."

"Well, thanks for being so patient."

"Patient? Vot iss patient? You are a friend of my zohn."

"Good-bye," I say.

"Are you married?" Mr. Brill asks.

"No," I say.

"Ah," he says kindly, "not yet. But soon, no? It iss good for a girl to be married. . . . Lehmann. I vill tell Jonathan."

"'Bye," I say.

"Good-bye," Mr. Brill says.

"Be well," I say, but he has hung up already.

Afterward, I sit in the chair from which I have made the phone call and don't budge. The muscles in my body, especially the ones I sit on, ache, and I know I would feel better if I got up, but I don't. My elbow rests on the table and I rest my cheek, in turn, on my hand: a thinking pose. It seems to me that I sit like this for some time, absolutely still; to someone coming in on me from behind, it might appear as if I were sleeping. I am staring at what appears to be the faintly scratched Formica surface of my desk but is actually somewhere far off. What I am staring at is nothing you can see—that amorphous triangle of inner space between my physical self, slumped in a nightgown on a chair; my thoughts; and the world outside both me and my thoughts about it. The *middle distance*, it is called, as though there were an exact location for the sense we have of the gap between ourselves and the universe.

Somewhere in the middle distance Mr. Brill tightens the belt on his robe and shuffles into the kitchen to get himself a *nosh*—a snack they call it in this country—from the cardboard box of cake in the refrigerator. He remembers Jonathan's near-perfect reading of the Torah at his bar mitzvah, the way he held on to his *tallis* with both hands, as though at the lapels of his suit, like a much older man. It had proved a better performance than his older brother's; Mr. Brill was honest enough to admit it to himself even then. And the way Jonathan's socks always fell down—black socks—even when he got older and cared about his looks. He had tried hard as a father, yelled a little more at Jonathan, true, but you couldn't account for one thing by the other. He feels a flicker of pain in his chest, but it passes. *Gas*, he thinks, *not a heart-attack. Please, God, just gas.* In the narrow kitchen, where an apple and a cluster of bananas rest on the gold and white speckled counter, he stands after he has turned the light off and twitches his shoulders, dismissing further mysteries, the whys of wherefores.

"Why, why, why," Lena says to me when I am six and want to know why the peas (Le Sueur, khaki-colored and tiny, packed in water) on my plate look like each other and the potatoes don't. Maybe they belong to the same family? "Don't ask so much, Hannah. Just eat."

Don't ask so much, and you'll do more. The heat gusts from the radiator as I sit immobile at my desk on a night in mid-December. If I concentrate very hard, I can remember when Jonathan Brill changed from one style of glasses, in tenth grade, to another, in eleventh. Sometime during the fall of that year, his small, rectangular tortoiseshell frame broke, and for a few weeks he wore the frame crisscrossed with Scotch tape to keep it together, as though it had suffered a wound that would heal with time. But someone, his mother or maybe one of the girls who used to giggle with him at the back of the class, must have nagged at him to get a new pair. In place of the old ones, he appeared one day in a pair of the then newly fashionable wire-rimmed glasses, larger and less angular. Sometime shortly after this I noticed his eyes, an acute blue with pinpoints for pupils, and the way his pants—black or navy straight-legged chinos—hung touchingly low on his slim hips.

Past, stand still and let me count you to see if you add up. If I remember Jonathan clearly enough—or simply imagine that I remember him—will that restore his presence? Or vitiate his absence? There is a corner of the earth, a sunlit clearing in a dream, where my memories are gathered. If memory could be given perimeters—a geographical location, like Minnesota or Cincinnati—this would be it. Grassy and strewn with daisies, the clearing is an image out of *Rebecca of Sunnybrook Farm* or *Anne of Green Gables*, with me in dimples and a gingham dress. Waiting to be reclaimed, orderly as a pile of memo slips on an office desk, are all the objects and people I have ever lost: my stubby fountain pen is here, and so is Willy; Sharon Levi is here, and my brown and white cashmere scarf; all the lost halves of my pairs of gloves are here, and so is Jonathan Brill.

Where do days go when they pass? Do they join other days that have passed, composing an Order of Lost Time? It is the sort of question I might have irritated Lena with as she bent over the bathtub, the sort of question that led me to collect my toenail clippings from the bathroom floor. Long before I knew the word for it, I became haunted by a sense of entropy. When were things used up beyond salvaging or repair? Nothing was disposable to my way of thinking, not even fast food or paper goods. As a child, an anal-retentive in the making, I believed everything contained a hidden treasure. Diamonds lay embedded everywhere, if I only looked hard enough—in the mud of the playground, in my glass of prune juice, in the turds that floated in the toilet bowl.

On one of those days that have passed into Lost Time, I am standing in the food concession at Wollman Skating Rink in Central Park. I keep swishing my index finger around the empty paper container that just seconds ago held my order of French fries, trying to dredge up whatever remains of salt and ketchup and French fry taste. I wobble in my skates on the rubbery floor, unable to stand around casually—as other girls my age do—on the tip of one blade, like a stork. Eric stands nearby in a gray-blue parka of velvety patchwork that my mother brought back from St. Moritz several years ago for Benjamin and that now belongs to him. Eric balances firmly on his skates; he doesn't have weak ankles as I do. My French fries have disappeared too quickly, but how can I be sure there is absolutely nothing left to entreat out of the paper container? I lick my index finger, which tastes tomato-y—essence of ketchup. My brother watches me; I must be about fourteen, and he is two years younger but he is stronger and doesn't look up to me at all.

"Why don't you throw it out?" he says.

"It's not finished," I say quickly.

"These Puerto Rican girls sure can skate. Even better than the blacks," he says. "You better stop getting into fights with them, before they really hurt you."

"I'm not coming here anymore," I say. "I'm going to Rockefeller Center from now on. It's so much prettier."

The Puerto Rican and black girls, who arrive in gangs of four or five and skate around the rink in one curving line, forcing people out of their path, scare me. I am always getting into fights with them just to prove that I don't feel outnumbered, and always end up having to be rescued by a uniformed attendant.

"But you won't know how to skate there, either," Eric says.

"None of the kids in my class go to this skating rink," I say, choosing to ignore his barb. "I don't know why Lena always drags us here."

"Ma's very democratic," Eric says. "She figures we should see the real world."

"Very democratic," I say. "It's just cheaper. Besides which, I don't like skating."

Eric is bent over one black skate, unlacing it with great concentration.

"I'm going as soon as I'm done," he says. "Are you gonna be ready or not?"

"Yes," I say, "at your command."

I wobble my way over to the large garbage bin that stands to the right of the counter where they take the food orders. I push the container through the swinging window of the disposal. It is filled almost to the top with crushed paper plates smeared with edible markings, and wilted napkins and punched-in paper cups with lipstick prints along their rims. The debris of the universe stares back at me, daring me to make sense of it, to let it go.

* * *

Eric's skating jacket wasn't the only thing that reminded me of velvet. There were foods that did, too. The first time I try herring in cream sauce, which my father loves only slightly less than he loves anything sweet, I say, "It tastes like velvet." The gray-green meat at the base of artichoke leaves also reminded me of velvet—soft but sturdy. Herring and artichokes intrigued my mind more than my palate, and for this reason I applied myself to tasting them whenever they were offered. How odd that they should taste the same as Eric's skating jacket looked.

Can it be that memories are so precious because they are so individual—no two sets exactly the same, like fingerprints? And does this mean that the better your memory, the closer to the tip of your tongue, the lonelier you'll be? No wonder Jonathan Brill's father wishes me a husband, someone with whom to share the burden of the past, to admit: *This is the way it was.* Without compliance from anyone other than ourselves, our memories are no more than arbitrary. They are possessions we rearrange endlessly on a shelf somewhere in our heads: was it a Sunday two summers ago, or would the moment fit in better a bit further forward or further back? Sometimes, like signposts from our childhood, our memories may still be there, existing in actuality. Indian Walk, the shoe-store where Lily did not get the pair of red patent-leather Shabbos shoes she coveted and where all of us got our closed-toe slippers, and Michael's, the children's haircutting salon that came to us and not we to it, stand where they did twenty years ago, Upper East Side institutions. This has, however, surprisingly little effect on the tentativeness with which I regard my memories.

And even if Mr. Brill should have his wish—every

woman assigned a man, the world paired off in couples—how can we be sure of a couple's compliance, their mutual recall? What if the couple in question gets it wrong—Maurice Chevalier and Hermione Gingold singing, "Ah yes, I remember it well" in *Gigi* (the movie I most wanted to live in), reconstructing different settings for the same climactic event, disagreeing about every detail of weather, dress, and place? What if Mrs. Brill was driven crazy by Mr. Brill's memories? My mother was there with me—she straddles my childhood like a colossus—but still she won't remember as I do, will never admit: *This is the way it was. This really happened.*

And if we are not remembered at all, is it as though we have never been? Isn't it worse than being forgotten? "Time is money," my mother says. Once you have spent your allotment of time, emptied the bank, does that mean you are worthless? It is that possibility, roaring with emptiness, that my grandmother—my mother's mother—must be afraid of when she tells me once again about her beautiful childhood home in Antwerp.

"My father was very rich, you know," she says to me, as though I were a stranger come to interview her for *The International Herald-Tribune.* "And very handsome. We lived wonderfully."

My grandmother leans heavily on my arm as we walk along a street in Jerusalem in late summer, the sun falling on the yellow stone of the houses. We are in Rechavia, the same leafy vicinity where my grandfather died reading Thomas Mann instead of a sacred text. I am a college girl from New York, come to visit my grandmother. A rebel of sorts, I am at odds with the articles of religious belief that are so important to her, but I have broken the deeper bond of filial belief not at all. I don't know what my grandmother knows and what she prefers not to. Does she know who her own daughter is, the spell she casts?

"Careful, Oma," I say, "there's a step here."

Oma, I call her, not *Grandma* or *Gran*. How American am I?

"My mother never entered the kitchen," she says, her breath coming out like a soundless whistling, "except to give the cook the menu. So different from today. Everyone knows how to cook now."

A cat slinks by us and circles a garbage pail.

"What was that?" my grandmother asks, raising her cane like a blackboard pointer.

Her eyes, an almost violet blue, are the first thing one notices in her face. She is justifiably proud of them, but they don't focus as well in the present as they do on the sights of the past.

"A cat," I say.

"Dirty creatures," she says, clicking her tongue. "We have too many of them here."

I look down at my grandmother's swollen ankles encased in stout laced shoes, and I wonder at the energy it takes to be old.

"I hate cats," I say. "They scare me. It must run in the family."

I am a modern grandchild, from the land of fast food and disposable goods. I know that you can't inherit hatreds and fears the way you can a nose or red hair, but still I wonder at the way I run from cats, stiffen at their very appearance—my mother's mild antipathy grafted onto me a thousandfold.

"You must never leave a baby alone with a cat," my grandmother says. "*My* mother told us that. The cat might get jealous and smother the baby."

As we walk slowly along the wide Jerusalem avenue

with its bank of benches, I shiver in the high heat, feeling fur on my neck. On and on it goes, the ingrained habits of seeing that are passed from one generation to the next. We are not even free to choose our own misgivings.

"The best one, not like they have today," my grandmother is saying. It is a narrative I have heard before, and I listen only halfheartedly. She is recounting the story of the secretarial school in England she was sent to ("the best one, not like they have today; you could run a company when you finished") so she could assist her father in his diamond business.

"I was never quite like other people," she says, squeezing my arm. "You're not, either, are you, my darling?"

"Oh, Oma," I say, laughing. "Probably not. I wish I were."

"Ach," she says. "Just like you always used to ask me if you were pretty when I came to stay. 'Oma, do you think I'm pretty?'" She repeats the words vehemently, as though someone has contested her: "Pretty. What does it mean? Silly girls are pretty."

We stop at an intersection, and my grandmother leans closer to me; her blue eyes, besieged by organic failure, stare murkily ahead. Small Israeli cars whiz by, the drivers mostly male and casual in rolled-up shirt sleeves, browned forearms exposed. It occurs to me that none of these people know of the house in Antwerp where my grandmother lived with her six sisters, or of the prefiguring ambitions that set her apart: the wish to be independent, her deep-seated distrust of the conventional notion of husband as founder. Did this distrust come about because she had witnessed the loss of her father's fortune, stolen by his partner from under her mother's eyes after his death? Or maybe her conviction about the importance of work, about independence, conveyed to me along with her passion for a regal level of worldly goods—shoes, *marrons glacés*, linens—had nothing to do with any clear-cut event at all but with some oblique coinciding of character and history.

The lives that haven't been written fill volumes. Who is my grandmother when she is not being my grandmother? I can't see beyond her role, her *Oma*-ness, the chest like a promontory, the many sisters who figure in her conversations—a ripe cluster of Belgian girlhood. *The Woman Within*: this is the title of a nonexistent book she could have been the subject of. The same question could be asked about my mother—who is my mother when she is not being my mother?—but I never think of her this way, as a daughter in her own right. In the sepia photograph of my mother as a newborn, as far away in time as Queen Victoria, her eyes are already the eyes she has now: pale, cool, about to enter into a German childhood, the eyes of an unbabied baby. To undo who I am, I would have to undo who my mother is and who her mother is before her. Like a Russian doll nesting ever smaller dolls inside of it, I house an infinity of selves.

A car honks, and I pull my grandmother quickly across the street.

"You must marry someone special," she says when we get to the other side. She stops to catch her breath. Inside the collar of her ecru blouse, her chest heaves, and the brisk scent of her cologne, 4711, wafts through the air. (4711—a name as mysterious in its numerology as my mother's perfume, Antilope, is mysterious in its association with the animal kingdom—is the only scent I have ever known my grandmother to wear. Why do neither of them wear perfumes that sound like perfumes? Perhaps this taste for indirection has been passed on, immutable as a dislike for cats.) "Someone who understands you," she adds.

"If he can stand me," I say. "It'll take years."

"Funny girl," she says. "I want to come to your wedding!"

"I'll speed it up just for you," I say.

"Yah," she says, linking her arm in mine as we start down the block. "Don't take too long. I waited till I was twenty-four."

"That was old then, Oma," I say reprovingly.

We pass two children sitting and solemnly licking ice cream on a bench, a boy and a girl, like the most compatible of couples.

"Here we are," my grandmother says as I push open the rusty iron gate leading to my uncle's apartment.

She is a head shorter than I, and when I kiss her soft, wrinkled cheek, the folds of her skin remind me of chamois.

Peekaboo, I see you—or don't I? Where has Jonathan Brill gone when I take my fingers away? Where is the Oma who used to be vigorously curious about the trends reported in the "Living" section of *Time* magazine, who used to savor fine things, who enjoyed the open spending of money in a way my mother never did. Lost in the mists of senility when I visit her again, three or four years later, she keeps asking me who I am and how many children I have.

"Hannah," I say, leaning across a great gap where she sits, shorter than I remember her, in the lobby of a Jerusalem hotel, her knees apart, the slack skin on her thighs peeking out from under her dress. "I'm Hannah, Oma. I'm not married. I don't have any children."

"Ach, yes," she says, shaking her head. "Of course."

Time is exact even if memory isn't; somewhere in memory, no more than seconds ago, the sun hangs again in a cloudless sky over a quiet street in Rechavia. My grandmother and I are about to enter her son's apartment, where coffee and cake await us.

I was to have been a young bride, obstacles banished, and my grandmother was to have stood there, in a dignified dress picked out for her by my mother at Bonwit's. Was to have. Should have. *Is*. In the present —the time in which we live as opposed to the time that is a grammatical construction—there is no conditional tense.

THIRTEEN

Where was my father?

My imagination, usually so busy, failed me when it came to him. I invent no one in his place, no alternate father visions, the way I do for my mother. He is too distant, or she too potent, a presence; or, more likely than either of these, he is too potent an absence. But this is something I begin to consider only years later, when I am ready to consider so predetermined a lack of choice.

It is again Friday night, but I no longer wear Lily's or Rachel's outgrown velvet jumpers. My newish breasts press against the scalloped opening of an embroidered caftan, a semi-hippie style bought in the Arab market in Jerusalem. I can no longer hear the word *bush*—Moses and the burning bush; a bird in the hand is worth two in the bush—without thinking, blushingly, of my own recently sprung undergrowth.

The world has turned scratchy with sexual possibility.

"Do you think he'll last?" my father asks.

My father, who inhabits the same apartment as I do, lives worlds away during the week. It is only on Shabbos that he surfaces, at the other end of the dining room table, to discuss what I think of as Current Events with someone male and powerful.

"For a while, Walter, like any politician," the guest, Mr. Hans, replies. "You and me—we could do better with one hand tied behind our backs."

Someone has been elected to high office somewhere, in Jerusalem or Paris or London or New York—it is all the same to me. None of this cares for my feelings, least of all my father. I look into my silver soup spoon, seeking the containable, the world inside me. I shift my spoon until my father's face is reflected in its curve, distorted but nonetheless there. After years of living with him, I am still looking for my father.

My father laughs, delighted by a skepticism that matches his own. "They say he's capable. Do you believe it?"

The heavy gold watch on Mr. Hans's wrist shines below his snowy white cuff. He nods his head, as though agreeing with himself in advance. "He knows how to get his way, there's no doubt about that. The financial disclosures alone would have ruined a weaker man. For the rest, wait and see is my opinion."

"He's tough, no doubt about it," my father says, taking a heap of rice from the bowl Louisa holds out to him. "And I think he knows how to handle the Americans."

"Not so much rice, Valter," my mother protests, ritually. "Louisa, don't let Mr. Lehmann have too much gravy."

I cross my ankles under the table, a grumpy fifteen-year-old. Does anyone realize I have *breasts*? Why does my father ignore all the circumstantial details that other men seem intrigued by—the bracelet of green, red, and blue stones that blinks, like a headlight, on the arm of Mr. Hans's wife, or the fact that I don't look exactly the same as I did only a year ago, that my body now bears visible signs of femaleness?

"The economy can't get any worse, that's for certain," Mr. Hans says. "What do you say?" He turns to Eric, who is sitting on his left, as if to solicit his opinion, and then turns back to my father.

"True," my father says. "And maybe he'll get things under control."

Lily holds out her hand in front of her like the woman in the Palmolive commercial and admires my mother's diamond ring, which she is wearing.

"It looks good on me, don't you think?"

No one listens to anyone in this family. We never have.

"It's too big," I say. "Or your fingers are too short. Or fat. Something."

The diamond, round and defined, signals blue, yellow, pink, and white in the combined glow of the candles and chandelier. Mr. Hans, who sounds to me as if he is insistently repeating himself, continues to talk to my father. My father is amorphous as the world outside my head, the world Out There.

"A good man," he says of someone Mr. Hans has proposed. "But he has no clout."

Between the two of them, they will remake the affairs of a country in which neither of them live but both have a stake in, half sentimental and half paternalistic. If I were a small foreign country, a Jewish state, would my father notice my breasts?

Mrs. Hans smiles at my mother. "Everything is so delicious," she says, although I notice she has left most of the fish salad and hasn't taken second helpings of anything.

"Don't be fooled," I want to say but don't. "My mother doesn't cook. She's not my real mother."

"Thank you," my mother says.

"What was the name of the actor who played Dobie Gillis on the 'Dobie Gillis' show?" Rachel asks.

"Maynard something," Benjamin says. "I think he killed himself."

"Really?" Rachel says. "But wasn't Maynard the name of another character on the show? Maynard G. Krebs. They always included his middle initial."

"Dwayne Hickman played Dobie Gillis," Eric says all-knowingly. "Dwayne Hickman."

"Benjamin's always making things up that he doesn't know," I say. "George Reeves is the one who killed himself."

"Everyone knows that," Benjamin says. "The guy who played Superman jumping out the window because he was afraid of heights. It's an old story, and that's not what I was talking about."

"Shut up," Eric says. "I'm trying to listen."

"Big shot," Benjamin says, snorting.

Eric flushes; "big shot" has hit the mark, reducing him to his own place on the left side of Mr. Hans, who spurns him in favor of my father.

"Pass the cookies," Lily says. "Please."

Rachel plucks a sugar cube with a pair of silver tongs from out of the bowl and puts it in her mouth, under her tongue, holding it in place until she can follow it with a bath of hot tea. I don't know where she developed this homely habit of sucking sugar while sipping tea, but whenever she does it, it is as though someone has slipped into her chair at the table. Instead of my sister—Rachel Lehmann of the glasses and brown hair—there appears in front of me the figure of an elderly Eastern European Jew. Frail and modest, he is a Jew I'm not actually acquainted with, but who is to be found in stories and novels, bent over a cup of tea at one of those large, well-lit cafeterias, Dubrow's or Famous, grasping a cube of sugar with the remnants of his teeth.

"Your children seem so marvelously close," Mrs. Hans says.

But hasn't she noticed that we are all miles apart even as we sit together at the Shabbos table? That Eric holds his tie up close and studies its pattern of polka dots as though someone has asked him for an exact count? That Arthur says nothing when he is here and that he disappeared from the table a while ago?

My mother smiles briefly—I think of it as her hostess smile—and says, "When they're not fighting."

"Well, they'll never be lonely," Mrs. Hans says. "So many! You must have had your hands full when they were little."

"You have children of your own?" my mother asks.

"Just two," Mrs. Hans says, as though she had secretly longed to produce a horde like my mother's. "A boy and a girl. My daughter's married."

"Oh, how nice," my mother says. "One of each."

"The lay of the land," my father is saying.

"Quite, quite," Mr. Hans says.

What Mr. and Mrs. Hans, securely enclosed in their guestdom, don't know is everything of importance.

What I have to go on are the words my father likes, words like *tough*, *clout*, and *order*. Just to think of the word *clout* makes me laugh; it sounds so much like what it's trying to be—a fist pounding on the table, a voice collaring, "Listen here, you." Although it is clear to me even when I am very young that my father has swallowed this word, like the whale swallowed Jonah, and that it now resides inside of him, I am not sure how *clout* works. For instance, do you need only to want it to have it?

I am twelve years old, my tanned feet poking out from a brand-new pair of Nimrod sandals—no more than a few crisscrossed straps of brown leather—and my hair swept off my face with a headband. I am in the midst of imagining that I look very Israeli, that I have grown up on a kibbutz and am not afraid of anything, when my father, fueled by some mechanism that I can't see, decides not to wait on the long, straggly checkout line in the lobby of our hotel in Jerusalem.

"Wait a minute," he says to me.

"Where are you going?"

"I'll be right back," he says, giving me his *Jerusalem Post* to hold. "Keep an eye out for your mother. She said she'll be down soon."

He strides forward, coming down hard on the outer side of his heels, his knees locking into the joints. He goes past groups of heavy-waisted women holding plastic flight bags that say TWA and EL AL and PERFECT TRAVEL, past silver-haired men in sunglasses wearing peaked sailor caps and bright, well-pressed clothes, as though the sandy, volatile Middle Eastern country they have come to see exists only as an image to be played with in their minds, a toy yacht.

"There's a line, sir. We're all waiting."

The woman who says this as my father walks by has a hairdo that looks as if it has been sprayed into immobility, and he heeds her reproach not at all. As I pretend to be caught up in the line of my Nimrod sandals, I take in the fact that my father is now signaling to someone behind the front desk and that the woman with the hairdo is agitating further.

"Arnie," she says, addressing a man wearing clothes the color of a beach ball—royal blue Bermuda shorts and a red and white checked shirt—"who does that guy think he is? There's a line here. This is a democracy!"

"Take it easy, Edith. Maybe it's an emergency."

Her husband stands several yards in front of her, and he talks to her from over his shoulder, as though it were imperative that he keep watch on the view ahead.

"This is a democracy!" the woman repeats. "We're all Americans here."

Her husband turns his head, and the two of them look back toward me. I smile at them sadly, hoping they will take me for an orphan, a young but diligent visitor, a reconnoiterer of foreign opinions—a reader of *The Jerusalem Post.*

"This is Israel," her husband says. "Wait till you get home."

I wonder what is to happen when she gets home. Is she the kind of woman who thrives on creating fusses wherever she goes, in supermarkets and movie lines? Has her husband become desperately peace-loving in the face of her willingness to take up arms? And what will she do when she discovers that my father isn't an American, after all?

"Well, I still think we should say something," she says, but she sounds pacified. "Where'd Sheila say she was going?"

"There she is now," her husband says, smiling broadly at the tall girl coming toward them. "We missed you, sweetheart."

"I just went to get a Coke. Mom, please, it's fine."

Sheila, who is very tanned and looks several years older than I do, shrugs off her mother's efforts to straighten the Peter Pan collar of her short-sleeved Villager blouse. Her mother's bangle bracelets click whenever she moves her arm, and I note enviously that Sheila is wearing a pair of elegant high-heeled sandals.

"God, their Coke is so bad! I can't wait to get home and taste real food again!"

Sheila doesn't pronounce *Coke* the way I do; she hugs the *o*, making it sound almost French: *coeuq*. Her mother seems to have completely forgotten my father's undemocratic behavior in the light of her daughter's return. She stands close to her, watching with an almost fearful affection, as though at any moment Sheila might go off again in search of another substandard refreshment.

"Daddy felt the same way about the ice cream here, didn't you, Arnie?"

"You girls," the husband says, shaking his head as though struck by his own powers of tolerance. "I can't take you anywhere."

"Don't be stupid, Daddy," Sheila says, giggling. "I *love* traveling."

I look over to the front desk, where a thickly mustached man—the same desk manager who has to be called out from some inner sanctum whenever I forget my room key—with whom my father has been in head-to-head conversation for the past ten minutes, suddenly lifts his hands, his shoulders thrust upward and elbows bent. There are dark ovals under the arms of his light blue shirt, and his gesture seems like a dramatization of defeat or frustration. But when he brings his hands back down, something has been decided, for my father pumps his hand like a victor. The deal has been decided in everyone's favor, which is conveniently his.

"Don't be stupid, Daddy, I *love* traveling." I practice saying this to myself as my father strides back toward me.

"All settled," he says.

What a wonderful purring tone it has: "Don't be stupid, Daddy. . . ." I could be a daughter in the movies or on TV—Sally Field with her smile that stretches like a rubber band, or pert-nosed Hayley Mills.

If I had said anything along these lines to my father, he wouldn't have known what to make of it, there being no precedent for this sort of exchange between us. In later years I will connect a recurring feeling of futility in myself to the recognition, while still a little girl, that my father was not seducible—that he took me in without being in any way stirred by the proposition that I existed. The fact that he was not in love with Lily or Rachel, either, should have been a source of consolation, but it wasn't.

My father is my mother's: it is that simple. What, I wonder over the years, would it be like to have a father who is in love with *me*? Once, for his birthday, I wrote a poem, which I read aloud. "My father is the midnight owl," it began and moved on from there to talk of his love of bananas and how he rummaged for them late at night.

Everyone was gathered around the dining room table at the beach house and listened with what seemed to be an air of incredulity. Or maybe I only imagined this response, out of my own unyielding embarrassment. My father sat in one of his sultanlike paisley dressing gowns, Sulka's latest whorling-patterned silk. After I finished reading the poem, he kissed my cheek, thrusting his lips out as though to stamp them upon my skin, and made some mild joke. Rachel said, "How nice, Hannah," and Eric said, "I really like it. Good stuff." So why did I end up in tears? I went upstairs and lay down on my bed, face into the pillow. I didn't know why I was crying so hard. I wanted my feelings to stay far away from me, to go bother some other girl; they had no recourse in this family. If only I could have split myself in two like Patty Duke did on her show—produce an identical cousin on whom I could fob off my worse self. . . . After a while I went back downstairs, where everyone was eating birthday cake, and no one commented on my disappearance. My mother passed me a piece of cake, vanilla with chocolate frosting, on a pink paper plate, with a spoon and napkin to match. There was nothing missing that you could see.

I imagine my father saved the piece of paper on which this poem was written, the way he saved all our stuff—diplomas (Rachel's and Benjamin's outnumbering the rest of ours), citations, birthday cards (Lily's being the most painstaking, with bits of yarn and colored chalk and verses in French), a scattering of report cards. His affection displayed itself best in this sort of chronicled remove, a passion for documentation. I bet if you looked for it today, you could find it somewhere in a box or file in his office downtown: a graying piece of blue-lined notebook paper where, in the spotty ink from a Bic pen, my squat adolescent handwriting composed a blurred image of a love poem.

But when I try and think of a clearer connection between myself and my father, then and now, I come up with the name of a TV show—one that eluded my actual viewing experience but that is known to me as a concept and as a name: "The Price Is Right." My father is always talking price; even when he is talking politics, he is talking price, value for your money. He reports on everything—all he has read, seen, and heard—with a succinct detachment, as though he were addressing a shareholders' meeting: "Seven up, three down. Trade today."

How, then, can I talk to him, ask for advice on my runny problems, problems that recognize no bottom line in their vast expenditures of feeling? When I knock on his study door seeking some of the lucidity I lack and that my mother keeps assuring me he can provide, he puts down his paper, folded into neat and very readable quadrants. Over the years I attempt these talks with my father, always at my mother's urging, about pending decisions—the decisions of a daughter. Should I go to summer camp? Should I travel to Europe on my own? And once, in my early twenties, in a never-to-be-repeated-flurry—should I marry? Invariably these talks would become monologues, my father waxing enthusiastic about the logic —or illogic—of going to summer camp, traveling to Europe, getting married. His enthusiasm is founded on facts, statistics—the making and unmaking of corporations. (About my marriage prospect he peered at me and said, "Just as long as you're not marrying him for his earning power." Buy me, sell me: it would be comic if I weren't the object.) I would sit on the very edge of the couch adjacent to his easy chair, silently nodding, crawled back under cover of mute agreement into some primordial part of myself that was beyond the call of reason. When I think back on them, it seems to me that all these occasions were fraudulent from the start, insoluble—and my father believed in solutions—because they arose from a basic and fatal incapacity on my part. Behind each and every occasion that presented itself for a decision, I felt only dread, a panic about the consequentiality, the separateness, that all decision-making implied—even tiny, girlish decisions. If only I could say to my father: "I can't move. I can never go anywhere even though I look perfectly fit because I can't leave my mother, your wife."

What I would most like to know, need to know, but don't ask is this: Am *I* value for his money? I don't think so, not at all, but can he trade me in for a more cost-efficient model? He is Pharaoh, and I am Joseph; the best I can do is to be of use, indispensable, point out that a famine is on the way and he would do well to set in supplies. My father likes people—children—who can be relied on to get things done. So it is that one winter, about the middle of January, he hits upon the perfect approximation, his form of affection.

It is the same winter I witness Beatrice screaming at the foot of the stairs and begin to have insomnia, a precursor of the pitfalls of adulthood. Come twelve, one o'clock in the morning, I can't fall asleep. Everything is keeping me awake: the library books, already overdue, I must remember to return; Lena, whom I'm afraid of; Naomi Litt, whom I want to like me but who only does so when she isn't "against" me; my mother, whom I'm afraid of; my arms, which aren't entirely smooth-skinned the way Rachel's are but are covered with a sprinkling of light brown hair, which may any day get worse and render me a full-scale freak, just like the Monkey Girl I have seen a photograph of in Benjamin's book of freaks (his favorite book after *The FBI Story*); my father, whom I'm afraid of; Lily, who is always watching me and who I wish would die instantly, clearing me from the necessity of submitting to her unfriendly, ready-to-be-jealous gaze;

the geography test that I haven't studied enough for and even if I did, it wouldn't help because I still have no idea where the different states go. (No matter how many times I study the filled-in map, all visual grasp flees my mind the minute I am confronted by the blank outline in Mrs. Gordon's class with the instructions: *Fill in the 50 states.* What am I to do with Oregon and Utah and Wyoming, reduced to one unlocatable jumble, but assign them haphazard places—tucking them in around other states whose neighbors I can't remember, Florida and Louisiana?) There is every reason in the world—in my world—to be awake at midnight, but most of all there is the dull clang of my self-dislike, striking the hour of awful truth like the most discordant of clocks: Hannah Lehmann, I am as I am, wrong. If I were right, it wouldn't be possible to feel such aversion to my own skin; I would have a mother other than mine, a mother who wouldn't say, unnaturally, "Your tears don't move me," when I cry. How can I feel right unless she is all wrong, and how can she be all wrong when I long for her, loathe and desire her, and don't think I will ever cease longing?

How did my father, having no direct link with me, decipher that now was the time to prove my case, that his youngest daughter—me, Hannah—was in some slow-dawning but nonetheless genuine fashion, imperiled? Did my mother, who was the usual conduit of news about "the children," good or bad, relay the symptoms of trouble? And whose idea was it to have my father, for a period of a few months, pay me a quarter every weekday evening to hang up his coat on one of the thick wooden hangers with the three initials—WLM—ornately engraved in the center? Whosever idea, it was an inspired one: I loved my stint as my father's personal hat-check girl, greeting him at the front door and then helping him off with his heavy, single-breasted black wool overcoat. There was also a double-breasted taupe coat of cashmere, and an English raincoat. To be paid for taking my father's coat from him as he shrugged it off and for then walking several feet to hang it up in the small downstairs closet was, most clearly, to be paid for doing nothing at all—for being me. Someone—a psychiatrist my mother consulted?—must have suggested that what I needed wasto feel singled out, special, loved. Although this undoubtedly was what Lily, Rachel, Benjamin, Eric, and Arthur needed, too, it was I who had begun to exhibit certain bothersome clues to a state of inner distress, small resistances in my natural functioning.

Interestingly enough, it wasn't Lily—whom I would have expected to complain about my special treatment—but Eric who was most resentful. "But she's not *doing* anything!" I could hear him say to my mother somewhere in the house when my father's key turned in the lock. "I could do the same thing even better!"

There wasn't much my mother could argue back under the circumstances, but once in a while I would hear her reply soothingly, "It's a girl's job," as though that had anything to do with anything.

I'm not sure why this odd ritual came to an end, but I think Eric's protests helped hasten its demise; it had been created to make me feel less overlooked, not to point up another child's similar sense of bereavement. While it lasted, though, I felt assuaged by the pretense that I worked, of an evening, at the "21" Club and that my father was a passing gentleman whose tip came about logically, as my due. Buy me, sell me—why, it made sense! The whole exchange took a matter of seconds, but it felt wonderfully clear-cut, without the web of emotion I generally spun around both my parents—

that hopelessly entangling skein of anger and need and pain.

I had heard about the "21" Club to begin with from my father. His on-the-town anecdotes were one of the things I liked about him, the snatches of songs he remembered from what I took to be his *bon vivant* days at "21," the Stork Club, and the Latin Quarter. "Sam, You Made the Pants Too Long" was his favorite tune; he would break into it when he was in an especially relaxed mood—on a Friday night without any guests—sing a raucous line or two, and then fade out. "That's all I remember," he would say, smiling broadly while looking around the table, as though he had just belted out a show-stopping number and was now expecting a storm of applause. "What can you do?" he'd say. "My memory's not so good anymore. I work too hard supporting all you kids." And then he'd try it once again, braying the music, hamming up the chorus, his voice strong but not particularly lilting. There were other songs he liked—"Get Me to the Church on Time," which he tried to do like Stanley Holloway, and "Two Ladies in the Shade of the Banana Tree," which he claimed had been made popular by a twin-sister singing team with a German-sounding name, whom none of us had ever heard of.

Once, to my amazement, as if to throw out a rope from my father's raft of memories to mine, these mythical sisters actually showed up on "The Ed Sullivan Show" while I sat watching it with Rachel and Eric. This was the only TV program we were allowed to watch regularly in those years, a fitting finish to the specialness that was Sunday. Eric loved the little talking mouse, Topo Gigio; it was what he watched the show for. Topo Gigio had only to pronounce Ed Sullivan's name, "Ed-tie, pu-leez, Ed-tie," to send Eric into howls of delight. Rachel and I watched all the acts with equal and indiscriminate passion, from jugglers to ventriloquists to torch singers like Nancy Wilson. Lily disdained the show altogether, and the only times Benjamin sat through the whole thing was when Ed Sullivan announced that one of his stable of wisecracking comedians would be on, Alan King or Rodney Dangerfield or George Carlin. That evening it was just the three of us, Rachel, Eric, and me (Arthur was too young to stay up during most of the Ed Sullivan period), when suddenly there they were: blonde and buxom and very guttural, the pair swayed their ample hips in unison as they harmonized the refrain of "Two Ladies in the Shade of the Banana Tree."

I was so excited to see them in living flesh that I went around singing their hit to myself for weeks afterward, stringing out the syllables in "ban-nah-nah tree" just as they had. I think I even convinced myself for a while that these sisters had been my father's girlfriends before he met my mother—while she had busied herself, under a different name, torturing Jewish children—part of a distant bachelor past in which he went incessantly to nightclubs, a white silk scarf dangling from under his coat collar. In actuality, although my father married late and was by far the oldest father among the fathers I knew—grandfatherly age, in fact—he was never quite the apogee of rakishness I would have liked to believe him to have been. The female whom he escorted most often to the clubs (pocketing matchbooks from each, just as he always snitched hand towels from the foreign hotels he stayed in) was undoubtedly my mother, during the two years of their on-again, off-again courtship. But the reality of who my father was—or had once been—didn't much matter at these moments when he was at his ease, taking jolly part in a culture that was recognizable to me rather than recounting with great sentiment some aspect of his youth in Germany that sounded alien and intrinsically unappealing. I came closest to loving my father when he sat in his white Shabbos shirt with one button opened at the neck, tieless, singing bits and pieces of American tunes. I could almost see him then as a harmless progenitor, safely consigned to caricature, a slightly tipsy but amiable fellow: Eliza Doolittle's father as played by Stanley Holloway in *My Fair Lady.*

What strikes me as odd in retrospect is not that there were things I liked about my father—the sandy feel of his cheeks after Shabbos, for instance, when he hadn't been able to shave for a day—but that they were highlighted so inordinately. Sitting on his lap, in my velvet jumper, I delighted in running my fingers across the grain of his grown-in bristles, his skin the texture of an emery board. When I am older and no longer invited to sit on his lap or so readily intrigued by analogous incidentals—something that looks or feels like something else, like Eric's skating jacket reminding me of artichokes—there are even fewer means of contact. Throughout the years of my adolescence, I recall my father taking note of me only when I get a haircut, as though each successive one were further demonstration of the erratic nature he suspects me of harboring—the demons of Beatrice come to haunt the next generation.

"I see you've cut your hair again," he says on a Tuesday night somewhere in my past. It is winter, the window sills are bejeweled with snow. We have bumped into each other in the kitchen: my father is scavenging for a banana and I am looking for a snack, a reprieve from my schoolwork. His tone is subtly preening, as though he prides himself on his unlikely but keen visual sense: he is a man who notices haircuts.

"Yes," I say. "Do you think it looks better than before?"

I am always trying to improve on "before"; before is never good enough. There is magic in "after," the same magic that will draw me in later years to lovers who don't like me as I am, who see in me a redoubtable object. In the land of "after," I will be unconditionally loved; I have only to find the entry to it, the inspiring aureole.

"I don't know," my father says. "I liked it longer. You look different."

"Really?" I say. "Don't you think I look better?"

My father unpeels a banana, dividing and conquering the yellow skin around the white fruit. I wonder for a moment how he would fare in a blizzard, bereft of warm clothes—I have just been lying upstairs on my bed, reading the second half of *King Lear* for an advanced English class the next day. Exposed to the elements, with Eric as his faithful Fool, would my father finally recognize he has misjudged me—his youngest daughter, pure as I am honest, his Cordelia?

"Maybe," he says, not unkindly. "Could be I'm just not used to it."

Mirror, mirror on the wall, who's the fairest of us all? It is not Lily or Rachel I'm competing with so much as myself—a reflection that will do me justice.

"See you," I say.

These discussions with my father about my appearance, minute as they are, make me feel shy—as if I had been picked out, flooded with light.

"Hair grows," he says.

"Yeah," I say, although I have just had mine cut expressly to counteract this tendency. I am holding a glass of juice and a rocky piece of streusel cake—the buttery crumbs of its topping now gone hard as pellets—to take upstairs with me.

"Your mother starves me," my father says, eyeing my cake.

"You don't look starved," I say.

He pulls his chest up with feigned dignity and says, "Appearances are deceiving."

"Poor man," I say, giggling. My father's abiding appetite is a family joke.

"Good night," he says, shaking his head and shuffling off to his study in his slippers; his feet under his Sulka pajamas are dimpled and white, the feet of a king.

The haircut my father was having difficulty adjusting to was very short, nearly androgynous. What I've looked for in hairdressers, from the age of fifteen up, has nothing to do with their skill at improving my looks. It has to do with a quality of attentiveness, an obsession with an abstract ideal of beauty—the beauty that will insure my father's undying devotion—equal to my own. The hairdressers I go to more than once are invariably fastidious and acutely homosexual. They know nothing of my quest; they know only of my hair and what they wish to do with it, a reflection of their whimsy rather than my need. I'm not even sure some of them—those with distant fathers of their own—might not have been sympathetic to my wish had I bothered to explain it. What I desired was a haircut—like the perfectly fitting glass slipper in the Cinderella story—that would transport me from my grungy state into a condition of chosenness: I am the belle of the ball, the one who wins the hand of the father-prince.

"Why don't you just take off?" Adam says. "Clear your head out for a while."

Adam's voice is tight and pitched slightly high; I imagine him in a room full of men with similar voices, chirping to one another like birds.

"Careful, love," Adam says. "Keep your chin down for me, won't you?"

"Sorry," I say, eager to render myself properly passive, a still life: *Girl Getting a Haircut.*

How many years later is it that I am still searching for the qualifying haircut, the touch-up that will make my self-portrait fetch an astronomical price? It is a late and rainy Thursday afternoon in March; I am in my early twenties. History should have deadened the impulse to transform myself, but once these things take hold, they don't let go. Outside the discreet glass doors of the salon, the cars and buses honk, roaring along Madison Avenue. Somewhere in the city my father pursues his life, sniffs at his fingernails, shakes his right ear out with his pinky as if it were hiding something, agrees to take a piece of a deal, doesn't think of me.

"Look at that kid, will you," Adam says.

"Where? I can't see."

"A beautiful kid. Angelic. He just went by. Some of the boys around here are so blond, natural blonds, they make me want to cry. In their little private-school uniforms and knee socks, those adorable little caps."

"They all look like they could be Hitler Youth to me," I say.

Adam laughs and taps my shoulder, as if to soothe a

cantankerous aunt. I wonder if my allusion is lost on him, whether he'd even care if he knew. Adam seems to judge everything exclusively in terms of aesthetics, for its eye-catching potential.

"This is going to be gorgeous," he says.

He bends closer and clicks his scissors in small, quick motions around my neck. There is loud, gasping music on the sound system and behind that another noise—the constant but muted roar of many blow dryers, going like enfeebled vacuum cleaners. A hairdresser who is a variant of Adam—who could be his cousin, with the same voice and look—cuts another customer's head, bent like a sacrificial offering, in the chair next to mine.

"Not *too* short, please," I say, suddenly anxious. "I mean, I like it short but not too short."

In truth I am quite happy to be at Adam's disposal, perfectly malleable. "I need a lover with an easy touch," moans a velvety-voiced singer on the radio, the most intimate of wishes amplified for all to hear. Adam's breath is cool on my neck, and I can feel his concentration. One day I will return home bald as an ostrich egg, confirming my father's fears that I am a casualty of heredity, sapped by indecisiveness—a stalk of grass turning in whichever direction the fashion savants, the Adams and the Yves St. Laurents, push me.

"Your hair's feeling just a lit-tle dry today," Adam says, lifting my head up with a finger under my chin to examine his handiwork. "You're using that conditioner I recommended, aren't you, darling?"

"Yes," I say. "It's great."

I have run out of the conditioner—which is concocted of costly ingredients like mink oil and essence of coconut that would seem to have no bearing on the strands of anyone's hair—but I don't dream of telling

Adam this. I want him to go on calling me "darling" forever.

"There," he says. "Fabulous. Take a look."

I am raised high in the cutting chair, dressed in the salon uniform—a neckless brown garment bearing a close resemblance to a hospital gown. There are damp swatches of hair scattered across the gown: I could be a mental patient gone berserk with a pair of scissors, looking for the heart of me.

"It's nice," I say. "Very."

When I look straight ahead into the mirrored wall, I see only myself, artfully disguised.

"The back," Adam says. "is sensational."

He passes me a small hand mirror to hold behind my neck. I tilt the mirror, catching a corner of the peach ceiling.

"I can never get the angle on these things right," I say.

Adam leans over and adjusts the mirror, then pumps on the pedal that lowers the chair. I descend slowly, gazing appreciatively at the back of my head.

"I really like that line," Adam says.

On the walls of the salon are blown-up photos of models with dazzling teeth and ingeniously tousled hair—women with names like Kelly and Dawn, who come from tiny towns in Texas and Washington, who are tall and thin, and who don't appear to be burdened by any pasts to speak of.

"Yes," I say, nodding, "it's beautiful."

The back of my haircut isn't so much beautiful as strikingly symmetrical—an undoubted enhancement to my overall appearance from a geometrical point of view.

"Work okay? You've got bags under your eyes, darling," Adam says, unpinning the towel that is wrapped bib fashion around my neck, and dusting me off.

"It's okay," I say noncommittally.

I'm not sure what it is that Adam thinks I do; I can't remember if I made up something high-powered when he first asked me months ago. I may have said I was the president of a cosmetics corporation, for all I know—something that would impress him, make him take extra care. I have a tendency to try and build myself up that way.

"Take my advice. Get away. Florida. The islands. Somewhere you can soak and do nothing. Get into yourself without any pressure. It always works for me."

Oh, to be Adam! If I got any more into myself, I'd come out the other end. Adam checks his appointment book while I stand up and gather my things; his trouser legs have razor-sharp creases, and he is wearing one of those thin Italian shirts that fit like a second skin.

"A-neee-ta!" he yells. "I need you, buttercup."

Anita is Adam's assistant, a short girl with a green streak in her hair. She hurries over, cracking her gum amiably.

"Blue Rinse is next," he says to her. "I thought she canceled on us."

This isn't the first time I have heard Adam mention his other "clients," as he calls them, but for some reason I am struck today by the disdain that edges his voice. Gone are the "darling" and "fabulouses," the solicitous advice about vacations, the finicky pride in his work. What arch nickname will I be reduced to when I am gone—Walter Lehmann's daughter, a mote in the hairdresser's contemptuous eye? The world is a treacherous place, and there is no home away from home.

"Nope," Anita says. "It wuzzn't huh. That old witch nevuh cancels."

"Shit," he says, and then he turns to me. "Sit back down for a sec, will you?"

I smile at Anita, who is dressed all in black, as I sit on the edge of the cutting chair, hoping to win her loyalty. But does she like me, neither family nor friend? Whenever she shampoos my hair, we talk about men and the programs she watches on her remote-control color TV. I really want to know what her life is like, what it feels like to be Anita, but maybe she only considers me garrulous—or, worse yet, nosy—one of Adam's "clients" to be humored.

"There," Adam says.

In the mirror he fluffs my hair around my ears, giving me wings.

FOURTEEN

As I get older, everything that ever happened—even a year or two back—seems long ago. This makes me impossibly sad, drives me to sit at coffee shop counters and to watch reruns of "Bewitched" and "Gidget" and —more for Lily's sake than for mine—"Ben Casey." (Aside from Theodore Bikel, drowsy-eyed Vince Edwards, who played Dr. Casey with a perpetual glower, was the only masculine figure I knew of who inflamed my sister's otherwise chaste romantic imagination.) It is as though I really believe I might make the time of my childhood stand still—alter the laws of nature like the prophet Joshua, who, as I learned at Melamed, had made the sun stand still over the valley—by reenacting its backdrops.

Why is it that the very people who should ache to leave their pasts behind them can't? Or is it only the deprived who suffer so acutely from nostalgia in the first place? I, for instance, who should want to leap unencumbered into a more felicitous present, hardly live in the here and now at all; I am back somewhere in time, glued to the image of my mother singing "Goodnight, Irene" as I lie in a narrow bed on a Thursday evening, Lena's day off. Could it be that the ratio of loyalty is an inverted one—the less there is to miss, the more we insist on missing it? If I had had more of my mother, less of her put-downs and more of her presence, would I remember with such fidelity the exact songs in her repertoire of international lullabies: "Irene," whose name I wanted instead of my own; "Kodderop," a bloodthirsty German ditty about an old lady who burned to death while smoking a pipe in her rocking chair; and a gentle Israeli boat song that began like the hooting of an owl—"Hoo hoohoo ha"—and made me feel homesick for a land I had not yet seen? I am sure those friends of mine born to natural mothers —mothers who clung like vines—those daughters glutted with mothering, do not remember with nearly so feverish a clarity.

Of course, the whole function of memory has often struck me as misconceived—a disservice to anyone over the age of five. It is only the very young, and then only if they're lucky, who can get away with thinking they are special—the insides of their heads as big as the globe. For isn't it only the very young (not the old, with their clutched-at narratives, the repeated tales of handsome fathers and beautiful Belgian sisters) whose memories we respect, listening intently as they breathlessly recount the plot of a fairy tale in excruciating detail? "An' then . . . an' then . . . an' then . . ."

In adults memory is nothing more than this: a shot in the dark against the deafening silence of the past—

this is what happened to me. I am twenty-six but I am really six, looking to be special.

When I was five or six, I used to think summer was another country—a difference in geography rather than climate. It was in summer that I got to see my cousins, the Schoenbaums, and it was from the bay behind their house that I thought I saw Holland. What I was looking at was only the other side of the bay, several hundred yards away, a point along the horizon, but to me it was a different world—peaceful and white, what Holland might be. At that age the Dutch girl's costume—from a trunk full of nurses' uniforms, Southern belle dresses, policeman and fireman outfits—was the one that fit me when we dressed up on Purim. Amid the welter of solemn Jewish holidays, it was only Chanukah and Purim that kept the interests of children in mind, and I liked the vision of myself as a smiling Dutch girl, dressed in wooden clogs and a pointed lace cap that curled up at the ends like the shoes of a jester.

The Schoenbaums were rather distantly related, some intricate denomination of kin such as third or fourth cousins twice removed, but for many of the summers of my childhood, they formed the image of a counterfamily: shadow-selves, who we might be if we weren't so ineffably ourselves. It was only during the summer that I got to see so much of them—could observe them for points of comparison with my own family, as I did with the Daleys—when they came out to a huge white house overlooking the bay, several long blocks from our house over on the beach side. (When we moved to the second house, the one with the swimming pool, the Schoenbaums were still only a short car ride away, but the summers I am speaking of preceded this move, when we were within walking distance.) Everyone in their family always seemed to be splashing around in some body of water or other—in the bay that fronted their house or in the ocean that was closer to ours or in the green, over-chlorinated water of the municipal swimming pool that we went to together on infrequent occasions.

I liked hanging around the Schoenbaums, but Lily and Rachel didn't, and even I never grew to feel comfortable around them as I had with the Daleys. Although the Schoenbaum children encouraged hanging around, that was all they encouraged; not one of them deigned to make you feel at home by any adaptation of manner, any gesture of inclusion. It was very much sink or swim. As a result I always felt slightly mousy around them—as if I had scuttled out from under a rock to come upon this boisterous group having a never-ending picnic in the sun.

The only member of their family who was even remotely hospitable—in the conventional way, I mean, taking note of me, recognizing that I was in fact a guest and not just an entranced spectator—was Mr. Schoenbaum. Mr. Schoenbaum was the sort of father who liked to spend Sundays horsing around with his children, honing their athletic skills. He would stand in the backyard, arms folded across his chest, and eye them proudly as they performed feats. Jimmy, the oldest, called out, "Hey, Pop! lookee here!" as he sped down the block on his prepossessing ten-speeder, hands behind his head, practically lolling. I admired Mr. Schoenbaum—he was as close to an alternate father vision as I ever got—but there was also something about him that made me uneasy. He reminded me of a circus trainer—a ringmaster—and I wondered why none of his children appeared to tire of his expectations. I guess what I was really wondering was what it would feel like to have those expectations turned on *me*. Mr. Schoenbaum had such an aggressively developed sense of play—"a wise-guy," was how my mother put it—that it seemed unlikely he would know when to stop kidding around.

Looked at from the outside, of course, the Schoenbaums and my parents had a lot in common. Mrs. Schoenbaum and my mother ordered their summer provisions from the same kosher grocery and the same bakery. We all attended the same noisy *shul* on Shabbos mornings. But where my father hated the lack of decorum in the *shul*—the way the adults in the congregation yielded to the adolescent boys, to Jimmy and his cohorts, allowing one of them to lead the congregation every other week—Mr. Schoenbaum loved it. He was a believer in chaos, in youthful energy. There were next to no rules in the Schoenbaum household, no enforced bedtimes or prohibitions about sweets, no limits on television watching. By contrast with the leadership-from-above style that governed our existence, theirs was a system with no apparent structure—a flourishing anarchy. Behind the scenes of this almost stagey freedom was Mr. Schoenbaum, a benign despot pulling the strings, but I wasn't to see this aspect of it until much later. What I saw at the time was that the very qualities that endeared Mr. Schoenbaum to his children and to most of the children he came in contact with irritated both my parents. My father avoided him as much as possible; my mother, however, maintained a tense friendship with the

Schoenbaums' mother, and there were visits between the two houses.

"None of my kids are the student type."

I overhear Mr. Schoenbaum say this to my mother on an afternoon when she is visiting along with me. They are both standing on the wide expanse of front porch that overlooks the bay, and my mother is holding her pocketbook over one arm as though she is prepared to leave at a moment's notice.

"Not like yours," he adds. "Top of the class."

Mr. Schoenbaum cannot believe he is fooling anyone—least of all my mother—with his tone of false deference: "Not like yours." For he is not admiring when he observes this; it is in the nature of a principle with him that his children are not cut out for school. Had one of his sons shown the grasp of a young Einstein, I'm sure Mr. Schoenbaum would have worked hard to engage his mind elsewhere—with something real and unhighfalutin, like baseball. What Mr. Schoenbaum means to imply is that we, the Lehmann children, are the odd ones out—deadheads, eggheads, orphans in spite of the evidence that our parents are alive, *without a father who teaches us how to swim.* (Or is it only in retrospect that I read this back into that moment, playing cat's cradle at the other end of the porch with Cecily Schoenbaum—her two straggly pigtails caught up in bows made of turquoise yarn, the same neon shade as her shorts? Wasn't this merely a dropped remark in the most casual of adult conversations, without intentions to judge my parents or to redeem me?)

"Each to his own," my mother says, shifting her weight uncomfortably, refusing to relax for even a moment.

"That's what makes horse racing," Mr. Schoenbaum says. "Your kids versus mine."

My mother, adrift in an idiom not her own (*horse racing*?), emits a small and mirthless laugh.

What I wanted, playing cat's cradle or *chamesh avanim* with Cecily—the latter game was an Israeli version of jacks, consisting of nothing more than five bronze-colored cubes the size of dice, heavy in the palm—was what I always wanted: to be redeemed, a Schoenbaum. To be a Schoenbaum meant that you weren't deterred by the paltry quality of your own hair, as Cecily wasn't. My hair was thicker and shinier, but it was mostly Lena's possession—washed and brushed and pulled tightly back by her into ponytails or headbands. Cecily, meanwhile, had a whole wardrobe of adornments with which to dote on her hair, and she washed it herself. When I disclosed the truth to her in one of our companionable moments, hadn't she said, "What a baby you are! You don't even wash your own hair!" —aghast at this evidence of my inferiority, an inferiority that, being a Schoenbaum, she had always suspected.

There are no rights in this matter of belonging: nothing in the world will make me a Schoenbaum. Just as there are no guarantees in this matter of alternate visions—everywhere there are blotches spoiling the portrait. I was always looking for perfect parent surrogates and always coming up short. Wasn't there always some catch? Years later Dr. Blue would have hands that sweated, and didn't I know, from an oft-repeated allusion of my father's, that Mr. Schoenbaum wore built-up shoes, the spring in his walk abetted by a false inch or two? What I hazily perceived, even without that condemning piece of knowledge, was that for me to have really and truly wanted to trade places with

Cecily Schoenbaum would have required either a suspension of disbelief concerning her father or a natural faith in his plausibility, the powers of his immunity.

Still, Mr. Schoenbaum must have had some glimmer of a messianic impulse, some divine intention of redressing this lack of faith when he tried one Sunday to shock me out of my cowardice in the water. I must have been eight or nine, still a tentative paddler, afraid to strike out without my float. A smattering of swimming lessons at the municipal pool had not dislodged my conviction that the only way to keep buoyant was via something—or someone—else. Who was the nice towheaded boy that my mother had hired to teach me and my siblings—in a group rather than individually, the same way we were given haircuts? ("The more the merrier" was an expression my mother not only understood but liked to use in reference to children—as though to be a child meant you were automatically consigned to life in a litter, like a puppy—whether it applied or not.) Lena's docile-making presence notwithstanding, Benjamin refused point-blank to try anything other than a dead man's float, propped from underneath by Kevin, the instructor, and Lily pretended that it felt painful when she kicked her legs without holding on to the side of the pool. Who was Kevin, after all—I mean, who was he *to me*, to any of us—that we should have turned brave and hearty under his coaxing? Possibly the only way to have changed my siblings' and my complete lack of trust in regard to the environment would have been to bring us up all over again, raise us to brandish our wills, stomp our feet, act like wild kids, the part of an approved-of troupe: a Schoenbaum.

So maybe Mr. Schoenbaum's intentions really were, as I would later try to convince myself they were, genial at bottom, and what went wrong was just that very possibility I had been afraid of all along: that he wouldn't know when to stop kidding around. Or maybe there was a spark of true malice at work, a wish to prove his bet—his method of grooming a stable of children—the winning one. But I would never know his real motives with any certainty; I knew only that the outcome was at my expense.

Somehow, in front of all his kids—including Harriet, Cecily's older sister, whom I secretly worshiped, who showed every sign of becoming a beauty, who was a real wise-ass, her father's favorite (if a man so besotted by fatherhood could be said to have a favorite)—Mr. Schoenbaum fooled me into believing that he wanted to show me a passing school of fish up close. I should have known better. He wasn't the naturalist type; his curiosity was purely familial. But there I was, obediently leaning over to where he was pointing ("Quick," he said, "before they get away; they rarely come this way"), when before I knew it he threw me into the water by my feet. I must have looked as though I were performing part of a tumbling act when I went in, head over heels—like someone who had been trained to defy gravity. But I had no acrobatic skills on land, much less in the water: I went under immediately, then flapped my arms wildly and started to scream. What flashed through my panicked brain was the punitive import of my mother's message whenever I expressed a wish to belong somewhere else, to be a Daley or a Schoenbaum: the wish was bad, and I was worse for having it. *No one will save me,* went my scrambled thoughts, *not even my parents, if they could. This is the price I pay for snuggling up to other people's families, to a father not my own.* I gulped in so much salt water that by the time Mr. Schoenbaum had his strong arms around my waist and was pulling me out, my face had turned blue.

When we got back on the dock, which was warm

beneath my soaked body and where I lay, immobile, like something caught—an ungainly fish—one of the Schoenbaum children pronounced me dead. But I wasn't; behind the burning sensation in my eyes, I could see clearly. Everyone was standing around and laughing as though I were the biggest joke. Mr. Schoenbaum came into view, his big head tilted, grinning down at me. "So you made it, kid," he said. I bit into his arm, right above his wrist. I bit him hard enough to leave a blue-brown-purple bruise, the insignia of my fury.

Families are a secret, the Schoenbaums as well as my own: behind the high walls of home, anything can go on; all screams are muffled. It is only rarely that a peephole opens—somehow or other the lock on the trunk is sprung—and we can see or listen in. At the municipal swimming pool where Keven tried in vain to convince Lily to let go of the side of the pool, on an August day when Cecily and Harriet Schoenbaum are there with my sisters and me, a mother drags a child about my age across her lap, pulls down his swimming trunks, and spanks him with her thong. *Slap! slap! slap!* goes the thong against the boy's exposed flesh. The curve of his buttocks is like Eric's, and I watch transfixed as the soft white of his flesh turns a stinging red.

The mother is sitting on a rusted iron bench against the whitewashed wall behind the lifeguard's station, the same bench you have to pass on your way in and out of the pool. The private has been made public; there are no fixed boundaries between the domains of one Lena and the other—the Lena at home, spanking Eric, and the Lena sitting innocently at the other end of the pool, a chaperone smoking a cigarette. It is as though she has become transparent: everyone can see who she really is, the lifeguard will have her arrested and handcuffed along with the other woman.

But nothing happens; there is no sounding of alarms. "I told you I'd fix your wagon," the mother says. "I told you to listen to me or else." She lets the boy up, and replaces the thong on her foot. Her toenails are painted red, the toenails of a witch. The boy is crying very hard as he pulls up his trunks, which are emblazoned with navy and white stripes.

I am standing nearby—I have turned deaf to the splashings around me, the shouts of "Watch me! *Watch* me!" as another perilous dive or intricate stroke is executed—when suddenly the boy's mother turns on me. "What are you gawking at?" she says. I blush. I can feel my face turn hot and crimson, like the boy's—like Eric's—bottom. I turn back to the other end of the pool, where Harriet Schoenbaum curls the soles of her feet over the edge of the diving board while Lily and Rachel look on. Can it be that they haven't even noticed the spanking? Inside my bathing suit I feel breathless with excitement. In the area between my stomach and the top of my thighs—the area that has no name, that is never referred to—I throb with a tension so exquisite, it feels like a pain I want to prolong forever. In the effort to make sense of what I experience, the confusion of realms—pain is pleasure, pleasure is pain—I give in to the evidence of my senses, an erotic flooding. I have no need to enter the pool, for it has entered me.

If families are a secret, I want to give mine away, to have no secrets. There is succor in exposure, although I have in fact immediate proof that after exposure everything remains as it was: the boy pulls up his bathing trunks over his blushing flesh and goes home, grows up to love—hate?—his mother. The Schoenbaum children will grow up, too—will have glided off into lives that have no points of convergence with my own. Each of them will marry young and produce abundant offspring who are, in turn, sporty and confident—tennis players and swimmers. Mr. Schoenbaum can rock on his fake heels; it is all a tribute to him, the many grandchildren who are wild with energy, to the happy lack of choice he dictated on that mild summer Sunday, the wind coming in gently off the bay: "None of my kids are students."

Since that day I have grown up as well, of course, and it was not long ago that Harriet Schoenbaum, her father's favorite, appeared in a dream of mine, hugely pregnant. We talk briefly, a nod at the past, and in one of those sympathetic consequences to be found only in the life of dreams—like Rita Katz being summoned up to have her eye makeup corrected—I realize I, too, am hugely pregnant. "When are you due?" Harriet asks. I name a date, and she says, "Really? Me, too." Harriet smiles at me—her twin—beautiful wise-ass Harriet. In a rush of joy, a blissful ripple in my unconscious, I suddenly know that my erotic impulses are no longer misbegotten, skewed toward a barren perversion of pleasure. There is no other career for me but to give birth to hundreds of athletically gifted children—to make Mr. Schoenbaum proud.

How do you ever know who you are—as distinct from who you might have been a year, ten years, another lifetime ago? My father might have been a modern Machiavelli, the shrewdness of a businessman applied to the business of state: *the end justifies the means*. My cousin Beatrice might have been anything, as my mother liked to say and always in the most pensive of tones.

I would like to have become the sort of person my father admires, the sort of person he imagines he himself might have become. (My father has a past, too. What has he done with it? Where does your past go if you agree to forget it? Does it pop up when you least expect it, a jack-in-the-box, drawing you into a maze of lapses, a hunt for lost pencils? The key to my father resides forever in the past, in the boy he was on the verge of becoming before he was yanked out of school, in his adolescent passion for hard data—the sites of battles and the names of field marshals gotten down pat, retrievable within seconds more than half a century later.)

To this day my father is not the least admiring of men like himself, who have thrived on the system of free enterprise. "It's all luck," he'll say of some magnate whose holdings dwarf his own not inconsiderable ones. "And decisiveness." (From his last remark I infer that he considers none of his children to be business material, least of all me.) I am curious about the men he knows, those businessmen who attend the Orthodox *shul* of my youth. It is in *shul* that I have my first taste of community life—the exposure of it, like living under the glare of constant sun: the unspoken rules of who sits next to whom and in what row, the acceptable color (white) and material (wool, not summer cotton) to be worn on Yom Kippur. These various fathers of various Lydia Blumfelds—by what magic do they arrange that their married sons and daughters shall inherit the right apartments and summer houses and clothes and schools, on and on, unto the tenth generation? By what cunning do they see to it that nothing gets lost in the transfer? *Why does nothing get lost in the transfer except me?* I look down the years to find myself sitting on a bench on upper Broadway, childless, cradled by shopping bags, throwing crusts to the pigeons. It is no use trying to understand my father by analogy to these men. What I understand about my father is that his instincts are different, less provincial but also less protective; they will not shelter me from harm as Mr. Schoenbaum's will shelter Harriet.

My father's admiration is reserved for politicians and journalists, those with direct access to either making or recording history. He reads three newspapers cover to cover and steadily disowns television, as though it were a gimmick whose reliability had yet to be proven. Throughout my growing up, he is given to predicting the outcome of presidential elections with incontrovertible statements. The rest of us might make guesses; he *knew.* When I was in high school, my father predicted —knew—that Hubert Humphrey would win against Richard Nixon. I remember that when Humphrey died not long afterward, I connected his death more with the fact that my father had been mistaken than with anything having to do with the politician himself—any sense of personal defeat he might have felt or illness he might have suffered from.

Over the years I have formed an impression of who my father is in his fantasy version of himself—who he might have been had his education not been aborted, had he gone on to university. In this fantasy my father is running the world; he is a clear-thinking assessor of international policy, someone asked to comment on global warfare for *The New York Times*. In a thickly accented English, he gives wry, brief opinions wherever they are solicited. If my father would watch TV, he would know that anything is possible, that he is only impersonating himself. He would know that he is the real Henry Kissinger, the contestant who looks to the right and left, pauses disingenuously, and then stands up to audience applause on "To Tell the Truth."

In the end and in the beginning, isn't it just luck of the draw? My mother says she wanted to be a doctor—a surgeon—if history hadn't stepped in her way and rendered her twice "orphaned," as she likes to describe it with her mocking sense of pathos.

"I would have made a good doctor," she always adds. "Although you can't expect to be an immigrant—twice—and have things work out."

My mother impressed upon all six of us an awed sense of her own untapped capabilities. Along with this she also conveyed a sense of our own advantaged position—extended schooling at our fingertips, no Hitler to wake us out of our dreams of self—and the extent to which we not only took it for granted but failed to live up to it in the way she would have. I never knew how completely my siblings bought the story of her lost glory, but I fully trusted my mother would have made a great doctor—standoffish but reliable, like Ben Casey. Although there was no evidence forthcoming to support her claim, this made no difference to me. She displayed remarkably little interest in, much less grasp of, the sciences or math, and none of her offspring showed much of a talent in these areas. What we did share, from Lily down through Arthur, was her marked interest in the abstract and the speculative, a quizzically detached interest in other people. All the same, I believed in her untested expertise the way I believed in each of the absolute tenets that she passed along—clarion judgments such as the one that Jews didn't make good surgeons, that "they didn't have the hands for it" (except, presumably, in her case). To this day I feel, uneasily, as though I must make up to my mother for what was rightly hers, and as a child I would bring her anything I had in the way of a triumph—a composition I was especially proud of, a friend who seemed "interesting" enough to pass her critical muster—as gifts that were her due.

Still, who's to say? There she was, stopped in her tracks, valedictorian of her Frankfurt class at age sixteen. . . . What might she have become had the war not intervened? It wasn't hard for me to believe that something large would have come of my mother if history had been kinder—something beyond her destiny as a local enchantress, a sorceress of the home.

The lives my parents, Walter and Margot Lehmann, didn't lead—it is all in the past, anyway.

("The past is nothing," says the narrow-featured magazine editor, a character in a French movie, a line that goes around and around in my head, like a dour refrain.)

But then, tell me this: If you take the past away—if you, in a bold instant, let it loose like the string on a balloon—isn't it like committing infanticide? What do you get instead? Isn't there only the gelatinous present, requiring the imprint of a personality that begins once again—the serpent biting the end of its own tail—in the past?

In the present there is a scientist who writes (in an arcane magazine I have subscribed to in a fit of loneliness, the same sort of bottom-of-the-barrel reasoning that leads me to enter sweepstakes) that there is no sound basis for believing in any genetically inherited trait other than shyness. There are many things this economical theory of personality doesn't explain. Why, for instance, whenever I find myself on a tennis court, does a feeling of futility, worse than sadness, overtake me? This feeling has nothing to do with the surroundings but with an acute sense I take from the game itself, of how dependent our lives are on someone else's foresight, or lack of it: the advantaged—years of tennis lessons, inculcated habits of discipline—separated out from the disadvantaged. Although I would like to believe that I can still be anything, I can see that certain possibilities have closed themselves off a long time ago, when other people were making decisions for me. I cannot become a champion skater—Peggy Fleming, who looked like Rachel would look if she knew how to cut figure eights or pirouette on one blade—or a ballerina if only I put my mind to it.

"Aw *right*," someone says at the far end of the tennis court, on a hot August Sunday. "Nice shot."

I am a grown-up, sitting on a stone bench under a vine-laced arch, a guest at a weekend house in Connecticut, watching two people play. Mosquitoes, thriving in the thickness of the heat, buzz in my ears, and when I stand up there will be a reddish blotch on the back of my thighs, the imprint of stone. The woman who has praised her partner's stroke is the friend of my friend Denise, my mother's idea of nonfamily taken to the limit: a friend of a friend, a stranger-and-a-half. She is a grown-up version of the Schoenbaum girls, lithe and impersonal; she is also a medical student, what none of the Schoenbaum girls were encouraged to be. She holds a siren yellow tennis ball in front of her, like the torch on the Statue of Liberty, and hits it with a combination of force and grace. The ball spins narrowly over the net, driven into place rather than simply landing. I watch her and imagine a high school coach in her background, a Vince Lombardi of a father who tirelessly drove her to lessons in a scuffed station wagon. Watching this woman, I wish for a kind of sustained interest, a parental investment, an individualized focus that did not exist; I think of the basement of the music school where I waited for Lily and Rachel, the smell of dirt that permeated it, all the skipped dance classes and abandoned piano lessons. While I waited for my sisters a pair of identical twins with long braids always ate salami sandwiches under the fond eye of their careworn mother, guardian of their hearty appetites. Without such a conscientious benefactor in my own background, I am like a sickly newborn in adult clothing, an infant who has failed to thrive.

"Yoo hoo. Wanna play?"

George, Denise's husband, shades his eyes with his hand against the sun. His calves are very muscular, and I think he tolerates me only because Denise's happiness is important to him.

"No thanks," I say. "I'm resting."

Hard to say, if someone should think to press the issue, what I'm resting from. Perhaps I have a brain tumor, undetected and unsympathized with. No wonder my thoughts are so painful, so stuck. When I die in a month or two, in the fall, they will sing of my bravery and note the unfanthomable quality of malaise that always marked my bearing: . . . *But other than that, nothing. How brave she acted! We all thought it was just the way she was. Habitually gloomy . . . If we had only known!*

"Steph? Another game? Or are you too drenched?"

Stephanie, the medical student, is a vision of coolness in her tennis outfit, white piped with navy blue—very "shick," as my mother would say. She leans over the net, her hands dangling. Oh, to be Stephanie!

"I'm zonked," she says.

"One more?"

Why is it always the obvious casualties who persist in enduring—the heat-stroke victims who keep on running the marathon? George's hair is plastered to his scalp, and his face is a mottled pink, the color of exertion.

"Sure you don't want to give it a try?" Stephanie looks over at me. She doesn't seem to like to use names much, has no urge to peg the universe to recognizable locutions.

"Not really," I said, shrugging apologetically. "Thanks."

She must think I'm a complete slug, Denise's leftover from less splendid days, crawled out from under a rock.

"Okay," she says. "*One* more. But that's all."

"Your thighs will love you," George says.

"Shmuck," Stephanie says, tossing her brown and beige hair.

I hit tennis balls with an unexpected power, but my game is a beginner's, erratic and too determined. I will play with Denise, but I don't like to play with total strangers. As I've gotten older, the world keeps getting more and more full of strangers.

I slap a mosquito against my neck and decide to go in. "See you later," I say loudly, pausing under the arch, giving them a chance to pick me out before I am recognized for who I really am. (Will the real Chris Evert please stand up?)

"Yah," George says, but Stephanie is crouched low, oblivious to everything except the ball that whizzes toward her.

On the way back to the house, I think suddenly of Willy, my father's driver—the back of his head beneath his chauffeur's cap, the half-inch or so of gray that crept out from under a wedge of sandy hair, his gloved hands on the steering wheel. It was years before I realized that Willy wore a toupee, that the bit of gray was the leading clue, and even then it was only after Eric pointed this fact out. Willy is dead now, of course, and it would probably astonish him to discover that I have never learned how to drive. Once, when I was in my late teens, eighteen or nineteen, he took me for a lesson in Central Park, where I drove the long, smooth car for a minute or two unaided, on my own. My mother was furious when I told her; she thought I might have killed somebody. Willy had offered to teach me some more, but my mother must have said something to him, and we never tried it again. At the time I remember Willy was most complimentary about my brief foray at the wheel. "Hannah," he had said, the gold fillings in his mouth outnumbering his uncapped teeth, "you'll do just fine, Hannah. Your future's in driving." I liked the way Willy always used my name, twice if he could—like lights along a dark highway, beams of familiarity.

FIFTEEN

Inside our own skins, every hurt, even the tiniest, is a direct hit, a frontal assault. To a child how much more so—Lena banged my head against the wall, and Benjamin got locked in the closet, placed there for having lied about something. This occurred frequently when he was eight or nine, and when he emerged he was always muffled, as though he had imbibed the hush of being inside a dark closet to his very soul. I remember I would walk around him carefully afterward, as though he were dangerous: a convicted felon, my older brother The Liar.

Benjamin enraged my mother because of his petty falsehoods—they were never necessary or important lies—and because he enraged my mother, he was the pawn in Lena's moods. Lena would have none of him when she was not so inclined, just as she would have none of me. When Benjamin was let out of the closet, he smiled helplessly, like an idiot, promising to tell the truth.

How it is that the misdemeanors that take place within families feel like imaginary crimes, even when they are real? Does this have something to do with the fact that in their aftermath no police sirens wail, no arrests are made? I can't remember which came first—thoughts of suicide or of killing my mother. They alternated with each other, flicking on and off like the light bulbs on a marquee. I first seriously entertained the idea of suicide when I was nine or ten. It seemed at once a way of soliciting the most drastic form of attention and a way of putting myself out of the misery that necessitated the attention—the intervention of Concerned Adults on Behalf of Mistreated Children—in the first place.

I envisioned myself jumping out the window and landing on the pavement, to be discovered by one of the doormen. If I had my choice, it would be Juan, the Brazilian. Juan was fond of me, more fond of me than of Lily or Rachel; it was only right to let him be the one to find me. (Years later, when I am in my twenties and he asks me if he can come and visit me in my own apartment, I am forced to reconsider the nature of his interest, the constant arm around my shoulder. He seems amused at the thought of my living in a small, unguarded apartment when I have the possibility of staying on as a tenant in one of the best of New York buildings.) Then, however, Juan was an all-kindly protector in my eyes, and I saw *his* eyes fill with tears. "Miss Hannah, she dead," I heard him reporting, shocked into the terse basics of language the way the boggle-eyed native would later report the fact of

Kurtz's being alive in my college copy of *Heart of Darkness*.

The fantasy continued. Shortly after my suicide would be the funeral, a restrained procession—I couldn't, even at that age, quite bring myself to imagine anyone in my family breaking out in violent fits of weeping, not even in fantasy. Surely, though, there would be some tender dabbing at the eyes, some shining reminiscences. (But *who* would put in a good word for me? Not Lily or Benjamin, I knew. And would Arthur, only six or seven, even remember me in the years to come? Would anyone feel *responsible*?)

"But they overlooked her so," someone standing in the crowd of mourners would say.

"That's because she was a middle child," Eric would answer, acting precocious, playing to the gallery. "Middle children are always overlooked."

"What a darling child that one is," someone else would murmur, "and so bright! How old is he?" (Oh! Was I to be robbed of any just compensation? Not to be granted the spotlight even at my funeral? Always to be usurped by a sibling, another child jostling my corpse?)

When it came to the moment of actual burial, of dropping me into the newly dug, child-sized grave, I saw marshes stirring in the wind and my brothers and sisters pale with guilt at the sorrow they had caused me. My mother was clenched and my father was in a business suit looking official, the way he always did. Above all there was me, calmly sitting in heaven, watching as Lena dropped a flower on my coffin.

What stopped me in the end wasn't the thought of the pain so much as the gore—*my* gore—blood and flesh and pink, mangled limbs. I kept worrying about one detail in particular: Would my head snap off from the impact and roll away, like a marble? The other thought that stopped me had an aspect of premature *realpolitik* to it, a suave grasp of the cards life had dealt me that would have given my pragmatic father cause for relief, a sense that his daughter wasn't entirely shrouded in imaginary mists. This was the knowledge—like a thorn in my side—that I was indeed one of six, not a doted-upon only child in whose wake there would be a yawning childlessness. No, the awful truth was that in my case the end didn't justify the means. The gap would be filled in quickly; I wasn't Sarah Crewe—the Little Princess, with her doting Papa—or any of those other lonely storybook children. There would be the presence of Lily, Rachel, Benjamin, Eric, and Arthur to assuage the loss of me, Hannah, but what I dreaded most was the possibility that my mother would decide, with true German efficiency—quicker than you could count *eins, zwei, drei* —to replace me with a newer and better model.

So my fantasies were kept in place—by the heartlessness of my perceptions about my relative importance to the family I was born into, if nothing else. Still, I was a decidedly unhappy ten-year-old. I was anxious about everything, hounded by guilt as though it were a live, ferretlike creature I had to appease with morsels of myself. For padding I gobbled up Ring Dings and Funny Bones, Devil Dogs and Yankee Doodles: I sought refuge in the icky sweetness of Drake's complete line of baked goods, the haven of its whipped fillings. (I was an obedient child; Drake's was kosher and Hostess wasn't. Twinkies and Snowballs, although I loved the pristine look of the latter—the white flakes of coconut on top of two orbs of white cake—were off-limits.) I should have gotten fat, but I didn't even become chubby, no matter how many packages I ate on the bus ride home from Melamed.

* * *

How do you lessen the pull of an obsession, except by replacing it with another? Without even realizing it, I began looking for a way out of the enchantment my mother had put me under—the spell that bound me, a desolate adjunct, to her side. Naomi Litt, fellow member of my fifth-grade class, became the alternate focus of my dread. She was the center of my universe, the universe in which I was No One—a misplaced person—without her permission to be Someone, her life-giving nod.

Naomi Litt had streaky light blonde hair—outstanding in that class of regular, Semitic browns and brunettes—and she was adopted. Her real parents were rumored to be non-Jewish, although it occurs to me in retrospect that this rumor was started by Naomi herself. What she had undeniably been granted by virtue of her birth, into whichever religious faith, was an atypically tiny and upturned nose (by the fifth grade I and many of the girls at Melamed had developed noses that were bumpy or long or broad-tipped—noses that flared with character, ripe for the plastic surgeon) and that moon-bright hair. "*Goyish* hair" was what Bertha, the stout head cook in the Melamed lunchroom, used to call it, giving substance to the rumor. "Hey, you with the *goyish* hair," she'd shout, even though Naomi didn't take the school lunches, "you want string beans?"

Toward the end of the week, Noami's hair had usually darkened with grease and gave off a distinct smell. I remember that I liked the smell—it seemed memorably pungent, like burnt chestnuts—and I used to lean forward to get a closer whiff when she was near me. It strikes me now that the dank perfume of Naomi's hair was an oddly sophisticated source of affection—as though I were a precocious seeker of the sensually exotic, a debauched lover, Flaubert preferring Egyptian whores with heavy bellies—but at the time anything that contrasted with my own state, positively or negatively, appealed to me. My hair never smelled of anything except a fainter or stronger aroma of Breck shampoo. I had started washing it myself only that year, and I had learned from Lena's pummeling techniques; each shampoo was more vigorous than the last, a stand against dirt, a show of force.

I felt about Naomi Litt the way I felt about my mother: I was both afraid of her and in love with her. I couldn't imagine being one without the other. She and I had a seesawing relationship, dependent for its upswings upon my total acquiescence to her wishes. In the Melamed lunchroom, at a table full of girls (the boys sat in a ghetto of their own), Naomi held court. She always brought lunch from home, in a brown paper bag neatly rolled over at the top. Although Melamed offered a hot lunch program, Naomi's lunch had obviously been planned with care by a mother who cut up vegetables and shopped for fresh fruit, whose concern for her daughter extended to the quality of food she ate when away from home. There were several years that I too brought lunch from home, consisting of sandwiches rapidly put together by Lena—slices of white bread smeared with jam or, for variation, with butter and chocolate sprinkles. Lena had next to no appetite herself, and her ideas about nutrition were even more scoffingly fundamental than my mother's. I guess she figured if you weren't starving, you were eating.

Naomi's lunches were models of wholesomeness, delicate teases to the palate: tuna fish sandwiches chunky with celery and pickles or egg salad vivid with pepper and parsley; a Baggie filled with cucumber and carrot sticks; an apple or an orange; and, to top it off, the added enticement of a Yodel or a box of animal crackers. These cookies came in a box that was in itself a treat to behold. Made of colorful cardboard that depicted assorted animals in their cages and printed with the announcement BARNUM'S ANIMALS, the box had instructions that enabled you to cut and fold it into a circus. The animal crackers inside were second in my affections only to Drake's cakes. I loved the pallid sweetness of their flavor, the different shapes you could maim just by taking a tiny bite in the right place —thereby severing the neck of a giraffe or denuding a camel of his hump. I had a deal with Naomi: in exchange for three of her animal cookies, I would tell her something noteworthy, an intriguing piece of information.

Did Naomi wish to know more about Julie Andrews? (We had both recently seen *The Sound of Music* and were in love with her.) I was already practiced in the art of influence; the made-up attributions to Eleanor Roosevelt and Christian Dior stood me in good stead. Julie Andrews, I triumphantly told Naomi as I nibbled the ear off a bear, just happened to be a relative of mine—an English cousin of my father's! Even Naomi, cool-eyed Naomi, was impressed, and I was instantly moved to invent further. Yes, I said, she had even stayed at my house for a Shabbos. At this revelation Naomi balked—part of the difficulty with my fabrications was that I could never figure out which thread would be the one to snap a listener's credulity —but I rose to the challenge. I gave her a complete account, remaining all the while cannily selective about the details: Julie Andrews had gone to *shul* with us in the morning, walking between my mother and me. Lily and Rachel had pretended not to be interested, I said, but Naomi understood that it was in the nature of older sisters to fein a lack of excitement in the presence of movie stars like Julie Andrews. When Naomi demanded to know what she had worn to *shul*, hoping to slip me up, I described a dress that sounded much like the Tyrolean costumes I had seen her wear in *The South of Music*—a dress with a dirndl skirt and an embroidered vest. Naomi nodded, recognizing the dress as the kind of outfit they would wear to *shul* in the Swiss Alps. She said she wished she had been there, and I said I would invite her the next time Julie Andrews came to stay.

I thought of Naomi as someone whose affection had to be won over and over again, like my mother's: I couldn't simply count on it. The surest way of winning it, again like my mother's, was by recourse to someone else's allure—someone impermeably worthy, other than myself. I could never be sure, however, how long any one phase of benignness would last; there was always the moment when I, Hannah Lehmann, became too evident. When Naomi Litt had enough of me, due to some small assertion of will on my part, she would signal to the others girls in the class—followers all—that they were to "get against" me. The signal—indicated by Noami's rolling her tongue inside her cheek until it bulged, then keeping it there for a minute or two while she turned to each of the girls—was one of the causes of the insomnia that began in those years; just the thought of its possible appearance the next day made me alert and wide-eyed with panic on any given night. To this day I can summon up the horror this signal induced, casting me adrift in a seemingly normal school day, throwing me out of the only society available to me. For the onset of the signal meant that I was to be ignored, frozen out as though I had been embalmed in loathesomeness. The only comparable oblivion I knew of were the times my mother refused to talk to me.

There was, in other words, a precedent for Naomi Litt's cruel caprice—a rather fatal precedent in terms of my response. My mother had whims of her own, and they were not particularly merciful. I don't think either Lily or Rachel ever tried to stand up to her by asking to be left alone, as I did. The first time I told my mother to "leave me alone," I must have been eight or nine, and she refused to talk to me—to so much as notice me—for several days afterwards.

"All right," she said, "I will." With that statement she closed the door on me, literally and metaphorically. Although she was there in the same house, there was no getting to her.

When she first devised this tactic—this ritual of ignoring—it threw me into a frenzy: I needed to ask her for bus money; I needed my mother in order to live. Maybe it wasn't all that strange for a child of that age to feel desperate; the odd part was that the frenzy never dissipated in later years. I was in high school when I made the mistake of saying "Shut up" to my mother for the first—and only—time. I had heard Rita Katz say it to her mother almost breezily, without blinking an eye, and her mother in turn seemed to think nothing of it. But my mother was not Mrs. Katz. After I told her to shut up, she didn't speak to me for ten days. *Ten.* I know because I counted them, piteously, like beads on a rosary. Instead of pleading with God when I woke up, I would wonder, *Is my mother talking to me today, or am I still cast out into darkness?*

The prolonged silence was broken only after I said I was sorry. I should have become accustomed to apologizing—that was how all my mother's silences, including the ones that began descending with lesser severity but greater frequency after I uttered the first blasphemous "Leave me alone," had been broken. From the start, however, it had made me uneasy to apologize to her, and as I grew older, it grew worse. Whenever I said I was sorry, I felt engulfed by humiliation—a feeling of abasement so acute, it bordered on the stimulating. But even after I was in college, a girl with breasts and cheekbones—three-quarters a woman—my mother's ability to write me out of existence in retaliation for something angry I said to her continued to shake me up, to fragment me into insignificance. Bits and pieces of me took the subway and walked to classes and conversed normally, but inside I was waiting for the moment when my mother would recall me to human life, the moment when I would feel whole again.

During those periods of my being ostracized by Naomi, one girl stayed friendly with me—the ever-loyal Ruth Samuel. Given that Ruth was unpopular herself, her allegiance to me made me feel more abandoned; I wasn't even sure that she had been considered important enough to be in on Naomi's plot. How long the exile went on and how effectively it was kept up are details that have blurred in my memory, but I will never forget the scene, repeated many times during that year, in which Naomi's ire would be finally assuaged. I will never forget it because, in an as yet childish form, the scene contained the kernel of the emotional style that would mark my adult life, especially when it came to romance. It was the apology to my mother raised, by some strange mathematics of anxiety, to a higher power. I would call up Naomi Litt three or four days into her latest boycott—as long as I could stand, virtual seconds before I began dissolving into nothingness, a carpet of tears—and implore her forgiveness. I can see myself sitting in a chair by the phone in the upstairs hall, my entire family within earshot, asking Naomi to absolve me from sin. "I'm sorry," I would say. "Do you forgive me?" There would be a long pause on her end. "Please," I would continue, breathless with the wish to please, to disavow my noxious self. "I'll never do it again. Forgive me."

It: there was no "it," of course. I was begging Naomi's forgiveness not for any specific offense I had committed but for the general crime she discerned in my being who I was. And if I were to say now that I cannot imagine the desperation that led me to such extremes—the lack of pride or the excess of need—that wouldn't be quite true. The truth is I *can* imagine such lack of pride. I have been capable of it since and am probably still capable of it. You can develop a taste for anything, after all; by the age of nine or ten, I had developed—or, more accurately, had been inculcated with—a taste for supplication. Didn't I bow and scrape to my mother all the time, enough to bend me permanently out of shape? When I get older, I will take to covering myself—applying a layer of gloss to the raw ooze where a sense of dignity should be—by saying that I don't understand the point of pride, its use, so to speak. It makes for an arresting line at those cocktail parties where I stand around, drinking vodkas and gins. When you are grown up, no one cares about your childhood; no one asks you to explain how you came to be.

What I mean is this: Obviously pride can prevent you from falling into the depths of humility, but what happens if what you want—who you happen to love—is on the other side of those depths, *beneath* them? If that object or person is more vital to you than being pride-smug but Naomi-less? It is a clever argument I conduct with myself, almost Jesuitical, but the truth is more slippery still. If I understood, even at a very young age, the purpose of pride, I couldn't fathom how its purpose could outdo my specific desire. Perhaps it was a disease I had caught from Beatrice—a simple but incurable deficiency of character, of that mysterious ingredient my mother called "will." Will, willpower, force of will—whatever you chose to call it, I lacked it. It's a difference I have observed between myself and other people, a difference I noticed very early on between myself and my siblings in regard to my mother. Where they had a shelf, something that resisted—an abutment of self-regard—I had only wide-open space inside of me, a pouch ready to be filled with her approval of my being.

After these scenes Naomi Litt and I made up. We went back to being friends, to seeing movies like *13 Frightened Girls* together over midwinter vacation, as if nothing had happened, as if my heart hadn't briefly been torn in two. At some point during the spring of that year, however, my mother decided to take action. I don't know if she simply tired of overhearing these hiccuping, whispered dramas, or if there was something more solicitous involved—an intuition of endangerment similar to the one that led to my father's tipping me a quarter for hanging up his coat. My mother telephoned Naomi's mother, a fat and genial woman, who had chauffeured us to Radio City Music Hall to see *13 Frightened Girls* and then taken us to lunch.

The tongue-signaling abated after that, but I wonder what Mrs. Litt made of my mother—and of me. Did she recognize her daughter's sadistic streak but laugh it off, consider it best handled by the children themselves? A mustached English teacher, Mr. Dreyfus, was also involved, and he, too, must have wondered at the unexpectedly official form an ongoing schoolgirl intrigue had taken. There are victims and victimizers in every fifth grade, and such crises hardly create a stir. What my mother was trying to do could not, in effect, be done, just as it would have been impossible for her to go to the principal of Melamed and demand that Benjamin become the most popular boy in his class. I was not to be the butt of a girlish conspiracy, even if I bore all the traces of being a natural butt.

Her intervention was limited in its success to an immediate situation, the case at hand. But there would be other situations. When I think of it now, it seems to me that my mother was trying to rescue me, albeit belatedly, from a process that had been put into motion while I was still in the cradle—a process that had begun with her: submission in the cause of redemption. I gravitated toward the tantalizingly indifferent, toward the girls and, much later, toward the men, who might or might not love me. But *if* they loved me! What a relief that provided—the suspense resolved once more in my favor! How much better than being loved by the amiable, the Ruths of the world!

Shortly after the phone call to Naomi Litt's mother, I started seeing Dr. Abeloff, a psychiatrist specializing in childhood disorders. Years later I learned that Dr. Abeloff's diagnostic tests had shown that I could go to Harvard (how were the tests to know that I couldn't leave home?) and that I was suffering from "pre-adolescent depression." It was a diagnosis almost as incisive as the one delivered to James Stewart in *Vertigo*, when he is told that he suffers from "severe melancholia and a guilt complex." Unfortunately, my psychiatrist did not wear a white coat.

Dr. Abeloff wore broadly striped suits, with a shirt and tie carefully selected to pick up on the subtlest hue of stripe. Nor did he promise, as James Stewart's doctor had, to deliver me cured in one year. Mostly he listened to me. I was undoubtedly encouraged to express my innermost feelings, to unburden myself, and I'm sure I spoke a lot about my mother and Lena, whom I hated, and Lily, who hated me, and Naomi Litt, and Eric, who beat me up, and Benjamin, whose goal in life was to prove how stupid I really was. Once, Dr. Abeloff offered me some Girl Scout cookies from the box that sat on the table near his chair. I ate a polite handful; they were salivatingly buttery, the essence of love, if love were a food. He urged me to keep on helping myself, and what I remember from that visit—one of the only sessions with Dr. Abeloff that has stuck in my mind, or in my belly—was that by the end of it, I had finished the entire box of cookies. All that was left were crumbs, and I even picked at these.

What did Dr. Abeloff make of my rampaging appetite? Did he utter something cryptic and benign, like, "We are hungry today, I see"? Or did he observe my cookie orgy quietly, note it to himself as a symptom? But if so, as a symptom of what? Of nature (my inborn voraciousness) or of nuture (the deprivation of my upbringing, its lack of vital sustenance)? Maybe he agreed with my mother, who told me even before I understood what the word meant, that I was "insatiable." If he had consulted with me, would I have been able to intervene on my own behalf, to explain that it was a relief to have a whole box of cookies thrust at me—an intoxication? That I was used to Lena's mingy dolings, two Smokey Bear cookies for each of us as a bedtime snack? And that it was an additional thrill, an incentive to run amok, to be an *only child*, not to have to share, to be the sole recipient? I might even have been Dr. Abeloff's daughter, for wasn't it paternal, undoctorlike, to be offering me an after-school snack in the first place? I was drunk on cookies, the plenitude of them, only for me: I *was* special, after all.

Dr. Abeloff died some years ago, before I could look him up and ask him these questions. My mother happened to read his obituary in *The New York Times* and reported to me that the doctor had sired three children of his own. "All psychiatrists have crazy children," she said. "I wonder how crazy his are."

But I barely remembered Dr. Abeloff by then. What had stayed with me were his Girl Scout cookies, and one other thing—a momentous revelation. I had told Dr. Abeloff, at the beginning of the fall of the second year in which I saw him, that I was worried I was a lesbian. And why, the doctor wanted to know, did I, a sixth grader, think I might be a lesbian? Well, I wasn't positive I knew what the word meant, I said, but I thought I knew. I had read the word just that summer, in a novel that had been left on someone's beach chair: "Priscilla was a lesbian, and her skin had the olive tone of someone who cried herself to sleep." I often cried at night, so I immediately identified with Priscilla on that score. But there was something else about the word *lesbian* that seemed applicable. But why?—Dr. Abeloff persisted. I hesitated; I knew being a lesbian had something to do with women loving other women. I had gone to sleep-away camp for the first time that summer, only to come home after three weeks because I couldn't breathe in my bunk bed away from my mother. Lily had tried to go to camp two years before, and the same thing had happened, and now she was smart enough to stay home in the summer, to sleep under the same roof as my mother. I also knew I didn't love my father or any of my brothers, but there was something less vague that was bothering me, something that I could pinpoint. I took the plunge. "I want to sleep with my mother," I said. Dr. Abeloff raised an eyebrow. (But did he then, or is it only the past playing tricks again, casting shadows, heightening the drama of a moment in my childhood that is gone forever, eclipsed by millions of other dramatic moments? Is there really no holding on to anything?)

"You want to sleep with your mother," Dr. Abeloff repeated after me, as if the repetition would keep him calm, remind him of who he was—a clinician, not a moralist—and prevent him from rising in his chair and stoning me.

What a case to be saddled with! As well as suffering from pre-adolescent depression, I appeared to be suffering from pre-adolescent perversion. He would never give me Girl Scout cookies again, I thought, as I looked at him from under my chin. But put this way, my words coming out of his mouth—"You want to sleep with your mother"—the declaration sounded not wrong, but off somehow. The truth wasn't nearly so bald.

"Well, not *with* her," I amended. "I want to sleep *next* to her, in the same bed."

"Ah, I see," Dr. Abeloff said, nodding. (Was he relieved to be spared the obligation to delve into the roiling waters of my twisted psyche, happy to have stumbled upon the most ordinary of Oedipal fixations instead?) "You want," he continued, "to sleep between your mother and your father, one on either side of you. Is that it?"

"My father," I said, "isn't there. He isn't part of us."

"But where is he? Doesn't your father usually sleep next to your mother?"

"Yes," I said. I was the one being patient now; Dr. Abeloff didn't understand anything. "But they don't sleep in the same bed."

My parents, as was required of Orthodox Jews who happened to be married to each other, slept in two twin beds pushed together. Dr. Abeloff seemed not to know the simplest facts.

"Oh, you mean they have separate bedrooms?" Dr. Abeloff, sitting across from me, puffed affably on his pipe.

"No," I said, sighing at the intricacy of it all. "They sleep in two separate beds that are next to each other."

"Right," he said, "in keeping with the laws. I'm sorry. I forgot."

"I don't think you pay attention to me," I said.

Dr. Abeloff chose not to reply, his pipe crammed into one corner of his mouth like a crowbar. "I still," he persisted, "don't understand where your father is when you're sleeping next to your mother, as you described."

Outside his office, down the hall that led from the waiting room to two other doctors' offices, came the unmistakable whooshing sound of a toilet being flushed. "He's gone," I said.

"Gone?" Dr. Abeloff screwed up his brow like Ben Casey. "Oh. You mean *dead*?"

"No," I said. "Just gone."

What I meant by this was that my father had faded from the air—disappeared in a *whoosh*.

"Ah, I see," he said.

But did he? I wondered if Dr. Abeloff had ever read the *Harold and the Purple Crayon* series when he was a child, if he knew that you could bring houses and airplanes into being just by drawing them. The trouble was, I couldn't imagine him as little boy; whenever I tried to, all I came up was a smaller version of the man sitting cross from me—a miniature Dr. Abeloff in gray Eton shorts like the ones my brothers used to wear, his eyebrows like unclipped hedges, sucking a pipe.

"You must be thinking about something important," Dr. Abeloff said, promptingly.

I was thinking about Louisa who worked wonders with the letters of the alphabet, like Harold: "Em, ah, crooked letter, crooked letter..." What a funny way to spell *Mississippi*.

"Hm?" Dr. Abeloff said. "Can't you tell me?"

"I wasn't thinking about anything," I said.

"I see," the doctor said.

"I see," said the blind man. That was Louisa's favorite expression, as much a part of her as Ida's chewing gum and Bible were a part of her. She liked to say it to herself while she patted meatballs into shape. The thought of it made me giggle. What Dr. Abeloff did not know, like the guests at the Friday night dinner table, was everything of importance.

SIXTEEN

"Family is all there is," says a fat woman to the woman sitting next to her. I sit across from the two of them on a bus going up Central Park West, on my way to a therapy session. Since I've stopped seeing Dr. Abeloff, a decade and a half ago, everyone has started seeing a psychiatrist. I no longer have to hide it, the way I felt I had to during those years when I was in and out of psychiatrists' offices while everyone else I knew was growing up normally, taking skating lessons and falling in love with the boy who sat across from them. Perhaps if I had gone to the sort of liberal private school —Dalton or Ethical Culture—where every other child has a weekly appointment to untangle the repercussions of his parents' divorce, I wouldn't have felt so strange. But at Melamed in those years, divorces were the exception, and visits to a psychiatrist were rarer still. I kept my after-school visits to myself, in a rare display of discretion.

"It's all you've got," the fat woman goes on companionably to her neighbor, who purses her lips and nods, wary of the intrusion. "There's nothing like family. Especially when the chips are down. My son looks after me now. I've got trouble with my health, you see."

"Nothing too serious, I hope," the other woman says. She is thinner and elegantly groomed; she barely moves her lips, determined to be civil without being encouraging.

"They had me in the hospital," the fat woman says, pulling the worn leather handbag in her lap closer toward her. Her chin nestles inside several other chins, one of which sprouts a large mole.

The other woman moves imperceptibly away in her seat and says, "I'm sorry to hear that."

The fat woman wheezes and says, "Family is what keeps you in the end. People are terrible. You can't count on them for nothing. But my son is good to me."

"You're lucky," the other woman says.

"I bet you have good children," her neighbor persists.

"Two daughters. They live nearby. And three grandchildren."

"That's wonderful."

"I enjoy them," the other woman says, as if suddenly at pains to differentiate herself, to establish an independent outlook. She crosses her thin, stalky legs at the ankles. "But I keep myself very busy. I go to museums, theater, the movies."

"By yourself ?"

"Yes. I like doing things by myself."

"I'd get awful lonely. You don't get lonely?"

A pack of boys, about the age I was when I started seeing Dr. Abeloff, gets on at the next stop. They cuff each other along the aisle, lunch boxes clanking, drowning out the women's conversation with their exclamations of "Yo!" and "Yo! Yo!" I suddenly wonder whether Dr. Abeloff would recognize me if he saw me now, a woman in her twenties, old enough to be a mother herself. If I were a member of an all but vanished primitive tribe, I would have been paired off years ago: a child bride, grinning from ear to ear, proud-breasted. But the things that haven't changed are greater than the things that have. Why am I still getting my own mother off my chest, week after week, the prime years of my life going into ungenerative airings? Maybe this was the mistake to begin with, learning to tell tales out of home: "I want to sleep with my mother." And Dr. Abeloff was only the first of many, my practice-confessor. How tentatively I spilled the beans in his office—with its view of the East River, its half-light, and the sweet, woodsy smell of his pipe. I was still a child then, with my family to protect; I kept the biggest secrets to myself.

"God be with you," the fat woman says lavishly, setting aside her knees so her neighbor can squeeze by.

"Keep well," the other woman says, a proper matron in a stiff wool coat with oversized buttons—the kind of coat my mother wears, referring to it as a "Ben Zuckerman coat" years after the designer has passed out of existence.

The things that have changed are all outside me: the strip of webbing you push to signal the driver that you want to get off has replaced the overhead cord, but when? The sound the strip makes—a muted *ping*—isn't even the same sound. The world rushes by, unyielding, cutting its losses.

* * *

In a taxi, sitting next to my father, I cross my legs. I am accompanying him to one of his hundreds of dinners, a fund raiser for a politician who furthers Jewish causes. There is a run in my pantyhose that stretches upward from my left ankle; I noticed it when I put the pair on but decided to wear them anyway. I am not good at cutting my losses; I am webbed in all around by dangling threads.

"Very pretty," my father says when he sees me, overlooking my run.

But there is so much else to overlook; I am marred by tiny imperfections. As I step into the cab, a fleck of dirt gets into my right eye, and it begins to tear furiously beneath my contact lens. I dab at my eye and come away with a smear of mascara on my hand, the evening's preparations undone in a moment by external forces, the world rushing by in a whimsy of wind and pollution.

"Shit," I say, hating my eyes for being myopic, my lenses for being uncomfortable, myself for being a woman rather than a man or a neutered creature. The trouble with being a woman is that you are supposed to enhance men—to add gaiety to their evening, like balloons, even if you feel heavy as stone. In profile my father's eyes look small and sparsely lashed, his skin porous. No one thinks to transform him into an Adonis, to require him to mascara his lashes or tint his cheekbones a delicate pink. Getting ready to go out in the evening always puts me on edge, makes me feel glaringly deficient—like walking into *shul* on Yom Kippur in a black dress. All the aids and tricks I have learned from magazines, the painstakingly penciled definition around my eyes, the smokey shadow on my lids—all this undoing of my genetic limitations doesn't fool anyone. Why can't I be incontestably beautiful, Grace Kelly lolling on a man's arm, a blonde in a camel coat adding luster to the evening just by the composition of her facial bones and the sheen on her skin, an undeniable visual asset?

"The Waldorf-Astoria," my father says loudly to the taxi driver. "The Waldorf. Straight across and down Park to Forty-ninth. The Waldorf."

My father repeats everything; he trusts no one. He leans back against the seat and turns to me. "New coat?"

"No," I say. "You've seen it many times."

My father is convinced that everything I wear is newly bought, another marker in my ongoing pattern of degeneracy.

"He doesn't seem to know English," my father says, gesturing forward with his hand. "Do you think he knows how to get to the hotel?"

"Yes," I say. "You told him."

A light turns red ahead of us, and the taxi jolts to a halt, the driver muttering to himself, my father falling against me. I look quickly at the photo on the dashboard and note the cabdriver's name: José Torres. It occurs to me that death could happen anywhere—at any time—picking off my father or me. Since I've gotten into my twenties, I've noticed that the people whose death I fear are greater in number than the people I hate.

"I'm tired, Hannah," he says. "*Sehr müde.* I work too hard." If my father ever thought to solicit my opinion, I would suggest to him that he is tired because it is very tiring to trust no one—neither daughters nor cabdrivers.

"Your mother isn't feeling so well," he says.

"I know," I say. "That's why I'm going with you to the dinner."

My father squeezes my arm, his gloved hand on my

coat sleeve, an embrace of leather and wool. Although he is as suspicious of me as Hamlet was of his mother, I am not Queen Gertrude. I don't lean over and poison his ear with the dark murmurings I have heard—things that have filtered down to me, family percolations. One of my father's aunts—a spinster who stayed home and nursed her sick mother even though this same mother openly disliked her ("Couldn't stand her guts," is how my mother puts it)—suffered from hysterical pregnancies. In the days before psychoanalysis and the excavation of childhood, how much more they have gotten used to! Fathers like Mongol conquerors and mothers who played favorites, all of it ingested whole, the unpalatable parts thrown up again in the most astonishing array of baroque symptoms: compulsions and phobias, tremors and paralyses, hysterical pregnancies and sexual aversions. Can it be this simple, a form of emotional Darwinism: you survive or you don't?

"What can you do," my father says out of nowhere, the philosophy of a man who has learned to take imbalance in his stride, who loses his footing only over small things, over pencils.

"We won't stay late," I say. "I hope."

As the taxi hurries through the crosstown transverse, trees rise on either side of the windows, and I glimpse a lone teenaged boy walking in the park. It is dark already, and somewhere among the trees danger lurks. Why is the boy walking in the park? Where is his mother? Families are monstrous, but without them there is no one to tell you not to go into Central Park at night.

At the dinner I will be introduced to resplendent couples the way I am always introduced at such occasions: as my father's daughter. Once again no one will know that I am not a chip off the old block, that I harbor black thoughts, doubt and malice. (But is anyone ever really a chip off the old block? Doesn't everything crumble, even monuments, when you look too closely?) At this dinner, I will find myself wondering, as I always do, about the workings of power. Power: this is what I should have learned from my father, imbibed at the knee of his noncommunications. But in order to understand power, you have to understand its precedents, like money. I don't understand money, either; I have been brought up not to. My father's father, Opa, who took time on Shabbos afternoons to study the Talmud in his *sefer*-lined study first with Benjamin and then with Eric—an aerie of Jewish learning on the Upper East Side—passed on his distrust to my father: money and women, a bad combination. (When I try and ask him anything directly on this subject, my father says,"Nu, Hannah? Since when the interest in business? I thought you liked to spend money.")

But Opa had little use for girls generally. If only I could have posed the question so it would have intrigued him, a question for those endlessly bickering Talmudic sages to mull over: "What is the earning power of a girl? By what scales shall she be weighed?" For there was something, undeniably, about the picturesquely rendered legalities and ethical parables of the Talmud that pulled on my imagination, the imagination of a girl: tales of carob trees that bore fruit in seventy years' time, from which could be deduced man's need for companionship; Lilliputian debates about the number of black hairs that would disqualify a red cow from being used for the purpose of purification of the dead. In other words, how red was red? An impenetrable logic and yet enviably insular. When I studied these arguments in Talmud class at Melamed, I envisioned myself in a world set to familiar background music—the tinkling piano chords of Lily's "Der Rebbe Elimelech," a world of busy kerchiefed women, forever plucking chickens, kind to their children.

How red is red? How rich is rich? Is there any connection between brains and money? Most of the people my parents know have money. Wealth is a family, too; it is a secret, barring its gates to nonmembers. In one of the ballrooms at the Waldorf-Astoria, crowded with round tables, my father sits at a dais, flanked by other corpulent and stiff-shirted men. Over a squeaking microphone someone is introducing his dear friend who is as generous as he is modest and a g-r-r-eat ballplayer. There is a scattering of laughter, and then a very bronzed man gets up, hands tucked in his pockets, and speaks lovingly into the microphone. Right here, then, is the Truth of Commerce revealed: a tan in coldest December and friends who joke about your minor prowess for hitting a softball instead of boasting about your major prowess for making millions of dollars. I have been misled all along; the truth has nothing to do with anything the literary men say—Keats with his "Truth is Beauty, Beauty Truth." What do girls know except what they read in books? My fate is sealed: I am doomed to hover, like a butterfly, on the rim of power.

"The squab is a bit tough, don't you think?" says the woman sitting next to me. She is taut with prettiness, and when she smiles, I am sure I can hear her jaw click, protesting the disruption. "I don't know why the kosher caterers are so much less good."

"I know," I say. "It's amazing when you think of how many of them there are."

I hear myself responding in blithe agreement, as though this woman and I have everything in common, as though it were crucial that she recognize me as a dinner companion with the same discriminating taste when it comes to poultry. How can she know that I am really Rosa Luxemburg, that I am a firebrand beneath my black silk dress and artful makeup: *Down with all charity dinners! Give philanthropy to the people! Let them eat squab! I am not my father's daughter!*

"I didn't catch your name," she says, jabbing her fork into the baby pigeon's breast, ready to do battle.

"Hannah," I say. "Hannah Lehmann."

"Oh," she says, the watch on her thin wrist sparkling with its galaxy of stones, "that's right. You're Walter Lehmann's daughter. I'm Lee. Lee Straus."

"Hello," I say. I hate her voice, its stentorian ring.

"My husband was going to try and make it," she continues, "if he could get away on time from a meeting with his board of directors. Do you go to a lot of these affairs?"

"No," I say. "I try not to. One has so little time these days."

I notice that my voice has taken on a slightly British intonation, a strangled politeness. Who is "one" if not me—the same "one" I had hauled out years ago when I wanted to impress my mother with the validity of my feelings? Does my neighbor recognize how young I really am despite the burst of tiny lines around my eyes—how the past lives on in me with savage disregard for the evidence of its passing?

"Oh," she says, giving a dry bark of a laugh. "You're doing your duty. Like a good little soldier."

"Duty?" I ask. "Do Americans really believe in

doing their duty? American children, that is? I always thought it was a European concept."

Who in the name of God am I? And who am I talking to? Lee Straus pulls at her left earlobe, which is weighed down by an enormous diamond pavé earring. I stare closely at the earring, the way it fractures the light from the chandelier above us into stabs of color, rays of the sun: *I am in pieces.* What does such a pair of wondrous earrings cost? And why is it only crazy people—poets like William Blake and the raspy folk singers like Arthur's Phil Ochs—who jabber about the inner life, the worth of feelings that no one can see ("There is no pain you are receiving")? Lee Straus is probably never in pain, her earrings an impenetrable buffer. I imagine myself ripping them off her ears at gunpoint, blasting the air above the dais with bullets, shouting slogans: "Unfair! Unfair! These earrings belong to the state and the state belongs to me! Long live Hannah Lehmann!"

"Your father seems very convivial," she says.

"He is," I say briefly. My father is off somewhere, shaking hands with a rabbi here, cracking jokes with a diplomat there. He likes to be at the center of things, a whirlwind, leaving me high and dry.

"I don't believe I've ever met your mother," Lee Straus says. "Of course, I don't come to many of these functions. Isn't your father very active?"

Over the din of the crowd—the rattling of silverware and clinking of glasses, the man standing behind my chair who slaps another man on the back and shouts, "You son of a gun!"—I could say anything, and its meaning would get lost: "My mother rarely goes out. She's mad, you see." Or: "Ever heard of Mrs. Rochester? Well, my mother takes after her. She's locked up in the attic." Or: "My mother's not my real mother. She's been deceiving me for years." Over the din of the crowd, I could live up to my mother's dire pronouncements on my character, the leak she detects in its crucible—prove myself constitutionally traitorous, unworthy of the name Lehmann.

"Yes," I say, "he is. You've probably bumped into the two of them somewhere or other."

A swearing waiter plunks a tiered silver plate of chocolate-coated fruit on the table. The elderly couple sitting across from me pass it back and forth to each other with great ceremony, as though they were sitting in a Japanese teahouse.

"Chocolate," my neighbor says, her thumb and forefinger curled around a plump strawberry. "Marvelous for the waistline."

I wish she'd stop talking. I hate everything about Lee Straus, and suddenly I find myself longing for my mother, who is comfortably reading in her bed, propped against the pillows. My mother is the source of my unease in the world and thus the only person who can make me feel at home in the world. "You and your great talks with strangers," she says. "Always ready to go off with the next one. Ever since you were a little girl you've acted like an orphan." I argue with the echo in my head, with my mother who is my shadow incarnate, whose voice only I can hear. But isn't it possible to be an orphan—to feel like one, at least—even with your parents alive and well and living in the same city?

"My, but it's late," Lee Straus says, "Edwin must be asleep for hours, lucky man."

The trouble with being an orphan is that you really *are*, like Blanche DuBois, dependent on the kindness of strangers; it's no longer a metaphor or a bit of ribaldry. And the trouble with my being a theoretical orphan is that behind my hasty confidings in friends (an openness so automatic as to be almost a tic)—who I am afraid of, who I don't like, what I was really doing on the day I claimed to be home sick—lies the thickest of paranoias: my mother's distrust of strangers (this category including all but the most immediate of family) made stronger by my wish to pretend it doesn't exist. "Americans," my mother often says, as though she has left Europe several days instead of forty years ago, "with their endless friends. Who needs friends? They don't give a hoot in the long run."

"It was so nice to meet you," I say to the woman I've been sitting next to all evening. Lee Straus, who doesn't give a hoot about me even in the short run, yawns and pushes back her thick, mocha-colored hair just as I spot my father coming toward me; his swaying gait, like a penguin's waddle, strikes me as peculiarly touching all of a sudden.

"Well, good night," she says. And turning to my father, who stands now with his hand on the back of my chair, she adds, "You have a lovely daughter."

"Yes," my father says, "she is."

For a moment, in a room full of tables formally attired in linen, it seems to me entirely possible that my father and I are wreathed in kinship, garlanded by love—plastic statuettes of devotion to be placed on top of a cake. Who am I this evening? Why, I am no other than Gale Storm, caught forever in a rerun of "My Little Margie," the cheeky but endearing daughter. Who says it need be any different? On the surface, if you don't look too hard, it isn't really any different. And what is the point of going beneath the surface, anyway?

"Come," my father says, offering me his arm, a gallant courtier. "I have the coat checks." I take his arm, closing us, like a museum after hours, to the public.

* * *

If blood is thicker than water, why do I spill so much, a crimson path for strangers to follow? Who will save you if not your own? "You have no loyalty," my mother says. "You would side with anyone against any of us."

It doesn't help me to scream. "Us? Who's *us*?" I know what she means, recognize that her greatest respect is given to those who are loyal to their families.

"But he is so *mishpochedik*," she will say protectively of a hapless cousin whose one virtue is that he keeps up an abiding interest in "family." In her mind I am consigned to a level of permanent ignominy for my refusal to act more *mishpochedik*, to take the pledge: my family, for better or worse, in good times and bad.

In the absence of love, one becomes very concrete (Benjamin growing up to think, *A bigger apartment will fix it*) or ferociously interior. I don't think it is so much a matter of choice as of temperament, but either way it is an attempt to wring justice. Even as a child I found solace in speculation, in flapping my wings and settling down to brood upon myself: could you be this if you were not that, and what would it be like to be that which was not this?

"Where Hannah go?" Arthur asks, banging his spoon against his highchair, a bib tied around his chubby neck.

It is Wednesday evening in what even I call the past. The six of us are eating supper at the kitchen counter, and Lily says, "Nowhere. She's just trying to get attention." She kisses the top of Arthur's curls, in love with his babyness; he is not yet a contender.

"*I* think she's nuts," Benjamin says. "And that's a fact."

"Wipe the ketchup off your cheek," Lena says to him. "And no one asked you, mister."

"Hannah's not eating her supper," Eric says. "Why do I have to ?"

"Hannah," Lena says, flicking her thumb and fore-finger against the base of my head, as though it were an acorn, "come back to earth."

I obediently pick up my fork and put a piece of fried fish in my mouth (fried fish, mashed potatoes, and spinach, Louisa's inflexible Wednesday menu, my least favorite), but I am not really eating. I float above the world in a Van Gogh sky, midnight blue, pitted with stars. It is dreamy up here. With a purple crayon I have drawn a place where everything is abundant, where there are no fights about who will get the last scoop of ice cream, no Lena to grimly divvy out small portions of dessert. It is a place where nothing you can feel is missing. Although I sit in a chair at the counter next to Rachel, I am not really here. I am off in a painted sky, recasting myself in more foolproof skin, guaranteed not to rust or scratch, aloof from hurt.

SEVENTEEN

"Max," I say to my nephew, only a little boy, but I depend on him. "Listen to this."

I am standing with him under a tunnel in the zoo in Central Park, the same zoo that Lena used to wheel Eric and me home from in the double Silver Cross carriage. How odd it is, really, that you can't stop the clock; even if I think I am turning its hands back, it will go on ticking from that second.

"You listening?"

Max looks at me with his small, serious eyes and nods his head rapidly up and down; no adult I know nods with so much deliberation. When I am with my nephew, I am never sure if I am paying attention to him or I am paying attention to myself as a child, reflected in him. (Lily would put it more harshly: "You were always moved by the vision of yourself being moved," she says, "even when you were little. When you read that poem out to Daddy for his birthday, that was typical. It was a nice poem and everyone congratulated you, but you had to be moved to tears—by yourself, for being his daughter and writing such a poem!")

"Ready?" I say.

"Yes," Max says raptly. He is in love with me the way no man will ever be.

After I make an echo, cupping my hands around my mouth and yodeling the way I remember Julie Andrews doing in *The Sound of Music*, Max wants to know where the echo goes.

"Back to where it came from," I say, in the half-earnest, half-indulgent tone of a grown-up speaking to a child.

But Max is more exact than I, intent on finding out the whys of wherefores. He goes over to a spot under the tunnel and points upward. "Here? Hannah, is this where it went?"

"Exactly," I say heartily, sounding like the over-expressive teachers who used to lead the kindergarten on the TV show "Romper Room."

Max turns on me a full, gap-toothed smile, and it occurs to me that he wants the echo to have a home.

"Let's go," he says, racing ahead.

"Not so fast," I yell, hoping people will mistake me for Max's mother. I am old enough to have children of my own, but now that I am old enough, I wish to be even older, anyone but myself: an old man snoozing in a red leather chair outlined with brass gussets at the Harvard Club, beyond the particular details of the life he has lived.

"Come on," Max says, galloping back toward me. "Hurry up."

His navy blue jacket keeps sliding off his shoulders, but he will not let me zip it up for him. Max likes to wear his jacket open, and inevitably it ends up more off than on, giving him a certain woebegone dash.

"Aren't you cold?" I say. "Let me close your jacket."

"Nope," he says. "I don't need to."

Who will Max be when he is my age? Now at four and a half, he is attentive in a way I associate mostly with women, waylaying people he meets with intimate questions, widening his eyes at the sorrows of baby animals stuck inside their cages.

"I don't like lions," he says, taking my hand as we stand and watch them being fed their dinner of fat, raw meat.

"Why not?"

My curiosity about Max's mental processes is boundless, as though he were of more startling coinage than he is, the product of someone other than my very own sister.

"They're not nice," he says. "Monkeys are better."

"Much better," I say.

Later, when we get outside, he looks into the faded autumn sky and announces with great and untested certainty that the evening is upon us. "It sounds like it's dark," Max says.

"She did not love you well," Dr. Klein says.

The late afternoon sun bounces off the windows in his office. I shade my eyes dramatically, as though I were Lawrence of Arabia peering across miles of hot desert.

"Is the sun bothering you?" Dr. Klein asks. "I can pull the shades down."

Dr. Klein—the latest in the series of psychiatrists I've seen—is young and eager, a natural nurturer.

"No," I say. "No, I mean yes, it is."

He unfolds his long legs and gets up to pull down the shades. I watch him carefully. I don't trust his offers; they fall short. He will not succeed in displacing my mother. Twice he has brought me a paper cup of water; today, when I tell him I am tired, he offers to make me a cup of tea.

"Is that correct?" I ask him.

I enjoy alerting Dr. Klein to the chinks in his professional armor.

"You mean will I lose my license because I offered you tea?"

He chuckles softly to himself. I wonder if he is considered a wit in psychiatric circles.

"Very funny," I snap. "Isn't it un-Freudian? Aren't you supposed to maintain a distance?"

"I don't know," he says.

Dr. Klein leans back in his brown vinyl chair and presses the cushiony tips of his fingers against each other, making a steeple. He has fragile, very white hands. I cannot imagine his hands doing anything forceful, tearing off a piece of bread or grabbing a breast. I can tell from past experience that he is about to impart one of his person-to-person, extratherapeutic tidbits of information—he always taps his fingertips together when he gets ready to share his life with me, a patient who is also a person.

"A friend of mine, Don Raab, an excellent clinician, was discussing just that issue with me the other night over beers."

"I never heard of him," I say. It irritates me that Dr. Klein sits in a brown chair and that his carpeting is shaggy and dusty, not at all the accoutrements to make a good impression. I wish he had an office like Freud's —the famous office I have seen in photographs: dignified and cluttered, filled with archaeological relics, plumped up with Persian rugs and antimacassars.

"Don suggested that the trouble with most therapists is that they're too comfortable with distance and not comfortable enough with intimacy. Perhaps that's why they go into the profession to begin with. What do you think?"

The doctor cocks his head at me as though he were genuinely curious, as though he were inviting the opinion of a reknowned colleague instead of a lowly patient: Dr. Hannah Lehmann, originator of the There-Is-No-Going-Forward Principle, an expert on the subject of human malaise.

"Nice of you to include me in your theoretical debates," I say.

"What is your irony protecting you from?"

Dr. Klein's question comes to me out of the blue, and for a moment I am unhinged.

"I want to be saved," I say.

Who will save you if not your own? And what happens if the people who are meant to save you are destined to destroy you?

"Ah, yes," he says. "The question is: From whom?"

For a second—shorter than that, really, it is but the briefest of tugs in my mind—there is a flip in my usual perspective, and I am overcome with affection for the doctor, for his utterly comprehending "Ah, yes." I feel mushy and wet, like a pile of leaves after they have been rained on. And then, in yet another shift, it occurs to me that love is expansive—that it notices things: Dr. Klein's hands strike me as beautiful, ravishingly gentle.

"From my mother," I say. (And now, I am suddenly sure of it, Dr. Klein will say the one thing to break the spell, utter some magical psychoanalytic truth that will set me free. I will be able to start over again—a downy ball waddling after the right mother duck, at last. How unfairly I have judged him, this redeemer among men!)

"Your mother?"

"Yes," I say, surprised by the questioning note in his voice. "That should be obvious." Surely this came as no news? Unless, as I had suspected all along, he didn't listen—really listen—to anything I said.

The doctor looks at me straight on, blinking slowly and calmly, reminding me of the sleepy-lidded hippopotamuses in the Central Park Zoo that Eric and I loved to watch when we were little. His lashes are thick and wheat-colored and there is no sign in his gray eyes of anything more surpassing than that they see me slouched in the chair across from him.

"But by your age," Dr. Klein says, continuing to gaze at me, "the problem resides within you. Your mother has no real power over you anymore, other than what you give her."

With these words, he changes before my very eyes —like one of those hideous transformations in a horror movie—from a paragon of understanding to an ape of backwardness. Can he really be so dense?

"Oh really," I say. And then I add more heatedly, "That's ridiculous. I don't think you ever pay attention to me. I can't dispossess myself of my mother like that. Maybe you can—of yours." (I immediately imagine his mother, sweet but negligible, standing over a hot stove and stirring soup—the mother I always wanted. With a mother like that, who couldn't take on the future?)

"You *can*," Dr. Klein says quietly, smiling. "Even your mother isn't invincible."

"But I can't. Sometimes they're just too strong."

"Where your mother ends," he says, "you begin."

"How Zen-ish," I say, stiffening. I am back where I always am. Hannah Lehmann: this is who I've always been and who I'll always be. How unbearable it is that you can only live your own life, never someone else's. . . .

"Maybe," the doctor says, looking tired, his hands drooping in his lap. "But I'd think about it if I were you."

What I'm thinking about is love. Or rather, the deception of love. Love, even only a glimmer of it, makes you look at things—like Dr. Klein's hands looked to me a few seconds ago—differently, in a way that makes you forget yourself. I am testing, always testing. One day I will come upon someone so inviolable that I will never doubt myself as seen—loved—through his eyes.

"Perhaps," Dr. Klein says, reading my mind, "you should think less about the possibility of being saved and more about the possibility of finding love. The odds are higher, for one thing."

"I do," I say. "All the time. I'd kill myself to be loved."

"That's not love," he says. "That's stopping the blood."

In the silence that follows this remark I wonder what would happen if I refused to leave Dr. Klein's office at the end of the session, if I held on to his feet so that he couldn't walk to the door. The doctor clears his throat and then there is only the sound of the rain hitting the air conditioner outside his window—*plash, plash, plash*—like drops of blood falling from the sky.

In the end, there are no compensations for having felt yourself to be unloved—except the ones of your own devising. For instance, if you have once been adored, isn't it possible that everything that comes after it is a letdown? Who could ever love Freud the way his mother did? "*Mein goldener Sigi*," she called him. No wonder he expected unwavering allegiance from his disciples. An old man, dying of a cancerous jaw, Freud still believed he was the golden boy: "You don't think it worth your while to love me," he told the woman poet who consulted him. But Freud must have had dreams, too, in which he murdered his father. Perhaps nothing clears us from the absolute longings of childhood, not even a happy childhood.

But again, maybe memory has gotten it all wrong, stored away in tissue paper borrowed feelings as well as actual experiences—what was feared and wished for as well as what happened. In my dreams, the dreams of adulthood, I kept stumbling upon the same dark rebus, an image of destruction. My mother, the Wicked Witch, is yelling at me, "You're crazy! Anyone can see you're crazy! You and your crazy psychiatrists!" "You're the crazy one!" I shout back. "Look what you've done."

But in my dream it is my mother who is damaged and I who remain unscathed; in dreams and fantasies my life is redeemed. I dream my mother's neck is burning; black furls of smoke go up from a gash in it like a crack in the neck of a china doll. I put on a brown wool dress and flat brown shoes, and then I realize they are looking for the woman who is wearing this dress; it is evidence, like spilled blood. When I wake up, I am in a double bed in a room that is not the room I had at home. The sheets are delicately flowered, and I am lightly covered with sweat, as though I have escaped from something. I slide a finger in the valley between my breasts and wipe away the moistness. It is very early in the morning, the moistness is only dew, and I curl up to sleep some more, relieved that my mother is unharmed.

* * *

"Dr. Klein says you did not love me well," I say to my mother when she calls several evenings after I have this dream. I savor the sound of it: *did not love me well*. How much nicer than *did not love me*, the extra beat of the comparative adding a sad music. ("You *need* to be sad," my mother has said to me more than once, airily dismissing more complex explanations, explanations that might implicate her. "Your psychiatrists don't understand that.")

"I know that," she says, unshaken.

In her acceptance is rejection. I am doing exactly what I'm not supposed to do, repeating everything to her. I want my mother with me for the ride, even though I am the honored passenger. I do not want to be burdened with all this insight. Insight is lonely, and it skirts the issue of culpability: *Look what you've done*. Insight means nobody is to blame.

"*Quatsch*," she says.

Quatsch: yet another of my mother's words for nonsense, resounding down my childhood like a rubber ball thumping down a flight of stairs. Putting a stop to further conversation, like *genug*. The German language seems to be full of such dismissive signals—upholding authority, discouraging exposure. Everything is nonsense.

"I did the best I knew how," she adds.

I say nothing. It is a mystery to me, the waves of emotion I keep breaking against her. I am a woodpecker, and my mother is a tree. Love. Hate. Emotions keep slipping off the end of my mind, to be followed by wholly different ones. Hate. Love. Which will do to wear her bark away? And who is torturing whom?

"Maybe you're not simple enough to be a good mother," I say.

There is a pause at the other end of the line, a shuffling of thought. What do we expect from our mothers but absolute fealty? *Meine goldene Hannah.*

"Maybe," my mother says. "Like who?"

"Grete," I said promptly, a line out of an old script. We have had this conversation, or a version of it, before.

"True," she says. "*Her* children love her."

Grete is a distant relative of my mother's, a stout, red-cheeked woman who lives on Staten Island. There is a blowsy quality about her that I associate with the women who leaned out of tenement windows in their housecoats on mild spring afternoons as I walked to the library. The library I took out books from as a child was on 68th Street, way over east—a neighborhood, close as it was to my house, that might as well have been another country for all the similarity it bore to the Upper East Side I knew. It was a world removed from quiet elegance, that sooty enclave behind Third Avenue, and in my mind it came to represent an idealized image of the past: a bustling, turn-of-the-century New York, where immigrants without money but not without merriment sucked on cubes of sugar with their tea.

"That's because she doesn't criticize them," I say.

When I was very young, I used to think of Grete as the little old woman who lived in the shoe, boundlessly maternal, with no needs of her own. Grete's husband learns Talmud all day, and they have many children, two more than my parents' six. She comes into the city every six months or so to have lunch with my mother at a kosher dairy restaurant on 47th Street. The two of them have been doing this for years, and they always end up in Bloomingdale's linen department, where my mother buys Grete sheets and pillowcases—like a dowry. My mother enjoys describing these outings, the patterns Grete picks: splashy prints, bright greens and pinks and blues, the antithesis of her on pristine taste.

"Strange what people like, isn't it?" she says when recounting their shopping trip. "I can't picture Samuel on those sheets, can you?"

"Not really," I say, laughing. I can barely remember what Grete's husband, Samuel, looks like, but I dimly recall a small, lushly bearded man: an ascetic, a Chasid, impossible to put together with the act of fathering, with wild sheets from Bloomingdale's.

"Grete's oldest daughter, Tziporah, is expecting any day," my mother says.

"Again? Isn't she only twenty?"

I act aghast, as I think befits a woman of my time, imbued with the newest ideas about the importance of career and the proper spacing of children. (The lack of space between myself and my siblings is a perverse source of pride for my mother. "I had the six of them in nine years," she is fond of saying, as though she's describing a race she has won.) But I don't really feel anything stronger than curiosity. What would it be like to be Tziporah instead of me, that and not this?

"Twenty-*one*," my mother says. "She got married at seventeen, after one date. What an enormous wedding!"

"I know," I say, interrupting her. "You told me. She's really pregnant *again*?"

"Why not? It's her third, better than anything else one could do. The more the merrier."

"It is *not*," I say. "Anyone can get pregnant. Your whole family procreates like guinea pigs."

"More power to them," my mother says staunchly, but the phone call has turned heavy with tension.

"You don't need me to have children," I say. 'Rachel has children. I'm sure the others will have them, too."

"I don't 'need' you to have children, period, Hannah, although I know you love to imagine I do. The world doesn't revolve around you." My mother's voice has become ominously crisp.

"I know that," I say. "Besides, maybe I don't want any. I would hate to ruin them."

"Well, you have nothing to worry about. You just go right on sitting there, bemoaning the past. What a luxury! By the time you're ready to have children, you'll be a grandmother."

"I don't understand why you have so much at stake in seeing to it that everyone has children. The whole world doesn't have to have children just because you did."

"I don't have anything at stake, thank you, Hannah, for your analysis. I just think it's marvelous to know what you want."

"Really," I say equably, as though I were talking to someone other than my mother. Do all mothers equate what their daughters should want with what they want —to see their lives confirmed, their choices repeated down to the color of the bed sheets?

"Yes, really," my mother says. "And I think we should both get off the phone now, don't you?"

"Okay," I say. " 'Bye, Ma."

"Good-bye," she says.

Does she sound dispirited? Have I punctured her full of holes this time? I can't tell. I want my mother to see the error of her ways, to admit that she did not love me well, to console me for a loss only she can make up for.

"Ma?"

"Yes?"

"Do you think I'll ever get married?"

I sound desperate, as though the odds are against it, as though I have lived a yawning half-century without a husband instead of a quarter of one.

"I suppose so," she says. "You can always get divorced."

"Thanks," I say. "That's a big help. Good-bye."

"Good-bye," she says, and then, relenting: "Don't worry. Everything will turn out fine."

"It won't," I say, disgusted to find myself in tears. Why is it always I who end up punctured?

"Don't be an idiot," my mother says. "There's nothing to cry about."

"Okay," I say, "Good-bye."

"Good-bye, Hannah," she says.

Desires that aren't met don't go away; they just become twisted. My love for my mother is not love; it is consuming, an addiction. There is something about our bristling conversations that is gratifying—almost sweet-tasting—as though we have come to this scarred place once again, my mother and I, arm in arm. What has developed over the time of our lives together is this: Hostility has become a form of seduction, and I have come to confuse the tenderness that is a bruise with the tenderness that is a kiss.

Somewhere in this story is a tragedy, but it is hard to see. How did others see me—see my family? Did my childhood friends or my parents' dinner guests even see beyond the building my family lived in, surrounded by a phalanx of doormen, sealed like a vault from the possibility of illicit entry? The rich are so private, more private than the poor or the middle class. They bury their losses. Whatever goes wrong goes on inside. It taxes the imagination to think of it—everything that money hushes up, the screams it drowns out. By the time I reached my teens, it seems to me that it would have been preferable to be poor, poor*er*. I had gotten hold of the idea—from books and from movies—that the poor let things out, aired their grievances like the wash, hung them on the line for all to see. If I were poor, my mother would stand on the fire escape in summer, and everyone for miles around would see what she was doing to me, that she had absorbed me like a sponge, made it so there was no "away" away from her. But my mother never wore rollers in her hair or walked around in bedroom slippers outside as though the world were her home. No pock-faced, leather-jacketed boy ever lounged against the neighborhood stoop and said, "Your old lady's crazy, isn't she?" Outside her own home you couldn't tell much about her.

How content we are to see people from the outside in, except those we are forced—from too close a proximity—to see from the inside out. Who will ever see my mother as I do: the consuming irritant of my life, my unrequited love?

Somewhere in this story is a tragedy, but it is nearly impossible to see. Look away for a moment and it is gone. Look back and it is there, a flicker in the corner of an eye—a tear, then another tear, dropping hotly. ("Your tears don't move me," my mother said.) I am —how old? Eleven? Twelve?—crying behind the locked door of my mother's bedroom. "Hysterical," I am called, like Beatrice. When I cry, in bouts so strong that they startle even me, my mother locks me in her bedroom until I finish. I cannot, do not want to imagine the humiliation of it—reduced to tears, literally.

When I am sixteen, set in a pattern of hopeless appeal, I take a pair of nail scissors while my mother is in her bathroom and make small cuts in my arm. I am seated on her bed with its fitted crewelwork spread, chosen by my mother and an elderly interior decorator named Mrs. Bowle. (Mrs. Bowle, like so many other people from my past, is dead now, but my mother still refers to her and her dicta with pride. "She had a passion for understatement," my mother says. "A true Wasp. She hated flocked wallpaper or anything but the simplest white lampshades. I suspect she was an anti-Semitic at heart. But I learned a lot from her.") My mother is going away—nowhere far, just to the beach house—but for some reason it is important to me that she stay with me this Friday afternoon. The sun pours through the windows in her bedroom as I make little nicks around my wrists, three o'clock on a Friday afternoon in my past that is not really the past but a small part of me still. I imagine myself dripping blood onto the rug—a pale yellow rug that picks up one of the subdued colors in the crewelwork bedspread. But the scissors, small as they are, hurt my skin, and I don't cut deeply enough to draw blood. I am determined but not determined enough; I lack willpower even when it comes to this. As I push the sharp point of the scissors in, I hate myself in advance for being a coward. My mother comes out of the bathroom.

"Look," I say, showing her my handiwork, ruining the effect by having to call attention to it. (But would she even notice otherwise? There is always so much to call her away from, my father and brothers and sisters, herself. There is no gaining her notice without jiggling her nerves.)

"What is that?" She asks this blankly; it is the same voice I have heard her use on Beatrice.

"I did it. With scissors. With these."

I hold the scissors, tiny silvery implements, up in the air: Look at me. *Look at me. Look what you've done.*

"Why?"

I am crying, beside myself with an emotion that is so basic it predates sadness or anger—like a baby's bawling for his mother's milk.

"Does it hurt?"

Before I can demonstrate the true Germanness of my character, impress my mother with my inherited stoicism, my offhand "not too much" (but she must know, surely, that there is no pain I will not suffer in her cause), the phone rings, loud and jangling. It will always be like this, the world intruding without a thought.

"Just a minute, Hannah," my mother says. She puts one hand over mine and reaches out her other to take the phone.

Just a minute? This is what happens when I try to make life stop, make the world stop whirring and huddle around my tears. Nothing happens; my mother takes the phone.

"Hello?"

My mother's voice goes up on the end like the top note in a bar of music, courteous as could be. The nicks on my wrist throb like paper cuts. I think of the silver hole puncher I love to use. Shaped like scissors, the puncher makes three perfect round holes in sheets of lined paper so they will fit into the rings of my looseleaf binder. Why can't I make myself into a perfect-fitting hole?

"Oh, hel-*lo*. . . . Yah, sure. . . . *Nein, ich hab's nicht vergessen. . . .*"

There is a pause, and I can hear a throaty female voice speaking in rapid German at the other end, a heartless language, the language of Ilse Koch. My mother laughs her best laugh, not the raucous one I'm used to but the one reserved for Friday night guests she doesn't know well.

". . . Next week. Of course . . . I'll call you then. . . . Perhaps we'll see you at the beach sometime this summer?"

Another spray of German follows, and then my mother repeats, "I'll call you then. Have a good Shabbos."

The traditional conclusion to Thursday and Friday phone calls between my mother and the people she talks to is "Have a good Shabbos," not "Have a good weekend." The world closes in, suffocatingly small, ignoring my particularity. Everyone is Jewish, everyone is German, everyone has no time for the *Quatsch* of my scene-making, my implacable needs. It occurs to me that my mother has no friends, no acquaintances even, who are other than she is. They are, the lot of them—the women on the other end of the telephone undoubtedly—toughened to the point of emotional obtuseness, immigrants acquainted with real horror: war and death and loss. My mother hangs up the phone with her usual vigor, practically banging it down into the receiver. She turns to me.

"Shall I get you a Band-Aid?"

"No," I say, my face clenched from crying. *A Band-Aid?* My mother is neutral as the camp nurse who some years ago diagnosed my incessant hiccuping as a symptom of homesickness.

"I don't know why you did it," my mother says. "I hope you do."

She gets up from the bed, where she has been sitting close to me. Under the hem of my gray and red pleated skirt, a hand-me-down from Lily, my knees are pinky white, shiny with health. I look down at my mother's feet, encased in gray pumps. They look enormous to me, like the feet of the selfish giant in Oscar Wilde's fairy tale must have looked to the children who wandered into the garden where he lived. If I could reach down and hold her feet, keep her from leaving me . . .

"I have to go," my mother says.

"I don't want you to," I say.

"Don't be silly," she says. "Daddy will be waiting for Willy to come back from the beach and pick him up at the office."

"But stay with me," I say.

"Hannah, I can't. Why don't you come along?"

Her voice has become warmer, like a hug.

"No," I say, hiccuping between sobs.

A doorman blows his whistle outside, and suddenly I think of the kids in my class, how most of them take their mothers for granted, how no one is in so much pain; not one of them can't get what I want the way I can't.

"No," I say. "*You* stay. I don't want to be out at the beach with all the others."

"They'll leave you alone," my mother says. "I'll tell Lily to be especially nice to you. And Rachel always is. The boys won't bother you; they're too busy with each other."

"I don't want to be left alone," I say.

What I want—what I can't get—is something organic, what my mother (but for what reason?) can't give me: potato love, natural as earth, scruffy and brown, clinging to your roots, helping you grow fit and firm.

"I have to go," my mother says, moving back toward the bed. "It can't be helped."

She puts an arm on mine. My arms, if you don't turn them over to where there are angry scratches—

blips in some indecipherable code—look perfectly normal, decked in flesh. I think of the color of blood, how shockingly vivid it is when it first spurts out.

"Okay," I say, giving up. Even the abject have to give up sometime.

"Louisa's here. Can you hear her? She's still cleaning up downstairs in the kitchen. I'll tell her to come up and check up on you before she goes, all right? You always liked Louisa."

Who, finally, will save you *from* your own? It is like the worst of nightmares, one of those awful dreams in which your life is endangered but when you open your mouth to scream, nothing comes out. And even if I could scream, the way Beatrice screamed . . . what then? My mother is a non-echo, failing to resound down the halls of my childhood.

"Hannah," my mother says, standing up, "it'll be fine. You'll see. Nothing's so terrible."

I nod mutely. Someone is taking my skin away.

"Okay," I say again.

From where she is standing, way up above, she leans over to kiss me, her mouth brushing against my cheek, the driest of kisses. "You can still come out with Daddy," she says. "I'll call you from the beach to see if you've changed your mind. Come."

I smile at my mother to show that I'm fine. My cheeks have that odd, stiff sensation they get after I've cried. It is the beginning of the Memorial Day weekend, and in two days I will turn seventeen, the right age for heartbreak.

EIGHTEEN

There is always more we can say about ourselves—the things that happen inside our skins, where it is hard to separate the feelings from the facts.

"Don't talk so much about yourself!" Didn't my mother say this to Lily and me all the time, fat-cheeked little girls, skipping along, our hands in hers? "An' then . . . an' then . . . an' then . . ." We recounted our fights in the playground as though they were the end of the world. Rachel was better, she never talked about herself. There was so much we could have said back then. These days, after Lily and I have one of our hours-long talks about the Tragedy of Our Family—it feels the way Pyrrhic victories always do: it doesn't make up for anything.

* * *

All the bells ring: too late. When I came across this line during college in a poem by John Berryman—who committed suicide, like his father before him—I copied it down on the cover of a notebook. But then again, I've always been drawn to sad music, the elegiac rather than the festive. Still, I wonder, if suicide does not run in your family, does that mean you are marked to live? The lure of killing myself remains to this very day, but I must admit I also consider other prospects: children of my own, a womb showily distended, the past irrevocably over. Just the other day when I took a walk in Central Park, on a Sunday afternoon, there was woman who looked a lot like me wheeling a baby carriage near the lion's cage. I am old enough now to wheel my own child, of course. Why, then, do I remain loyal to the pain of childhood, skulk at the passing of days? What must it feel like to be the woman wheeling the baby carriage—to be endowed with such a facility, such a graceful acceptance of present history?

I would love to find someone whose memories matched mine, little hurt for little hurt, who remembers the clammy feel of that summer afternoon years back after the rain stopped. Everything that once happened is both long ago and omnipresent, sticks under my skin like burrs. The first movie I ever saw, with Lily and Rachel and my mother, was a grainy semidocumentary called *Third Man Up the Mountain*—the sort of hortatory account that appealed to my mother, reminded her of her own childhood. The second or third or possibly eighth movie I saw was with Lily, Rachel, Benjamin, and Eric in the shabby movie house out near the beach, the one next to the drugstore. It was raining that afternoon, and we were all wearing slickers that rustled when we moved. It was Lena's day off, and because we were on our own, we took the opportunity of going into the drugstore first to buy candy. Lily liked licorice twists, and Rachel usually bought Tootsie-Roll Pops or Good-and-Plenty. I always picked Lik-m-aid, a slightly acidic-tasting sugared powder that came in little packets. There were assorted flavors, cherry and grape and lemon, but they all tasted the same to me. What I liked was throwing my head back and pouring the candy down my throat—the sting it left on my tongue.

The theater was warm and damp, with lots of little kids sitting on their slickers, making noise. The movie we saw that afternoon was called *101 Dalmatians*. It was an animated cartoon, and it featured a character with black hair that wiggled out of her skull like snakes. Her name was Cruella De Vil, and she reminded me of my mother. There were also oodles of spotted dogs in that movie; they scrambled all over the screen. While we were walking home, Eric insisted that he had counted each and every dalmatian, and that there really had been exactly one hundred and one of them.

"Bull!" Benjamin says loudly, from where he straggles behind, running his hand along the bushes as we pass. "That's a lie."

"No, it's not." Eric says. "I counted them."

"You couldn't have."

"How would you know?"

I am walking next to Eric, and Lily and Rachel are walking together ahead of us. From the back my sisters look very shlumpy in their baggy shorts and stretched-out-T-shirts, slickers slung over their shoulders.

"Because there wasn't enough time." Benjamin has

caught up with us now, his feet practically on top of mine.

"*I* count quickly," Eric says. "Unlike some retards I could name."

A timid sun is beginning to break through a patch in the clouds. The air is muggy, and there are flies buzzing all around.

"I hope there's ice cream for a snack," Rachel says.

"Me, too," I say.

There is something ardent—almost lovelorn—about our collective interest in food, as though we lived in Oliver Twist's orphanage.

"If the two of you don't stop it," Lily says, "I'm telling, and you won't come with us to the movies anymore."

"He started," Eric says, punching Benjamin in the chest again. Although smaller than Benjamin, he is fierce and wiry.

"Shut up. *You* did," Benjamin says, coughing. He flails out, hitting the air.

"Lily," I say. "Didn't Cruella De Vil remind you of someone?"

My hair is pulled tightly into a ponytail, making my scalp ache. My rain slicker is heavy and uncomfortable, and I am beginning to fall behind the others.

"Lena?" she asks from up ahead.

"Come on," I say. "You know."

"I *know* who you meant, I thought so, too. But don't go and tell her, like you always do."

"I do not," I say.

But Lily is right, of course. I confide everything in my mother, even my fears about her—that she is really Ilse Koch or Cruella De Vil—as though she could banish these fears simply by being privy to them. But isn't there some validity to this line of attack? Isn't it only the devil who can convince you that she isn't the devil, that she's only the devil in disguise? How can you undo the terrible things you know about people, about your own family, except by asking them to tell you that the terrible things you know aren't true?

"Who wants to race me home?" Rachel asks.

"No one," Lily said. "It's too hot."

"Cool Joe," I say out loud, even though no one is walking next to me. I am trying it out.

I have heard two girls use this phrase about the lifeguard at the municipal swimming pool: "He thinks he's a cool Joe," one girl said to the other in that taunting voice girls of a certain age use.

"Hey," Benjamin says, stopping his fight with Eric. "Get this: Hannah's talking to herself!" My brother doubles over with laughter, as if he has just said something riotously funny.

"You kiddin'," Eric says.

"Nope, I just heard it."

"Stop it, boys," Rachel says from up ahead, but she and Lily are almost at the end of the block.

"Hannah, whadya say?" Eric asks.

"Cool Joe," I repeat for his benefit.

"What's that?"

"An expression. *You* wouldn't have heard of it."

Eric and Benjamin slow their steps and look at each other. Then they shake their heads in unison, as though they were two cops on the same beat, a madcap TV duo.

"Loony," Eric says. "Loony bin."

But Benjamin and he are friends again, so my purpose as a foil has been served. I can see they're not going to push me any further, set me going like a wind-up toy, as they sometimes do. The two of them laugh together some more, cuffing each other lightly.

"Ready or not," Eric says to Benjamin. "Bet I'll beat you home."

"Bet you two Yankee cards you won't," Benjamin says, lining up next to him. They both limber up as though they were really about to go somewhere, bouncing on their knees and crouching low.

"I'll be the judge," Rachel says.

Standing next to Lily, she shades her eyes, taking her role very seriously. There is nothing that suits Rachel's personality more than being a judge of unimportant competitions—the perfect neutralist position.

"Ready?" my sister barks at my two brothers, cupping her hands around her mouth like a megaphone.

"Yep," Eric yells.

"No cheating," Benjamin says.

"One . . . two . . . three . . ." Rachel counts and then pauses dramatically. "Go!"

They dash off, passing Lily and Rachel within seconds.

"Eric's winning," Rachel shouts after them.

Ahead of me on the pavement is a rainbow, a tiny, glistening circle of color. The sun is out fully now, and in the distance the four o'clock siren sounds, a mournful howling. Lily and Rachel turn the corner, out of sight, and for the rest of the block there is nothing in the world but me and the solid houses of Long Island, under a sky that is clearing into a turquoise blue.

Whoever believes our stories, anyway? Isn't belief only this: a matter of instinct, choosing one version over another? Even my brother's memories don't match mine. What's interesting is that when I ask Eric if he remembers going to see *101 Dalmatians*, he says he does, but he insists that I am wrong about our having been on our own that day. Lena accompanied us everywhere, he says, to miniature golf, everywhere. They're not details I would bother to argue with him about, but the discrepancy makes me feel lonely.

It has always been this way, more or less. When I was very young, I used to feel lonely for my mother—for all of her—even when she stood next to me. There was something deeply remote about the woman who sat in my childhood at the oval dining room table under a glistening chandelier, chin in her hand, staring into space.

What space does my mother stare into? What is it that she sees? I stand in the kitchen, peeking at her through the little window in the swinging door that leads to the dining room. I am seven, ten, sixteen, twenty-six. That woman sitting there still is my mother, although I think half of her is inside of me. I want to rescue her from the solitude that is hers and that has become mine. For isn't the other side of tragedy—any tragedy—always another tragedy, the begetting tragedy? We are all daughters of yet other daughters, and everywhere are strewn the mothers with broken hearts. Now that I am grown up, I am afraid of so many things—cats and matches, cars and travel, of leaving anywhere for anywhere else. At some predetermined moment I was designated as the carrier of my mother's unspoken fears. And my yearnings—could they be but shadows of her own? Or maybe this is only what I'd like to believe, a way of stopping up gaps. For the half of my mother that is not me is like the dark side of the moon, unknowable.

How do you get free of an obsession that's become a part of you, as necessary as air? When I went to sleep-away camp, a ten-year-old with the sober eyes of someone much older, I couldn't breathe in the morning for loss of my mother. I couldn't believe she went on without me, that I went on without her, that she would be there when I returned at the end of that August. I cried every morning before the rest of the camp got up, at the back of the bunks near the smelly toilets. I sent my mother supplicating letters. *I love you so much*, I wrote. *I miss you terribly. Please let me come home.* I circled the imprint of my tears on the page, little stains that looked like stars—like drops of water. *These are my tears*, I wrote underneath.

My mother tore up the first of these letters into jagged pieces, clues in a scavenger hunt, and sent them back to me with the following notice: *This is what I will do with each and every one of these letters.* My head was a rubber ball, being bounced against walls, but I was impervious to all hurt except the hurt of being without her.

Someone tried to get me to stay—Mr. Slotnick, the camp owner, I think it was—promising me trunks of the underwear line he owned. (Years later I told people Mr. Slotnick had owned Fruit of the Loom, but what I know to have been absolutely true is that he sat by the lake and tried to coax me.) "You have such beautiful hair," he said, "Why don't you stay? You'll be the belle of the ball. I'll see to it." My father never spoke this way to me, but I guess I must have been, in my way, a beguiling child—a girl to turn a businessman tender.

I would have none of Mr. Slotnick's offers though; I continued to write heartsick letters, and after three weeks I prevailed: Willy arrived to pick me up in a long, crowd-stopping car, the talk of the camp. (Years later I will bump into people who have only to hear my name to recall this chariot of a car, with its own helmsman. It seems that Camp Kulanu—an Orthodox camp, its name the Hebrew for "all of us"—had never borne witness to such a splendid exit before or since.) When I arrived at the beach house, my trunk neatly repacked with the underwear and socks and T-shirts and shorts in which Lena had sewn labels with my name, HANNAH LEHMANN, just three weeks before, my mother wasn't home. Lena greeted me at the door, balefully. "Traitor," she said, as though I had fled a war. Lily came down the stairs, clearly unhappy to see me, and my father acted as if I had never been away when he came home that evening.

In enchantment, the thralldom of love, there is no time, no chronology, no year by which to date things. The enchantment I am under is stifling, a witch's cloak. My mother is the Wicked Witch, but she is also the object of desire. She is the first I have known of love—of the deception of love. I don't believe the world is any different away from her.

"Where did you get these tits?" Robert, who is a lawyer, cups my breasts from where he lies beneath me, and then lets them fall. His hands are dry and thin-fingered, distant hands that don't give anything away. "Huh? How come you're not saying anything? Can't you tell me?"

"No," I say, giggling.

We are lying on Robert's wide platform bed in an apartment on a street that has a church and trees and birds that chirp in the morning, like a street on a movie set. There are curls of reddish dust on the floor around the bed—they have been there since the first time I saw this room—and in one of the drawers that are built into the bed's headboard, hidden under some old legal documents are several magazines with women leaning over on the cover, baring bottoms that are as high and glossy as the ones on prize stallions.

"How come you're not talking now?" Robert says, his fingers trailing across my breasts and down my body. "You always like to talk. Tell me something."

"Like what?" All that's important to me is that Robert like my body, make it forget itself. If I say too much when we're in bed there is a good chance we'll get into an argument and then Robert will pull his hands away, leaving me to my own company. Anything I say can rub him the wrong way; there are so many things he doesn't like about me.

"Tell me what you are," he says. "I bet you can't even tell me."

"I could," I say, "but you wouldn't understand. Your mind's too thick."

After a year of knowing Robert, of knowing how he objects to the most basic facts of my life—the wealth of my background, my family's looming presentness, the way I talk to people (there's something wrong, according to him, about the way I talk to people)—I have found it easier to be intentionally provocative than to stumble onto his annoyance unawares.

"Oh really," he says. "Is that so?"

He sounds amused, and I put a hand on his thigh—high up, at a spot where it is no longer scratchy with hair. I love the areas on his body where the skin is soft, no longer the skin of a lawyer but of a little boy. I am about to continue my explorations when Robert puts a hand over mine.

"Uh, uh. What would you do for it?"

I lie back on the pillow and stare at the ceiling over his bed; the paint on it is a scuffed white, the same color as dirtied saddle shoes. I look at the ceiling and pretend I haven't heard the question because it is part of our unspoken pact that I act as though I don't enjoy being made to beg.

"Okay," he says, his voice curt where a second ago it was breathy. "In that case you can go home."

Robert is lying on his side, propped up on one

elbow, his mouth tight. Behind him, through the slats in his venetian blinds, the sky is black.

"I don't want to," I say. There is a long, meandering crack in the ceiling and I follow it with my eyes from one end to the other several times, as though it were a path to something, a telling line of breakage.

"I don't want to," he says, mimicking me.

"Don't," I say, turning on my side, leaning across to kiss his cheek.

"You are a piece of pathos," Robert says, ducking out of my reach. "Do you know that? A rich piece of pathos."

What the crack in the ceiling won't tell me is what I already know: how I got here, from what misguiding compass I take direction.

"No, I'm not," I say.

Robert chuckles. When he laughs—always with this restrained, ungenerous chuckle—I realize what I have gotten myself into. There are two clues I have to how I really feel about Robert—more than clues, really, portents of the truth. One clue is his laugh and the other is that the room gets smaller when he calls. I mean this literally; when I pick up the phone in my apartment and the voice on the other end is Robert's, I feel the walls shrink around me.

"Then you'll do what I tell you."

"That depends."

How I feel about Robert is this: afraid. Also: excited.

"I'm not asking you to name your terms," he says.

"Spoken like a true lawyer," I say.

I am lying on my stomach and he is lying on his back. To an observer who happened in on the two of us, we would probably look like a couple in love, making the sweetly desultory conversation lovers make.

"I want you to crawl on the floor."

"No," I say.

"But you know you will."

Somewhere in this very city is a nice man meant for me, a man without fetishes, a man not meant for me.

Robert caresses my bottom, a prelude to the main theme.

"I love your ass," he says, and raises his hand.

Later on—I am red-assed as a baboon, he has started a flood inside me—he turns me over and enters me.

"Do I own you now?" he whispers into my ear. "Do I?"

"Yes," I say, "yes."

When Robert is inside me he feels like velvet, but when it is over I am alone again. I wake up often in his bed, unaccustomed to the early hour at which he goes to sleep. In the morning he has his set routines, undeviating even to the brand of soap he uses from month to month. He doesn't really like having me around then, but before I go I stand in his doorway, sliding the zipper on my jacket up and down, stalling. I study objects I've noticed many times before—his worn orange sofa, the matted sheepskin hanging on his wall, the round table with its ugly quartet of chairs—as though in them I might find a way to make myself feel at home.

"What's the matter, chickadee?" he says. He is still in his black terry robe, in an unusually good mood about some case he thinks he'll win. Robert loves to win; when things don't go his way professionally, he crumples like a used-up piece of paper.

"Nothing," I say, but I don't leave. How can I explain to him that it seems to me I am forever on the verge of leaving? Even arrivals are a form of departure—whiffs of future absences.

"I'll give you a call later," he says, scratching his chin, making a sound like sandpaper.

"Will you miss me today?" I have never figured out the point of pride.

"Here," he says, leaning over, smelling of Dial soap. "Till we meet again. A memento."

When I get home that morning, I see in the bathroom mirror that Robert's good-bye bite has left its mark: a blue-brown-purple bruise, the insignia of love. It occurs to me then that for certain people the normal spectrum of emotions narrows itself down to a blinding intensity: love creates the same violence as hate and desire the same color as fury.

Oh yes, we are all still here, where we started.

It is a Sunday in January, a cold and unfriendly day. In the living room—redecorated some years ago in the quietest of schemes, my mother's tutelage in understatement displayed in her choice of plain styles and cloudy colors, nothing too fashionable or too clamorous—we gather to celebrate Max's fifth birthday.

"Murgatroid," Eric says, his boots planted wide apart on the carpet, like anchors.

"Say it again," my nephew says, delighted.

"Eric," Rachel says, "don't get him all excited."

David, her husband, stands toward the back of the living room, taking pictures with his bulky camera.

"Hannah," he says to me, "smile. Look at the boidy."

I grimace at him, baring my teeth like a cheetah. David loves to take pictures, although I have heard my mother say more than once that with an expensive camera like his, you would think he'd learn how to focus.

"I want you to say it again," my nephew says.

Max is entranced by Eric, who treats him as if he were a poodle—or a serf.

"Murgatroid," Eric says, then leans over and pokes Max lightly. "You're a murgatroid, fathead."

"You are," Max says. His skin is pale, and his small eyes glisten with excitement.

I watch them from where I sit. My niece Ella is ensconced on Lily's lap. Everyone is wearing party hats, conical and silly-looking, even my father. My mother has filled the antique Chinese bowls with jelly beans, and on the sideboard in the living room there is an array of presents wrapped in paper decorated with monkeys holding balloons.

"Birfday," Ella says, squirming. "My birfday."

"It's mine," Max says patiently, as though he's gone over this ground hundreds of times before. "Yours is in *June*."

"It's my birfday," Ella says again. My niece, not yet three, is possessed by fierce powers of desire. I wonder if one day she might become a surgeon.

"Of course it is, you knutch," Lily says. "Every day is your birthday."

Ella looks delighted and leans against my sister contentedly.

Knutch: that word my mother used to use when we were little, signaling her affection, her good mood. When she called me "knutch," everything seemed suddenly wonderful. In the present we all use it in our turn, absently, on Max and his sister.

"And now we'll sing 'Happy Birthday,' " my father announces. Underneath his *yarmulke*, the fringe of hair circling his bald head is no longer gray but white.

"I brought my guitar," Eric says.

"Well, get it then," my mother says. "What a nice idea."

Eric goes to the hall closet, and while he is gone, his

fiancée, Linda, leans shyly against the chair he has vacated.

"You look very pretty," my mother says formally, giving a guttural roll to the *r* in *pretty.*

"Thank you," Linda says, blushing.

My brother returns with his guitar and bangs some chords as everyone joins in the singing, Lena and Arthur and Eric's fiancée and my sisters' husbands. Max hops around on one foot, beside himself with pleasure.

"Play something good," I say to Eric when we are done. "Play 'Beast of Burden.'"

"What's that?" my father asks.

The young, in the form of his children, render my father paranoid; he is convinced that whatever he can't grasp—a harmless remark of mine to Eric—is explosive in nature, part of a plot to overthrow the world.

"It's not meant for guitar," Eric says.

"You only know things with easy cords," I say. "A, E, G, C."

My brother strums the opening of a song I recognize.

"You must have gotten that from TV," my father says. "You watch too much TV."

"TV is very important," Benjamin says. "It's the most influential medium in the country."

"Here we go again," Lily says. Her husband, Stan, sits next to her on the couch, smiling inscrutably. What does he think of all of us? Every family must strike every other family as unutterably strange.

"TV's junk," my father says. "*Drek*. No one of any importance watches it."

"The bride cuts the cake," Rachel says. "Let's have the birthday cake."

The flames crackle in the fireplace, there are bowls of flowers scattered around the living room, and the curtains are drawn against the world's intrusion. It is, in its way, a beautiful setting.

"Yeah, cake," Max says. "Let's eat my birthday cake."

"Cake," Ella pipes up.

"Enough arguing, Valter," my mother says.

In the last few years the contours of her face have weakened, especially around the eyes. She is not the sort of woman to indulge her vanity, to place herself under a surgeon's knife, like most of the women she knows. But then we, too, are all grown up now, unrecognizable as the children we once were.

"We've been thro-u-gh," Eric sings in his husky, oddly riveting voice, "some things together, with trunks of memories still to come. . . ."

"What a nice song," my mother says, always partial to Neil Young.

"We've found things to do in stormy weather," my brother goes on singing. "Long may you run."

"Long may you ru-u-un," Max sings along with his favorite song. "Long may you run. . . ."

"It's *my* birfday," Ella says, watching all of us at our own level, in Lily's arms. "Free years old."

But it has begun to dawn on her that it's not. Arthur, who is the only one of us who never seems to be present, even when he is standing in the same room, leans in close to her.

"Happy birthday, dear El-la," he chants to her ear quickly. "Happy birthday, dear El-la."

"And now in Hebrew," my father says. "Everyone together."

As we sing the Hebrew version—"Yom Huledet Sameach"—Lena stirs the logs in the fireplace with a poker, sending a shower of sparks up the flue. Her hands are still capable—strong hands, the hands that spanked, conveying a tenderness in their very brutality. What I learned long ago, in the midst of the family that circles me now, is that there is a sweetness to pain, a seduction.

"Cheers," my father says, holding up a glass of juice. *"L'chayim."*

I take a glass from the tray on the sideboard and clink it with his, a guest at a party where there are no real guests. I am twenty-six years old, and somewhere in another part of the city, the man in whose bed I sometimes lie pulls absently at his bottom lip; he is not thinking of me.

"*L'chayim*," I say.

"*L'chayim tovim ulshalom*," Eric declaims rapidly with mock fervor.

"Max will lead us into the dining room," my mother says.

My nephew lifts his legs high and marches in, like a storm trooper on parade. The rest of us follow after him, haphazardly.

"Look at this!" Max shouts. "Will you look at *this*!"

"Me," Ella shouts, beaming with happiness. "Look at me!"

My mother has bought presents for Ella, too; she is good that way. Although I think of her as creating the gaps in me—the disowned longings—there are also the things she didn't overlook. Who's to say, finally, why the balance has tipped the way it has?

About my mother I feel an ancient sadness, a whistling in my bones. Desires that aren't met don't go away, they just get twisted. When I'm not speaking to my mother, in a show of independence, I dream about her. In my dreams I am still looking for both my parents, my father and my mother. They are dreams of being reborn: in a large, floating house an older man, craggy and tanned as my father never is, has left drawings of women—unfashionably full-figured women whose bodies resemble mine more than they do the bodies in *Vogue*—scattered on his desk. I hide from him, this Léger of my dreams, in a little room. He comes looking for me, and when he finds me, I explain why I'm there: to find *him*, the neatest and most satisfying of tautologies.

In another dream—but no, it is in another life, the next one or the one preceding this—I am racing my past to the finish line. There are warm breezes on the other side; I will learn to ride them, a beginner once again. My mother is waving, the sun behind her, and me, I am running, freer than can be, my arms wide open.

About the Author

Daphne Merkin grew up in New York City and attended Barnard and Columbia University. Her fiction has been published in *The New Yorker, Partisan Review, Encounter*, and *Mademoiselle*. She has been the book and film critic for *The New Leader* and is a contributing editor at *Partisan Review.*